Also by Sally Thorne

SECOND FIRST IMPRESSIONS
99 PERCENT MINE

ATTENTION: ORGANIZATIONS AND CORPORATIONS
HarperCollins books may be purchased for educational, business,
or sales promotional use. For information, please e-mail the Special
Markets Department at SPsales@harpercollins.com.

THE
HATING
GAME

SALLY THORNE

wm
WILLIAM MORROW
An Imprint of HarperCollinsPublishers

"The Hating Game Epilogue" copyright © 2019 by Sally Thorne.

Excerpt from *Second First Impressions* copyright © 2021 by Sally Thorne.

First William Morrow mass market printing: April 2021
First William Morrow paperback printing: August 2016

Print Edition ISBN: 978-0-06-306353-2
Digital Edition ISBN: 978-0-06-243960-4

Cover design and illustration by Connie Gabbert

William Morrow and HarperCollins are registered trademarks of HarperCollins Publishers in the United States of America and other countries.

21 22 23 24 25   CPI   10 9 8 7 6 5 4 3 2 1

Praise for

The Hating Game

" 'Hating someone feels disturbingly similar to being in love,' says Lucy Hutton, who can't stand fellow executive assistant Joshua. There's only one place this could go . . . but it's good fun getting there." —*People*

"Five feet tall and a total oddball, Lucy carries the plot by being engagingly self-deprecating, quick-witted and funny. . . . The chemistry between Lucy and Joshua is also gratifying, with both seeming like fully conceived characters rather than passive stereotypes. . . . A vibrant take on an old standard." —*The New York Times Book Review*

"If you miss romantic comedies, the kind that were so funny you would pay $15 to see them in the theater . . . this novel will make you very happy indeed. . . . The rising tension and Thorne's biting dialogue will make you wish for the romantic comedies of days gone by—or just more books like this one." —NPR Books

"Sally Thorne satisfies hearts longing for laughter in their love stories. . . . Their battle of wits is tremendously fun— acerbic and sexy and filled with tension. The result is a wicked, witty romance that will capture readers' hearts long before Joshua manages to capture Lucy's."

—Sarah MacLean,
New York Times bestselling author

"A brilliant, biting, hilarious new voice. *The Hating Game* will take the rom-com world by storm. One of the best I've read, ever."

—Kristan Higgins,
New York Times bestselling author

In loving memory of Ivy Stone

Acknowledgments

This book is my dream come true.

I have had a wonderful cheer squad of friends encouraging me to pursue this dream: Kate Warnock, Gemma Ruddick, Liz Kenneally, and Katie Saarikko. Each has played their part to support, push, and inspire me. You're all pretty special.

Thank you to Christina Hobbs and Lauren Billings for supporting my writing endeavors and for introducing me to my lovely agent, Taylor Haggerty from Waxman Leavell Literary Agency. Taylor, thank you for helping me to achieve this dream.

Thanks to the friendly and efficient people at Harper-Collins, especially my editor, Amanda Bergeron, for making me feel like one of the family.

Speaking of family, I want to send love to my parents, Sue and David, my brother, Peter, and my husband, Roland. Rol, thank you for believing in me. Even though my pug, Delia, cannot read, she has been remarkably supportive and I will love her until the end of time.

Carrie, whoever or wherever you are: That one word, *nemesis,* was such a gift. You gave me the prompt that sparked this entire book. I am very grateful that you did.

THE HATING GAME

Chapter 1

I have a theory. Hating someone feels disturbingly
similar to being in love with them. I've had a lot
of time to compare love and hate, and these are my
observations.

Love and hate are visceral. Your stomach twists at
the thought of that person. The heart in your chest beats
heavy and bright, nearly visible through your flesh and
clothes. Your appetite and sleep are shredded. Every interaction spikes your blood with a dangerous kind of
adrenaline, and you're on the brink of fight or flight.
Your body is barely under your control. You're con-
sumed, and it scares you.

Both love and hate are mirror versions of the same
game—and you *have* to win. Why? Your heart and your
ego. Trust me, I should know.

It's early Friday afternoon. I'm imprisoned at my
desk for another few hours. I wish I was in solitary con-
finement, but unfortunately I have a cellmate. Each tick
of his watch feels like another tally mark, chipped onto
the cell wall.

We're engaged in one of our childish games, which
requires no words. Like everything we do, it's dread-
fully immature.

The first thing to know about me: My name is Lucy Hutton. I'm the executive assistant to Helene Pascal, the co-CEO of Bexley & Gamin.

Once upon a time, our little Gamin Publishing was on the brink of collapse. The reality of the economy meant people had no money for their mortgage repayments and literature was a luxury. Bookstores were closing all over the city like candles being blown out. We braced ourselves for almost certain closure.

At the eleventh hour, a deal was struck with another struggling publishing house. Gamin Publishing was forced into an arranged marriage with the crumbling evil empire known as Bexley Books, ruled by the unbearable Mr. Bexley himself.

Each company stubbornly believing it was saving the other, they both packed up and moved into their new marital home. Neither party was remotely happy about it. The Bexleys remembered their old lunchroom foosball table with sepia-tinted nostalgia. They couldn't believe the airy-fairy Gamins had survived even this long, with their lax adherence to key performance indicator targets and dreamy insistence on Literature as Art. The Bexleys believed numbers were more important than words. Books were units. Sell the units. High-five the team. Repeat.

The Gamins shuddered in horror watching their boisterous new stepbrothers practically tearing the pages out of their Brontës and Austens. How had Bexley managed to amass so many likeminded stuffed shirts, far more suited to accountancy or law? Gamins resented the notion of books as units. Books were, and always would be, something a little magic and something to respect.

One year on, you can still tell at a glance which company someone came from by his or her physical appearance. The Bexleys are hard geometrics, the Gamins are soft scribbles. Bexleys move in shark packs, talking figures and constantly hogging the conference rooms for their ominous Planning Sessions. Plotting sessions, more like. Gamins huddle in their cubicles, gentle doves in clock towers, poring over manuscripts, searching for the next literary sensation. The air surrounding them is perfumed with jasmine tea and paper. Shakespeare is their pinup boy.

The move to a new building was a little traumatizing, especially for the Gamins. Take a map of this city. Make a straight line between each of the old company buildings, mark a red dot exactly halfway between them and here we are. The new Bexley & Gamin is a cheap gray cement toad squatting on a major traffic route, impossible to merge onto in the afternoon. It's arctic in the morning shadows and sweaty by the afternoon. The building has one redeeming feature: Some basement parking—usually snagged by the early risers, or should I say, the Bexleys.

Helene Pascal and Mr. Bexley had toured the building prior to the move and a rare thing happened: They both agreed on something. The top floor of the building was an insult. Only one executive office? A total refit was needed.

After an hour-long brainstorm that was filled with so much hostility the interior designer's eyes sparkled with unshed tears, the only word Helene and Mr. Bexley would agree on to describe the new aesthetic was *shiny*. It was their last agreement, ever. The refit definitely fulfilled the design brief. The tenth floor is now a cube of glass, chrome, and black tile. You could pluck your eyebrows using any surface as a mirror—walls, floors, ceiling. Even our desks are made from huge sheets of glass.

I'm focused on the great big reflection opposite me. I raise my hand and look at my nails. My reflection follows. I stroke through my hair and straighten my collar. I've been in a trance. I'd almost forgotten I'm still playing this game with Joshua.

I'm sitting here with a cellmate because every power-crazed war general has a second in command to do the dirty work. Sharing an assistant was never an option, because it would have required a concession from one of the CEOs. We were each plugged in outside the two new office doors, and left to fend for ourselves.

It was like being pushed into the Colosseum's arena, only to find I wasn't alone.

I raise my right hand again now. My reflection follows smoothly. I rest my chin on my palm and sigh deeply, and it resonates and echoes. I raise my left eyebrow because I know he can't, and as predicted his forehead pinches uselessly. I've won the game. The thrill does not translate into an expression on my face. I remain as placid and expressionless as a doll. We sit here with our chins on our hands and stare into each other's eyes.

I'm never alone in here. Sitting opposite me is the executive assistant to Mr. Bexley. His henchman and manservant. The second thing, the most *essential* thing anyone needs to know about me, is this: I hate Joshua Templeman.

He's currently copying every move I make. It's the Mirror Game. To the casual observer it wouldn't be immediately obvious; he's as subtle as a shadow. But not to me. Each movement of mine is replicated on his side of the office on a slight time delay. I lift my chin from my palm and swivel to my desk, and smoothly he does the same. I'm twenty-eight years old and it seems I've fallen through the cracks of heaven and hell and into purgatory. A kindergarten classroom. An asylum.

I type my password: IHATEJOSHUA4EV@. My previous passwords have all been variations on how much I hate Joshua. For Ever. His password is almost certainly IHateLucinda4Eva. My phone rings. Julie Atkins, from copyrights and permissions, another thorn in my side. I feel like unplugging my phone and throwing it into an incinerator.

"Hello, how are you?" I always put an extra little bit of warmth into my voice on the phone. Across the room, Joshua's eyes roll as he begins punishing his keyboard.

"I have a favor to ask, Lucy." I can almost mouth the next words as she speaks them.

"I need an extension on the monthly report. I think I'm getting a migraine. I can't look at this screen any longer." She's one of those horrific people who pronounces it *me-graine*.

"Of course, I understand. When can you get it done?"

"You're the best. It'd be in by Monday afternoon. I need to come in late."

If I say yes, I'll have to stay late Monday night to have the report done for Tuesday's nine A.M. executive meeting. Already, next week sucks.

"Okay." My stomach feels tight. "As soon as you can, please."

"Oh, and Brian can't get his in today either. You're so nice. I appreciate how kind you're being. We were all saying you're the best person to deal with up there in exec. *Some people* up there are total nightmares." Her sugary words help ease the resentment a little.

"No problem. Talk to you Monday." I hang up and don't even need to look at Joshua. I know he's shaking his head.

After a few minutes I glance at him, and he is staring at me. Imagine it's two minutes before the biggest interview of your life, and you look down at your white shirt. Your peacock-blue fountain pen has leaked through your pocket. Your head explodes with an obscenity and your stomach is a spike of panic over the simmering nerves. You're an idiot and everything's ruined. That's the exact color of Joshua's eyes when he looks at me.

I wish I could say he's ugly. He should be a short, fat troll with watery eyes. A limping hunchback. Warts and zits. Yellow-cheese teeth and onion sweat. But he's not. He's pretty much the opposite. More proof there's no justice in this world.

My inbox pings. I flick my eyes abruptly away from Joshua's non-ugliness and notice Helene has sent through a request for budget forecasting figures. I open up last month's report for reference and begin.

I doubt this month's outlook is going to be much of an improvement. The publishing industry is sliding further downhill. I've heard the word *restructure* echoing a few times around these halls, and I know where that leads. Every time I step out of the elevator and see Joshua I ask myself: Why don't I get a new job?

I've been fascinated by publishing houses since a pivotal field trip when I was eleven. I was already a passionate devourer of books. My life revolved around the weekly trip to the town library. I'd borrow the maximum number of titles allowed and I could identify individual librarians by the sound their shoes made as they moved up each aisle. Until that field trip, I was hellbent on being a librarian myself. I'd even implemented a cataloging system for my own personal collection. I was such a little book nerd.

Before our trip to the publishing house, I'd never

thought much about how a book came to actually exist. It was a revelation. You could be paid to find authors, read books, and ultimately create them? Brand-new covers and perfect pages with no dog-ears or pencil annotations? My mind was blown. I loved new books. They were my favorite to borrow. I told my parents when I got home, *I'm going to work at a publisher when I grow up.*

It's great that I'm fulfilling a childhood dream. But if I'm honest, at the moment the main reason I don't get a new job is: I can't let Joshua win this.

As I work, all I can hear are his machine-gun keystrokes and the faint whistle of air conditioning. He occasionally picks up his calculator and taps on it. I wouldn't mind betting Mr. Bexley has also directed Joshua to run the forecasting figures. Then the two co-CEOs can march into battle, armed with numbers that may not match. The ideal fuel for their bonfire of hatred.

"Excuse me, Joshua."

He doesn't acknowledge me for a full minute. His keystrokes intensify. Beethoven on a piano has nothing on him right now.

"What is it, Lucinda?"

Not even my parents call me Lucinda. I clench my jaw but then guiltily release the muscles. My dentist has begged me to make a conscious effort.

"Are you working on the forecasting figures for next quarter?"

He lifts both hands from his keyboard and stares at me. "No."

I let out half a lungful of air and turn back to my desk.

"I finished those two hours ago." He resumes typing. I look at my open spreadsheet and count to ten.

We both work fast and have reputations for being

Finishers—you know, the type of worker who completes the nasty, too-hard tasks everyone else avoids.

I prefer to sit down with people and discuss things face-to-face. Joshua is strictly email. At the foot of his emails is always: Rgds, J. Would it kill him to type Regards, Joshua? It's too many keystrokes, apparently. He probably knows offhand how many minutes a year he's saving B&G.

We're evenly matched, but we are completely at odds. I try my hardest to look corporate but everything I own is slightly wrong for B&G. I'm a Gamin to the bone. My lipstick is too red, my hair too unruly. My shoes click too loudly on the tile floors. I can't seem to hand over my credit card to purchase a black suit. I never had to wear one at Gamin, and I'm stubbornly refusing to assimilate with the Bexleys. My wardrobe is knits and retro. A sort of cool librarian chic, I hope.

It takes me forty-five minutes to complete the task. I race the clock, even though numbers are not my forte, because I imagine it would have taken Joshua an hour. Even in my head I compete with him.

"Thanks, Lucy!" I hear Helene call faintly from behind her shiny office door when I send the document through.

I recheck my inbox. Everything's up to date. I check the clock. Three fifteen P.M. I check my lipstick in the reflection of the shiny wall tile near my computer monitor. I check Joshua, who is glowering at me with contempt. I stare back. Now we are playing the Staring Game.

I should mention that the ultimate aim of all our games is to make the other smile, or cry. It's something like that. I'll know when I win.

I made a mistake when I first met Joshua: I smiled at him. My best sunny smile with all my teeth, my eyes sparkling with stupid optimism that the business merger wasn't the worst thing to ever happen to me. His eyes scanned me from the top of my head to the soles of my shoes. I'm only five feet tall so it didn't take long. Then he looked away out the window. He did not smile back, and somehow I feel like he's been carrying my smile around in his breast pocket ever since. He's one up. After our initial poor start, it only took a few weeks for us to succumb to our mutual hostility. Like water dripping into a bathtub, eventually it began to overflow.

. I yawn behind my hand and look at Joshua's breast pocket, resting against his left pectoral. He wears an identical business shirt every day, in a different color. White, off-white stripe, cream, pale yellow, mustard, baby blue, robin's-egg blue, dove-gray, navy, and black. They are worn in their unchanging sequence.

Incidentally, my favorite of his shirts is robin's-egg blue, and my least favorite is mustard, which he is wearing now. All the shirts look fine on him. All colors suit him. If I wore mustard, I'd look like a cadaver. But there he sits, looking as golden-skinned and healthy as ever.

"Mustard today," I observe aloud. Why do I poke the hornet's nest? "Just can't wait for baby blue on Monday."

The look he gives me is both smug and irritated. "You notice so much about me, Shortcake. But can I remind you that comments about appearance are against the B&G human resources policy."

Ah, the HR Game. We haven't played this one in ages. "Stop calling me Shortcake or I'll report you to HR."

We each keep a log on the other. I can only assume he does; he seems to remember all of my transgressions. Mine is a password-protected document hidden on my personal drive and it journals all the shit that has ever gone down between Joshua Templeman and me. We have each complained to HR four times over this past year.

He's received a verbal and written warning about the nickname he has for me. I've received two warnings; one for verbal abuse and for a juvenile prank that got out of hand. I'm not proud.

He cannot seem to formulate a reply and we resume staring at each other.

I LOOK FORWARD to Joshua's shirts getting darker. It's navy today, which leads to black. Gorgeous Payday Black.

My finances are something like this. I'm about to walk twenty-five minutes from B&G to pick up my car from Jerry ("the Mechanic") and melt my credit card to within one inch of its maximum limit. Payday comes tomorrow and I will pay the credit card balance. My car will ooze more oily dark stuff all weekend, which I will notice by the time Joshua's shirts are the white of a unicorn's flank. I call Jerry. I return the car and subsist on a shoestring budget. The shirts get darker. I've got to do something about that car.

Joshua is currently leaning on Mr. Bexley's door-frame. His body fills most of the doorway. I can see this because I'm spying via the reflection on the wall near my monitor. I hear a husky, soft laugh, nothing like Mr. Bexley's donkey bray. I rub my palms down my forearms to flatten the tiny hairs. I will not turn my head to try to see properly. He'll catch me. He always does. Then I'll get a frown.

The clock is grinding slowly toward five P.M. and I can see thunderclouds through the dusty windows. Helene left an hour ago—one of the perks of being co-CEO is working the hours of a schoolchild and delegating everything to me. Mr. Bexley spends longer hours here because his chair is way too comfortable and when the afternoon sun slants in, he tends to doze.

I don't mean to sound like Joshua and I are running the top floor, but frankly it feels like it sometimes. The finance and sales teams report directly to Joshua and he filters the huge amounts of data into a bite-size report that he spoon-feeds to a struggling, red-faced Mr. Bexley.

I have the editorial, corporate, and marketing teams reporting to me, and each month I condense their monthly reports into one for Helene . . . and I suppose I spoon-feed it to her too. I spiral-bind it so she can read it when she's on the stepper. I use her favorite font. Every day here is a challenge, a privilege, a sacrifice, and a frustration. But when I think about every little step I've taken to be here in this place, starting from when I was eleven years old, I refocus. I remember. And I endure Joshua for a little longer.

I bring homemade cakes to my meetings with the division heads and they all adore me. I'm described as "worth my weight in gold." Joshua brings bad news to his divisional meetings and his weight is measured in other substances.

Mr. Bexley stumps past my desk now, briefcase in hand. He must shop at Humpty Dumpty's Big & Small Menswear. How else could he find such short, broad suits? He's balding, liver-spotted, and rich as sin. His grandfather started Bexley Books. He loves to remind Helene that she was merely *hired*. He is an old degenerate, according to both Helene and my own private observations. I make myself smile up at him. His first name is Richard. Fat Little Dick.

"Good night, Mr. Bexley."

"Good night, Lucy." He pauses by my desk to look down the front of my red silk blouse.

"I hope Joshua passed on the copy of *The Glass Darkly* I picked up for you? The first of the first."

Fat Little Dick has a huge bookshelf filled with every B&G release. Each book is the first off the press; a tradition started by his grandfather. He loves to brag about them to visitors, but I once looked at the shelves and the spines weren't even cracked.

"You picked it up, eh?" Mr. Bexley orbits around to look at Joshua. "You didn't mention that, Doctor Josh."

Fat Little Dick probably calls him *Doctor Josh* because he's so clinical. I heard someone say when things got particularly bad at Bexley Books, Joshua masterminded the surgical removal of one-third of their workforce. I don't know how he sleeps at night.

"As long as you get it, it doesn't matter," Joshua replies smoothly and his boss remembers that he is The Boss.

"Yes, yes," he chuffs and looks down my top again. "Good work, you pair."

He gets into the elevator and I look down at my shirt. All the buttons are done up. What could he even *see*? I glance up at the mirrored tiles on the ceiling and can faintly see a tiny triangle of shadowed cleavage.

"If you buttoned it any higher, we wouldn't see your face," Joshua says to his computer screen as he logs off.

"Perhaps you could tell your boss to look at my face occasionally." I also log off.

"He's probably trying to see your circuit board. Or wondering what kind of fuel you run on."

I shrug on my coat. "Just fueled by my hate for you."

Josh's mouth twitches once, and I nearly had him

there. I watch him roll down a neutral expression. "If it bothers you, *you* should speak to him. Stand up for yourself. So, painting your nails tonight, desperately alone?"

Lucky guess on his part? "Yes. Masturbating and crying into your pillow tonight, *Doctor Josh*?"

He looks at the top button of my shirt. "Yes. And don't call me that."

I swallow down a bubble of laughter. We jostle each other in an unfriendly way as we get into the elevator. He hits B, but I hit G.

"Hitchhiking?"

"Car's at the shop." I step into my ballet flats and tuck my heels into my bag. Now I'm even shorter. In the dull polish of the elevator doors I can see that I barely come halfway up his bicep. I look like a Chihuahua next to a Great Dane.

The elevator doors open to the building foyer. The world outside B&G is a blue haze; refrigerator cold, filled with rapists and murderers and lightly sprinkling rain. A sheet of newspaper blows past, right on cue.

He holds the elevator door open with one enormous hand and leans out to look at the weather. Then he swings those dark blue eyes to mine, his brow beginning to crease. The familiar bubble forms in my head. *I wish he was my friend.* I burst it with a pin.

"I'll give you a ride," he forces out.

"Ugh, no way," I say over my shoulder and run.

Chapter 2

It's Cream Shirt Wednesday. Joshua is off on a late lunch. He's made a few more comments to me lately about things I like and do. They have been so accurate I'm pretty sure he's been snooping through my stuff. Knowledge is power, and I don't have much.

First, I conduct a forensic examination of my desk. Both Helene and Mr. Bexley despise computerized calendars, and so we have to keep matching paper schedule books like we're Dickensian law clerks. In mine, there's only Helene's appointments. I obsessively lock my computer, even if I go to the printer. My unlocked computer in the vicinity of Joshua? I may as well hand him the nuclear codes now.

Back at Gamin Publishing, my desk was a fort made of books. I kept my pens in the gaps between their spines. When I was unpacking in the new office, I saw how sterile Joshua kept his desk and felt incredibly childish. I took my Word of the Day calendar and Smurf figurines home again.

Before the merger, I had a best friend at work. Val Stone and I would sit on the worn-out leather couches in the break room and play our favorite game: systematically defacing photographs of beautiful people in magazines. I'd add a moustache onto Naomi Campbell. Val would then ink out a missing tooth. Soon it was an onslaught of scars and eye patches and bloodshot eyes and devil horns until the picture was so ruined we'd get bored and start another.

Val was one of the staff who was cut and she was furious I didn't give her some kind of a warning. Not that I would have been allowed to, even if I had known. She didn't believe me. I turn slowly, and my reflection spins off twenty different surfaces. I see myself in every size from music box to silver screen. My cherry-red skirt flips out and I pirouette again once, just for the hell of it, trying to shake away the sick, troubled feeling I get whenever I think of Val.

Anyway, my audit confirms that my desk has a red, black, and blue pen. Pink Post-its. One tube of lipstick. A box of tissues for blotting my lipstick and tears of frustration. My planner. Nothing else.

I do a light shuffling tap dance across the marble superhighway. I'm in Joshua Country now. I sit in his chair and look at everything through his eyes. His chair is so high my toes don't touch the ground. I wiggle my butt a little deeper into the leather. It feels completely obscene. I keep one eye permanently swiveled toward the elevator, and use the other to examine his desk for clues.

His desk is the male version of mine. Blue Post-its. He has a sharp pencil in with his three pens. Instead of lipstick he has a tin of mints. I steal one and put it in the tiny, previously useless pocket of my skirt. I imagine myself in the laxative section of the drugstore trying to find a good match and have a good little snicker. I jiggle his desk drawer. Locked. So is his computer. Fort

Knox. Well played, Templeman. I make a few unsuccessful guesses at his password. Maybe he doesn't hate me 4 eva.

There's no little framed photo of a partner or loved one on this desk. No grinning, happy dog or tropical beach memento. I doubt he esteems anyone enough to frame their likeness. During one of Joshua's fervent little sales rants, Fat Little Dick boomed sarcastically, *We've got to get you laid, Doctor Josh.*

Joshua replied, *You're right, boss. I've seen what a bad drought can do to someone.* He said it while looking at me. I know the date. I diarized it in my HR log.

I get a little tingle in my nostrils. Joshua's cologne? The pheromone he leaches from his pores? Gross. I flip open his day planner and notice something; a light code of pencil running down the columns of each day. Feeling incredibly James Bond–ish, I raise my phone and manage to take one single frame.

I hear the cables in the elevator shaft and leap to my feet. I vault to the other side of his desk and manage to slam the planner shut before the doors spring open and he appears. His chair is still spinning gently out of the corner of my eye. Busted.

"What are you doing?"

My phone is now safely down the waistband of my underwear. Note to self: Disinfect phone.

"Nothing." There's a tremor in my voice, convicting me instantly. "I was trying to see if it's going to rain this afternoon. I bumped your chair. Sorry."

He advances like a floating Dracula. The menace is ruined by the sporting-goods-store bag loudly crinkling against his leg. A shoebox is in it, judging from the shape.

Imagine the wretched sales assistant who had to help

Joshua choose shoes. *I require shoes to ensure I can ef-*
fectively run down the targets I am paid to assassinate
in my spare time. I require the best value for my money.
I am size eleven.

He looks at his desk, his computer's innocuous log-in
screen, his closed planner. I force my breath out in a
controlled hiss. Joshua drops his bag on the floor. He
steps so close his leather shoe touches the tip of my little
patent heels.

"Now why don't you tell me what you were actually
doing near my desk?"

We have never done the Staring Game this close. I'm
a pip-squeak at exactly five feet tall. It's been my lifelong cross to bear. My lack of height is an agonizing
topic of conversation. Joshua is at least six-four. Five.
Six. Maybe more. A giant of a human. And he's built out
of heavy materials.

Gamely, I maintain eye contact. I can stand wherever
I like in this office. Screw him. Like a threatened animal trying to look bigger, I put my hands on my hips.

He's not ugly, as I've mentioned, but I always struggle to work out how to describe him. I remember eating
my dinner on the couch a while back, and a soft-news
piece came on the TV. An old Superman comic book
sold for a record price at auction. As the white-gloved
hand turned the pages, the old-fashioned drawings of
Clark Kent reminded me of Joshua.

Like Clark Kent, Joshua's height and strength are
all tucked away under clothes designed to conceal and
help him blend into a crowd. Nobody at the *Daily
Planet* knows anything about Clark. Underneath these
button-up shirts, Joshua could be relatively featureless
or ripped like Superman. It's a mystery.

He doesn't have the forehead curl or the nerdy black

glasses, but he's got the strong masculine jawline and sulky, pretty mouth. I've been thinking all this time his hair is black but now that I'm closer, I can see it is dark brown. He doesn't comb it as neatly as Clark does. He's definitely got the ink-blue eyes and the laser stare, and probably some of the other superpowers, too.

But Clark Kent is such a darling; all bumbling and soft. Joshua is hardly the mild-mannered reporter. He's a sarcastic, cynical, Bizarro Clark Kent, terrorizing everyone in the newsroom and pissing off poor little Lois Lane until she screams into her pillow at night.

I don't like big guys. They're too much like horses. They could trample you if you got underfoot. He is auditing my appearance with the same narrowed eyes that I am. I wonder what the top of my head looks like. I'm sure he only fornicates with Amazons. Our stares clash and maybe comparing them to an ink stain was a tad too harsh. Those eyes are wasted on him.

To avoid dying, I reluctantly breathe in a steady lungful of cedar-pine spice. He smells like a freshly sharpened pencil. A Christmas tree in a cold, dark room. Despite the tendons in my neck beginning to cramp, I don't permit myself to lower my eyes. I might look at his mouth then, and I get a good enough view of his mouth when he's tossing insults at me across the office. Why would I want to see it up close? I wouldn't.

The elevator bings like the answer to all my prayers. Enter Andy the courier.

Andy looks like a movie extra who appears in the credits as "Courier." Leathery, midforties, clad in fluorescent yellow. His sunglasses sit like a tiara on top of his head. Like most couriers, he enriches his workday by flirting with every female under the age of sixty he encounters.

"Lovely Luce!" He booms it so loud I hear Fat Little Dick make a wet snort as he jolts awake in his office.

"Andy!" I return, skittering backward. I could honestly hug him for interrupting what was feeling like a whole new kind of strange game. He has a small parcel in his hand, no bigger than a Rubik's cube. It's got to be my 1984 baseball-player Smurfette. Super rare, very minty. I've wanted her forever and I've been stalking her journey via her tracking number.

"I know you want me to call from the foyer with your Smurfs, but no answer."

My desk phone is diverted to my personal cell, which is currently located near my hip bone in the waistband of my underwear. So that's what the buzzing feeling was. Phew. I was thinking I needed my head checked.

"What does he mean, Smurfs?" Joshua narrows his eyes like we're nuts.

"I'm sure you're busy, Andy, I'll let you get out of here." I grab at the parcel, but it's too late.

"It's her passion in life. She lives and breathes Smurfs. Those little blue people, yea big. They wear white hats." Andy holds two of his fingers an inch apart.

"I know what Smurfs are." Joshua is irritated.

"I don't live or breathe them." My voice betrays the lie. Joshua's sudden cough sounds suspiciously like a laugh.

"Smurfs, huh? So that's what those little boxes are. I thought maybe you were buying your tiny clothes online. Do you think it's appropriate to get personal items delivered to your workplace, Lucinda?"

"She's got a whole cabinet of them. She's got a . . . What is it, Luce? A Thomas Edison Smurf? He's a rare one, Josh. Her parents gave it to her for high school graduation." Andy blithely continues humiliating me.

"Quiet now, Andy! How are you? How's your day going?" I sign for the package on his handheld device with a sweaty hand. Him and his big mouth.

"Your parents bought you a Smurf for graduation?" Joshua lounges in his chair and watches me with cynical interest. I hope my body didn't warm the leather.

"Yeah, yeah, I'm sure you got a car or something." I'm mortified.

"I'm fine, sweetheart," Andy tells me, taking the little gizmo back from me and hitting several buttons and putting it in his pocket. Now that the business component of our interaction is completed, he pulls his mouth into a beguiling grin.

"All the better for seeing you. I tell you, Josh my friend, if I sat opposite this gorgeous little creature I wouldn't get any work done."

Andy hooks his thumbs into his pockets and smiles at me. I don't want to hurt his feelings so I roll my eyes good-humoredly.

"It's a struggle," Joshua says sarcastically. "Be glad you get to leave."

"He must have a heart of stone."

"He sure does. If I can knock him out and get him into a crate, can you have him delivered somewhere remote?" I lean on my desk and look at my tiny parcel.

"International shipping rates have increased," Andy warns. Joshua shakes his head, bored with the conversation, and begins to log on.

"I've got some savings. I think Joshua would love an adventure vacation in Zimbabwe."

"You've got an evil streak, haven't you!" Andy's pocket makes a beep and he begins to rummage and walk to the elevator.

"Well, Lovely Luce, it's been a pleasure as always. I will see you soon, no doubt, after your next online auction."

"Bye." When he disappears into the elevator, I turn back to my desk, my face automatically faded to neutral.

"Absolutely pathetic."

I make a *Jeopardy!* buzzer sound. "Who is Joshua Templeman?"

"Lucinda flirting with couriers. Pathetic."

Joshua is hammering away on his keyboard. He certainly is an impressive touch typist. I stroll past his desk and am gratified by his frustrated backspacing.

"I'm nice to him."

"You? Nice?"

I'm surprised by how hurt I feel. "I'm lovely. Ask anyone."

"Okay. Josh, is she lovely?" he asks himself aloud. "Hmm, let me think."

He picks up his tin of mints, opens the lid, checks them, closes it, and looks at me. I open my mouth and lift my tongue like a mental patient at the medication window.

"She's got a few lovely things about her, I suppose."

I raise a finger and enunciate the words crisply: "Human resources."

He sits up straighter but the corner of his mouth moves. I wish I could use my thumbs to pull his mouth into a huge deranged grin. As the police drag me out in handcuffs I'll be screeching, *Smile, goddamn you.*

We need to get even, because it's not fair. He's gotten one of my smiles, and seen me smile at countless other people. I have never seen him smile, nor have I seen his face look anything but blank, bored, surly, suspicious, watchful, resentful. Occasionally he has another look on his face, after we've been arguing. His Serial Killer expression.

I walk down the center line of the tile again and feel his head swivel.

"Not that I care what you think, but I'm well liked here. Everyone's excited about my book club, which you've made pretty clear you think is lame, but it will be team building, and pretty relevant, given where we work."

"You're a captain of industry."

"I take the library donations out. I plan the Christmas party. I let the interns follow me around." I'm ticking them off on my fingers.

"You're not doing much to convince me you don't care what I think." He leans back farther into his chair, long fingers laced together loosely on his generic, flat abdomen. The button near his thumb is half-loose. Whatever my face does, it makes him glance down and rebutton it.

"I don't care what *you* think, but I want normal people to like me."

"You're chronically addicted to making people adore you." The way he says it makes me feel a little sick.

"Well, excuse me for doing my best to maintain a good reputation. For trying to be positive. You're addicted to making people hate you, so what a pair we are."

I sit down and tap my computer mouse about ten times as hard as I can. His words sting. Joshua is like a mirror that shows me the bad parts of myself. It's school all over again. Tiny, runt-of-the-litter Lucy using her pathetic cuteness to avoid being destroyed by the big kids. I've always been the pet, the lucky charm, the one being pushed on the swings or pulled in a wagon. Carried and coddled and perhaps I am a little pathetic.

"You should try not giving a shit sometime. I tell you, it's liberating." His mouth tightens, and a strange shadow clouds his expression. One blink and it's gone.

"I didn't ask for your advice, Joshua. I get so mad at myself, letting you drag me down to your level all the time."

"And what level are you imagining me dragging you down to?" His voice is a little velvety and he bites his lip. "Horizontal?"

Mentally I hit Enter in my HR log and begin a new line.

"You're disgusting. Go to hell." I think I'll go treat myself to a basement scream.

"There you go. You've got no problem telling me to go to hell. It's a good start. It kind of suits you. Now try it with other people. You don't even realize how much people walk all over you. How do you expect to be taken seriously? Quit giving the same people deadline extensions, month after month."

"I don't know what you mean."

"Julie."

"It's not every month." I hate him because he is right.

"It's every single month, and you have to bust your ass working late to meet your own deadline. Do you see me doing that? No. Those assholes downstairs give it to me on time."

I dredge up a phrase from the assertiveness self-help book I keep on my nightstand.

"I don't want to continue this conversation."

"I'm giving you some good advice here, you should

take it. Stop picking up Helene's dry cleaning—it's not your job."

"I am now ending this conversation." I stand up. Maybe I'll go and play in the afternoon traffic to let off steam.

"And the courier. Just leave him alone. The sad old guy thinks you're flirting with him."

"That's what people say about you." The unfortunate retort falls out of my mouth. I try to rewind time. It doesn't work.

"Is that what you think you and I do? Flirt?"

He reclines back in his chair in a way I can never manage to do. The back of my chair doesn't budge when I've tried to recline. I only succeed in rolling backward and bumping into the wall.

"Shortcake, if we were flirting, you'd know about it." Our eyes catch and I feel a weird drop inside. This conversation is running off the rails.

"Because I'd be traumatized?"

"Because you'd be thinking about it later on, lying in bed."

"Been imagining my bed, have you?" I manage to reply.

He blinks, a new rare expression spreading across his face. I want to slap it off. It looks like he knows something I don't. It's smug and male and I hate it.

"I bet it's a very small bed."

I'm nearly breathing fire. I want to round his desk, kick his feet wider, and stand between his spread legs. I'd put one knee on the little triangle of chair right below his groin, climb up a little, and make him grunt with pain.

I'd pull his tie loose and unbutton the neck of his shirt. I'd put my hands around his big tan throat and squeeze and squeeze, his skin hot underneath my fingertips, his body struggling against me, cedar and pine spicing the air between us, burning my nostrils like smoke.

"What are you imagining? Your expression is filthy."

"Strangling you. Bare hands." I can barely get the words out. I'm huskier than a phone-sex operator after a double shift.

"So *that's* your kink." His eyes are going dark.

"Only where you're concerned."

Both his eyebrows ratchet up, and he opens his mouth as his eyes go completely black, but he does not seem to be able to say a word.

It is wonderful.

IT'S A BABY-BLUE shirt day when I remember the photo I took of his planner. After I read the Publishing Quarterly Outlook Report and make an executive summary for Helene, I transfer the photo from my phone to my work computer. Then I glance around like a criminal.

Joshua has been in Fat Little Dick's office all morning, and weirdly the morning has dragged. It's so quiet in here without someone to hate.

I hit Print, lock my computer, and clatter down the hall. I photocopy it twice, making the resolution darker and darker until the pencil marks are better visible. Needless to say, I shred all unneeded evidence. I wish I could double-shred it.

Joshua's begun locking away his planner now.

I lean against the wall and tilt the page to the light. The photograph captures a Monday and Tuesday a couple of weeks back. I can see Mr. Bexley's appointments easily. But next to the Monday is a letter. *D*. The Tuesday is an *S*. There is a tally of tiny lines adding up to eight. Dots next to times near lunchtime. A line of four X's and six little slash marks.

I puzzle covertly over this all afternoon. I'm tempted to go to security and ask Scott for the security tapes for this time period, but Helene might find out. It'd definitely be a waste of company resources too, over and above my illicit photocopying and general slacking.

The answer doesn't come for some time. It's late afternoon and Joshua is back in his regular seat across from me. His blue shirt glows like an iceberg. When I finally work out how to decode the pencil marks, I slap my forehead. I can't believe I've been so slow.

"Thanks. I've been dying to do that all afternoon," Joshua says without taking his eyes from his monitor.

He doesn't know I've seen his planner and the pencil codes. I'll simply notice when he uses the pencil and work out the correlation.

Let the Spying Game begin.

Chapter 3

I don't get quick results with the Spying Game and by the time Joshua is dressed in dove gray I'm at my wit's end. He has sensed my heightened interest in his activities and has become even more furtive and suspicious. I'll have to coax him out. I'm never going to see the pencil in motion if all he does is half frown at his computer.

I start a game I call You're Just So. It goes like this. "You're Just So . . . Ahh, never mind." I sigh. He takes the bait.

"Handsome. Intelligent. No, wait. Superior to everyone. You're coming to your senses, Lucinda."

Joshua locks his computer and opens his planner, one hand hovering over the cup with the pens and pencils. I hold my breath. He frowns and slaps the planner shut. The gray shirt should make him look like a cyborg, but he ends up looking handsome and intelligent. He is the worst.

"You're Just So *predictable*." Somehow I know this will cut him deep. His eyes become slits of hatred.

"Oh, am I? How so?"

You're Just So basically gives both players free rein to tell the opponent how much they hate each other.

"Shirts. Moods. Patterns. People like you can't succeed. If you ever acted out of character and surprised me, I'd die of shock."

"Am I to take this as a personal challenge?" He looks at his desk, apparently deep in thought.

"I'd like to see if you attempt it. You're Just So inflexible."

"And You're Just So flexible?"

"Very." I fell right into that one, and it's true. I could get my foot up to my face right now. I recover by raising an eyebrow and looking up at the ceiling with a smirk. By the time I lock eyes with him again, my mouth is a neutral little rosebud, mirrored off a hundred glittering surfaces.

He drops his eyes slowly down to the floor, and I cross my ankles, belatedly remembering I kicked off my shoes earlier. It's hard to be a good nemesis when your bright red toenails are showing.

"If I did something out of character, you'd die of shock?"

I can see my face mirrored on the paneling near his shoulder. I look like a black-eyed, wild-maned version of myself. My dark hair falls around my shoulders in jagged flames.

"Might be worth my while then."

Monday to Friday, he turns me into a scary-looking woman. I look like a gypsy fortune-teller screaming about your imminent death. A crazed lunatic in an asylum, seconds from clawing her own eyes out.

"Well, well. Lucinda Hutton. One flexible little gal." He is reclining in his chair again. Both feet are flat on the floor and they point at me like revolvers in a Wild West shootout.

"HR," I clip at him. I'm losing this game and he knows

it. Calling HR is virtually like tapping out. He picks up the pencil and presses the sharpened tip against the pad of his thumb. If a human could grin without moving their face, he just did it.

"I meant, You're Just So flexible in your approach to things. It must have been your wholesome upbringing, Shortcake. What do your parents do again? Could you remind me?"

"You know exactly what they do." I'm too busy for this nonsense. I grab a stack of old Post-its and begin to sort them.

"They farm . . ."

He looks at the ceiling, pretending to be wracking his brains.

"They farm . . ." He leaves it dangling in the air for an eternity. It's agony. I try not to fill in the silence, but the word that amuses him so much comes out of my mouth like a curse.

"Strawberries." Hence the nickname Strawberry Shortcake. I indulge myself in molar grinding. My dentist will never know.

"Sky Diamond Strawberries. *Cute*. Look, I've got the blog bookmarked." He does two double-clicks with his mouse and swivels his computer screen to face me.

I cringe so hard I sprain something internally. How did he find this? My mom's probably calling out to my dad right now. *Nigel, honey! The blog's had a hit!*

The Sky Diamond Daily. Yes, you heard right. Daily. I haven't checked it in a while because I can't keep up. Mom was a journalist with the local newspaper when she met Dad, but she quit to have me, and then they opened the farm. When you know her backstory, the daily entries make a sad kind of sense. I squint at Joshua's screen. Today's feature story is about irrigation.

Our farm supplies three local farmers' markets as well as a grocery chain. There's a field for tourists to pick their own and Mom sells jars of preserves. In hot weather, she makes homemade ice cream. Sky Diamond was certified organic two years ago, which was a pretty big deal for them. Business ebbs and flows, dependent on the weather.

When I go home I still have to take my turn at the front gate, explaining to visitors the flavor differences between Earliglow and Diamonte strawberries. Camino Reals and Everbearers. They all sound like the names of cool old cars. Not many people look at my name badge and make the connection with the farm's name. The Beatles' fans who do are deeply, smugly pleased with themselves.

I bet you can guess what I eat when I'm homesick.

"No. You didn't. How did you—"

"And you know, there's the nicest family picture somewhere . . . here." He clicks again, barely needing to glance at the screen. His eyes light with evil amusement as he watches me.

"How nice. It's your parents, right? Who's this adorable little girl with black hair? Is it your little cousin? No . . . It's a pretty old picture." He makes the picture fill his entire screen.

I'm turning redder than a flippin' strawberry. It's me, of course. It's a photo I don't think I've ever seen. The blurred treeline in the background orients me instantly. I turned eight when my parents put those new rows into the west quarter block. Business was picking up then, which accounts for the pride in my parents' smiles. I'm not ashamed of my parents, but it never ceases to amuse those who were raised in the city. Most white-collar jackasses like Joshua find it so *quaint* and *cute*.

They imagine my family as simple folk, hillbillies on the side of a hill covered in rambling vines. For people like Joshua, strawberries come from the store prepackaged in plastic boxes.

In this picture, I'm sprawled at my parents' feet like a foal. I'm wearing stained, dirty short overalls and my crinkly dark hair is a scribble. I have my patchwork library satchel looped around my body, no doubt crammed with The Baby-Sitters Club and old-fashioned horse stories. One of my hands is in a plant, the other filled with berries. I'm flushed from sun and possibly a vitamin C overdose. Maybe it's why I'm so small. It stunted my growth.

"You know, she looks a lot like you. Maybe I should send the link in an all-staff email to B&G, asking them who they think this wild little girl could be." He is visibly trembling with the need to laugh.

"I will kill you."

I do look completely wild in this photo. My eyes are lighter than the sky as I squint against the sun and do my best big smile. The same smile I've been doing all my life. I begin to feel a pressure in my throat, a burning in my sinuses.

I stare at my parents; they're both so young. My dad's back is straight in this photo, but each time I go home he's a little more stooped over. I flick my eyes to Joshua, and he doesn't look like he wants to laugh anymore. My eyes prick with tears before I stop to think of where I am and whom I'm sitting opposite.

He turns his computer screen back slowly, taking his time closing the browser, a typical male, awkward at the sight of female tears. I swivel and look up at the ceiling, trying to make them drain back down to where they came from.

"But we were talking about me. What can I do to be more like you?" An eavesdropper would think he sounds almost kind.

"You could try to stop being such an asshole." It comes out in a whisper. In the reflection on the ceiling I see his brow begin to crease. Oh lord. *Concern*.

Our computers chime a reminder: All-staff meeting, fifteen minutes. I smooth my eyebrows and fix my lipstick, using the wall as my mirror. I drag my hair down into a low bun with difficulty, using the hair elastic on my wrist. I ball up a tissue and press it into the corner of each eye.

The unsaid word *homesick* continues to rattle inside my chest. *Lonely.* When I open my eyes, I can see he's standing and can see my reflection. The pencil is in his hand.

"What?" I snap at him. He's *won*. He's made me cry. I stand up and grab a folder. He grabs a folder too, and we're seamlessly into the Mirror Game. We each knock lightly twice on our respective boss's door.

Come in, we are simultaneously beckoned.

Helene is frowning at her computer. She's more a typewriter kind of woman. She used one sometimes before we moved here, and I loved hearing the rhythmic clacking of keys from her office. Now it's in one of her cabinets. She was afraid of Fat Little Dick mocking her.

"Hi. We've got an all-staff in fifteen, remember? Down in the main boardroom."

She sighs heavily and raises her silver-screen eyes to me. They're big, dark, expressive and sparsely lashed under fine eyebrows. I can detect no trace of makeup on her face bar a rose lipstick.

She moved here with her parents from France when she was sixteen and even though she's now in her early fifties, she still has the remnants of a growly purr in her voice.

Helene doesn't notice that she is elegant, which makes her even more so.

She wears her hair in a short, neat cut. Her short nails are always painted cream pink. She buys all of her clothes in Paris before visiting her elderly parents in Saint-Étienne. The plain wool sweater she's wearing now probably cost more than three full carts of groceries.

In case it's not painfully clear, I idolize her. She's the reason I stopped wearing so much eye makeup. I want to be her when I grow up.

Her favorite word is *darling.* "Darling Lucy," she says now, holding out her hand. I put the folder into it. "Are you all right?"

"Allergies. My eyes are itchy."

"Hmm, that's no good."

She scans the agenda. For bigger meetings we'd do a bit more preparation, but the all-staffs are pretty straightforward since the division heads are doing most of the talking. The CEOs are there mainly to show involvement.

"Alan turned fifty?"

"I ordered a cake. We'll bring it out at the end."

"Good for morale," Helene replies absently. She opens her mouth, then hesitates. I watch her try to choose her words.

"Bexley and I are making an announcement at this meeting. It's very significant for you. We'll talk about it straight after the meeting."

My stomach twists. I'm fired for sure.

"No, it's good news, darling."

The all-staff meeting goes according to plan. I don't

sit next to Helene during these meetings, but instead prefer to sit with the others, mingling in. It's my way of reminding them I'm part of the team, but I still feel their reserve with me. Do they honestly imagine me snitching to Helene about their shitty days?

Joshua sits beside Fat Little Dick at the head of the table. Both are disliked and seem to sit together inside a bubble of invisibility.

Alan is pink and pleased when I bring out the cake. He's a crusty old Bexley from somewhere in the bowels of the finance section, which makes me feel even better about making the effort for him. I've passed a pretty frosting-covered peace offering over the fence between the two camps. It's how we Gamins roll. In Bexleyville they probably mark birthdays with a new calculator battery.

The room is crowded with latecomers leaning against the walls and perched on the low windowsill. The buzzing chatter is overwhelming compared to the silence of the tenth floor.

Joshua hasn't touched the wedges of cake that sit within arm's reach. He's not a snacker or even an eater. I fill our cavernous office with the rhythmic sounds of my carrot crunching and apple biting. Ziplocs of popcorn and little pots of yogurt disappear into my bottomless pit. I demolish tiny crunchy smorgasbords every day, and in contrast Joshua consumes peppermints. He's twice my size for heaven's sake. He's not human.

When I checked the cake, I'd groaned out loud. Of ALL the possible cake decorations the bakery could have used. You guessed it.

A consummate mind reader, Joshua leans forward and takes a strawberry. He scrapes away the icing and looks at the little blob of ivory on his thumb. What will he do? Suck it? Wipe his thumb with a mono-grammed handkerchief? He must sense my anticipation because his eyes cut to me. My face heats and I look away.

I quickly ask Margery about her son's progress learn-ing the trumpet (slow), and Dean's knee surgery (soon). They're flattered that I remember, and reply with smiles. I guess it's true that I'm always observing, listening, and collecting trivia. But not for any nefarious purpose. It's mainly because I'm a lonely loser.

I catch up with Keith regarding his granddaughter (growing) and Ellen's kitchen renovation (nightmarish). All the while, the following plays in the back of my head in a loop. *Eat your heart out, Joshua Templeman. I'm lovely. Everyone likes me. I'm part of this team. You're all alone.*

Danny Fletcher from the cover design team signals to get my attention from across the boardroom table. "I watched the documentary you recommended."

I wrack my brains and come up blank. "Oh, um? Which?"

"It was a couple of all-staffs ago. We were talking about a documentary you'd watched about da Vinci on the History Channel. I downloaded it."

I make a lot of small talk in my role. It never oc-curred to me anyone was listening. There's an intricate sketch in the margin of his notepad and I sneakily try to look at it.

"Did you enjoy it?"

"Oh, yeah. He was pretty much the ultimate human being, wasn't he?"

"No argument there. I'm such a failure—I haven't in-vented anything."

Danny laughs, bright and loud. I look from his notepad to his face. This is probably the first time I've looked at him properly. I get a little kick of surprise in my stomach when I flip off the autopilot switch. *Oh*. He's cute.

"Anyway, did you know I'm finishing up here soon?"

"No, why?" The little flirt-bubble inside my stomach bursts. Game over.

"A buddy and I are developing a new self-publishing platform. My last day is in a couple of weeks. This is my last all-staff."

"Well that's a shame. Not for me. For B and G." My clarification is as subtle as a love-struck schoolgirl.

Trust me to not notice a cute guy in my midst. He's been sitting right opposite me, for heaven's sake. Now he's leaving. Le sigh. It's time I took a proper look at Danny Fletcher. Attractive, lean, and in shape, with soft blond curls cropped close to his head. He's not tall, which suits me fine. He's a Bexley, but not of the typical variety. His shirt, while crisp like a birthday card, is rolled at the cuffs. His tie is subtly patterned with tiny scissors and clipboards.

"Nice tie."

He looks down and grins. "I do a LOT of cutting and pasting."

I look sideways at the design team, mainly Bexleys, who all dress like funeral directors. I understand his decision to leave B&G, the most boring design team on this planet.

Next, I look at Danny's left hand. Every finger is bare, and he drums them lightly against the table.

"Well, if you ever want to collaborate on an invention, I'm available." His smile is mischievous.

"You're freelancing as an inventor as well as reinventing self-publishing?"

"Exactly." He clearly appreciates my clever wordplay.

I've never had anyone flirt with me at work. I sneak a look at Joshua. He's talking to Mr. Bexley.

"It'll be hard to invent something the Japanese haven't thought of."

He considers for a moment. "Like those little mops babies can wear on their hands and feet?"

"Yes. Have you seen those pillows shaped like a husband's shoulder for lonely women to sleep on?"

His jaw is angular and shadowed with silvery stubble, and he has one of those slightly cruel mouths, until he smiles. Which he does now, looking right into my eyes.

"Surely you don't need one of those, do you?" He drops his tone, below the chatter of everyone else. His eyes are sparkling, daring me.

"Maybe." I make a rueful face.

"I'm sure you could find a human volunteer."

I try to get us back on track. Unfortunately, it comes out sounding like I'm propositioning him. "Maybe it would be fun to invent something."

Helene is tapping her papers into order and reluctantly I turn in my chair. Joshua is glaring at me with angry eyebrows. I use my brainwaves to transmit an insult to him, which he receives and pulls himself up straight.

"One more thing before we depart," Mr. Bexley says. Helene tries to not scowl. She hates when he acts like he's solely chairing meetings.

"We have an announcement about a restructure in the executive team," Helene continues seamlessly, and Mr. Bexley's lips tighten in annoyance before he cuts over her.

"A third executive position is being established—chief operating officer."

Joshua and I both do electric-shock jolts in our seats.

"It will be a position below Helene and myself. We want to formalize the position that oversees operations, leaving the CEOs free to focus on more strategic things."

He casts a thin-lipped smile at Joshua, who nods intently back at him. Helene catches my eye and raises her eyebrows meaningfully. Someone nudges me.

"It will be advertised tomorrow—details on the recruitment portal and the Internet." He says it like the Internet is a newfangled contraption.

"It's open to both internal and external applicants." Helene stacks her papers and rises.

Fat Little Dick stands to go, and selects another slice of cake. Helene follows him, shaking her head. The room once again explodes into noise and the cake box is dragged across the table. Joshua stands by the door, and when I stubbornly remain seated, he slinks off.

"Looks like you've got some work to do," Danny says to me. I nod and gulp and wave good-bye to the room in general, too overwhelmed to make a graceful exit. I break into a run when I leave the room, taking the stairs two at a time. I see Mr. Bexley's door close as I hotfoot it into Helene's and skid to a halt, swinging the door shut behind me and banging it closed with my backside.

"What's the reporting line?"

"You'd be Josh's boss, if that's what you're asking."

A sensation of pure elation floods me. Joshua's BOSS. He'd have to do everything I say, including treating me with some respect. I am at risk of wetting my pants right about now.

"It's got disaster written all over it, but I want you to have the job."

"Disaster?" I sink into a chair. "Why?"

"You and Josh do not work well together. Chalk and

cheese. Adding in a power dynamic like that . . ." She clucks doubtfully.

"But I can do the job."

"Of course, darling. I want you to have the job."

My excitement grows as we talk about the role. Another restructure is looming, but I'd have a direct hand in it this time. I could save jobs instead of cutting them. The responsibility is greater and the raise is substantial. I could go home more often. I could get a new car.

"You should know, Bexley wants Josh for the job. We had a big fight over it."

"If Joshua becomes my boss I will have to resign." It comes out of my mouth instantly. It's like what someone in a movie would say.

"All the more reason for us to get you the job, darling. If I had my way we would have just announced your promotion."

I nibble my thumb. "But how is it going to be a fair process? Joshua and Mr. Bexley are going to sabotage me."

"I thought of that. An independent panel of recruitment consultants are doing the interviews. You'll be competing on an even playing field. There'll be applicants from outside B and G too. Probably a pretty strong field. I want you to be prepared."

"I will be." I hope.

"And part of the interview is a presentation. You'll need to get started on it. They want to hear your thoughts on the future direction of B and G."

I'm itching to get back to my desk. I need to update my CV. "Do you mind if I work on my application during my lunch breaks?"

"Darling, I don't care if you work on it all day until

it's due. Lucy Hutton, chief operating officer, Bexley and Gamin. It sounds good, doesn't it."

A grin spreads across my face.

"It's yours. I feel it." Helene makes a motion of zipping her lip. "Now go. Get it."

I sit at my desk and unlock my computer to open my woefully outdated CV. I'm lit up inside by this new opportunity. Everything about today has changed. Well, almost everything.

I notice a shape standing over me after I've been editing for several minutes. I breathe in. Spicy cedar. His belt buckle winks at me. I do not break my keystrokes.

"The job is mine, Shortcake," Joshua's voice says.

To stop myself from standing up and punching him in the gut I'm counting one, two, three, four . . .

"Funny, that's what Helene just told me." I watch his backside walk away in the glossed surface of my desk, and vow that Joshua Templeman is going to lose the most important game we've ever played.

Chapter 4

Off-white stripes today, and I've got a big red cross in my planner for Friday. I would bet a hundred dollars there's an identical red cross in Joshua's. Our job applications are due.

I'm half-insane from rereading my application. I've become so obsessed with my presentation I've started dreaming about it. I need a break. I lock my screen and watch with interest as Joshua does the same. We are aligned like chess players. We fold our hands. I still haven't seen his pencil in motion.

"How You Doing, Little Lucy?" His bright tone and mild expression indicates we're playing a game we almost never play. It's a game called How You Doing? and it basically starts off like we don't hate each other. We act like normal colleagues who don't want to swirl their hands in each other's blood. It's disturbing.

"Great, thanks, Big Josh. How You Doing?"

"Super. Gonna go get coffee. Can I get you some tea?" He has his heavy black mug in his hand. I hate his mug.

I look down; my hand is already holding my red polka-dot mug. He'd spit in anything he made me. Does he think I'm crazy? "I think I'll join you."

We march purposefully toward the kitchen with identical footfalls, left, right, left, right, like prosecutors walking toward the camera in the opening credits of *Law & Order*. It requires me to almost double my stride. Colleagues break off conversations and look at us with speculative expressions. Joshua and I look at each other and bare our teeth. Time to act civil. Like executives.

"Ah-ha-ha," we say to each other genially at some pretend joke. "Ah-ha-ha."

We sweep around a corner. Annabelle turns from the photocopier and almost drops her papers. "What's happening?"

Joshua and I nod at her and continue striding, unified in our endless game of one-upmanship. My short striped dress flaps from the g-force.

"Mommy and Daddy love you very much, kids," Joshua says quietly so only I can hear him. To the casual onlooker he is politely chatting. A few meerkat heads have popped up over cubicle walls. It seems we're the stuff of legend. "Sometimes we get excited and argue. But don't be scared. Even when we're arguing, it's not your fault."

"It's just grown-up stuff," I softly explain to the apprehensive faces we pass. "Sometimes Daddy sleeps on the couch, but it's okay. We still love you."

In the kitchen I am hanging my tea bag into my mug when the urge to laugh almost knocks me over like an ocean wave. I hold on to the edge of the counter and soundlessly shake.

Joshua ignores me as he moves around preparing his coffee. I look up to see his hands opening the cupboard miles above my head, and I feel the heat of his body inches from my back. It's like sunshine. I'd forgotten that other people are warm. I can smell his skin. The urge to laugh fades.

I haven't had any human contact since my hairdresser, Angela, gave me a head massage, probably eight weeks ago. Now I'm imagining leaning back against him and letting my muscles go slack. What would he do if I fainted? He'd probably let me crumble onto the floor, then nudge me with his toe.

Another freeze-frame snaps through my brain. Joshua grabbing me, stopping me falling. His hands on my waist, fingertips digging in.

"You're so funny," I say when I realize I've been silent for a bit. "So very funny." I swallow audibly.

"So are you." He goes to the fridge.

Jeanette from HR materializes in the doorway like a dumpy frazzled ghost. She's a nice lady, but she's also sick of our shit.

"What's going on?" She has her hands on her hips. At least, I think she does. She's shaped like a triangle underneath the jingling Tibetan poncho she must have bartered for on her last spirit quest. She's a Gamin, natch.

"Jeanette! Making coffee. Can I tempt you?" Joshua wags his mug at her and she waves her hand irritably. She hates him deeply. She's my kind of lady.

"I got an emergency call. I'm here to referee."

"No need, Jeanette. Everything's fine." I dunk my tea bag gently, watching the water turn brick red. Joshua dumps a spoonful of sugar into my mug.

"Not quite sweet enough, are you?"

I make a fake laugh at the cabinet in front of me and wonder how he knows how I take my tea. How does he know *anything* about me? Jeanette is fisheyed with suspicion.

Joshua looks at her mildly. "We're making hot beverages. What's new in the human resource field?"

"The company's two worst serial complainants should not be left alone together." A corner of her poncho gestures to the kitchen.

"Well, that's a bind. We sit in a room together alone, all day. I spend between forty and fifty hours a week with this fine woman. All alone." He *sounds* pleasant, but the subtext to his dialogue was *Fuck Off.*

"I've made several recommendations to your bosses about that," Jeanette says darkly. Her subtext reads the same.

"Well, I'll be Lucinda's boss soon," Joshua replies and my eyes snap to his. "I'm professional and can manage anybody."

The way he enunciates *anybody* implies he thinks I am mentally deficient.

"Actually, I'll be *your* boss soon." I am syrupy sweet. Jeanette's little hands appear from under her poncho. She rubs her eyes, making a mess of her mascara.

"You two are my full-time job," she says softly, despairingly. I feel a stab of guilt. My behavior is unbecoming of a soon-to-be senior executive. Time to repair this relationship.

"I know in the past, communication between myself and Mr. Templeman has been a little . . . strained. I'm keen to address this, and strengthen team building at B and G." I use my best smooth professional voice, watching her face pinch suspiciously. Joshua flicks his eyes toward me like laser beams.

"I've drafted a recommendation for Helene outlining a team-building afternoon for corporate, design, executive, and finance." We call it CDEF for short, or the Alphabet Branch. This is my latest brainstorm.

How excellent would this sound in the interview? Very excellent.

"I will cosign to show my commitment," Joshua says, the goddamn hijacker. My wrist trembles with the need to flick hot tea in his face.

"Don't you worry about a thing," I tell Jeanette as we stand in front of her. "It'll all be fine." Her poncho jingles sadly as we stride off.

"When I'm your boss, I'm going to work you so fucking hard." Joshua's voice is dirty and rough.

I am struggling to keep up with him now, but I make myself. Some of my tea spatters onto the carpet. "When I'm *your* boss, you're going to do everything I say with a big smile on your face." I nod politely at Marnie and Alan as we pass them.

We round the corner like racehorses.

"When I'm your boss, any more than three mistakes in your financial calculations will result in an official warning."

I mutter under my breath but he still hears me. "When I'm your boss, I'm going to be convicted of murder."

"When I'm your boss, I'm implementing a corporate support uniform policy. No more of your weird little retro costumes. I've already got it circled in the Corporate Wear catalog. A gray shift dress." He pauses for effect. "Polyester. It's supposed to be knee length, so it should reach your ankles."

I am insanely sensitive about my height and I absolutely hate synthetic fibers. I open my mouth and a cute animal growl comes out. I hustle ahead and bump the glass door open to the executive suites with my hip.

"Is that what it would take for you to stop lusting after me?" I snap and he looks up at the ceiling and lets out a huge sigh.

"You got me, Shortcake."

"Oh, I've got you all right." We're both breathing a little harder than the situation warrants. We each set down our mugs and face off.

"I will never work for you. There'll be no polyester dress. I'll resign if you get it. It should go without saying."

He looks genuinely surprised for a fraction of a second. "Oh, really."

"Like you wouldn't quit if I got it."

"I'm not sure." He's gimlet-eyed with speculation.

"Joshua, you need to resign if I get it."

"I don't quit things." His voice gets a galvanized edge to it and he puts a hand on his hip.

"I don't quit things either. But if you're so certain you're going to get it, why would you have a problem with promising to resign?" I watch him mull this over.

I want him to be my subordinate, skittish with nerves as I review a piece of his work, which I'll tear up. I want him on his hands and knees at my feet, gathering up the torn shreds, burbling apologies for his own incompetence. Crying in Jeanette's office, berating himself for his own inadequacies. I want to make him so nervous he's tied in knots.

"Okay. I agree. If you get the promotion, I promise to resign. You've got your horny eyes on again," Joshua adds, turning away and sitting down. He unlocks his drawer and takes out his planner, busily sorting through the pages.

"Mentally strangling me again?"

He is making a mark with his pencil, a straight single tally, when he notices me.

"What are you smirking about?"

I think he makes a mark in his planner when we argue.

"I'D BETTER GET to bed." I'm talking to my parents. I'm also gently cleaning the two-dollar eBay Smurf I got a few weeks back with a baby's toothbrush. *Law & Order* is on in the background and they are currently pursuing a false lead. I've got a white clay mask on my face and my toenail polish is drying.

"All right, Smurfette," my parents chime like a two-headed monster. They haven't worked out they don't have to sit cheek to cheek to fit onto the video-chat screen. Or maybe they have, but they like it too much.

Dad is dangerously suntanned, bar the white outline of his sunglasses. It's a sort of reverse-raccoon effect. He's a big laugher and a big talker, so I get a lot of glimpses of the tooth he chipped while eating a rack of ribs. He's wearing a sweatshirt he's had since I was a kid and it makes me ridiculously homesick.

My mom never looks properly at the camera. She gets distracted by the tiny preview window where she can see her own face on screen. I think she analyzes her wrinkles. It gives our chats a disconnected quality and makes me miss her more.

Her fair skin can't cope with the outdoors, and where Dad has tanned, she has freckled. We have the same coloring, so I know what will happen if I give up the sunscreen. They dapple every square inch of her face and arms. She even has freckles on her eyelids. With her bright blue eyes and black hair, tied up in its usual knot on top of her head, she always gets a second glance wherever she goes. Dad is enslaved by her beauty. I know for a fact, because he was telling her roughly ten minutes ago.

"Now, don't worry about a thing. You're the most determined person there, I'm sure of it. You wanted to work for a publisher, and you did it. And you know what? Whatever happens, you're always the boss of Sky Diamond Strawberries." Dad's been explaining at great length all the reasons why I should get the promotion.

"Aw, Dad." I laugh to cover the leftover bubble of emotion I've been feeling since the blog meltdown in front of Joshua. "My first act as CEO is to order you both to bed for an early night. Good luck with Lucy Forty-two, Mom."

I caught up with the last ten blog entries while I ate dinner. My mom has a clear, factual style of writing. I think she would have been working somewhere major one day if she hadn't quit. Annie Hutton, investigative journalist. Instead, she spends her days digging up rotting plants, packing crates for delivery, and Frankensteining hybrid varieties of strawberries. To me, the fact she gave up her dream job for a man is a tragedy, no matter how wonderful my dad is, or the fact that I'm sitting here now as a result.

"I hope they don't turn out like Lucy Forty-one. I've never seen anything like it. They looked normal from the outside, but completely hollow on the inside. Weren't they, Nigel?"

"They were like fruit balloons."

"The interview will go fine, honey. They'll know within five minutes that you live and breathe the publishing industry. I still remember you coming home after that field trip. It was like you'd fallen in love." Mom's eyes are full of memories. "I know how you felt. I remember when I first stepped into the printing room of a newspaper. The smell of that ink was like a drug."

"Are you still having trouble with Jeremy at work?" Dad knows Joshua's actual name by now. He just chooses to not use it.

"Joshua. And yes. He still hates me." I take a fist of cashews and begin eating them a little aggressively.

Dad is flatteringly mystified. "Impossible. Who could?"

"Who even could," Mom echoes, reaching up to finger the skin by her eye. "She's little and cute. No one hates little cute people." Dad seamlessly agrees with her and they begin talking as though I'm not even here.

"She's the sweetest girl in the world. Julian's clearly got some sort of inferiority complex. Or he's one of those sexists. He wants to bring everyone else down to make himself feel better. Napoleon complex. Hitler complex. Something's wrong with him." He's ticking them off on his fingers.

"All of the above. Dad, put the Post-it note over the screen so she can't see herself. She's not looking at me properly."

"Maybe he's hopelessly in love with her," Mom offers optimistically as she looks properly into the camera for the first time. My stomach drops through the floor. I catch a glimpse of my own face; I am a clay statuette of frozen horror and surprise.

Dad scoffs all over the place. "Ridiculous way of showing it, don't you think? He's made that place a misery for her. I tell you, if I met him, he'd have to do some groveling. You hear that, Luce? Tell him to shape up or your dad's gonna get on a plane and have a few words with him."

The image of them face-to-face is weird. "I wouldn't bother, Dad."

It's the segue Mom needs. "Speaking of planes, we could put some money in your account so you could book a flight to visit us? We haven't seen you in so long. It's been a long time, Lucy."

"It's not the money, it's getting the time," I try to say, but they both begin talking over me at once, in an unintelligible combination of begging, pleading, and arguing.

"I'll come as soon as I can get some time, but it might not be for a while. If I get the promotion I'll be pretty busy. If I don't . . ." I study the keyboard.

"Yes?" Dad is sharp.

"I'll have to get another job," I admit. I look up.

"Of course you would. You would never work for that jackass Justin," he says. "It would be good to have her home though," Dad tells Mom. "The books are not adding up. We need some extra brainpower."

I can see Mom is still fretting about my job situation. She's a penny pincher, and she's been living on a farm long enough that in her imagination the city is a heinously expensive, bustling metropolis. She's not far off. I make a good wage, but after the bank sucks my rent payment out, I'm stretched pretty tight. The thought of getting a roommate fills me with dread.

"How will she . . ."

Dad shushes her and waves his hands to dispel the mere thought of failure like a puff of smoke. "It'll be fine. It'll be Johnnie unemployed and sleeping under a bridge, not her."

"That will never happen to her," Mom begins, alarmed.

"Have you made up with that friend you used to work with? Valerie, wasn't it?"

"Don't ask her, it upsets her," Mom scolds. Dad raises his hands in surrender and looks at the ceiling.

It's true; it does upset me, but I keep my tone even. "After the merger, I managed to meet her for a coffee, to explain myself, but she lost her job and I didn't. She couldn't forgive me. She said a true friend would have given her warning."

"But you didn't know," Dad begins. I nod. It's true. But what I've been grappling with ever since is, should I have somehow tried to find out for her?

"Her circle of friends were starting to become my friends . . . and now here I am. Square one again." A sad, lonely loser.

"There are other people at work to be friends with, surely," Mom says.

"No one wants to be friends with me. They think I'll tell their secrets to the boss. Can we change the subject? I talked to a guy this week." I regret it immediately.

"Oooh," they intone together. "Oooh." There is an exchanged glance.

"Is he nice?"

It's always their first question. "Oh, yes. Very nice."

"What's his name?"

"Danny. He's in the design section at work. We haven't gone out or anything, but . . ."

"How wonderful!" Mom says at the same time that Dad exclaims, "About time!"

He puts his thumb over the microphone and they begin to buzz to each other, a hornet swarm of speculation.

"Like I said, we haven't gone on a date. I don't know exactly if he wants to." I think of Danny, the sideways look he gave me, mouth curling. He does.

Dad speaks so loudly the microphone gets fuzzy sometimes. "You should ask him. It's got to beat sitting in the office for ten hours a day slinging mud at James. Get out and live a little. Get your red party dress on. I want to hear you have by the time we Skype next."

"Are you allowed to date colleagues?" Mom asks,

and Dad frowns at her. Negative concepts and worst-case scenarios do not interest him. However, she does raise a good point.

"It isn't allowed, but he's leaving. He's going to free-lance."

"A nice boy," Mom says to Dad. "I've got a good feeling."

"I really should go to bed," I remind them. I yawn and my clay face mask cracks.

"Night, night, sweetie," they chime. I can hear Mom say sadly "Why won't she come home—" as Dad clicks the End button.

The truth? They both treat me so much like a visiting celebrity, a complete and utter success. Their bragging to their friends is frankly ridiculous. When I go home, I feel like a fraud.

As I rinse my face, I try to ignore my Bad Daughter Guilt by deciding on the items I would take if I have to live under a bridge. Sleeping bag, knife, umbrella, a yoga mat. I can sleep on it AND do yoga to keep myself nimble. I could get all of my rare Smurfs into a fishing tackle box.

I have the copy of Joshua's desk planner on the end of my bed. Time to do a little Nancy Drewing. It's disturbing that a piece of Joshua Templeman has invaded my bedroom. My brain stage-whispers *Imagine!* I guillotine the thought.

I study the copy. A tally—I think those are the arguments. I make a note of this on the margin. Six arguments on this particular day. Sounds about right. The little slashes I have no idea about. But the X's? I think of Valentine's cards and kisses. None of those are going on in our office. This has got to be his HR record.

I fold up my laptop and put it away, then brush my teeth and get into bed.

Joshua's jibe about my work clothes—my "weird little retro costumes"—has prompted me to find the short black dress from the back of my wardrobe to wear tomorrow. It's the opposite of a gray ankle-length shift dress. It makes my waist look little and my ass look amazing. Thumbelina meets Jessica Rabbit. He thinks he's seen small clothes? He ain't seen nothing.

Little runts like me usually come across as cute rather than powerful, so I'm pulling out all the stops. The fishnet tights are so fine they feel like soft grit. My red heels that boost me up to a towering five-feet-five inches.

There's not going to be a single mention of strawberries tomorrow. Joshua Templeman is going to spray his coffee out his nose when I walk in. I don't know why I want him to—but I do.

What a confusing thought to fall asleep with.

Chapter 5

Falling asleep with his name in my head is probably the reason for my dream. It's the middle of the night, I'm lying on my stomach and I press my cheek into my pillow. He's braced over me, pressed against my back, warm as sunlight. His voice is a hot whisper, right in my ear as he twists his hips to grind himself against my butt.

I'm going to work you so fucking hard. So. Fucking. Hard.

I get a full impression of his heaviness and size. I try to push back against him again to feel it again, but he mutters my name like a reprimand and crawls up higher, his knees straddling my hips. His fingertips smooth along the sides of my breasts. His exhale steams against my neck. I can't get a decent lungful of air. He's too heavy and I'm too turned on. Sensitive, forgotten parts of me blaze to life. I scratch my fingertips against the sheets until they burn with friction.

The realization that I'm having a dirty dream about Joshua Templeman suddenly jars me and I teeter on the edge of waking, but I keep my eyes shut. I need to see where my mind takes this. After a few minutes, I sink back in.

I'll do anything you want, Lucinda. But you'll have to ask.

His tone is that lazy one he sometimes uses when he looks at me with that certain expression. It's like he's seen me through a hole in a wall and knows what I look like, down to my skin.

I twist my head, and see his wrist braced by my head, the sleeve of a business shirt loose with no cuff link. I can see an inch of wrist; hair, veins, and tendons. The hand bunches into a fist and the mere thought of him being overcome makes me clench inside.

I can't see his face. Even though this may destroy everything, I roll over onto my back, the blankets and sheets beginning to twist me up. I'm tangled up in his arms and legs. I realize I'm turned on, and the realization that I am probably wet hits me as I look into his brilliant navy eyes. I let out a theatrical gasp of horror. A husky laugh is his reply.

I'm afraid so. He doesn't look sorry.

There's so much delicious weight, pressing me down. Hips and hands. I move against Dream-Joshua sinuously, feeling him bite back a groan, and I realize something shocking.

You want me desperately.

The words echo out of my mouth, true and undeniable. A kiss on the pulse in my jaw confirms what I already know. It's stronger than attraction; darker than wanting. It's a restlessness between us that has never had a true outlet, until now. The cream sheets are blazing hot against my skin.

You're tied up in fucking knots over me. I feel hands sliding along my body, weighing curves, buttons popping and seams unfurling. I'm being peeled, inspected. Teeth bite, and I'm being eaten. I have never had anyone burn for me like this. I'm shamefully turned on and even though I'm on my back, the look in his eyes confirms it's me who is winning this game. I try to tug him down to kiss me, but he evades and teases.

You've known all along, he tells me and his blazing smile tips me over the edge. I tremble awake. I jolt my hand away from the seam of my damp pajamas, my face burning red in the darkness. I can't decide what to do. Finish the job, or take a cold shower? In the end, all I do is lie there.

The hanging shape of my black dress at the foot of my bed is menacing and I stare at it until my breathing slows. I look at my digital clock. I have four hours to repress this memory.

IT'S SEVEN THIRTY A.M. on a Cream Shirt Day. The reflection in the elevator doors confirms my trench coat is longer than my tiny dress, so I look like a high-class call girl, en route to a hotel penthouse with only lingerie on underneath.

I had to get the bus today. I could barely climb from the curb onto the first step without showing my underwear, and as the doors closed behind me, I knew this dress was a catastrophic lapse in judgment. The enthusiastic set of honks from a passing truck as I teetered up the sidewalk to B&G confirmed it. If Target were open this early, I'd duck in and buy some pants.

I can get through this. I will need to remain seated for the entire day. The elevator doors open and of course Joshua is at his desk. Why does he always have to be at work so flippin' early? Does he go home? Does he sleep in a morgue drawer in the boiler room? I suppose he could ask the same of me.

I was hoping I'd have a minute or two alone here in the office to get settled in for a long day of remaining seated. But there he is. I hide myself behind the coat rack and pretend to rifle through my handbag to buy myself some time.

If I focus on the dress as my main issue, I can ignore the flashbacks to last night's dream. He lifts his eyes from his planner, pencil in hand. He stares at me until I begin to untie the belt on my trench coat, but I can't continue. The blue of his eyes is even more vivid than in my dream. He's looking at me like he's busy reading my mind.

"It's cold in here, no?"

Mouth pursing into a kiss of irritation, he waves his hand in circles as if to say *Get on with it*. Fortifying myself with a deep breath, I take off the coat and hang it on my special padded hanger. I feel the friction of the tiny fishnet diamonds between my thighs as I walk toward our desks. I'm pretty much wearing a swimsuit.

I watch his eyes drop to his planner, dark lashes making a half-moon shadow on his cheeks. He looks young, until he looks up and his eyes are a man's, speculative and hard. My ankle wobbles.

"Wowsers," he drawls, and I watch his pencil make some kind of mark. "Got a hot date, Shortcake?"

"Yes," I lie automatically and he puts the pencil behind his ear, cynical.

"Do tell."

I try to perch my butt nonchalantly on the edge of my desk. The glass is cold against the backs of my thighs. It's a dreadful mistake but I can't stand back up now, I'll look like an idiot. We both stare at my legs.

I look down at my bright red heels and I can see faintly up my own dress, the tiles are polished so bright.

I let my hair fall across my eye. If I focus on this stupid dress, I can forget how my brain wants him to lick me, bite me, undress me.

"What's up?" For once his voice sounds normal. "What's happened?"

I pick vaguely at an irregular diamond on my thigh. The dream is surely written all over my face. My cheeks are getting warm. He's wearing the cream shirt, soft and silky as the sheets in my dream. My subconscious is a deviant. I try to make eye contact but chicken out and manage to saunter around to my chair. I wish I could saunter out of here, all the way home.

"Hey." He says it more sharply. "What's up? Tell me."

"I had a . . . dream." I say it like someone might say, *Grandma's dead.* I sit down in my chair, pressing my knees together until the bones grind.

"Describe this dream." He has the pencil in his hand again and I am like a terrier watching the motion of a knife and fork. We start playing Word Tennis. Whoever can't think of a reply first loses.

"Your face has gone all red. All the way down your neck."

"Quit looking at me." He's correct, of course. This mirror-ball office confirms it.

"Can't. You're right in my line of vision."

"Well, try."

"It's not often I see such an interesting choice of thigh-revealing attire in the workplace. In the HR manual for appropriate business attire—"

"You can't take your eyes off my thighs long enough to consult the manual." It's true. He looks at the floor but after a second the red sniper-dot from his eyes recommences at my ankle bone and slides up.

"I have it memorized."

"Then you'll know that thighs are not an appropriate topic of conversation. If I get my polyester sack dress I guess you'll be kissing them good-bye."

"I look forward to it. Getting the promotion, I mean. Not your thighs— Never mind."

"Dream on, pervert." I type in my password. The previous one expired. Now it's DIE-JOSH-DIE! "It's my job, not yours."

"So who's your date with?"

"A guy." I'll find one between now and the end of the workday. I'll hire a guy if I have to. I'll call a modeling agency and ask for the catch of the day. He'll pick me up in a limo out front of B&G and Joshua will have egg on his face.

"What time is your date?"

"Seven," I hazard.

"What location is your date?" He slowly makes a pencil mark. An X? A slash? I can't tell.

"You're very interested; why is that?"

"Studies have shown that if managers feign interest in their employees' personal lives it increases their morale and makes them feel valued. I'm getting the practice in, before I'm your boss." His professional spiel is contradicted by the weird intensity in his eyes. He's truly captivated by all of this.

I give him my best withering look. "I'm meeting him for drinks at the sports bar on Federal Avenue. And: You're never going to be my boss."

"What a total coincidence. I'm going there to watch the game tonight. At seven."

My clever fib was a tactical error. I study him but can't tell where his face ends and the lie begins.

"Maybe I'll see you there," he continues. He is diabolical.

"Sure, maybe," I make my voice bored so he can't tell I'm simultaneously fuming and panicking.

"So this dream—a *man* was in it, right?"

"Oh, yes indeed." My eyes travel across Joshua without my permission. I think I can see the shape of his collarbone. "It was highly erotic."

"I should compose an email to Jeanette," he says faintly after a pause and a throat-clearing rasp. He does a poor imitation of typing on his keyboard without even looking at the screen.

"Did I say erotic? I meant esoteric. I get those mixed up."

He narrows one eye. "Your dream was . . . mysterious?"

Here goes nothing. It's time to take my chances with the human lie detector.

"It was full of symbols and hidden meaning. I was lost in a garden, and there was a man there. Someone I spend a lot of time with, but this time he seemed like a stranger."

"Continue," Joshua says. It's so strange to talk to him when his face isn't a mask of boredom.

I cross my legs as elegantly as I can manage and his eyes flash under my desk, then back to my face.

"I was wearing nothing but bedsheets," I say in a confiding tone, then pause.

"This is strictly between us, right?"

He nods, spellbound, and I mentally high-five myself for winning Word Tennis.

I need to prolong this moment; it's not often I gain the upper hand. I put on lipstick using the wall as a mirror. The color is called Flamethrower and it's my trademark. Vicious, violent, poisonous red. Slit-wrists red. *The color of the devil's underpants,* according to Dad. I have so many tubes that I always have a tube within a three-foot radius. I am black and white, but thanks to Flamethrower, I can be Technicolor. I live in terror of it being discontinued by the manufacturer, hence my hoarding.

"So I'm walking through this garden and the man is right behind me." Today I am a pathological liar. This is what Joshua Templeman does to me.

"He's right behind me. Like, up against me. Pressed up against my ass." I stand and slap my own butt loud enough to make my point. The words ring so true, because mostly it *is* true. Joshua nods slowly, his throat constricting in a swallow as his eyes trail down my dress.

"I seem to recognize his voice." I pause for thirty seconds, blotting my lips, holding it up to admire the little red heart-shaped mark on the tissue before scrunching it and putting it in the wastebasket near my toes. I start reapplying.

"Do you always have to do that twice?" Joshua is growing irritated by this stilted storytelling. He taps his fingertips impatiently on the desk.

I wink. "Don't want it kissing off, now do I?"

"Who is this date with, exactly? What's his name?"

"A *guy*. You're changing the subject, but that's okay. Sorry for boring you." I sit down and click the mouse until my computer whirs to life.

"No, no," Joshua says faintly, like he is completely out of air. "I'm not bored."

"Okay, so I'm in the garden, and it's . . . all reflective. Like it's covered in mirrors."

He nods, elbow sliding forward on the desk, chin in hand. He is inching his chair back.

"And I . . ." I pause, and glance at him. "Never mind."

"What?" He barks it so loud I bounce an inch out of my seat.

"I say, *Who are you? Why do you want me so badly?* And when he tells me his name, I was so shocked . . ."

Joshua dangles from the end of my fishing line, a glossy fish, flipping and irrevocably hooked. I can feel the expanse of air between us vibrating with tension.

"Come over here, I need to whisper it," I murmur, glancing left and right although we both know there's nobody for miles.

Joshua shakes his head reflexively and I look at his lap. He's not the only one who can stare underneath the desk.

"Oh," I say to be a smartass, but to my astonishment color begins to burn on Joshua's cheekbones. Joshua Templeman is turned on in my presence. Why does it make me want to tease him even more?

"I'll come over and tell you." I lock my computer screen.

"I'm fine."

"I have to share it." I walk over slowly and put my hands on the edge of his desk. He looks at my fishnet legs with such a tormented expression I almost feel sorry for him.

"This is unprofessional." He glances at the ceiling for inspiration before finding it. "HR."

"Is that our safe word? Okay." In this fluorescent lighting he looks irritatingly healthy and gold, his skin even and unblemished. But there's a faint sheen on his face.

"You're a little sweaty." I take the Post-its from his desk and plant a big, slow kiss on top. I peel it off and stick it in the middle of his computer screen.

"I hope you're not coming down with something." I walk away toward the kitchen. I hear the wheels on his chair make a faint wheeze.

LIVE A LITTLE.

Danny's cubicle is stripped down and a little chaotic. Packing boxes and stacks of paper and files are everywhere.

"Hi!"

He jolts and makes a jagged gray smudge on the author photograph he was Photoshopping. Real smooth, Lucy.

"Sorry. I should wear a bell."

"No, it's okay. Hi." He hits Undo, Save, and then swivels, his eyes sliding up and down me as fast as lightning, before getting snagged on the hemline of my dress for an extra few seconds.

"Hi. I was wondering if you'd come up with any inventions for us to get started on?"

I can't believe how forward I'm being, but I'm in a desperate situation. My pride is at stake here. I need someone sitting next to me tonight on a barstool or Joshua will laugh his ass off.

A smile spreads across his face. "I've got a half-finished time machine I could get you to take a look at."

"They're pretty straightforward. I can help you out."

"Name the time and place."

"The sports bar on Federal? Tonight, seven o'clock?"

"Sounds great. Here, I'll give you my number." Our fingers graze when he gives it to me. My, my. What a nice boy. Where on earth has he been all this time?

"See you tonight. Bring, um, blueprints." I weave back through the cubicles and climb the stairs back to the top floor, mentally dusting my hands.

Time to work. I drop back into my seat and begin work on the proposal outlining our desire to run a team-building activity. I put two signature spaces at the bottom, sign my name, and dump it into his in-tray. He takes a full two hours to even pick it up. When he does, he reads it in about four seconds. He slashes his signature onto it and flicks it into his out-tray without a glance. He has been in a weird mood this afternoon.

I steeple my fingers and commence the Staring Game. It takes about three minutes but he eventually heaves a sigh and locks his screen. We stare so deep into each other's eyes we join each other in a dark 3-D computer realm; nothing but green gridlines and silence.

"So. Nervous?"

"Why would I be?"

"Your big date, Shortcake. You haven't had one in a while. As long as I've known you, I think." He indicates quotation marks with his fingers at *big date*. He's positive it's all a lie.

"I'm way too picky."

He steeples his fingers so hard it looks painful. "Really."

"Such a complete drought of eligible men here."

"That's not true."

"You're searching for your own eligible bachelor?"

"I—no—shut up."

"You're right." I drop my eyes to his mouth for a split second. "I've finally found someone in this godforsaken place. The man of my dreams." I raise my eyebrow meaningfully.

He makes the connection to our early-morning conversation seamlessly. "So your dream was definitely about someone you work with."

"Yes. He's leaving B&G very soon, so maybe I need to make a move."

"You're sure about it."

"Yes." I can't remember the last time he has blinked his eyes. They are black and scary.

"You've got your serial killer eyes on again." I stand and take my proposal from him. "I'll get you a copy for Fat Little Dick. Don't screw this up for me, Joshua. You've got no concept of how to build a team. Leave this to the expert."

When I return he's a little less dark looking, but his hair is messed up. He takes the document, which I have stamped COPY.

He looks at the document, and I can see the exact moment he has his idea. It's the sharp pause that a fox makes as it mooches past the unlatched gate of a henhouse. He looks up at me, his eyes glittering. He bites his bottom lip and hesitates.

"Whatever you're thinking, don't."

He takes a pen and writes something across the bottom. I try to see, but he stands and holds it so high a corner touches the ceiling. I can't risk standing on tiptoes in this dress.

"How could I possibly resist?" He rounds his desk and touches his thumb under my chin as he brushes past.

"What have you done?" I say to his back as he walks into Mr. Bexley's office. I scuttle into Helene's, rubbing my chin.

"I agree," she says, laying the document aside. "This is a good idea. Did you see how the Gamins and Bexleys sat apart in the team meeting? I'm tired of it. We haven't done anything as a team since the merger-planning day. I'm impressed that you and Joshua came together."

I hope my weird brain doesn't file away her last filthy-sounding sentence.

"We are working out our differences." I have no trace of lie in my voice.

"I'll talk to Bexley at our four o'clock battle royale. What are your ideas?"

"I've found a corporate retreat that's only fifteen minutes off the highway. It's one of those places with whiteboards all over the walls."

"Sounds expensive." Helene makes a face, which I had already anticipated.

"I've run the numbers. We were under the training budget for this financial year."

"So what will we do at this corporate love-in?"

"I've already come up with several team-building activities. We'll do them in a round-robin style, rotating each group so teams get regularly mixed up. I'd like to be the facilitator for the day. I want to end this war between the Bexleys and Gamins."

"People absolutely hate team activities," Helene points out.

I can't argue. It's a corporate truth universally acknowledged that workers would rather eat rat skeletons than participate in group activities. I know I would. But until business team-building models make a significant advance, it's all I've got.

"There's a prize at the end for the participant who's made the biggest effort and contributes the most." I pause for effect. "A paid day off."

"I like it," she cackles.

"Joshua is planning something though," I warn. She nods.

She enters the Colosseum at precisely four. As usual, I can hear them shouting at each other.

At five, Helene comes out of Mr. Bexley's office and arrives at my desk in an irritated state. "Josh," she tosses over her shoulder, her voice colored with dislike.

"Ms. Pascal, how are you?" A halo floats above his head.

She ignores him. "Darling, I'm sorry. I lost the coin

toss. We've gone with Josh's idea for team building. What is the thing called? Paintballs?"

Sweet baby Jesus, no. "That wasn't the recommendation. I should know; I wrote it."

Joshua nearly smiles. It shimmers like a holograph over his face. It vibrates out of him in waves. "I took the liberty of providing an alternative to Mr. Bexley. Paintballing. It's been shown to be an effective team-building activity. Fresh air, physical activity . . ."

"Injuries and insurance claims," Helene counters. "Cost."

"People will pay twenty dollars of their own money to shoot their colleagues with paintballs," he assures her, staring at me. "It won't cost the company a cent. They'll sign waivers. We'll split into teams."

"Darling, how does it help team building to separate people and give them paint guns?"

While they argue in fake-polite voices, I seethe. He's hijacked my corporate initiative and taken it down to a juvenile, base level. Such a Bexley thing to do.

"Perhaps we'll see some unlikely alliances form," he tells Helene.

"In that case, I want to see you two paired together," Helene says archly and I could hug her. He can't paintball his own teammate.

"Like I said, unlikely alliances. Anyway, let's not fluster Lucinda before her *hot date*."

"Oh, really, Lucy?" Helene taps my desk. "A date. I expect a full report in the morning, darling. And come in late if you wish. You work too much. Live a little."

Chapter 6

At six thirty P.M. my knee begins jiggling.

"Will you be late?"

"None of your business." Goddamn it, will Joshua ever leave? He's worked an eleven-hour day and still looks as fresh as a daisy. I want to lie facedown on my bed.

"Didn't you say seven? How are you getting there?"

"Cab."

"I'm headed there too. I'll give you a ride. I insist." Joshua's face has been the picture of amusement throughout this little exchange. He's waiting for me to fess up about lying. It feels good to know I have Danny as the ace up my sleeve.

"Fine. Whatever." My fury over the team-building hijack has burned away, leaving a husk. Everything is spiraling slowly out of control.

I head to the ladies room, makeup bag in hand. My footsteps echo in the empty corridor. I haven't had a date in a long time. I'm too busy. Between work, hating Joshua Templeman, and sleeping, I have no time for anything else.

Joshua cannot believe anyone would want to spend time in my company. To him I'm a repugnant little shrew. I carefully draw my eyeliner into a tiny cat's-eye. I wipe off my lipstick until only the stain is left. I put a spray of perfume into my bra and give myself a little wink and a pep talk.

I have a dangly pair of earrings in the side pocket of my makeup bag and I hook them on. Office to evening, like those magazine articles. I'm tugging up my bra when I bump squarely into Joshua outside the bathroom. He is holding my coat and bag in hand. The shock of making contact with his body clashes through me.

He looks at me strangely. "Why'd you do all that?"

"Gee, thanks." I hold my hand out and he hooks my bag onto it. He holds on to my coat and pushes the elevator button.

"So I get to see your car." I try to break the silence. That thought is more nerve-racking than seeing Danny. It's such an enclosed space. Have Joshua and I ever even sat next to each other before? I doubt it.

"I've been imagining it for so long. I've been thinking it's a Volkswagen beetle. A rusty white one, like Herbie."

"Guess again." He is hugging my coat idly. His fingers twiddle the cuff. Against his body it looks like a kid's jacket. I feel sorry for this poor coat. I hold my hand out but he ignores me.

"MINI Cooper, early 1980s. Kermit green. The seat won't go back so your knees are on either side of the steering wheel."

"Your imagination is quite vivid. You drive a 2003 Honda Accord. Silver. Filthy messy inside. Chronic gearbox issues. If it were a horse, you'd shoot it." The elevator arrives and I step in cautiously.

"You're a way better stalker than I am." I feel a chill of fear when I see his big thumb push the B button. He looks down at me, his eyes dark and intense. He's clearly deliberating something.

Maybe he'll murder me down there. I'll end up dead in a Dumpster. The investigators will see my fishnets and heavy eye makeup and assume I'm a hooker. They'll follow all the wrong leads. Meanwhile, Joshua will be calmly bleaching all my DNA off his shoes and making himself a sandwich.

"Serial killer eyes." I wish I didn't sound so scared. He looks over my shoulder at his reflection in the shiny wall of the elevator.

"I see what you mean. You've got your horny eyes on." He spirals his finger dramatically over the elevator button panel.

"Nope, these are my serial killer eyes too."

He lets out a deep breath and pushes the emergency stop button and we judder to a halt.

"Please don't kill me. There's probably a camera." I take a step backward in fright.

"I doubt it." He looms over me. He raises his hands and I start to lift my arms to shield my face like I'm in some awful schlocky drive-in horror movie. This is it. He's going to strangle me. He's lost his sanity.

He scoops me off the floor by my waist and balances my ass on the handrail I've never noticed before. My arms drop to his shoulders and my dress slides to the top of my thighs. When he glances down he lets out a rough breath which sounds like I'm strangling *him*.

"Put me down. This isn't funny." My feet make little ineffectual spirals. This isn't the first time a big kid's thrown his weight around with me. Marcus DuShay in third grade once slung me onto the hood of the principal's car and ran off laughing. The plight of the little humans. There is no dignity for us in this oversize world.

"Visit me up here for a sec."

"What on earth for?" I try to slide down but he spans his hands on my waist and presses me against the wall. I squeeze his shoulders until I come to the informed conclusion that his body is extravagant muscle under these Clark Kent shirts.

"Holy shit." His collarbone is like a crowbar under my palms. I say the only idiotic thing I can think of. "Muscles. Bones."

"Thanks."

We are both desperately out of breath. When I press my leg against him for balance, his hand wraps around my calf.

When he puts one hand on my jaw and tilts my head back, I wait for the squeeze to start. At any moment, his warm palm will snap tight and I'll begin to die. Nose to nose. Breath against breath. One of his fingertips is behind my earlobe and I shiver when it slides.

"Shortcake."

The sweet little word dissolves and I swallow.

"I'm not going to kill you. You're so dramatic." Then he presses his mouth lightly against mine.

Neither of us closes our eyes. We stare at each other like always, closer than we've ever been. His irises are ringed blue-black. His eyelashes lower and he looks at me with an expression like resentment.

His teeth catch my bottom lip in a faint bite, and goose bumps spread. My nipples pinch. My toes curl in my shoes. I accidentally touch him with my tongue when I check for damage, although it didn't hurt. It was too soft, too careful. My brain is whirring hopelessly with explanations of what is happening, and my body begins to better its grip.

When he leans in again and begins to move his

mouth against mine, softly plying it open, the penny drops.

Joshua. Templeman. Is. Kissing. Me.

For a few seconds I'm frozen solid. It seems I've forgotten how to kiss; it's been so long since it's been a daily activity. Not seeming to mind, he explains the rules with his mouth.

The Kissing Game goes like this, Shortcake. Press, retreat, tilt, breathe, repeat. Use your hands to angle just right. Loosen up until it's a slow, wet slide. Hear the drum of blood in your own ears? Survive on tiny puffs of air. Do not stop. Don't even think about it. Shudder a sigh, pull back, let your opponent catch you with lips or teeth and ease you back into something even deeper. Wetter. Feel your nerve endings crackle to life with each touch of tongue. Feel a new heaviness between your legs.

The aim of the game is to do this for the rest of your life. Screw human civilization and all it entails. This elevator is home now. This is what we do now.

Do not fucking stop.

He tests me and pulls back a fraction. The cardinal rule broken. I pull his mouth back to mine with my hand fisted at the scruff of his neck. I'm a quick study and he's the perfect tutor.

He tastes like those spearmints he's always crunching. Who chews mints? I tried it once and burned my mouth out. He does it to annoy me, flickers of amusement in his eyes at my irritated huff. I nip him now in retribution, but it urges him closer against me, body hard, warming me everywhere we connect. Our teeth chink together.

What the fuck is happening? I ask silently with my kiss.

Shut up, Shortcake. I hate you.

If we were actors in a movie we'd be bumping against walls, buttons flying, the fishnet of my stockings shredded, and my shoes falling off. Instead, this kiss is decadent. We're leaning against a sunlit wall, dreamily licking ice cream cones, rapidly succumbing to heat stroke and nonsensical hallucinations.

Here, come a little closer, it's all melting. Lick mine and I will definitely lick yours.

Gravity catches me by the ankle and begins to drag me off the handrail. Joshua hoists me up higher with a hand on the back of my thigh. From this tiny loss of his mouth I growl in outraged frustration. *Get back here, rule breaker.* He's wise enough to obey.

The sound he makes in reply is like *huh*. The kind of amused sound people make when they discover something unexpected yet pleasing. That I-should-have-known sound. His lips curve and I touch his face. The first smile Joshua's ever had in my presence is pressed against my lips. I pull back in astonishment, and in one millisecond his face has defaulted back to grave and serious, albeit flushed.

A harsh burr comes from the elevator speaker, and we both jolt when a tinny voice *ahems*. "Everything okay in there?"

We freeze in a tableau entitled *Busted*. Joshua reacts first, leaning over to press the intercom.

"Bumped the button." He slowly sets me down onto the ground and backs away a few paces. I hook my elbow on the handrail, my legs sliding out on roller skates.

"What the fuck was that?" I wheeze with the last of my air.

"Basement, please."

"Right-o." The elevator slides down about three feet

and the doors open. If he'd waited another half second, it would have never happened. My coat is in a crumpled mess on the floor, and he picks it up, dusting it off with surprising care.

"Come on."

He walks off without a backward glance. My earrings are caught in my hair, tangled by his hands. I look for an exit. There are none. The elevator doors snap shut behind me. Joshua unlocks an arrogantly sporty black car and when I reach the passenger door we face each other. My eyes are big fried eggs. He has to turn away so I don't see him laugh. I catch the reflection of his white teeth on a nearby van's rearview mirror.

"Oh dear," he drawls, turning back, dragging his hand over his face to wipe away the smile. "I've traumatized you."

"What . . . what . . ."

"Let's go."

I want to sprint away but my legs won't hold me up.

"Don't even think about it," he tells me.

I slide into his car and nearly fall unconscious. His scent is intensified in here perfectly, baked by summer, preserved by snow, sealed and pressurized inside glass and metal. I inhale like a professional perfumer. Top notes of mint, bitter coffee, and cotton. Mid notes of black pepper and pine. Base notes of leather and cedar. Luxurious as cashmere. If this is what his car smells like, imagine his bed. Good idea. Imagine his bed.

He gets in, tosses my coat on the backseat, and I look sideways at his lap. Holy shit. I avert my eyes. Whatever he's got there is impressive enough to make my eyes slide back again.

"You've died of shock," he chides like a schoolteacher.

My breath is shaking out of me, and he turns to look at me, eyes poison-black. He raises his hand and I flinch back. He frowns, pauses, then twists my closest earring carefully back into position.

"I thought you were going to kill me."

"I still want to." He reaches for the other earring, and his inner wrist is close enough to bite. Painstakingly, he tugs the caught strands of hair until my earring hangs properly again.

"I want to. So bad, you have no idea."

He turns the car on, backs out, and drives as though nothing happened.

"We need to talk about this." My voice is rough and dirty. His fingers flex on the steering wheel.

"It seemed like the right moment."

"But you *kissed* me. Why would you do that?"

"I needed to test a theory I've had for a while. And you really, *really* kissed me back."

I twist in my seat and the lights ahead go red. He slows to a stop and looks at my mouth and legs.

"You had a theory? More like, you were trying to mess me up before my date." Cars behind us are beeping and I look over my shoulder. "Go."

"Oh, that's right, your date. Your imaginary fake date."

"It's not imaginary. I'm meeting Danny Fletcher from design."

The look of shocked surprise on his face is magnificent. I want to commission a portrait artist to capture it in oils, so I can pass it down to future generations. It. Is. *Priceless.*

Cars begin to pull out from either side behind us, horns bleating and wailing. A string of road-rage obscenities manage to jerk him from his stupor.

"What?" He finally notices the green light and accelerates sharply, braking to avoid hitting a car swerving in front. He wipes one hand over his mouth. I've never seen Joshua so flustered.

"Danny Fletcher. I'm meeting him in ten minutes. That's where you're driving me. What is wrong with you?"

He says nothing for several blocks. I stare stubbornly at my hands and all I can think about is his tongue in my mouth. In my *mouth*. I estimate there's probably been about ten billion elevator kisses in the history of mankind. I hate us for the cliché.

"Did you think I was lying?" Well, technically I was lying, but only at first.

"I always assume you're lying." He changes lanes in an angry swerve, an ominous black thundercloud of temper settling over him.

Here's a fact. Hating someone is exhausting. Each pulse of blood in my veins takes me closer to death. I waste these ending minutes with someone who genuinely despises me.

I drop my lids so I can remember it again. *I'm shimmering with nerves, heaving a box onto my desk at the newly minted B&G building, tenth floor. There is a man by the window, looking out at the early-morning traffic. He turns and we make eye contact for the first time.*

I'm never getting another kiss like that again, not for the rest of my life.

"I wish we could be friends," I accidentally say out loud. I've held those words in for so long it feels like I've dropped a bombshell. He's so silent I think maybe he didn't hear me. But then he casts me a look so contemptuous that I feel a painful twist inside.

"We'll never, ever be friends." He says *friends* like he'd say the word *pathetic*.

When he slows the car at the front of the bar I'm out and running before he's even come to a complete stop. I hear him shout my name, annoyed. I register that he calls me Lucy.

I see Danny at the bar, bottle of beer dangling from his fingertips, and I pinwheel through the crowd and fall into his arms. Poor old Danny, who has turned up early like a gentleman, with no idea what kind of crazy woman he's agreed to spend an evening with.

"Hi." Danny is pleased. "You made it."

"'Course!" I manage a shaky laugh. "I need a drink after the day I've had."

I hoist myself like a jockey onto the barstool. Danny signals to the bartender. Identical baseball bats swing on huge screens positioned above the bar. I feel the memory of Joshua's mouth on mine, and I press my shaking fingertips to my lips.

"A big gin and tonic. As big as you can, please."

The bartender obliges and I empty half of the contents into my mouth and maybe a little down my chin. I lick the corners of my mouth and I still taste Joshua. Danny catches my eye as I lower the glass.

"Is everything okay? I think you need to tell me about your day."

I take a good look at him. He's changed into some dark jeans and a nice button-down check shirt. I like that he's made an effort to go home and change for me.

"You look nice," I tell him honestly, and his eyes spark.

"And you look beautiful." His tone is confidential. He leans his elbow on the bar and his face is open and without malice. I feel a weird bubble of emotion inside my chest.

"What?" I wipe my chin. This man is looking at me like he does not hate me. It's bizarre.

"I couldn't exactly tell you at work. But I've always thought you were the most beautiful girl."

"Oh. Well." I probably turn bright red and I feel a tightness in my throat.

"You don't take compliments well."

"I don't get many." It's the honest truth. He just laughs.

"Oh, sure."

"It's true. Unless it's my mom and dad on Skype."

"Well, I'll have to change that. So. Tell me all about you."

"I work for Helene, as you know," I start uncertainly.

He nods, his mouth quirking.

"And that's about it."

Danny smiles, and I nearly reel backward off my barstool. I'm so badly socialized I can barely converse with normal human beings. I want to be at home on my couch with all of the pillows piled on my head.

"Yes, but I want to know about *you*. What do you do for fun? Where's your family from?"

His face is so open and guileless. I think of children before the world ruins them.

"May I go and freshen up first? I came straight from the office." I swallow the other half of my glass. The faint mint on my tongue deadens the flavor.

He nods and I make a beeline in the direction of the bathrooms. I lean against the wall outside them and take a tissue from the front of my bra and press it to the corners of my eyes. *Beautiful.*

A shadow darkens the hall, and I know it's Joshua.

Even in the furthest corners of my peripheral vision, his shape is more familiar than my own shadow. He's holding the coat I left in his backseat.

I burst out laughing, and I keep laughing until the tears stripe down my face, almost certainly ruining my makeup.

"Fuck off," I tell him, but he only comes closer. He takes my chin and studies my face.

The memory of the kiss floats up between us, and I can't look him in the eye. I remember the groan I made into his mouth. Humiliation kicks in.

"Don't." I slap him away.

"You're crying."

I hug myself. "No I'm not. Why are you even here?"

"Parking is a nightmare around here. Your coat."

"Oh, my coat. Sure. Whatever. I'm too tired to fight with you tonight. You win."

He looks confused so I clarify. "You've seen me laugh, and cry. You made me kiss you when I should have slapped your smug face. You've had a good day. Go and watch the game and eat pretzels."

"Is that the prize you think I'm playing for? To see you cry?" He shakes his head. "It's really not."

"Sure it is. Now go away," I tell him more forcefully. He backs away and leans against the opposite wall.

"Why are you hiding here? Shouldn't you be out there charming the shit out of him?" He looks in the direction of the bar and rubs his hand over his face.

"I needed a minute. And it's not always that easy, trust me."

"I'm sure you won't have any trouble."

He doesn't sound sarcastic. I wipe my tears and look at the tissue. Quite a bit of mascara on it. I heave a shuddery sigh.

"You look fine." It's the nicest thing he's ever said to me.

I begin patting my hand along the wall, trying to find the portal to another dimension, or at least the door to the ladies room. Anything to get away from him. He puts his hand into his hair, his face twisting with agitation.

"I shouldn't have kissed you, okay. It was a fucking stupid move on my part. If you want to report me to HR—"

"That's your problem? You're scared I'm going to report you?" My voice is raising loud enough that bar patrons turn. I take a deep breath and when I speak again I am quieter.

"You've broken me down so completely, I can't even handle it when a guy tells me I'm beautiful."

Dismay spreads across his face.

"That's why I'm crying. Because Danny told me I'm a beautiful girl, and I nearly fell off the barstool. You've *ruined* me."

"I . . ." he begins to say, but he's got nothing. "Lucy, I—"

"There's nothing left you can do to me. You win today."

From the look on his face, I think I've landed a punch. His shadow recedes along the floor, and then he's gone.

Chapter 7

I call Helene in the morning to say I'm not hungover but I'm having a few personal issues and I'll be in a little late. She is kind and tells me to rest and take the day off.

Rest, and finish up your job application because, darling, it's due tomorrow.

I'm missing out on a pale yellow shirt today. It's the color of nursery walls when the unborn baby's gender is a surprise. It's the color of my cowardly soul.

Last night after Joshua slid away from me, his face twisted with guilt and regret, I tidied myself up and sat back down with Danny and salvaged the evening. Danny and I have some things in common. His parents have a hobby farm, so my revelation that I grew up in a strawberry patch didn't garner the usual amount of amused, patronizing scorn.

It gave me the courage to talk more about it than I usually would. We swapped stories of life on a farm. I watched the expressions slide across his face like clouds. We hung out for hours, laughing like old friends, as comfortable as a pair of slippers.

I should be happy and excited. I'm should be polishing my job application. I should be thinking about a second date. I end up doing the one thing I shouldn't. I lie in bed with my eyes closed, replaying the kiss.

Shortcake, if we were flirting, you'd know about it.

Maybe he forgot I was Lucinda Hutton, people-pleasing Strawberry Shortcake, and I morphed into something different for him. An enclosed space, different makeup, my dress short and my perfume fresh. In a moment ruled by insanity, I was the object of his lust from the time it took us to travel from tenth floor to basement. And he was definitely mine.

I needed to test a theory I've had for a while. What theory? How long is a while? If I were some kind of human experiment, he could have had the decency to give me his conclusion.

When I think about his teeth biting softly down on my bottom lip, I get a clenching flutter between my legs. When I think of his hand on the back of my thigh, I have to reach down and feel where his fingers spread. The hardness of his body? I can skip breathing for a bit. I wonder how I tasted to him. How I felt.

I'm loafing around in my pajamas at three P.M., paralyzed by the looming application deadline, when my door buzzer startles me. My first thought is it's Joshua, come to drag me back to work. Instead, it's a deliveryman with flowers. A huge bouquet of lipstick-red roses. I pinch open the little envelope and the card says three whole words.

You're always beautiful.

There's no signature but it doesn't need one. I can imagine Jeanette's expression softening as she hands Danny a Post-it note detailing my address with a muttered, *You didn't get this from me.* Even HR ladies break the rules for love.

I text him: *Thank you so much!!*

He replies almost instantly: *I had a great time. I'd love to see you again.*

I reply: *Definitely!*

I stand, hands on hips, looking at the flowers. The ego boost couldn't have been timed better. I turn back to my computer. That job will be *mine*. And Joshua will be gone.

"Let's get this finished."

HE'S A BIG blur of mustard out of the corner of my eye when I walk in on Friday. I hang my coat and walk straight into Helene's office. For once she's in early. I could enfold her in my arms and squeeze.

"I'm here," I tell her. She waves me in and I close the door behind me.

"Is it in?" I nod.

"Joshua's is too. And two external applicants so far. How was your date? Are you all right?"

She's always the picture of composure. Today she's wearing a blazer over what is probably a pure silk T-shirt, tucked into a wool skirt. Nothing as common as cotton for Helene. I hope when she dies she bequeaths her wardrobe to me.

I ease into a chair. "It was fine. Danny Fletcher in design. I hope that's okay; he's finishing up next week to freelance."

"Shame. He does good work. Seeing him won't be a problem."

My mind flashes to kissing Joshua in the elevator. That's a problem, all right.

"But something happened," Helene surmises.

"I had a huge argument with Joshua before the date, and it rattled me. I woke up feeling unstable. Like if I came in here we'd both be wheeled out by paramedics, drenched in blood."

Helene is eyeing me speculatively. "What was the argument about?"

Maybe it isn't such a good idea to vent about my personal issues with Helene. I'm terminally unprofessional. My cheeks heat and when I can't think of a lie, I abbreviate.

"He thought I was lying about having a date. I'm so lame."

"Interesting," she says slowly. "Have you thought about this very hard?"

I shrug. Only obsessively, to the point where I couldn't sleep.

"I'm upset with myself for letting him push my buttons. You have no idea how hard it is, sitting opposite him, trying to resist his constant attacks."

"I've got some idea. It's called brinkmanship, darling." She gestures at the wall with her thumb.

She's the perfect person to confide in. Mr. Bexley is on the other side of her wall right now, plotting ways to assassinate her. She follows my eyeline. We hear a faint honking sneeze, a fart sound, and some grumbling.

"Why would he assume you were lying? And why did it upset you so much that he did?" Helene is drawing spirals on her notepad and I feel a little hypnotized. She's turned into my therapist.

"He thinks I'm such a joke. He's always laughing about what my parents do. I'm sure he laughs at where I went to school. My clothes. My height. My face."

She nods patiently, watching me try to untangle these complicated thoughts.

"It bothers me to know he thinks that of me. That's the bit that trips me up. All I want is his respect."

"You prize your reputation of being likable and approachable," she supplies. "Everyone likes you. He is the only one who resists."

"He lives to destroy me." Maybe I'm getting a little overdramatic.

"And you, him," she points out.

"Yes. And this isn't the person I want to be."

"Don't interact with him today. You could take the vacant office down on the third floor for a few days. We could divert the phones."

I shake my head. "Tempting, but no, I can deal with it. I'll draft the quarterly report and keep to myself. I'll forget he exists."

I can still remember the taste of his mouth. I breathed his hot exhalations until my lungs were filled with him. His air was inside my body. He taught me things in the space of two minutes that the span of my lifetime did not. Forgetting his existence is going to be a challenge, but this job is nothing but challenges.

I gently close Helene's office door and gather myself. I turn and there he is, slouched at his desk.

"Hey." I get a flatter version of How You Doing?

"Hello," I respond stiffly and walk on tiny stilts to my desk.

What he says next astonishes me. "I'm sorry. I'm so, so sorry, Lucy."

I believe him. The memory of his raw expression as he stumbled away from me at the bar has made it near impossible to sleep for two nights in a row. Now is the moment. I could take us back to our normal status quo. I could snap at him; he'd snap back. But that's not the person I want to be.

"I know you are." We both nearly smile and we look at each other's mouth, the ghost of the kiss jangling between us.

He's not his immaculate self today. He's a little rough around the edges, probably from a few bad nights' sleep. His mustard shirt is the ugliest color I have ever seen. His tie is badly knotted, his jaw is shadowed with stubble. His hair is a mess and has a devil's horn on one side. He's practically a Gamin today. He looks divine and he's looking at me with a memory in his eyes.

I want to run until my legs give out. I want to sweep everything off his desk with my arm. I can feel my clothes touching my bare skin. That's how Joshua's eyes make me feel when he looks at me.

"Let's put our weapons down, okay?" He raises his hands to show he's unarmed. His hands are big enough to encircle my ankles. I swallow.

To hide my awkwardness, I mime taking a gun out of my pocket and toss it aside. He reaches into an imaginary shoulder holster and takes out a gun, putting it on his planner. I unsheathe an invisible knife from my thigh.

"All of them." I indicate under the desk. He reaches down to his ankle and pretends to take a handgun out of an ankle holster.

"That's better." I sink into my chair and close my eyes.

"You're deeply weird, Shortcake." His voice is not unkind. I force my eyes open and the Staring Game almost kills me. His eyes are the blue of a peacock's chest. Everything is changing.

"Are you going to report me to HR?"

Something in my chest folds painfully. So *that's* why he looks like shit. He's had a hellish day yesterday, anticipating being marched out of the building by security upon my return. My empty desk would have been terrifying. He sat there, visualizing the moment he is locked in jail for being a molester of tiny women. I understand now. Stupid me.

"No. But can we please never mention . . . *it* . . . again?" It comes out of me a little hoarse. I'm letting him off the hook, instead of taunting him with the prospect. Another step toward being the person I'd like to be. Regardless, he frowns like he's been deeply insulted.

"That's what you want?"

I nod, but I'm such a little liar. *All I want to do is kiss you until I fall asleep. I want to slide in between your sheets, and find out what goes on inside your head, and underneath your clothes. I want to make a fool of myself over you.*

Mr. Bexley's door is ajar so I speak as quietly as I can. "It's freaking me out."

He can see that it's the truth. I've got desperate, crazy eyes. He nods and just like that: Control, A; Delete. The kiss never happened.

I pray for a diversion. A fire drill. Julie calling me to say she would never meet a deadline ever again. I'm not the only one praying for the floor to cave in.

"How was your . . . date?" His voice is faint, his knuckles white. Being nice to me is a lot of effort.

"Fine. We've got a lot in common." I try in vain to wake my computer.

"You're both extremely small." He's frowning at his own computer as if this is the worst conversation he's ever been party to. Being friends with me does not come naturally.

"He didn't even tease me about the strawberries. Danny is . . . nice. He's my type." It's all I can think of to say.

"Nice is what you want, then."

"It's all anybody wants. My parents have been begging me for ages to find myself a nice guy." I keep my voice light, but inside, a little bubble of hope is rising. We're talking like friends.

"And did Mr. Nice Guy drive you home?"

I know what he's asking me. "No. I got a cab. By myself."

He breathes out heavily. He rubs his face in exhaustion, then looks at me through his fingers. "What shall we play now?"

"What about Normal Colleagues? Or the Friendship Game? I've been dying to try either of those." I look up and hold my breath.

He sits up straight and glowers at me. "Both would be a waste of time, don't you think?"

"Well, ouch." If I say it sarcastically, he won't know I'm serious. He opens his planner, pencil in hand, and begins making so many annotations that I blink and turn to my computer. I can't care about his stupid planner anymore. His pencil, my spying experiment. It all ends right now. It's all been a waste of time.

I tell myself to be glad.

TODAY IS A magnificent black T-shirt day. Write today in your diaries. Tell your grandchildren stories about it. I tear my eyes away, but they slide back moments later. Underneath that T-shirt is a body that could fog an elderly librarian's glasses. I think my underwear is curling off me like burning paper.

It's a week after the kiss that I never think about. Bexley & Gamin's Alphabet Branch is being herded onto a bus like cattle.

"Waivers," Joshua is saying over and over as people slap them into his hand. "Waivers to me. Cash to Lucinda. Hey, this isn't signed. Sign it. Waivers."

"Who's Lucinda?" someone farther back in the line asks.

"Cash to *Lucy*. This ridiculously small person right here. Hair. Lipstick. Lucy."

I know someone who is going to be riddled with paint shortly. The line surges forward and I'm nearly flattened against the bus.

"Hey, I didn't tell you to trample her."

Joshua whips them all back and rebalances me beside him like a bowling pin, the warmth of his hand searing through my sleeve. Julie then touches my other elbow and I nearly jump out of my skin.

"Sorry for missing the deadline the other day. I can't wait to have a proper night's sleep. I'm like a zombie."

She hands me her twenty and her nails have French tips. I curl my slightly chipped nails into my palms.

"I was hoping for a favor," she says, and over her shoulder I see Joshua tense, ear tilted to our conversation like a satellite. Eavesdropping is unbecoming. I draw Julie away a little, my hand outstretched as people continue to slap twenties into it.

"Okay, what is it?" Already my stomach is sinking.

"My niece is sixteen, and she needs to do an internship. Her school counselor thinks it would help her to gain some perspective. She can't skip classes and sleep all day, you know? Teenagers have no idea of the concept of work."

"You could talk to Jeanette, she could arrange something." I take someone else's cash. "They always want to work with the design team."

"No, I want her to do an internship with *you*."

"Me? Why?" I'm seized with the urge to run away.

"You're the only person here who'd be patient enough with her. She's a little bit opinionated."

This is a world first, but I wish Joshua would interrupt. Something happen. Please. I am beaming messages his satellite ear is not receiving. *Joshua, Mayday, Mayday, I will do anything for you if you interrupt.*

"She's got a lot of issues. Drugs, and a few other things. Please, would you do it? It'd mean a lot to her mother, and it might get her back on track."

"Well. Can I think on it?" I avert my eyes from Joshua who has abandoned eavesdropping and has now turned to face us, hand on hip.

"I need to know now. She's meeting with her school counselor in half an hour. She's meant to have something lined up." Julie looks at me, her mouth curled in an expectant smile.

"How long would it be for? Like, a day?"

Julie takes a step closer, squeezing my arm painfully in her beautiful hand.

"It'd be for two weeks during the next school break. You're such a sweetheart. Thank you, I'll text her now. She won't be happy but you'll bring her around."

"Wait," I begin, but she's already climbing onto the bus.

"Well, that went well. You know what I would have told her?" Joshua says.

I stick a hand into my hair. My scalp feels hot and prickly. "Shut up."

"I'd have said one little word. It's simple, you should try it sometime. Say it with me. No."

"Hey," Danny says with a smile as he joins the queue.

"No. Hi." I do my cutest grin. I hope he's wearing sunscreen on his pretty silver-blond skin. "You made it. I guess paintballing is a good way to celebrate your last day."

"Yeah, it'll be fun. Mitchell said I didn't have to

come, but I wanted to. The team took me out for a farewell lunch too."

I know most of this; we've been emailing all week, and I helped him carry some boxes to his car. The little envelope icon on my toolbar has been giving me little twinges of excitement. I've been hot and restless all morning. Light-headed. I definitely have a crush.

"Waiver," Joshua interjects. Danny hands him the paper, not taking his eyes from me.

"I love your hair today," Danny tells me and I duck my head, flattered. It's the correct thing to say to me. I'm ridiculously vain about my hair. My conditioner is probably worth more per ounce than cocaine.

"Thanks, it's gone a little crazy. I think it's a bit humid."

"Well, I like it a little crazy." Danny touches the haywire curls resting on my upper arm. We make eye contact and start laughing.

"I'll bet you do, sleazebag." I shake my head.

"Give her the money, then get on the bus," Joshua says slowly, like Danny is very simple indeed. They exchange an unfriendly look. I take his twenty and give him a Flamethrower smile in return.

"Wanna be teammates?"

"Yes," I say at the same time as Joshua barks, *No*. He sure is good at saying that word.

"Teams are pre-allocated," he snaps, and Danny shoots me a look that clearly says, *What's up his ass?*

"I was hoping to—" Danny begins, but Joshua shoots him his own look: *Whatever you're trying? Don't.* The last person in the line gives me their cash, and we are left standing in a fog of weird tension.

Chapter 8

"I'll talk to you in a bit," Danny promises me and boards the bus. I don't blame him. Joshua has his arms crossed like a nightclub bouncer.

"What the hell was that about?" I ask Joshua. He shakes his head.

Helene and Mr. Bexley swerve out in their respective Porsche and Rolls to meet us there. Of course, they're not going to participate in the team building. They're going to sit on the balcony overlooking the paintball park and drink coffee and hate each other's guts.

"Let's go," Joshua says and pushes me onto the bus. There are only two seats left, and they're right up front. Joshua has reserved them with stacks of clipboards. Danny leans into the aisle and shrugs regretfully.

Joshua sent the branch an email instructing us to change into old casual clothes at lunch. Things we won't mind ruining. I'm wearing skintight jeans and a stretched-out vintage Elvis T-shirt. It used to belong to my dad. Fat, jumpsuit Elvis, microphone raised to his lips. It slides loosely off my shoulder. The look I was trying to emulate was Kate Moss at a music festival. Judging by Joshua's face when he saw me, I'm a tragic loser. He did, however, look at the emerald-green strap of my sports bra. I know that for a fact.

Joshua also got changed into casual clothes. While he folded his black business shirt neatly on his desk like a retail assistant, I caught my reflection on the wall diagonal to him; a slack-jawed mask of idiotic lust. Firstly, Joshua is wearing jeans. They're all beaten-up and worn, with ice-blue paint flecks, and they pull taut across his thighs as he sits. I can't fault those jeans.

Next, he's wearing a T-shirt. The soft, threadbare cotton melts all over his torso as he slouches. The shapes going on under that T-shirt are . . . The sleeves are cutting gently into biceps that are making me . . . But it's his flat stomach that I'm . . . The skin is all gold like—

"May I help you with something?" He smoothes down the T-shirt. My eyes slither along behind his hand. I want to scrunch up that T-shirt into a bowl and eat it with a dessert spoon.

"I never thought you'd wear . . ." I gesture vaguely at his fabulous torso.

"You thought I'd be paintballing in Hugo Boss?"

"Hugo Boss, eh? Didn't they design the Nazi uniforms?"

"Lucinda, I swear." He closes his eyes for nearly a full minute. He pinches the bridge of his nose. I'd swear he's trying to not laugh, or scream.

I cross my eyes at him, poke my tongue out, and say, *"Derrrr."* He doesn't crack. Defeated, I twist up and look over the seats until I see Danny's ruffled hair. We wave to each other and pull identical faces to indicate how unhappy we are with our seatmates. Then it occurs to me my boobs are probably a couple of inches from Joshua's head and I slide back down.

"You and him? It's getting a little pathetic." Joshua is testy.

The word cuts me deep. *Pathetic*. He's called me that before. We've circuited back neatly to the same place we're most comfortable. I had wondered how things would play out after the kiss, after the tears, the wounded sadness in his eyes. The apology. The silence that has stretched through each day since.

According to Joshua, we're back to hate, and I can't do it much longer. I can't keep it going. It's taking too much out of me. What was once as easy as breathing is now an uphill battle. I'm so tired I'm aching.

"Sure. I'm pathetic." I watch the road ahead, and the Staring Game is going on, one-sided. I ignore him. No one can see us except the driver, if she chose to look, but she's got traffic to contend with.

"Shortcake."

I ignore him.

"Shortcake."

"I do not know anyone by that name."

"Play with me for a minute," he says it softly, right in my ear. I turn my face to his and try to regulate my breathing.

"HR," I manage. His face is so close to mine I can taste his breath, hot mint sweetness. I can see the tiny stripes in his irises, tiny unexpected sparks of yellow and green. There are so many blues I think of galaxies. Little stars.

"Are your roses still alive?"

Is there anything this man does not know? I try to not notice that our elbows are touching a little. Elbows are not erogenous. At least, I didn't think they were.

"Who'd you hear about them from?"

"Well, everyone knows Danny Fletcher is your dream man. Roses and whatnot. Candlelit lunches for two in the work kitchen." He looks at my lips, and I lick them. He looks at my bra strap, and my knees press together.

"Who's your source?"

His eyes are getting darker. The pupil is eating the blue, and I think of his elevator eyes. Murderous eyes. Passionate eyes. Crazy-person eyes.

"Inside source? Like magazines have for celebrities? Are you a *celebrity,* Lucinda?"

"I don't know how you know so much."

"I'm perceptive. I know everything."

"You know I have roses in my bedroom because of what, body language? Mind reading? You're so full of shit. You probably look through my window with a long-range telescope."

"Maybe I have the apartment opposite yours."

"You wish you did, you creep." I'm beginning to feel the first prickles of sweat on my spine. If he did, I'd probably be the one sitting in the dark with binoculars.

"Well? Are they?"

"They wilted. I had to toss them out this morning."

His hand slides down my arm, slowly, softly, pressing the goose bumps flat. His hand is so cold I glance up at his face. His face is set to a default frown.

"You're pretty hot."

"Yeah, but that's common knowledge." I'm sarcastic as I pull away. The bus jolts around a corner and a little wave of dizziness blurs my vision and nausea turns my stomach over. I'm not getting sick. My body is probably reacting to the stress of the job application process, the kiss, and the murder-glint in Joshua's eyes.

"Looking forward to being annihilated?"

I manage the best retort I can.

"I'm going to destroy you. The Hating Game. You versus me. It's the only way this can possibly end."

"Right," Joshua barks abruptly, standing up and kneeling in his seat to address our colleagues. They all reluctantly stop talking, and I sense mutiny is afoot.

I kneel up too, and wave at everyone. They all smile. Good little cop, universally despised cop. I notice the Gamins are sitting to the left, the Bexleys to the right.

"There will be a total of six challenges today," Joshua begins.

"Seven if you include him," I add and get some cheap laughs. He scowls sideways at me.

"Six teams of four. Each challenge you'll be in a different group. The aim is to get to know your colleagues in an outdoor, active environment. As teams you'll come up with strategies to get the flag first."

There are blank faces, and he sighs heavily. "Seriously? No one here has ever done paintball? You will be trying to get the flag before the opposing team. Main rule is no paintballing the flag marshals. Or each other's faces, or groins."

Darn it, that's all I've been dreaming about.

"Marion, Tim, Fiona, Carey, you are flag marshals. You are assessing the team participation from the vantage point beside the flag. Scoring people, if you will."

I'm slightly impressed. I was a bit concerned imagining those four heaving their heavy, pain-riddled, aging bodies across a paintball course. Carey and Marion nod to each other self-importantly as Joshua passes back four clipboards. I wish he'd discussed all of this with me. He's in complete control and I don't like it.

"After we finish, we will convene up on the deck for coffee and to discuss what we've learned about each other today." He slithers back down into his seat.

"Any questions?" I look around and a few hands are raised.

"Do we get overalls?"

Joshua says something under his breath that sounds like *fucking morons*. I'll field this one.

"You'll each get a protective suit and a helmet to protect your eyes and face." I feel Joshua's sigh at my hip sink through my T-shirt.

"Yes." I point, and Andy lowers his hand.

"How much do paintballs hurt?"

"A lot," Joshua says from his seat.

"Remember, folks, the aim isn't to hurt each other." I glance down at Joshua. "No matter how bad you want to!"

"Are you two on opposing sides?" someone at the back calls, causing laughter.

Our reputation for hatred has gotten a little out of hand, and most of it is my fault. I have to quit with the hating-Joshua jokes.

"This is designed to bring us all together. We'll all be on each other's team at some point, like in a work situation. Even Joshua and I will find some common ground today. Anyway. The grand prize!" Everyone sits up straight.

"The prize," Joshua interrupts loudly from his seat, "is an extra leave day credited to you. That's right—a free day off. But you have to earn it displaying outstanding commitment to your team."

There's a buzz among the group. A free day off. A day release from jail. It dangles above them all like a brass ring.

Paintball Shootout is located in a small pine plantation. The ground is dusty and stark. The trees ache for death. A crow circles overhead, making ominous creaking noises. Everyone straggles into a lumpy circle near the gates.

A guy in camouflage Paintball Shootout coveralls poses like an army sergeant beside Joshua. They both have the same tall, muscled, marine body types. Maybe Joshua spends his every spare moment here. They're brothers in arms. Comrades who've seen some seriously painty shit go down in this barren wasteland. When they both stare expectantly at me, I realize I'm supposed to be standing up front too.

Joshua demonstrates how to put the suit and protective gear on and everyone watches with keen interest. Sergeant Paintball fields the slew of stupid questions with practiced patience. We all receive our suits, helmets, kneepads. Then we're armed.

We are adults undertaking a team-building activity in a professional capacity, so naturally we spend several minutes horsing around, striking poses with our paintball guns and making sound effects. Joshua and Sergeant Paintball watch us like orderlies at a mental facility. Alan, recent Birthday Boy, pretends to mow us all down. "Pew, pew, pew," he intones in his grave baritone. "Pew, pew."

I scramble out of the path of one fake skirmish and start to feel undersized and feeble. I look at all the long legs and eyes lit with paint-lust. Maybe tensions will boil over. They'll all go rogue, Gamins versus Bexleys, swapping paintball guns for AK-47s.

Sweat is starting to bead on my brow and upper lip and whatever is going on with my stomach, it's bad. My lipstick is a faded pink Popsicle stain and my hair is stuffed into a heavy helmet. The smallest suit they had is still so big that people laugh when they see me. Such elegance. Such grace. I am going to need to concentrate really hard on getting through this afternoon.

Helene waves to me. She is standing on an observation deck, wearing a white visor, cream linen shirt, and white cigarette pants, sipping Diet Coke through a straw. Only Helene would wear white to a paintball park. Mr. Bexley is sulking about something and remains seated, arms crossed, a bullfrog in khaki.

"Have fun, everyone," Helene calls. "And remember, we can see you!" With that eerie Big Brother comment ringing in our ears we begin.

Joshua reads out the first teams and I'm on his. We stride out with our teammates, Andy and Annabelle. Two Gamins, two Bexleys. Our opposing team files out, a similar ratio. He must have sorted each team like this.

I should have opened my mouth this last week to ask him about the arrangements, but the awkwardness between us has been insurmountable. Plus, since my corporate retreat idea was completely destroyed I've felt lackluster and sulky about everything. He hijacked it, he can damn well organize it.

But as I realize the air is filled with palpable excitement, I realize my grand idea has now become his achievement. I'm such an idiot.

I spot Marion with the flag. She waves merrily with a pen gripped between her teeth, clipboard in hand, and binoculars hanging on her chest. She is taking her faux-important job seriously.

"What's the plan, team?" I can't see our opposition.

"Stick together or spread out?" Annabelle is unsure.

"Hmm, I'd say probably stick together, given this is a team-building challenge." I prop myself up on some slender pine branches and wish I could wipe my face. In this suit I'm so hot I feel faint.

"We should pick one person who'll be going for the flag, and protect them," Andy says, which is a good idea.

"I like it. Who's going to do it?"

They both peep furtively at Joshua, clearly fearful of him. Somehow, the helmet doesn't look stupid on him. His gloved hand looks big enough to punch through a brick wall. He should be miniaturized and sold in toy stores for violent little boys.

"Annabelle," Joshua decides. "And if she gets shot, we'll go for the flag in alphabetical order, first names."

Great. Meaning Andy, Joshua, and then Lucy. Basically, no one is protecting me at all. I'm cannon fodder. We file out and take cover. Andy sees my rising panic and smiles kindly. "We'll all look after you Luce, don't worry."

I knew somehow Joshua would find a way to screw with me. I am coming out of this bruised, battered, and paint-splattered. And I can't even shoot him until I'm rotated onto another team.

There's a horn blast, and I'm crawling on hands and knees up an incline awkwardly, the loose dirt making me slide. I am moving first. It makes sense, given our strategy. I'll scout the way forward. I'm the most expendable.

My arms won't seem to hold me up properly and I collapse onto my stomach. Annabelle runs ahead of me with windmill limbs and zero strategy or stealth. I kneel up and try to call her back. A hand clamps on my calf and I'm dragged backward until Joshua flops down next to me, gun in hand. He motions at me to lie down.

"Don't," I hiss at him.

"You'll get shot in the face if you pop up like that."

"Why didn't you let me then?"

His hand spreads across my lower back, pinning me firmly to the ground. In the privacy of my mind I can admit the weight of his hand is delicious. The slivers of fabric between our skin begin to glow.

"What's wrong with you, anyway?"

"Nothing's wrong." I try to squirm away.

"You look terrible."

"Thanks. We have to cover Annabelle." I edge up to see her tottering awkwardly among slender tree trunks, completely exposed. Andy is gallantly leaping after her. The flag is an orange scrap in the distance.

I'm up and running, Joshua behind me. I fall behind a boulder and spot Marnie on the opposing team. Raising my gun, I fire off a couple of rounds, clipping her in the shoulder. She says a disappointed, "Aw," and walks off.

When I look at Joshua he looks mildly impressed. "Badass."

Annabelle is out of sight. The air is filled with cracks, pops, and cries of pain. After a few short runs, I find Andy kneeling on the ground trying to tie his boot lace with a big splat of paint on his chest.

"Oh, Andy!"

He looks up at me with the weary eyes of a Vietnam vet who knows he's about to die, blood geysering from a pulpy stomach wound. He grasps at my knee. "Go save her."

He has been watching too many action movies, but so have I judging by the swell of responsibility and protectiveness inside me. I will save Annabelle.

"I'm going to get a Coke," Andy tells me, ruining the moment.

I keep running. My breath feels short and I'm fogging my goggles a little. I hear a crack and jump behind a pyramid of barrels, which drum with the sound of shots. I look down. Nothing on me so far. I assume I'd feel it. I check the backs of my legs.

"You're clear," Joshua calls. I look over at him, crouched nearby behind a big tree stump. He's holding his paintball gun in a cool way, pointed straight at the sky. I try to copy him and begin to drop it.

"Dork," he comments unnecessarily. He must have strong wrists.

"Shut up."

Annabelle is crouched behind a miserable, suicidal sapling. I watch her raise her gun and take out Matt from the opposition. I let out a yelp of delight and she turns and gives me the thumbs-up, grinning widely as she waves me forward. The flag is fluttering about thirty yards away. She is abruptly shot in the center of her back and yips in pain. I don't need to even look at Joshua to know that he is shaking his head at me.

"Off you go then. I'll protect you. Just you and me now, buddy. Age before beauty."

"Great. I'm a dead man." He makes the short run to my barrel hideout and checks his ammo, glancing over his shoulder.

"Were your parents in the military?" It would explain a lot. The rigid behaviors, the brisk, impersonal manner. Addiction to rules and sequences. His neatness and economy in everything he does. He's now got a lack of friends and the inability to connect. I bet his parents had frequent foreign postings. He bounces a quarter off his perfectly made bed.

"No," he tells me, checking my gun for me. "They're doctors. Surgeons. Well, they were."

"Are they dead? You're an . . . orphan?"

"Am I what? They're retired. Alive and well."

"Huh. Are you from here?" The tip of my gun is resting in the dirt. I'm too tired. I hope I get shot. I need a rest.

"Only me and my brother live in the city." He frowns at me and taps my gun with his. "Hold your gun up."

"There's *two* of you? Heaven help us." I try to obey but my arms are watery.

"You'll be pleased to know we're nothing alike."

"Do you see him much?"

"No." He assesses the course in front of us.

"Why not?"

"None of your business." Sheesh.

I can see Danny in the distance stalking through the trees in the skirmish happening on the next rotation over, a dividing rope between us. I give him a wave and he lifts a hand in response, a smile spreading. Joshua raises his gun and shoots him twice on the back of the thigh with sharpshooter accuracy, then sniffs derisively.

"What gives? I'm not against you," Danny shouts. He calls out to his flag marshal and resumes, this time with a slight limp.

"That was unnecessary, Joshua. Very bad sportsmanship."

We begin to move forward, and he's bent low at the waist, surprisingly light on his feet as he sidesteps a volley of shots, bumping me backward behind a tree. The flag is dangling close by, but there are still two of our opponents out there.

"Quiet," we hiss to each other in unison and look at each other. The worst place to play the Staring Game is in the middle of a live paintball session.

I have to lean my helmet back against the tree to look up at him properly. His eyes are a color I've never seen. The thrill of live action combat electrifies him. He looks away to check behind us, a scowl darkening his face. How do I ever manage to keep my composure under those fierce eyes?

We're pressed together. My skin instantly sensitizes, and when I glance sideways I get a peripheral glimpse of his curved, heavy bicep. My heart stutters when I remember how it felt to have his hand on my jaw, cradling it, tilting me up to meet his mouth. Tasting me like something sweet. He is looking at my mouth and I know he is remembering the exact same thing.

Chapter 9

Y ou're sweating." Joshua frowns. Maybe not then. I can hear a twig crack and realize someone is approaching behind us. I raise my eyebrows in askance and Joshua nods. My moment is here and he needs to get the flag. I grab handfuls of his paintball suit and swing him around behind me against the tree.

"What are you—" he starts to say behind my back, but I'm scanning the terrain for the ambush. I'm Lara Croft, raising her guns, eyes burning with retribution. I can see the shape of the enemy's elbow behind the barrels.

"Go!" I yell. I fumble in my thick gloves for the trigger. "I'm covering you!"

It happens instantly. *Pop, pop, pop.* Pain radiates through me—arms, legs, stomach, boob. I howl, but the shots keep coming, white splats all over me. It's complete overkill. Joshua pivots us neatly and blocks the shots with his body. I feel him jolting as he takes more hits and his arm rises to cradle my head. Can I freeze time and take a nap right here?

He turns his head and shouts angrily at our assailant. The shots stop, and nearby I hear Simon crow with triumph, standing on top of the mound and waving the flag. Dammit. My one job and he wouldn't even let me do it.

"You should have gone. I was covering for you. Now we've lost." Another wave of nausea nearly knocks me over.

"Sor-reeee," Joshua says sarcastically. Rob is approaching, gun lowered. I'm making whimpering noises. The pain is throbbing in points all over me.

"Sorry, Lucy. I'm so sorry. I got a bit . . . excited. I play a lot of computer games." Rob takes a few steps back when he sees Joshua's expression.

"You've really hurt her," Joshua snaps at him, and I feel his hand cup my head. He's still pressing me against the tree, knee braced between mine, and when I look to my left I see Marion watching us with her binoculars. She drops them and writes something on her clipboard, a grin curling her mouth.

"Off." I give him an almighty shove. His body is huge and heavy and I'm so boiling I want to rip my suit off and lie in cold paint. We're all panting a little as we walk back to the starting point under the balcony. I'm limping and Joshua takes my arm brusquely, probably to move me on faster. I see Helene up ahead, lowering her sunglasses. I wave like a sad cartoon kitten; *womp, womp.*

Casualties abound. People groan as they press the painted parts of their bodies gingerly. Dozens of reenactments are taking place. I look down and realize my front is almost solid paint. Joshua's front half is fine, but his back is a mess. Trust us to be opposites.

When I strip off my gloves and helmet, Joshua gives me his clipboard and a bottle of water. I raise it to my lips and it seems to be empty quickly. Everything feels weird. Joshua asks Sergeant Paintball if they have any aspirin.

Danny picks his way through our fallen comrades to join me. I'm acutely aware of how disgusting I must look. He looks at my front. "Ouch."

"I'm seriously one big bruise."

"Do I need to avenge you?"

"Sure, that'd be great. Rob from corporate is the definition of trigger happy."

"Consider him taken care of. And what was that, Josh? You shot me in the leg and I was in a completely different game."

"Sorry, I got confused," Joshua says, insincerity ringing in his tone.

Danny shades his eyes and Joshua smirks up at the sky. Our colleagues stumble and flail, paint slicked and in pain, unsure of what to do next. Things are rapidly starting to disintegrate. I consult the clipboard. I see he's written me on his team for every rotation, probably at Helene's request. She'd never know. She's doing a Sudoku puzzle. I quickly use a pencil and change it before calling out the next teams. People clump together, complaining.

"Wait, they're getting the first-aid kit. You'd better sit the rest of the afternoon out. Something's wrong with you," Joshua says. I glance up at Helene again, and then look at everyone around me. I could be in charge of this bunch soon. This afternoon is an audition, no doubt about it. I'm not going to fail it now.

"Yeah, you've been telling me since the day we met. Enjoy the rest of your afternoon." I walk off without a backward glance into my new team.

It feels like the longest afternoon of my life, but it

also goes by in a flash. The feeling of being stalked and watched is unnerving, and in our small teams we do form instant bonds. I shove Quintus from accounts receivable into a bunker as pink pellets rain down over us.

"Go! Go!" I roar like a SWAT team leader as Bridget goose steps through to the flag, bursts of paint clipping at her heels. The extent of how sick I am reveals itself during my third rotation, after I snatched the flag. I knew it was deeply tragic of me to feel so triumphant, but honestly I felt as though I'd scaled Everest. My teammates screamed, and big basketball-player Samantha—a Bexley—picked me up off the ground and swung me in a circle. I threw up a little in my mouth.

My arms shake from the strain of holding the gun. Everything feels slightly surreal, as if at any moment I'll awake from a bad afternoon nap. The sky overhead is a silver-white dome.

I look at the faces surrounding me, shining with sweat. I feel such a kinship with these people. I watch a Gamin high-five a Bexley as they burst out laughing. We're all in it together. Maybe Joshua had a good idea with this, after all. Maybe the only way to truly unite people is through battle and pain. Confrontation and competition. Maybe surviving something is the point.

Where *is* Joshua, anyway? I don't see him for the rest of the afternoon except for the team rotation breaks. With every person stalking through the trees my eyes would play tricks. I'd see him kneeling down, reloading, and taking shots. I'd see the shape of his shoulders and the curve of his spine. But then I'd blink and it would be someone else.

I'm expecting that one fatal shot. A big red splat, straight to the heart.

"Where's Joshua?" I ask the flag marshals and they shrug. "Where's Joshua?" I ask everyone I pass. "Where's Joshua?" The answers start to get clipped and irritated.

I tug at my paintball suit despite the rhythmic pops and cracks of live fire. I pull down the neckband ineffectually, baring half an inch of sweaty skin to the cold air. Then I throw up. It's nothing but water and tea. I didn't feel like lunch today. Or breakfast. I kick sand over it and wipe my mouth on the back of my hand. The planet is circling too quickly so I hold on to a tree.

The air is beginning to chill as the final horn sounds and we all trudge back to HQ. Everyone is visibly exhausted and there is a great deal of fuss as we strip out of our suits. Everybody is complaining. Sergeant Paintball looks like he's evaluating his life choices. Joshua is standing with one hand on his hip and I instinctively raise my gun. It's time.

Lucy versus Joshua, total annihilation.

He walks over to me, completely unperturbed by my action-man pose and takes the gun. I pull my helmet off. He steps behind me and his fingers slide in the sweat on the nape of my neck. It's like he's touched a live wire and I make a weird gurgle. He grips the zipper of my suit and slashes it down my back. I hop around to get it off, batting away his hands.

"You're sick," he accuses. I shrug noncommittally and weave up the stairs to where Helene and Fat Little Dick wait.

"Looks like some excellent teamwork went on," Helene says. We let out a weak cheer, propping each other up. I lift the edge of my T-shirt. My bruises are purple. The smell of coffee makes me feel ill. I make my way to the front. Joshua's been running this little show for too long. I can salvage this.

"Can I call our four flag marshals to stand and discuss the acts of teamwork and bravery they witnessed?"

The flag marshals make their observations and I try to hold it together. Apparently, Suzie caused a commotion, allowing her teammate to slip up and get the flag.

"I got four shots for that," Suzie calls, patting her hip and wincing.

"But you took the shots for your team," Mr. Bexley says, rousing himself out of his stupor, which I am beginning to suspect is caused by prescription drugs. "Good work, young lady."

"And speaking of bravery," Marion says, and my stomach sinks. "Little Lucy here did something quite remarkable."

A cheer goes up and I wave it away. If one more person calls me little, small, or *ridiculously small* I am going to karate chop them.

"She took at least ten rounds for a colleague today, protecting him from someone who was going a little overboard. That person remains nameless." She looks pointedly at Rob and he cowers lower to the ground like a guilty dog. Other people frown at him.

"She's standing in front of her colleague, arms outstretched, protecting him to the death!" Marion mimes my actions, arms scarecrow straight, body jolting from the shots. She's a good actress.

"And to my surprise, I see it's none other than Josh Templeman that Lucy is protecting!"

A big laugh breaks out. People swap amused looks and two girls from HR elbow each other.

"But—but then! He swings her around to protect *her* and takes paintballs in the back! Protecting her! It was quite something."

Another fun fact: Marion reads romance novels in the kitchen at lunchtime. I catch Joshua's eye, and he wipes his forehead roughly on his forearm.

"It seems paintball has brought us *all* together today," I manage to say and everyone claps. If this were a TV episode, we've just reached the little moral conclusion: Stop hating each other. Helene is pleased; her lips are pursed in a knowing smile.

The Day Off Prize is awarded to Suzie, and she accepts her little mock certificate with a deep bow. Deborah has taken some good action shots on her camera and I ask her to email them to me for the staff newsletter.

Helene catches me by the elbow. "Remember, I'm not in on Monday. I'll be meditating under a tree."

Everyone heads down to the bus, and I'm gratified to see it's now harder to tell who's Gamin and who's Bexley. Everyone looks like a train wreck; bedraggled clothes and red, sweaty brows. Most of the women have panda eye makeup. Despite the physical discomfort, there's a new sense of camaraderie.

Helene and Mr. Bexley peel out again like Wacky Racers. A few people are being picked up by spouses, and there's a confusing swirl of cars and dust. The bus driver puts down her newspaper at our approach and unlocks the door.

"Please hold on for a few minutes," I tell her, and jog back inside. I make it to the bathroom and am violently sick. Before I can feel like it's completely out of my system there's a sharp rap on the bathroom door. There's only one person I know who could knock so impatiently, and put so much irritation into it.

"Go away," I tell him.

"It's Joshua."

"I know." I flush again.

"You're sick. I told you." He jiggles the doorknob lightly.

"I'll get home by myself. Go away."

There's a silence and I figure he's gone back to the bus. I throw up again. Flush again. I wash my hands, leaning my legs against the sink until the splash-back soaks into my jeans. Elvis clings to me damply.

"I'm sick," I confide to my reflection. I'm fevered, eyes glittering. I'm blue and gray and white. The door is creaked open, and I squawk in fright.

"Holy shit." Joshua's eyebrows pinch together. "You look bad."

I can barely focus my eyes. The floor is spinning. "I can't make it. That bus trip. I can't."

"I could call Helene. She could come back, she couldn't have gotten far."

"No, no, I'll be okay. She's driving to a health retreat. I can take care of myself." He leans on the doorframe, his brow creased.

I steel myself, cupping a little cold water in my hand and slosh it over the back of my neck. My hair has been unraveling from its bun and sticks to my neck. I rinse my mouth. "Okay, I'm all right."

As we walk back, he pinches the little joint of my elbow between two fingers like a bag of garbage. I can feel the avid eyes watching us from the tinted bus windows. I think of the two girls nudging each other and shake him loose.

"I could leave you here and drive back and get you, but it would take an hour, at least."

"You? Come back and get me? I'd be here all night."

"Hey. Don't talk like that anymore, all right?" He's annoyed.

"Yeah, yeah, HR." I wobble up onto the bus.

"Oh dear," Marion calls loudly. "Lucy, you're looking awful."

"Lucy!" Danny calls from the rear of the bus. "Saved you a seat!" He's so far back in the bus it telescopes claustrophobically. If I sit back there I will absolutely vomit on everyone. *Sorry*, I mouth at Danny and sit in the front seat and close my eyes.

Joshua presses the back of his hand to my damp forehead and I hiss. "Your hand is cold."

"No, you're burning up. We need to get you to a doctor."

"It's almost Friday night. What are the chances of that happening? I need to go to bed."

The trip home is pretty bad. I'm trapped in an endless, unmarked period of time. I'm a bug in a jar being shaken by a kid. The bus is swaying, hot, airless, and I feel every bump and curve. I focus on my breathing and the feeling of Joshua's arm pressed against mine. At one particularly sharp corner he uses his shoulder to support me upright in my seat.

"Why?" I ask uselessly. I feel him shrug.

We're unloaded in front of B&G. A few women cluster around me and I try to understand what they're saying. Joshua is holding me by the scruff of my damp T-shirt and tells them it's fine.

He has a lively debate with Danny, who keeps asking me, "Are you sure?"

"Of course she's fucking sure," Joshua thunders. Then we're alone.

"Did you drive?"

"Jerry needs another weekend. The mechanic. I'll get a bus."

He moves me forward; a heaving, sweating marionette. My mouth tastes like acid. His grip drops from my neck to loop a finger into the loop on the back of my jeans, the other on my elbow. I can feel his knuckle pressing above my butt crack and I laugh out loud.

The stairs to the basement parking lot are steep and I balk, but he pushes me on, hands tightening. He uses his swipe card to get us in and steers me steadily toward his black car. I can smell car fumes and oil. I can smell everything. I dry-retch behind a pole and he hesitantly lays a hand between my shoulder blades. He rubs it around a little. I shudder through another volley of nausea.

Joshua guides me to the passenger seat. He slings the bag I'd forgotten about into the backseat. He idles the car and I glimpse myself in a side mirror, my head rolled to the side, a dark flush on my cheekbones, gleaming with sweat, my mascara smudged.

"Now. Are you gonna be sick in the car, Shortcake?" He doesn't sound impatient, or annoyed. He opens my window a few inches.

"No. Maybe. Well, possibly."

"Use this if you need to," he tells me, handing me an empty takeout coffee cup. He puts the car into reverse. "Tell me where to go, then."

"Go to hell." I start laughing again.

"So that's where you came from."

"Shuddup. Go left." I navigate him to my apartment building. I keep my eyes closed, and count my breaths, and do not vomit. It is quite an achievement.

"Here. Out front is fine."

He shakes his head and in defeat I direct him to my empty parking space. He has to help me climb out of the car and I sag against him. My cheek momentarily rests on something like his chest. My hand grips something like his waist.

He hits the button and we stand at opposite sides of the elevator car, and the Staring Game is overlaid with hot, sweaty memories of the last time we did this together.

"Your eyes were like a serial killer that day." I must have vomited out my filter.

"So were yours."

"I like your T-shirt. So much. It's magnificent on you."

He's mystified as he looks down at himself. "It's nothing special. I . . . like yours too. It's as big as a dress."

The elevator doors open. I lurch out. Unfortunately, he follows.

"I'm here," I lean on my door. He digs my keys from my bag and unlocks the door.

I've never seen anyone so desperate to be invited inside. His head pokes in farther. His hands are hanging on to the doorframe like he's about to fall in.

"It's not what I expected. It's not very . . . colorful."

"Thank you, good-bye." I push into the kitchen and seize a glass. Then I drink straight from the faucet.

"I think we could find an after-hours clinic," Joshua says behind me, and takes the glass before I can drop it. He pushes my toaster straight against the wall and to fill in the awkward silence he folds a dishcloth. His fingernail picks at a crumb glued to the countertop. Oh man, he's one of those people who love to clean. He wants to roll up his sleeves and bleach and scrub.

"It's so messy, isn't it?" I point at a mug with a lipstick mark. He looks at it longingly and we simultaneously begin to try to get past each other in the tiny space.

"Let me take you to a doctor."

"I need to lie down. That's all."

"Is there anyone you want me to call?"

"I don't need anyone," I announce proudly. I hold my

hand out for my key. He holds it out of reach. *I don't need anyone to look after me. I can get through this. I'm alone in this world.*

"Alone in this world? So dramatic. I'll go to the drugstore and see what I can get you."

"Sure, sure. Have a nice weekend."

As the door snicks shut, I reconfirm that my apartment is a bit of a disaster zone, cluttered, and yes, a little colorless. My dad calls it the Igloo. I haven't had enough time yet to put my stamp on the place. I've been too busy. The Smurf cabinet takes up a large part of the living room wall, dark without the special lights switched on. Thank goodness Joshua left.

My bed looks like I've been having disturbing, sexual dreams, which is accurate. The sheets are all rumpled and twisted, and the side where a man should be is strewn with books. Lingerie straps and Smurf-patterned underwear peek out of drawers like lettuce from a burger. I take the copy of Joshua's planner from my nightstand and hide it.

My shower is wonderful, torturous, endless. I turn it cold and freeze. I turn it hot and burn inside my skin. I drink the spray. I goop a big pile of shampoo on the top of my head and let it rinse away. An indication I must be near death is I can't be bothered to condition.

My head spins with nonsensical images, and I lean against the tiles and remember what it was like to lean against a tree with Joshua Templeman shielding me with his body.

In the privacy of my mind I can imagine whatever I want, and they aren't progressive, twenty-first-century thoughts.

They're depraved, brutal cavewoman thoughts. In my mind, he's electric with the animal instinct to protect me, his heavy muscle braced over my body. He absorbs each impact and it is his privilege. He's injected sharp and hard with nature's superdrug, testosterone.

I'm wrapped in him, safe from anything the world wants to throw at me. Anything painful or cruel will have to get through him before it has any chance of touching me. And it will never happen.

"Alive?"

I scream when I realize that resonating voice isn't in my imagination and cling to the tiles.

"Don't come in!" I did close the door. Thank you, guardian angels. I cross my arms over all of my X-rated zones.

"Of course I won't," he snaps.

"I am completely naked. Bruises . . ." I'm a Monet watercolor; purple water lilies floating in green. He says nothing.

"Well, go out. Into the living room."

My skin hurts when I towel myself. I crack the bathroom door open and hear silence. I scurry out and find underwear, a heinous beige bra, shorts, and an old crappy pajama top with a picture of a cute dinosaur on it, his drowsy eyes half closed. Underneath him reads: SLEEPYSAURUS.

I'm naked and putting on clothes, separated from Joshua by only a wall. I love you, wall. What a good wall. I toss myself so hard into bed the mattress squeaks, and it's the last thing I hear.

I WAKE UP in a volcano. "No! No!"

"I'm not poisoning you. Quit squirming." Joshua's hand is behind my neck as he presses two pills onto my tongue. I swallow water and then he lowers me flat.

"My mother always gave me lemonade. And she'd sit

with me. Whenever I woke up, she'd still be there. Did yours?" I sound like I'm five years old.

"My parents were too busy on shift looking after other sick people to do that stuff for me."

"Doctors."

"Yep, except me." An edge in his voice denotes a sore topic.

I feel his hand on my forehead, fingers light and stiff. "Let's do a temperature check."

"I feel so fucking stupid." My voice is garbled due to the thermometer he's put into my mouth. He must have bought it, because I don't own one. I'm currently inside a moment destined to become the most cringe-worthy memory of my life.

"You'll never let me live this down." That's what I try to say. Thanks to the thermometer it comes out like I've got a head injury.

"Sure I will. Don't chew the thermometer," he replies quietly, taking it out of my mouth.

"We don't want you to get over one hundred four." In the low evening light, his eyes are darkened navy as he assesses me almost clinically, before smoothing his hand over my forehead again, softly, not checking my temperature. My pillow is adjusted a little. His eyes are not the man I know.

"Okay. Please stay for a minute. But you can leave if you want."

"Lucy, I'll stay."

When I eventually dream, it's about Joshua sitting on the edge of my mattress, watching me sleep.

Chapter 10

I'm vomiting. Joshua Templeman is holding a large Tupperware container under my face—the one I usually carry cakes to work in. I can smell the sweet-plastic residue of icing and eggs. I throw up more. His wrist is holding up my limp head, my hair gathered in his fist.

"This is so disgusting," I groan in between heaves. "I'm so— I'm so—"

"Shh," he replies and I fall asleep, shuddering and gasping, while he wipes my face with something cold and damp.

The clock says 1:08 A.M. when I sit upright again. A wet compress falls into my lap. I jerk in fright at the weight on the bed next to me.

"It's me," Joshua says. He's sitting against my headboard with his thumb in a Smurf price guidebook. He's got no shoes on and his socked feet are casually crossed at the ankles. The other books have been stacked neatly on my dresser.

"I'm so cold," I chatter. I put my hand into my hair; it's still damp from my shower. He shakes his head. "You have a fever. It's getting worse."

"No, cold," I argue. I stumble into the bathroom,

leaving the door ajar. I pee, flush, and then realize how unladylike I was. Oh, well. He's seen and heard almost everything now. There's nothing left to do but fake my own death and start a new life.

I use my finger to rub some toothpaste on my tongue. Gag. Repeat.

I hear cotton unfurling, the snap of elastic, and the creak of mattress, and through the crack in the door I watch him put fresh sheets on the bed. I'm a soggy, disgusting mess, but I still manage to watch his bent-over backside.

"How You Doing?" He looks at me under his arm and hauls the last corner of the sheet into place. My lucky mattress is being manhandled.

"Oh, just fine. How You Doing?" I fall into bed, and claw the blankets up onto me. The mattress depresses heavily beside me and his hand is on my forehead.

"Ah, that's nice."

His hand feels like the sort of temperature I should be striving for. Everything we do is tit for tat, so I raise my hands up and put them on his forehead.

"Okay." He is amused.

I'm touching my colleague Joshua on the face. I'm dreaming. I'll wake up on the bus with him sneering at the trail of drool on my chin. But a minute ticks by, and I don't.

I slide my hands down, over sandpaper grit on his jaw, remembering how he cradled my face in the elevator. No one has ever held me like that. I open my eyes and I could swear he shivers. I touch his pulse. It touches me back.

I have my hands on his throat now, and I remember how badly I wanted to strangle him once. I spread my hands lightly around his neck, just to check the fit, and he narrows one eye.

"Go ahead," he tells me. "Do it."

His throat is way too big for my tiny hands. I feel a tension shimmering through him, a tightening in his body. There's a sound in his throat.

I'm hurting him. Maybe I'm strangling him to death right now. Color is sweeping up his neck. When he pins me with his eyes, I know something's coming. I am not prepared when it happens.

The world explodes apart as he begins to laugh.

He's the same person I stare at every weekday but lit up. He's plugged into the mains and electric. Humor and light radiate from him, making his colors glow like stained glass. Brown, gold, blue, white. It's a crime I've never seen these smile lines before. His mouth is in an easy curve, perfect teeth and a faint dimple bracketing each corner.

Each laugh gusts from him in a husky, breathless rush, something he can no longer hold in, and it's as addictive to me as the taste of his mouth or the smell of his skin. His amazing laugh is something I need now.

If I'd ever thought he was good-looking before, in passing or noticed in irritation, I never knew the full story. When Josh smiles, he is blinding. My heart is pounding and I frantically catalog this moment in the half-light. It's the only one I'll get, while delirious with fever.

If only I could hold on to this moment. I already feel the sadness that will hollow me out when it ends. I want to tell him, *Don't leave yet.* My fingers must be flexing, because he laughs until the mattress is shaking beneath us. A diamond wet sparkle of light in the corner of his eye is a bullet to my heart. I'll be able to replay this beautiful, impossible moment in my memory when I'm a hundred years old.

"Go ahead, kill me, Shortcake," he gasps, wiping his eye with his hand. "You know you want to."

"So bad," I tell him, like he once told me. I've got a tightening in my own throat and I can barely get the words out. "So bad, you have no idea."

MY PAJAMAS ARE soaked with sweat when I jolt awake and there is a third person in my bedroom. A man I've never seen before. I begin screaming like an injured monkey.

"Calm down," Josh says into my ear. I scramble into his lap and press my face into his collar bone, huffing his cedar scent so hard I probably suck out his ghost. I'm about to be taken to a scary medical facility, away from the safety of my bed and these arms.

"Don't let them, Josh! I'll get better!"

"I'm a doctor, Lucy. How long and what symptoms?" The man puts on some gloves.

"She wasn't one hundred percent this morning. High color, distracted, and she got worse throughout the day. Visibly sweaty since lunchtime, and she didn't eat. Vomiting at five P.M."

"And then?" The doctor continues to select things from his case, lining them on the end of my bed. I watch suspiciously.

"Delirious by eight. Trying to strangle me with her bare hands by one thirty. Burning up closer to one hundred four, and now she's one hundred five point six."

I squeeze my eyes shut when the unfamiliar rubber hands feel the glands in my throat. Josh rubs my arms soothingly. I'm sitting between his thighs now, feeling his solid weight behind my shoulder blades. My own human armchair. The doctor presses his fingertips into my abdomen and I make crying sounds. My top is peeled up a few inches.

"What in the hell happened here?" They both simultaneously let out a sympathetic hiss of breath.

"We had a paintball day at work. Even my back isn't as bad as this." Josh's fingers stroke the skin and I sweat even more. "Poor Shortcake," he says in my ear. There's no sarcasm.

"Have you eaten out at any restaurants?"

I wrack my brains. "Thai takeout for dinner. Not today. Yesterday maybe."

When the man frowns it's so familiar. "Food poisoning is a possibility."

"Could be a virus," Josh argues. "The time frame is a little long."

"If you're so capable of diagnosing her, why even call me?"

They begin bickering about my symptoms. To my ears, they sound like guys talking about sports, and the city's current viruses are the teams. I watch them through slitted eyes. I didn't even know doctors would do house calls, especially at two thirty-nine in the morning. He's midthirties, tall, dark haired, blue eyed. He's clearly thrown a jacket over his pajamas.

"You're good-looking," I tell the doctor. My lost filter should be a secondary diagnosis.

"Wow, she must *really* be delirious," Josh says acridly, wrapping his arm across my collarbones. The squeeze renders me immobile.

"Funny, he's usually called the good-looking one." The doctor says it wryly as he searches in a kit bag at the foot of the bed. "Oh, calm down, Josh."

"You're his BROTHER," I say in childlike wonder when the rusted cogs in my brain clunk into place. "I thought he was an experiment gone wrong."

They look at each other and Josh's brother laughs. "She's so cute."

"She's . . ." I feel Josh shake his head. He adjusts me a little against his chest, and my fevered brain interprets it as a snuggle.

"I'm pathetic. He tells me constantly. What's your name?"

"I'm Patrick."

"Patrick Templeman. Holy shit. You're the actual Dr. Templeman."

I'm still sitting in Josh's lap, my head in the curve of his neck, probably covering him in sweat. I try to struggle off but I'm held tight.

"I am indeed Dr. Templeman. One of them, anyway." The amusement fades from his face and he coughs and begins to turn away. I catch his sleeve to try to see how much of Josh is in his features. He stills obediently, but his eyes flick to Josh, who is tense as a brick wall behind me.

"Sorry, yes. Josh is better looking." There's a pause before both brothers laugh. Patrick isn't remotely offended and Josh's arm relaxes.

"Can you tell me embarrassing things about him?"

"When you're feeling better, you bet. Keep her fluids up, Josh. She's small enough that she'll dehydrate."

"I know." Together they coax me to swallow a sour medicine. I am laid flat against the bed and the two leave the room, shutting the door, but their voices still reach me.

"You would have been good at this," Patrick says, rattling in his medical kit. "You've done all the right things for her." Josh sighs heavily. I'm sure he's just crossed his arms.

"Don't get defensive. So, next hard topic. Were you going to give me an RSVP? Ever?"

"I was going to." He's lying.

"Well, you can give me one now. And don't pretend you don't know the date; I know for a fact Mom gave you the invite in person. We didn't want it to go 'missing' like the engagement party invite." *Josh, you little weasel.*

Patrick is thinking the same thing. "RSVP right now. Mindy needs to know. For such minor details as catering. Seating."

"I'm busy at the moment," Josh tries, but Patrick cuts him off.

"Imagine how it'll look if you don't turn up."

Josh says nothing and Patrick perseveres. "I know it's going to be hard."

"You expect me to walk in there like nothing happened?"

Patrick is confused. "But you'd bring Lucy, wouldn't you?"

I ponder this in the dark. Why on earth would it be hard for Joshua to attend his own brother's wedding?

"She's not my girlfriend. We work together." Josh sounds irritated. I wish that didn't give me such a punch in the gut, but it does.

"You could have fooled me."

"Yeah, well, she's more on the market for a nice guy. Aren't they all."

There's a loaded silence. "How many more times do I have to say—"

"No more times." Josh is the king of shutting down a conversation. There's more silence. I can almost hear them both looking at my bedroom door.

Patrick's voice is lowered now and I can't hear anything except huffy arguing. Hating myself desperately, I climb silently out of bed, careful to keep my feet in the shadows. I'm a disgusting little snoop.

"I'm asking you to come to my wedding and make your mother happy. Make *me* happy. Mindy is stressed as hell thinking there's some sort of family feud happening."

Josh sighs, heavy and defeated. "Fine."

"So, that's a yes? *Yes, please, Patrick, I'd love to come to your wedding? I accept your gracious invitation?*"

"Yes. That."

"I'll mark you down with a plus one. If she survives the night."

I grip the wall in horror until I hear Josh say sarcastically, "Ha-ha."

IT'S NOW SOME time before dawn and my room is ice blue. I'm propped into a sitting position, gulping messily what I realize is lemonade. Did he go to the convenience store across the road? The sweet-sour taste of childhood nostalgia and homesickness makes me almost choke.

He takes the glass and eases me back down against the pillows with his arm behind my shoulders. His touch was uncertain yesterday, but now he smooths his palms and fingertips across me with no hesitation. He looks wrecked with tiredness.

"Josh."

His eyes flicker with surprise. "Lucy."

"Lucinda," I whisper archly. He turns away to smile, but I catch his sleeve.

"Don't. I've already seen it." I'm never getting over his smile.

"Okay." I can tell he's confused. He's not the only one. I've been staring at Joshua for so long, he's become a color spectrum unto himself. He's my days of the week. The squares on my calendar.

"White, off-white stripes, cream, non-gender-specific yellow, disgusting mustard, baby-blue, robin's-egg, dove-gray, navy, black." I tick them off on my fingers.

Josh is alarmed. "You're still delirious."

"Nope. Those are the shirt colors you have. Hugo Boss. Haven't you ever been to Target?"

"What the hell is the difference between white and off-white?"

"Ecru. Eggshell. They're different. There was one single time you surprised me."

"And when was that?" He asks the question as indulgently as a babysitter. I kick my heel in temper against the mattress.

Why aren't I draped in a black negligee at least? I have never been this unattractive. I'm wearing SLEEPY-SAURUS. I look down. I'm wearing a red tank top. Holy shit. He changed me.

"The elevator," I blurt. I want to reroute this moment, back to a time I was halfway attractive. "You surprised me then."

He looks at me carefully. "What did you think?"

"I thought you were trying to hurt me."

"Oh, great." He sits back, embarrassed. "Clearly my technique is a little rusty."

I snatch his sleeve with superhuman strength and sit

up a little. "But then I realized what you were doing. Kissing. Of course. I haven't kissed in ages."

He frowns. "Oh, really." He stares down at me.

I elaborate so forcefully my voice shakes. "It was *hot*."

"I never heard from HR or the cops, so . . ." He trails off, looking at my lips. I'm twisting my hands into his T-shirt. It stretches around my fists. It's so soft, I want to wrap my entire body in it.

"Is my bed everything you imagined?"

"I wasn't expecting so many books. And it's a little bigger than I pictured."

"What about my apartment?"

"It's a tiny little pigsty." He's not being mean about it. It's true.

"Do you think Mr. Bexley and Helene make out in the elevator?" As long as he keeps answering my questions, I'll keep asking them.

"Guaranteed. I'm sure they have vicious hate-sex after each quarterly review." His eyes are tipping into black and he unravels his T-shirt from my hands as I catch a glimpse of half an inch of stomach—*hard* and *hair*. Now I'm sweating more.

"I bet when you shower, water pools right up . . . here." I put my finger into his collarbone. "I'm thirsty. I'll dehydrate." He lets out a breath and it blows right through me.

"Let's be just like them when we grow up, Josh. We could start a new game. Imagine. We could play games forever."

"Let's talk about it when you're not crazy with fever."

"Yeah, right. When I'm not sick you'll hate me again, but for now we're good." I take his hand and put it on my forehead to hide my sudden despair.

"I won't," he tells me. He smoothes his hand away, over my hair.

"You hate me so much, and I can't take it much longer." I'm pathetic. I hear it in my voice.

"Shortcake."

"Stop calling me Shortcake." I try to roll onto my side but he presses the heels of his palms lightly against my shoulders. I stop breathing.

"Watching you pretend to hate that nickname is the best part of my day."

When I don't reply, he almost smiles and releases me. "It's time to tell me about the strawberry farm."

It's a sore point—and it's also not the first time he's asked. I might be about to give him fodder to tease me with for a long time.

"Why?"

"I've always wanted to know. Tell me everything about strawberries." His soft, cajoling whisper will be the death of me.

In my mind I'm almost back there, under the big canvas umbrella with the torn corner, talking to tourists while their kids run on ahead, buckets clanking. The alien hum of cicadas fills the air. There's never silence.

"Well. Alpines are also called 'Mignonette,' and they grow wild in France on the hillsides and they're as big as your thumbnail. They have amazing flavor intensity for their size."

"Tell me another."

I open my eyes to slits. "Strawberries are not a joke. I've gotten shit from almost everyone I've ever met about it."

"It's such a cute thing about you."

The word *cute* lights up like neon in my dim bedroom and I'm so rattled I begin babbling.

"Fine. Okay, Earliglows. They grow so quickly. One day you're walking along at sunset next to nothing but green . . . the next morning they're all there. Little red buds, getting brighter. By dinnertime they're done, like red Christmas lights."

When Josh sighs, his eyes close for a second. He's exhausted. "Which are your favorites?"

"Red Gauntlets. They were in the rows closest to the kitchen and I was too lazy to go much farther. I had a big pink smoothie every morning."

He sits in silence, and his eyes are definitely not the man I know. They're wistful, lonely, and so beautiful I have to close mine.

"I swear, I can still feel the seeds between my teeth. Chandlers are my dad's favorite. He says he paid for my college tuition with them."

"What's your dad like? He's Nigel, right?"

"You and that blog. He worked so hard to send me to school. I can't begin to tell you. He cried on the back porch the day I left for college. He said . . ."

I trail off. The squeeze in my throat makes it impossible to go on.

"What did he say?"

I sidestep. "I haven't thought about this for so long. I haven't been home in eighteen months now. I missed Christmas, because Helene went back to France to see her family, and I wanted to cover for her."

"I didn't go home either."

"Oh, yeah. My parents mailed me a big care package, and I ate shortbread and opened presents on the floor of my living room watching infomercials. What did you do?"

"Pretty much the same. What did he say to you, then? Your dad, on the back porch?" He's a dog with a bone.

I can't relay that entire conversation; I'll start crying. I might never stop. My dad, his elbows on knees, the tears making clean lines down his tanned, dusty face. I abbreviate the conversation into a sanitized nutshell.

"That his loss was the world's gain. And my mom, she couldn't stop bragging, telling everyone about her daughter going off to college . . . She's making a new variety of strawberry, and they're all called Lucies."

"According to the blog, Lucy Twelve was quite good. Tell me more."

"I don't understand your fascination with that blog. Mom was a newspaper writer, but she had to give it all up."

"For what?"

"For my dad. She was doing a piece on the effects of some heavy rain on agriculture, so she went out to a local orchard. She found my dad in a tree. His dream was to own a strawberry farm, and he couldn't do it alone."

"Do you think she made the wrong decision?"

"Dad always says, *She picked me.* Like an apple, right out of the tree. I love them, but I think it's a sad story sometimes."

"You could ask her sometime. She probably doesn't regret a thing. They're still together, and it means you're here."

"Dad calls you other names starting with J, but never your real name."

"What?" He looks alarmed. "You've told your dad about me?"

"He's mad at you for being so mean. Julian and Jasper and John. One time, he called you Jebediah and I nearly peed myself. You'd have to grovel to my dad, that's for sure."

Josh looks so disturbed I decide to cut him a break and change the subject.

"When I'm homesick I can smell warm strawberries. Which is pretty much all the time." I watch him scrambling to try to unscramble these nonsensical statements.

"Did you play out there in the fields? When you were a kid?"

"You've seen the blog picture. It's pretty clear I did." I turn my face away. Me, knees stained pink from berry juice, tangled mane of hair, eyes bluer than the sky. Wild little farm girl.

"Don't be embarrassed." He gently puts his fingertips on my jaw and turns me back. "You in your little overall shorts. You look like you've been outside for days. All dirty and wild. Your smile hasn't changed."

"You never see my smile."

"I bet you had a tree house."

"I did, actually. I practically lived up there."

His eyes are bright with an expression I've never seen. I close my eyes for a second to rest them. He checks my temperature and when his hand lifts away from my forehead I complain. He touches my hand.

"I've never thought where you come from is inferior."

"Oh, sure. Ha-ha. Strawberry Shortcake."

"I think where you came from—Sky Diamond Strawberries—is the best place I can imagine. I've always wanted to go there. I've Google mapped directions. I've even looked up the flight and hire car."

"Do you like strawberries?" I don't know what else to say.

"I love strawberries. So much, you have no idea." He sounds so kind that I feel a wave of emotion. I can't open my eyes. He'll see I have tears in them.

"Well, it's out there, waiting for you. Pay the lady

under the umbrella and take a bucket. Mention me for a discount, but you'll get an interrogation on how I'm doing. How I'm *really* doing. If I'm lonely, if I'm eating properly. Why I won't take the time to come home."

I think of the job applications, side by side in a beige folder. A wave of exhaustion and dizziness hits me. I want to be asleep, that lovely dark place where these anxieties and sadness can't follow me. I start to feel like I'm slowly spinning.

"What should I tell her?"

"I'm so scared. It's all going to end soon, one way or another. I'm hanging on by my fingernails. I have no idea if their investment in me will ever pay off. And I'm so lonely sometimes I could cry. I lost my best friend. I spend all my time with a huge frightening man who wants to kill me, and he's probably my only friend now, even though he doesn't want to be. And it breaks my heart."

His mouth presses on my cheek. A kiss. A miracle. Josh's warm breath, fanning my cheek. His fingertips slide into my palms, and my fingers curl into his.

"Shortcake. No."

I'm twirling through endless loops, and I tighten my grip on his hands.

"I'm so dizzy . . ." I am, but I also need this conversation to end.

"I need to ask you something." Sometime later, his voice cuts through the hazy darkness.

"It's not fair to ask now, but I will. If I could think of a way to get us out of this mess, would you want me to do it?"

I'm still holding on to him like he's the only thing stopping me from falling off the planet. "Like how?"

"However I could. Would you want me to?" If

he would be my friend for the days left, it would be enough. It would be wonderful enough to burn away the negativity.

That smile would be enough.

"This is the part of the dream where you smile, Josh."

He sighs, frustrated. He holds me still, and as I orbit away into sleep, I whisper it through the fog of sleep.

"Of course I would."

Chapter 11

I sit up cautiously in a bedroom lit bright by sun. Artifacts of illness are strewn everywhere. Towels, washcloths, my Tupperware container washed clean. Glasses and medication and a thermometer. My SLEEPYSAURUS pajama top is hanging from the hamper. So is the red tank. My paintball clothes lie in a puddle and need to be burned.

I suck the thermometer to confirm what I already know: The fever has broken.

I'm wearing a blue tank top now. I clutch the mattress as vulnerability makes a long overdue appearance. I feel my shoulder and realize I'm still wearing my bra. I thank all available gods. But still. Joshua Templeman has seen all the rest of my torso skin.

I peer out into the living room. He's still here, sprawled out on the couch, one big-socked foot dangling off the end of the couch.

I grab fresh clothes and stumble into the bathroom. Good gracious. My mascara didn't wash off properly in my shower and instead melted down my face into an Alice Cooper Halloween mask. I also have Alice Cooper hair, which I contain in a bun. I change, wash my face as fast as I can, and gargle mouthwash. At any moment I expect a knock on the door.

This feeling is worse than a hangover. It's worse than waking up after a nude karaoke performance at the office Christmas party. I said too much last night. I told him about my childhood. He knows how lonely I am. He's seen everything I own. He's got so much knowledge the power will fog out of him in toxic clouds. I have to get him out of my apartment.

I approach the couch. It's a three-seat sofa but he can't remotely fit on it. He jolts before I can get a glimpse of him sleeping.

"I think I'm going to be okay."

My magazines are stacked. There are no high heels under the coffee table. Joshua has tidied my apartment. He's lying a few feet from my huge wall cabinet filled with Smurfs, stacked four and five deep. He turned the lights on, and it's illuminated proof that I'm mental. He stands up and the room gets a lot smaller.

"Thank you for sacrificing your Friday night. I don't mind if you want to leave."

"Are you sure?" He is fussily pressing the backs of his fingers on my forehead, cheek, throat. I am definitely feeling better, because when he touches my throat my nipples pinch in response. I cross my arms over my chest.

"Yes. I'll be okay now. Go home please."

He looks down at me with those dark blue eyes and the memory of his smile is overlaid across his solemn face. He looks at me like I'm his patient. I'm no longer elevator-kiss worthy. Nothing like a little vomit to destroy chemistry.

"I can stay. If you can manage to stop freaking out." There's a kind of pity on his face and I know why.

It's not all one-sided—I've seen a hidden part of him too during this endless night we've survived. There's patience and kindness beneath his asshole façade. Human decency. Humor. That smile.

His eyes have flecks of light in their depths and his eyelashes look as if they'd curl against the pad of my little finger. His cheekbones would fit in the curve of my palm. His mouth, well. It'd fit me just about everywhere.

"Your horny eyes are back," he tells me, and I feel my cheeks heat. "You must be feeling better if you can look at me like that."

"I'm sick." I say it primly and I hear his husky laugh as I turn away. He goes into my bedroom and I take several gulps of air.

"You're a little sicko all right." When he reappears he's holding his jacket, and I realize he's spent the entire night dressed in his paintball clothes. And he doesn't even stink. How is it fair?

"I need to . . ." I'm getting frantic. I grab at his elbow when he toes on his shoes by the door.

"Yeah, yeah, I'm leaving. You don't need to pick me up and throw me out. See you at work, *Lucinda*." He rattles a bottle of pills at me.

"Go back to bed. Two more next time you wake up." He hesitates again, reluctance written all over his face. "Are you sure you'll be okay?" He touches my forehead again, rechecking my temperature though surely it couldn't have changed in thirty seconds.

"Don't you dare tease me about this on Monday."

The word *Monday* rattles between us, and he takes his hand away. I think that's our new safe word.

"I'll pretend it never happened, if that's what you want," he tells me stiffly and I feel a sinking in my gut.

The last time I asked that of him it was about the kiss; he kept that promise pretty well.

"Don't try to use anything against me. The job interviews, I mean."

The look on his face probably melts the paint off the wall behind me.

"Knowing the consistency of your vomit will give me the edge. For fuck's sake, Lucinda."

When the door bangs behind him and silence expands to fill my apartment, I wish I had the courage to call him back. To say thank you, and to apologize for the fact that yes, he's right as always.

I am completely freaking out. To avoid thinking about it, I sleep.

When I open my eyes again I have a new perspective. It's Saturday evening and the sunset is making the wall at the foot of my bed a glorious honey-peach candle-glow. The color of his skin. My bedroom blazes with the force of my epiphany.

I stare at the ceiling and admit the astonishing truth to myself.

I don't hate Joshua Templeman.

IT'S WHITE SHIRT Monday, six thirty A.M. I'm so washed out I should call in sick, and Helene isn't in anyway, but I need to see Joshua.

Rest assured, I have microanalyzed every moment he was in my apartment, and I know I need to apologize for throwing him out like that. He was nothing but decent and kind to me. We were teetering on the edge of friendship, and I ruined everything with my sharp mouth. When I recall eavesdropping on Josh's conversation with Patrick I feel sick with guilt. I wasn't meant to hear any of that.

How do I properly thank a colleague for helping me vomit? My grandma's vintage etiquette handbooks won't help me with this. A thank-you note or a pound cake won't quite cut it in this instance.

I stare at myself in the bathroom mirror. The week-end's sickfest has bleached me of color. My eyes are puffy and bloodshot. My lips are pale and flaky. I look like I've been trapped down a mineshaft.

My kitchen is now as neat as a pin. He has sorted my mail into a tidy pile on the counter. I claw open the top envelope with one hand while I dunk a herbal tea bag with the other. It's a friendly little note to advise me that my rent is going up. I squint at the new monthly figure and my inhalation probably rattles the Smurfs on their shelves. My rash announcement to quit B&G now feels infinitely more terrifying.

How can I even attempt to face an interview panel at a different company and try to articulate what makes me so good at my job? I try to think of all the things I do well, but all I can think of is pranking Joshua. I'm childish and so unprofessional.

I sit down heavily and try to eat a mouthful of dry cereal from the box. Then I wallow in low spirits and self-doubt a little more.

I open an Internet browser and begin clicking my way through a depressingly barren recruitment website. I'm relieved to be interrupted by my phone buzzing with Danny's caller ID. Weird. Maybe he has a flat tire.

"Hello?"

"Hi. How are you feeling?" His tone is warm.

"I'm alive. Barely."

"I tried to call you a few times on Friday night, but I kept getting Josh. Man, he's such an asshole!"

"He helped me out." I hear how stiff my voice is and

realize I'm beginning to prickle in defensiveness. What the hell is happening?

He held me while I threw up. And called his brother in the middle of the night. He washed my dishes. And I'm pretty sure he watched me sleep.

"Oh. Sorry, I thought we hated him. Are you going to work today?"

"Yeah, I'll go."

"I'm downstairs in the lobby if you, um, want me to drive you."

"Really? Isn't today your first day of freedom?"

"Well, yeah. But Mitchell's written me a letter of recommendation and I need to pick it up. It's no trouble to give you a ride."

"I'll be down in five." I check to make sure my gray wool dress is zipped up. Putting lipstick on my haggard face would look ridiculous.

"Hi," Danny calls when I step out of the elevator. He's holding a bunch of white daisies. My emotions balance on a tightrope between delighted and embarrassed.

It seems he's on the tightrope right next to me. I'd have to be blind to not see the split-second pop of crestfallen surprise in his eyes. As sweaty and gross as I was on Friday, I still looked better than this.

He blinks away his reaction and offers me the flowers. "Are you sure you shouldn't stay home?"

"I look worse than I feel. Should I . . ." I gesture at the elevator. I take another look at him. He's wearing a Matchbox Twenty concert T-shirt, and the sunglasses on the top of his head have ugly white frames. We stand awkwardly and stare at each other.

"You could always put them on your desk at work."

"Okay, I will." It seems like a bad idea but I'm all flustered. If I take the flowers upstairs, I'll have to invite him up. We walk out to the pavement and I breathe my first fresh air in days.

I need to snap out of it. Danny has been nothing but thoughtful this morning. I shade my eyes from the sun. Maybe I can try being thoughtful too. Maybe the convenience store sells olive branches?

"I need to grab something. I'll be right back."

As I pay for Joshua's thank-you gift plus an overpriced red adhesive bow, I can see Danny leaning patiently against his car. I stuff the present into my bag and scurry back across the street.

He opens the door to his red SUV and helps me in. I watch him round the hood. In casual clothes, he looks younger. Slimmer. Paler. As he straps himself in and starts the car, I realize I haven't properly thanked him for the red roses. I am a girl with no manners whatsoever.

"I loved the roses." I look at the little bouquet on my lap.

"The daisies?" He pulls into traffic.

"Yes, these are daisies. A good choice for someone recovering from an epic vomit weekend."

I wish I hadn't said something so gross, but he laughs.

"So. Josh Templeman. What's his deal?"

"The devil sent his only son to earth." Weirdly, I feel guilty.

"He's got a big-brother protective vibe going on." Danny is fishing and I know it.

I am noncommittal. "He does?"

"Oh, yeah. But don't worry. I'll tell him my intentions are honorable." He throws me a sideways grin but a sense of deep disappointment is starting to echo through me. The sparky little flirtatious feeling in my chest has died.

Am I like a little sister to Joshua? It's not the first time a guy has said that to me. Ancient embarrassments echo through me. He'd kissed me in the elevator; that goes against this theory. But he'd never tried again, so maybe it's true. I remember telling him how *hot* the elevator kiss was and wince.

"He didn't tell me you'd tried to call. Thanks for checking on me."

"I didn't think he'd pass on my messages. But it doesn't matter. I'd like to take you out again. Dinner this time. You look like you need a good meal."

I have to appreciate his perseverance in the face of my weirdness and present appearance. Just because I have developed a fascination with Joshua, doesn't mean I should say no. I look at Danny. If I'd thrown a torn-up wish list into a fireplace, he's the guy Mary Poppins would have delivered. "Dinner sometime would be nice."

He parks in a twenty-minute zone and I sign him in as a visitor. As the elevator doors open I realize too late he has delivered me all the way to the tenth floor.

"Thanks."

He steps out with me and tugs me to a halt. "Take it easy today."

He straightens the collar of my coat, his knuckles brushing my throat. I resist the urge to look to my left. Either Joshua is at his desk, witnessing this tableau, or he's not in yet. The tension of not knowing is excruciating.

"Dinner? What about a little dinner tonight? Couldn't hurt?"

"Sure," I agree just to get him to leave. He gives me the daisies with a little flourish, and I manage a smile. I slowly pivot.

Once upon a time, this moment would have been a triumph. I've had daydreams like this. But when I see

Joshua sitting at his desk, sharply tapping paperwork into straight stacks, I wish I could rewind time.

We're playing a new game. While I don't know the rules, I do know I've made a major misstep. I lay the daisies on the end of my desk, and shrug out of my coat.

"Hi, buddy," Danny says to Josh, who slouches down into his chair. It's a boss-type power pose he has perfected.

"You don't work here anymore." Josh isn't one for pleasantries.

"I gave Lucy a ride in and thought I'd come by and make sure I'm not treading on your toes."

"What do you mean?" Josh's eyes grow knife-sharp.

"Well, I know you're pretty protective of Lucy. But I've been treating you right, haven't I?"

I'm floundering under their collective gaze. "Sure, of course."

For a guy facing off against someone Joshua's size, Danny certainly does have a remarkable amount of courage. He tries again.

"I mean, you've clearly got some kind of problem. You were a real asshole on the phone on Friday."

"She'd got vomit on her tank top. I had enough to deal with without being her secretary."

"Your protective big-brother thing is something we need to talk about."

"Voices down," I hiss. Mr. Bexley's door is open.

"Well, no one is good enough for my kid sister." Joshua's voice is heavy with sarcasm, but I still deflate. This morning is the absolute worst.

"And you're right. I don't work here anymore, so I'm free to date Lucy if I want." Danny looks past me at my desk and raises his eyebrows. "Well, well. What do you know. Romance isn't dead."

Joshua scowls darkly and picks at his thumbnail. "Get out before I throw you out."

Danny kisses my cheek, and I am almost certain he did it because of our audience. It was a petty move on his part.

"I'll call you later today about dinner, Luce. And we'll probably need to talk more, Josh."

"Bye, man," Joshua says in a fake voice. We both watch Danny get in the elevator.

Mr. Bexley makes a bull-calf bellow from his office and I finally notice the red rose on my keyboard.

"Oh." I'm a complete and utter moron.

"It was there when I got in." I've more than a thousand hours in the same room as Joshua and the lie in his voice is crystal clear. This rose is velvet-red perfection. In comparison, the daisies look like a tangle of weeds growing in a sewer.

"They were from you? Why didn't you say so?"

Mr. Bexley bellows again, more annoyed. Josh continues to ignore him and impales me with his glare. "You should have had Danny stay with you. Not me."

"He's . . . We're just . . . It's . . . I don't know. He's nice." Olympic-level floundering.

"Yeah, yeah. Nice. The ultimate quality in a man."

"It's right up there. You were *nice* to me on the weekend. You were *nice* to send me roses. But you're back to being a total fuckwit." I am hissing like a goose by this point.

"Doctor Josh," Mr. Bexley interrupts from his doorway. "My office, if you can possibly spare me a moment. And mind your language, Miss Hutton." He huffs off.

"Sorry, boss, I'll be right there," Joshua says through gritted teeth. We're both blazingly frustrated and mere seconds away from mutually strangling each other. He sweeps past my desk and whips away the rose.

"What is wrong with you!" I make a grab for it and a thorn drags across my palm.

"I only sent you those fucking roses because you looked so cut-up after our fight. This is why I don't do nice things for people."

"Ow!" I look at my palm. A stinging red line is forming. I'm holding drops of blood. "You scratched me!"

I catch him by the cuff and squeeze his wrist in a death grip.

"Thank you, Nurse Joshua, you were wonderfully kind. And thank your gorgeous doctor brother."

He remembers something. "I have you to blame for the fact I now have to go to his wedding. I'd nearly gotten out of it. That's your fault."

"*My* fault?"

"If you hadn't been sick, I would never have seen Patrick."

"That makes no sense. I never asked you to call him."

He examines the line of blood I've left on his cuff with a look of complete and utter revulsion. He stuffs a tissue into my palm.

"Just wonderful," he tells me, tossing the ruined rose in the trash. "Disinfect that." He disappears into Mr. Bexley's office.

I open my inbox and see our interviews have been scheduled for next Thursday. My stomach makes a little heave. I think of my rent. I look at the empty desk opposite me.

I then lift up my mouse pad where I have hidden the little florist's card from the bunch of roses. I'd peeked at it last week whenever Joshua wasn't looking.

I stare at the card and wonder how I could have ever thought it was from Danny. It's Josh's handwriting; but I didn't notice the way the letters slashed and swooped.

You're always beautiful.

There's one red petal on my desk and I press it onto the pad of my thumb and breathe it in deep while the daisies blur at the corner of my eye. My palm stings and itches. Josh is absolutely right. I've somehow injured myself due to my own carelessness.

I sit and breathe in the scent of roses and strawberries until I can trust myself not to cry.

Chapter 12

I feel childish as I look at his rolled-up white cuffs, one of which now contains my DNA. He's glowering at his computer screen and has not spoken a word to me in hours. I've royally fucked up.

"I'll dry clean your shirt," I offer, but he doesn't acknowledge me. "I'll buy you a new one. I'm so sorry, Josh—"

He cuts me off. "Did you think it'd all be different today?"

I feel a lump begin to squeeze in my throat. "I'd hoped so. Don't be mad."

"I'm not mad." His neck is red against his white collar.

"I'm trying to tell you I'm sorry. And I wanted to say thank you, for everything you did for me."

"And are those pretty daisies for me, then?"

I remember. This might fix everything. "Wait, I did get you a present."

I pull the little plastic cube topped with the red bow from my purse. I present it to him like a boxed Rolex. His eyes spark with an unidentified emotion before he reassumes his frown.

"Strawberries."

"You said how much you love them." The word *love* has probably never been said in this office, and it gives my voice a weird little tremor. He looks at me sharply.

"I'm surprised you remember anything at all." He puts the strawberries into his out-tray and logs back onto his computer.

After several more minutes of silence I try again.

"How can I pay you back for . . . everything?" The balance has shifted dramatically between us. I'm in his debt now. I owe him.

"Tell me what I can do. I will do anything."

What I want to say is, *Speak to me. Engage with me. I can't fix anything if you ignore me.*

I watch him continue to type, his face expressionless as a crash test dummy. Stacks of sales figures are to his right and he slashes a green highlighter across them. Meanwhile, I am at complete loose ends with no Helene.

"I'll clean your apartment for you. I'll be your slave for the day. I'll . . . bake you a cake."

It's like a soundproof pane has dropped in between us. Or maybe I've been erased. I should let him do his work in silence, but I can't stop talking. He can't hear me anyway, so it won't matter if I say this next thing out loud.

"I'll go with you to the wedding."

"Be quiet, Lucinda." So he *can* hear me.

"I'll be your designated driver. You can get drunk. You can get so drunk and you'll have the best time. I'll be your chauffeur."

He picks up his calculator and begins to tap. I persevere.

"I'll drive you home and put you to bed, like you did for me. You can vomit into Tupperware and I'll rinse it. Then we'll be even."

He rests his fingertips on his keyboard and closes his eyes. He seems to be reciting a string of obscenities in his mind. "You don't even know where the wedding is."

"Unless it's in North Korea, I'll go. When is it?"

"This Saturday."

"I'm free. It's settled. Give me your address and I'll pick you up and everything. Name the time."

"Pretty presumptuous of you to assume I won't have a date."

I nearly open my mouth to retort that I know for a fact I'm his plus-one. Just in time, my cell phone rings. Danny. I swivel my chair a full one hundred eighty degrees. Hasn't he ever heard of texting?

"Hi, Lucy. Feeling any better? Are we still on for dinner?"

I drop my voice to a whisper. "I'm not sure. I have to go pick up my car and I've been feeling pretty shitty."

"I've heard so much about this car of yours."

"I think it's silver . . . that's as much as I can remember of it."

"I've booked a table for seven tonight. Bonito Brothers. You said you like it?"

There's not much choice left then. It's hard to get a reservation there. I try not to sigh.

"Bonito Brothers is good. Thanks. I won't have a huge appetite but I'll do my best. I'll meet you there."

"See you tonight."

I hang up and sit facing the wall for a bit.

"Danny Fletcher has a clichéd evening in store for you. Italian restaurant, checkered tablecloth. Probably a candle. He'll push the last meatball to you with his nose. Second date, right?"

"Let's change the subject." I pretend to start typing. My screen fills with error messages.

"Most guys would try for a kiss on the second date."

That stops me in my tracks, and the look in my eye is probably crazy. The idea of Joshua making an effort on a second date is inconceivable. Joshua on a date, period.

I imagine Josh, seated across from a beautiful woman, laughing and smiling. The same smile he once gave me. His eyes lit up, anticipating a good-night kiss. I've got a dark ball of pressure burning in my chest. I try to clear my throat but it doesn't work.

I'm not the only one looking a little crazy. "Just say it. You look like you're about to explode."

"Do yourself a favor and stay home tonight. You look *terrible*."

"Thank you, Doctor Josh. Why does Fat Little Dick call you that, anyway?"

"Because my parents and brother are doctors. It's his way of reminding me I've failed to reach my potential." His tone indicates I am the town simpleton, and he gets to his feet. I trail after him down the hall toward the copy room. He doesn't slow so I grab him by the arm.

"Wait a minute. I'm trying to fix this. You're right, you know. I did come in here today hoping these last days together might be different."

He opens his mouth, but I steamroll ahead. He's letting me hold him against the wall, but we both know he could pick me up like a chess piece if he wanted to.

Some heeled shoes are clopping toward us sedately as a Clydesdale and my frustration mounts. I need to clear this up, *now*, or I am going to have an aneurism.

The cleaner's closet will have to do. It's thankfully unlocked, and I walk in and stand among the chemicals and vacuum cleaners.

"Get in here."

He obeys reluctantly and I pull the door shut and lean on it. We remain silent as the heels round the corner and continue past.

"This is cozy." Josh kicks his toe against a bulk quantity of toilet paper. "Well? What?"

"I've screwed up. I know I have."

"There's nothing to screw up. You've pissed me off. The status quo is maintained."

He leans an elbow on a shelf to drag his hand tiredly through his hair, and his shirt slides up an inch or so out of his trouser waistband. We're so close I can hear the fabric stretch and slide over his skin.

"I thought maybe the war might be over. I thought we might be friends."

His eyes flash with disgust, so I might as well put it all out there. "Josh, I want to be *friends* with you. Or something. I have no idea why, because you're awful."

He holds up a finger. "There's an interesting couple of words in among what you just said."

"I say a lot of interesting words. And you never hear any of them." I ball my hands until the knuckles crack, and the realization hits me across the head.

The reason for my rising distress is this: I will never see his hidden softness again. I think of his hands braced on either side of my pillow, talking me through the fever. His hands passing easily over my skin.

Right now he looks like he'd burn me at the stake. He was my friend once, for one delirious night, and it's all I'll ever get.

"Or something," he uses his fingers to add quotations. "You said you wanted to be friends, or something. What exactly does *or something* entail? I want to know my options."

"It probably entails not completely hating each other. I don't know." I try to sit on a stack of boxes and they crush underneath me so I stand back up.

"So, what is he, your boyfriend?" He has hands on hips and the small room shrinks to microscopic.

He's close to me now. Whatever divine soap Josh uses, I need some. I'll keep a bar of it in my top drawer to scent my lingerie. I feel my cheeks beginning to heat.

"You couldn't care less if I date Danny. You can't believe any guy would want to be with me."

Instead of replying, he holds out his hand, palm up. His shirt sleeves are still rolled, and I look at the strong tendons and cords in his wrists. I notice for the first time he has those muscly-guy raised veins in his inner arms.

"Touching at work is against HR policy." My throat is bone dry. *Not touching me should be illegal.*

He stares expectantly at me until I slide my hand into his. It's hard to resist someone holding out his hand this way, and it's completely impossible if it's Joshua. I register the heat and size of his fingers before he turns over my hand to inspect the scratch on my palm, handling my hand like an injured dove.

"Seriously though, did you clean this? Rose thorns can have fungus on them. The scratch can get infected." He presses around the wound, fussing and frowning. How can he be these two different men? A second realization hits me. Perhaps I am a determining factor. The concept is scary. The only way I can get him to drop his guard is to drop mine. Maybe I can change everything.

"Josh."

When he hears me shorten his name, he folds up my fingers and gives me my hand back. It's time to try this. I pray I'm not wrong.

"I wanted you there on Friday night. You, and only you. And if you don't want to be friends with me, I'll try to play the Or Something Game with you."

There's a long pause and he doesn't react. If I've misjudged this, I will never live it down. My heart is pulsing uncomfortably fast.

"Really?" He is skeptical.

I push him against the door and feel a thrill when I hear the thud of his weight against it.

"Kiss me." I whisper it and the air gets warmer.

"So the Or Something Game involves kissing. How interesting, Lucinda." He passes his fingers through my hair, raking it gently away from my face.

"I don't know the rules yet. It's a pretty new game."

"Are you sure about that?" He looks down to watch my hand spread out over his stomach.

I push at the hard flesh. It doesn't remotely give. "Are you wearing a bullet-proof vest?"

"I've got to in this office."

"I really am sorry for hurting your feelings, and for throwing you out of my apartment. Josh." When I use his shortened name, it's a little peace offering. It's an apology.

Frankly, it's a pleasure. It lets me imagine he's my friend. My friend, who lets me run my palms up his torso in a cleaner's closet. I wish he'd run his hands up mine.

"Apology accepted. But you can't expect me to be a nice guy when another man walks you into the office, and kisses you and gives you flowers. It's not the way this game works between you and me."

"I have never had the faintest clue on how it works." I swallow heavily. He touches his fingers underneath my chin, raising my face to his.

"I thought you were so clever, Lucinda. I must be wrong."

I rise on tiptoes and my hands slide onto his shoulders and grip. When I press my fingernails into him, his throat constricts in a swallow and I manage to land one glancing, openmouthed kiss across it. I can feel the effect it has; his hands flex, his hips tilt toward me. Something heavy presses into my stomach.

This is the best game I've ever played in my entire life.

His hand settles on my lower back and I arch against him and manage to get one hand on the nape of his neck.

"Is there any reason we're not kissing yet?"

"The height difference, mainly." He's trying to conceal the fact he's got an erection hard enough to dent a tin can. It's an impossible task. I smile and try to tug him down to my mouth.

"Well, don't make me climb up there."

His mouth belongs on mine, but he doesn't move down farther. His face tightens with indecision and restrained lust. I imagine he's mulling over the work implications.

"We're barely working together for another two weeks. So what does it matter?" I congratulate myself on my casual tone.

"What a romantic proposition." His tongue emerges and licks the corner of his mouth. He wants to. It's obvious he does. But yet he still resists.

"Put your hands on me."

Instead of grabbing me, he puts out his hands, offering them to me like I just did to him. Then he just stands there. His chest rises and falls.

"Put them on yourself."

Nothing ever goes the way I expect it will. I take one of his hands and lay it on my side. The other, I decide to slide around to my butt. Both squeeze me, but they don't move. Basically, I'm feeling myself up, hardly aided by him at all.

"Is this to get around the HR rules? No more HR threats. It's a complete waste of breath at this point." Saying it was a waste of *my* breath. I need all the oxygen I can get. The heat of his hands on me burns through my clothes.

I push his hand down to where my butt meets thigh. He has to bend down a lot and it gets his mouth much closer. Now, I pull his other hand up from my ribs to the side of my breast. He looks like he's about to pass out. My ego is nearly too big to fit in this room.

"So this is what sex with you would be like." I can't resist teasing him. "I was hoping you'd participate a little more."

He finally says something. "I'd participate. So well, you wouldn't walk straight the next day."

More footsteps pass. I'm in a room smaller than a jail cell and Josh has his hands on me. Too bold for my own good, I lift his hand and press his fingertips into my cleavage, just to see what happens.

"That's okay, walking is overrated."

Whatever control he has on himself slips significantly and his hand regains its autonomy. He puts a hand under my knee to lift my leg. His fingertips stroke up under the hem of my dress, making a smooth line up my outer thigh to the side of my underwear. His fingertip touches the elastic and I shiver. Between my breasts, his fingers dip and stroke. Then he puts my foot back on the ground, and both his hands in his pockets.

"I want you to do something for me. I want you to have your cute little date with Danny, and I want you to kiss him."

Even as he says it, his mouth twists in distaste. I drop back down to my regular height. We've said some fucking unbelievable things to each other recently, but that was completely out of left field.

"What? Why?" I drop my hands from his shoulders.

The sinking feeling has started. He's been messing with me all along. He sees the alarm in my eyes and halts my retreat with a hand on my elbow.

"If it's better than our elevator kiss, case closed. Date him. Plan a spring wedding in a gazebo at Sky Diamond Strawberries."

I begin to protest but he cuts me off. "If it isn't as good, you have to admit it to me. To my face. Verbally. Honestly. With no sarcasm." Every loophole is neatly closed.

"It's weird you want me to." I take a step back and knock over a broom.

"The Or Something Game doesn't resume until you tell me that no one kisses you like I do."

"Can I just tell you now?" I tiptoe up again but he won't have a bar of it.

"No way am I going to be your little experiment before you choose Mr. Nice Guy. So yes, I want you to kiss Danny Fletcher tonight and report back on the result. If it goes great, then good luck to you."

"You certainly are biased against nice guys."

He adds one more caveat. "One last thing. If kissing him isn't as good as kissing me, you can't kiss him again." He opens the door and pushes me out. Mr. Bexley is clomping along sullenly, so I pull the door shut quickly behind me. He does a double take when he sees me come out of the janitor's closet.

"I was looking for some glass cleaner. There are fingerprints all over the office."

"Have you seen Josh? He's not anywhere. Everything's falling apart and he's gone."

"He's gone to get you coffee and donuts. You've been so busy. Promise you'll act surprised."

Mr. Bexley perks up, puffs, and grumbles all in one guttural sound. Then he looks at my dress and its contents with such a leisurely perusal I put my hands on my hips in annoyance. He doesn't notice.

"You're looking a little flustered, Miss Hutton. I don't mind a young lady looking a bit pink in the cheeks. You should smile more, though."

"Oops, my phone is ringing," I say, even though it isn't. "Remember, act surprised when Josh gets back."

"I can be surprised," he tells me and heads to the men's bathrooms. He's got a newspaper in one hand. Josh can take a leisurely meander downstairs now.

I keep my composure until I get back to my desk, but then I let myself do what I've desperately needed to: I pant for air. I huff like I've run a half marathon. Sweat is beading on the back of my neck and my face is dewy. My fingers are burning hot from touching the cotton covering his skin. I fog up half the shiny surfaces of the tenth floor before I am composed enough to even sit.

I'm so turned on I wish I could knock myself unconscious until it passes.

Joshua returns twenty minutes later, bearing donuts and coffee. He still beats Mr. Bexley back from the bathroom.

"Nice save," Joshua tells me, putting a hot chocolate

and a strawberry donut beside my mouse pad. "Impressive thinking on your feet."

I stare at the gorgeous pink donut like we've fallen through a wormhole while he disappears into his boss's office. In the space of twenty minutes self-doubt has begun to erode my confidence that I can handle the Or Something Game. He's too big, too clever, and my body likes him way too much. I'm desperate to try to lay some kind of ground rules. When he sits at his desk and sips his coffee, it all comes out in a vulgar blurt.

"If the Or Something Game involves sex, it'll be a one-time deal. Once. One meaningless time only." I clap my hand over my mouth.

He narrows an eye cynically and begins eating the strawberries I gave him. It's mesmerizing. I never see him eat anything.

"One." I hold up one finger.

"Just once? You're sure? Would you at least buy me dinner first?" He leans back in his chair, enjoying this exchange. He bites, chews, swallows, and I have to look away because frankly, it's sexy as hell.

"Sure, we can hit the drive-thru for a Happy Meal."

"Gee, thanks. A burger meal and toy before we went and did it. Once." He sips at his coffee and looks at the ceiling. "Couldn't you at least spring for a fancy Italian restaurant? Or do you *want* me feeling cheap?"

"Once." I put several knuckles into my mouth and bite them until it hurts. *Shut your mouth, Lucy.*

"Can you define what one time would involve?" He rests his chin on his palm and closes his eyes, yawning. You'd think we were talking about a work presentation, not a naked, dirty game in my bed.

"Did your parents never give you the birds and bees talk?" I sip my hot chocolate.

"I'm trying to understand the rules upfront. You make up an awful lot as you go along. Could you email them to me?"

Mr. Bexley walks between us, breaking the moment, and makes an unconvincing sound of surprise when he sees his coffee and donuts on his desk.

"I'll be in, one minute," Joshua calls to him.

To me he says, "Once, huh? You'd restrain yourself?" I see the edge of his mouth lift in a little smile, and he begins to click on his computer screen.

"Don't look so self-satisfied," I hiss as quietly as I can. "It's not a guarantee it'll ever happen."

"Don't act like it's only me who wants this. This isn't some favor you'd be doing me. It's the pretty big favor you'd be doing yourself."

He doesn't seem to be making a sleazy reference to what lies beneath his zipper, but I look there anyway. I can't seem to stop talking.

"To kill off this weird sexual tension between us, then yes, it would be only once. Like I said, what does it matter?"

He blinks hard, opens his mouth to speak, then seems to reconsider. For a guy who's just been told by a woman she's considering having sex with him, he looks a little disappointed.

"Then I guess I'd better make it count, Shortcake." A promise and a warning. I bite my donut nearly in half so I don't have to reply.

I got the upper hand, defining the terms a little. He stands and picks up his coffee. It's a signal of retreat. But then he slams the tennis ball back into my court, forcing the decision back onto me so squarely I have to admit, I'm impressed.

He writes something on a blue Post-it note. His spiky

black letters swoop and slash; ink spreading a little into the veins of paper.

He writes down something I never dreamed I'd ever know. I have no idea if it's for the purpose of picking him up before the wedding, *or something.* I can't ask because my mouth is so full.

He sticks it onto my computer screen. His home address.

Chapter 13

I keep half expecting your big brother to storm in here any moment, and haul you off. You're out on a school night and all," Danny says as I slush my spoon halfheartedly in lemon gelato.

"I'm sure he's idling his car out front, ready to run you over." It only comes out half like a joke. The waitress comes to check on us. Again, we reassure her of how delicious everything is. Everything's flippin' perfect. Checked tablecloth and candles. Romantic music and me cleaned up nicely in a red dress and lipstick. The only thing keeping me from dozing off is the little sharp nervous feeling in my stomach when I think of the near-inevitable kiss tonight.

"I need to ask. Are you . . . single? Available? I'm getting a vibe. You and he aren't . . . ?"

"Yes, no. No! No vibe. Absolutely no vibe. I'm single." Then I repeat it a couple more times. Danny's expression is doubtful. The lady doth protest way, way too much.

A slice of panic opens in my gut. If anyone suspected me and Josh of being involved in any way, there'd be repercussions. Reputation-wise. HR-wise. Dignity-wise. I remember the amused looks and nudges at the post-paintball meeting and cringe to think the horse may have bolted.

"There's been heaps of office hookups. Samantha and Glen. Phew, that was a disaster." Danny grins. He's a gossip, I can tell. He raises his eyebrows, hoping I'll have my own juicy scandal to share, but I shake my head.

"No one talks to me at work. They think I'll snitch."

"Is it true Josh completed first-year medical school?"

"I don't know. His parents and brother are doctors, though."

"We always lived in hope he'd quit Bexley Books and go be a proctologist or whatever."

I have to laugh.

"So, did you have a bad breakup in the past or something?" Danny looks genuinely curious. "I guess I'm trying to work out why you're single."

"I haven't had any time to date and I haven't put in enough effort to make new friends after losing touch with people from Gamin after the merger. My job has taken over my life. Working for a CEO isn't your typical nine-to-five."

"So, what was that rose on your desk?" He raises his eyebrows expectantly.

"It was a joke."

He waits for me to elaborate but when I don't, he gives up and changes the subject. "Did you get your application in for the new exec position?"

"It's in. Interviews are next week."

"Is there a big field?"

"The shortlist for interviews is just me, a couple of externals, and my good buddy Joshua Templeman. Four applicants in total."

"You've been waiting a long time for this," Danny

surmises. Maybe I've got my crazy-intense eyes on again.

"Helene has been big on developing me. When we were Gamin Publishing, I was earmarked to transfer into the editorial team after a year of working for her." I hear how bitter my voice is.

Danny considers. "It's not uncommon to get into publishing any way you can. Even if it means taking an admin role. Half the people here didn't start out in their dream job. It was smart to jump on any opening you could."

"No, that's not my issue. I really am glad I've moved into a business role."

"But then the merger happened."

"Yes. So many people lost jobs; I was lucky to keep mine. Even if it's meant staying in the same role. I lost my best friend." I make it sound like she's dead now.

"Chief of operations will look pretty impressive on your CV, especially at your age."

"Yes." I breathe, imagining it in Arial font. Then I imagine it on Joshua's CV, and the delicious daydream turns sour. "I'm preparing a presentation for the interview. It's something I've been thinking about for a long time. I haven't been in the position to be as influential as I'd like. The timing's always been off. I want to set up a formal project to get the backlist into ebook format. Repackaging the whole book, covers, the works. I think getting this new role will give me the leverage I've been lacking."

"Sounds like you'll be needing lots of support in terms of cover design. Keep me in mind," Danny says. He rummages in his pocket and gives me his new business card. A lady at the next table looks at him sideways like, *What a douche.*

He signals for the check and hands over his credit card.

"Oh, thank you," I squeak awkwardly and he smiles.

We walk to my car. "Sorry I talked so much about work."

"It's no problem. I used to work there, remember. So. This is it. Your car." Danny stops, frames his hands around the car. "It's incredible."

"Isn't she?" I lean on the door. "Free at last, free at last."

"Did you just quote Martin Luther King Jr. in relation to your car?"

"Um. Yes, I guess I did . . ."

He bursts out laughing. "Man, you're awesome."

"I'm an idiot."

"Don't say that. I'd like to kiss you. Please," he adds courteously.

"Okay." We lock eyes. We both know this is it. The moment of truth. Either Danny blows my mind, or I have to pump up Josh's ego.

We look like a pretty little Valentine's card. The road is slicked with rain; a streetlight rings us in white. My red party dress is the focal point, and a man with the angelic white-blond curls is bending me back a little, his pale blue eyes dropping to look at my mouth. His height means we clinch together perfectly.

His breath is light and sweet from his dessert, and his hands spread respectfully at my waist. When his lips touch mine, I implore myself to feel something. I wish on every single shooting star overhead. I pray for the first dizzying kick of lust. I kiss Danny Fletcher again and again until I realize lust is never coming.

His mouth tips mine open a little, although he keeps his tongue in his mouth like the gentleman he is. I put my hand on his shoulder. His frame, which looked so fit and muscular at first glance, feels as light and insubstantial as chicken bones. I bet he couldn't even lift me off the ground.

We both pull back.

"Well." My hopes are absolutely dashed and I think he knows it. He studies my face. It was like kissing a cousin. All wrong. I want to do it again, to be sure, and when I move forward he takes a half step back and drops his hands from me.

"I enjoy spending time with you," he begins. "You're a great girl."

I finish his sentence for him. "Can we just be friends, though? I'm sorry."

His face shows disappointment that he didn't get to say it first, relief and a little slice of irritation that makes me like him less.

"Sure. Of course. We're friends."

I take my car key out. "Well, thanks for dinner. Good night."

I watch him walk away, his hand raised in farewell. He flips his car keys into his palm, his stride a little slow. An expensive meal exchanged for a bad kiss.

Well, you win the Kiss Competition, Joshua Templeman. I was afraid you would.

A tiny thundercloud is brewing inside me. This was a limp, dull, waste of an evening.

But the worst part? If Joshua did not exist, it would have been a fine date by my standards. Perfectly agreeable. I've had worse dates and far worse kisses. Even though the chemistry wasn't ideal, we could have built on it. The only opportunity I've had in recent memory and it was ruined.

It was like Joshua was sitting at a third chair at our

romantic little table, watching, judging. Reminding me of all the things I was missing. When I looked at Danny's mouth, I begged myself to feel something.

When the streets get too unfamiliar, I pull over and spend countless minutes battling with my GPS settings, my clumsy fingers pressing all the wrong buttons, a blue square of paper between my teeth.

I call the GPS woman the worst names I can think of. I beg her to stop. But she doesn't. Like a total bitch, she directs me to Josh's apartment building.

I'm definitely not going into his building. I'm not totally pathetic. I park on a side street and look up at the building, wondering which glowing square represents him.

Josh, why have you ruined me?

My phone buzzes. It's a name I've barely ever seen on my screen.

Joshua Templeman: Well? Suspense, etc.

I lock my car and pull my coat tighter as I walk. I try to think of how to reply. I've got nothing, frankly. My pride is ridiculously wounded. I should have tried harder tonight. Convinced myself a little more. But I'm so tired of trying.

I compose a reply. It is an emoticon of a smiling poo. It sums everything up.

I decide to make one full lap of his apartment building, praying I'm not abducted in the meantime. I don't need to worry too much. The rain has cleared the streets of all but the most dedicated of stalkers. My red heels echo loudly as I complete my reconnaissance.

It's strange, walking along, trying to look at things through someone else's eyes, let alone your sworn enemy's. I look at the cracks on the pavement, and wonder if he treads on these when he takes a walk down to that little organic grocery store. I wish I lived near a store like that; maybe I wouldn't eat so much macaroni and cheese.

I've always suspected people in our lives are here to teach us a lesson. I've been sure Josh's purpose is to test me. Push me. Make me tougher. And to a certain degree it's been true.

I pass a pane of glass, and pause, studying my reflection. This dress is as cute as a button. I've got color back in my cheeks and lips, most of it cosmetic. I think of the roses. I still can't reconcile it. They were from Joshua Templeman. He walked into a florist, of his own volition, and wrote three words on a card that changed the state of play.

He could have written anything. Any of the following would have been perfect.

I'm sorry. I apologize. I messed up. I'm a horrible asshole. The war is over. I surrender.

We're friends now.

But instead, those three little words. *You're always beautiful.* The strangest admission from the last person on earth I'd expect. I let myself think the thought I've been blocking so admirably.

Maybe he's never hated me. Maybe he's always wanted me.

Another chirp from my pocket.

Joshua Templeman: Where are you?

Where, indeed. Never you mind, Templeman. I'm skulking behind your building, looking at Dumpsters, trying to decide if that's your regular cafe across the street or if you ever walk in the tiny park with the little fountain. I'm looking at the way the light shines off the pavement and looking at everything with these brand-new eyes.

Where am I? I'm on another planet.

Another text.

Joshua Templeman: Lucinda.
I'm getting annoyed.

I don't reply. What's the use? I need to chalk tonight up as another awkward life experience. I look down the street and can see my car at the end of the block, waiting patiently. A cab cruises past, slows, and when I shake my head it speeds off.

Is this how stalking begins? I look up and see a moth circling a streetlight. Tonight, I understand that creature completely.

One pass along the front of his building and I'm done. I'll turn my head to look at where the mailboxes are. Perhaps I might want to leave him a death threat. Or an anonymous dirty note, wrapped in a pair of underpants the size of a naval flag.

I lengthen my stride to pass by the front doors, catching a glimpse of the tidy lobby, when I see someone walking ahead of me. A man, tall, beautifully proportioned, hands in pockets, temper and agitation in his stride. The same silhouette I saw on my first day at B&G. The shape I know better than my own shadow.

Of course, on this new planet I've traveled to, there is no one but Josh.

He glances over his shoulder, no doubt hearing my insanely loud shoes stop in their tracks. Then he looks again. It's a double take for the record books.

"I'm out stalking," I call. It doesn't come out the way I'd intended. It's not lighthearted or funny. It comes out like a warning. I'm one scary bitch right now. I hold my hands up to show I'm not armed. My heart is racing.

"Me too," he replies. Another cab cruises past like a shark.

"Where are you actually going?" My voice rings down the empty street.

"I just told you. I'm going out stalking."

"What, on foot?" I come closer by another six paces. "You were going to walk?"

"I was going to run down the middle of the street like the Terminator."

The laugh blasts out of me like *bah*. I'm breaking one of my rules by grinning at him, but I can't seem to stop.

"You're on foot, after all. Stilts." He gestures at my sky-high shoes.

"It gives me a few extra inches of height to look through your garbage."

"Find anything of interest?" He strolls closer and stops until we have maybe ten paces between us. I can almost pick up the scent of his skin.

"Pretty much what I was expecting. Vegetable scraps, coffee grounds, adult diapers."

He tips his head back and laughs at the tiny stars visible through the clouds. His amazing, exhilarating laugh is even better than I remembered. Every atom in my body trembles with the need for *more*. The space between us is vibrating with energy.

"You *can* smile." It's all I can say.

His smile is worth a thousand of anyone else's. I need a photograph. I need something to hold on to. I need this entire bizarre planet to stop spinning so I can freeze this moment in time. What a disaster.

"What can I say? You're funny tonight." It fades off his face as I take a step back.

"So giving you my address was the only thing I needed to do to find you out here? Maybe I should have given it to you on our first day."

"What, so you could run me over with your car?"

I creep a little closer until we meet under a streetlight. I've spent over eight hours looking at him today, but out of the office context, he looks brand-new and strange.

His hair is shiny and damp and there is a glow on his cheekbones. The cotton T-shirt he's wearing is a washed-out navy, probably softer than a baby's bed-sheets, and the cold air is probably nipping his bare forearms. Those old jeans love his body and the button winks at me like a Roman coin. The laces on his sneakers are loose and nearly undone. He is an absolute pleasure to look at.

"Date didn't go so well," he surmises.

To his credit he doesn't smirk. Those dark blue eyes watch me patiently. He lets me stand there and try to think of something. How can I get myself out of this situation? Embarrassment is starting to catch up with me again, now that the joking between us is fading away.

"It went okay." I check my watch.

"But not great, if you're outside my building. Or are you here to report good news?"

"Oh, shut up. I wanted to . . . I don't know. See where you live. How could I resist? I was thinking about putting a dead fish in your mailbox one day. You saw where I live. It's unfair and uneven."

He won't be distracted. "Did you kiss him like we agreed?"

I look at the streetlight. "Yes."

"And?"

While I dither he puts his hands on his hips and looks down the street, apparently at his wit's end. I wipe the back of my hand across my lips.

"The date itself went fine," I begin, but he steps close and cradles my jaw in his hands. The tension is crackling like static.

"Fine. Fine and great and nice. You need something more than *fine*. Tell me the truth."

"Fine is exactly what I need. I need something normal, and easy." I see disappointment in his eyes.

"That's not what you need. Trust me."

I try to turn my face away, but he won't allow it. I feel his thumb trace across my cheek. I try to push him away but end up tugging him closer, his T-shirt in my fists.

"He's not enough for you."

"I have no idea why I'm even here."

"You do know." He presses a kiss to my cheekbone, and I rise to my tiptoes, shivering. "You're here to tell me the truth. Once you stop being a little liar."

He's right, of course. He's always right.

"No one can kiss me like you do."

I have the rare privilege of seeing Josh's eyes flash bright from something other than irritation or anger. He steps closer and pauses to assess me. Whatever he sees in my own eyes seems to reassure him, and he wraps his arms around me and lifts me clear off my feet. His mouth touches mine.

We both let out twin sighs of relief. There's no point in lying about why I'm here on the wet pavement outside his building.

It starts as nothing more than breathing each other's air, until the pressure of our lips breaks into an openmouth slide. I said earlier, *What does it matter?* Unfortunately for me, this kiss matters.

The muscles in my arms begin to quiver pathetically at his neck and he holds me tighter until I can feel he's got me. My fingers curl into his hair, and I tug the silky thickness. He groans. Our lips sink luxuriously into kisses. Slip, tug, slide.

The energy that usually lashes ineffectively inside each of us now has a conduit, forming a loop of electricity between us, cycling through me, into him. My heart is glowing in my chest like a bulb, flashing brighter with each movement of his lips.

I manage to take a breath and our slow, sexy slide is cut into a series of broken-up kisses, like gentle bites. He's testing, and there's a shyness there too. I feel like I'm being told a secret.

There's a fragility in this kiss I would never have expected. It's the same as the knowledge that one day this memory will fade. He's trying to make me remember this. It's so bittersweet my heart begins to hurt. Just as my mouth opens and I try to slide my tongue, he ends the kiss on a chaste note.

Was that a last kiss?

"My signature second-date kiss." He waits for a response but he must see from my face I'm not capable of human language right now.

He continues to hold me in a comfortable hug. I cross my ankles and look at his face like I've never seen this person before. The impact of his beauty is almost frightening up this close, with those eyes flashing bright. Our noses brush together. The sparks are in my mouth, desperate to reconnect with his.

I picture him on a date with someone else, and a punch of jealousy gets me right in the gut.

"Yeah, yeah. You win," I say once I regain my breath. "More."

I lean forward but he doesn't take the hint. As gorgeous as it was, it was only a fraction of what he's capable of. I need the intensity of the elevator.

A middle-aged couple walking arm in arm pass us by, breaking our little bubble. The woman looks back over her shoulder, her heart in her eyes. We clearly look flippin' adorable.

"My car is that way." I start to squirm and point.

"My apartment is that way," he points upward and carefully puts me on the ground like a milk bottle.

"I can't."

"Tiny. Little. Chicken." He's got my number, all right. My turn to try out some scary honesty.

"Fine. I admit it. I'm scared shitless. If I come upstairs, we both know what will happen."

"Pray tell."

"*Or Something* will happen. That one time I was talking about. We won't make it to the interviews next week. We'll both be crippled in your bed, with the sheets in rags."

His mouth lifts in what I think is going to be one hell of a heart-exploding smile so I turn and point myself in the direction of my car. I lift one foot and begin to run.

Chapter 14

N o you don't," he tells me. He walks into the building lobby with me under his arm like a rolled-up newspaper. He even checks his mailbox.

"Relax. I'm just going to let you see my apartment, so that we're even."

"I always thought you'd live underground somewhere, near the earth's core," I manage to say as he hits the button for the fourth floor. Watching his finger gives me flashbacks. I look at the red emergency button and the handrail.

I try to discreetly smell him. I bypass discreet and press my nose against his T-shirt and suck in two brimming lungfuls. Shameful addict. If he notices he doesn't comment.

"Uncle Satan didn't have any apartments available in my price range."

It's a big elevator and there's no reason for me to remain under his arm like this. But four floors is such a short distance, there's hardly any point in removing my arms from his waist. He's got his fingertips in my hair.

I spread my hands slowly, one across his back, the other across his abdomen. Muscle and heat and flesh. I'm pressing my nose back against his ribs, inhaling again.

"Creep," he says mildly, and we are walking down the hall. He unlocks a door and I am teetering in the doorway of Joshua Templeman's apartment. He strips off my coat like a banana peel. I brace myself.

He hangs my coat near the door. "Come in, then."

I am not sure what to expect. Some kind of gray cement cell maybe, devoid of personality, a huge flat-screen TV, and a wooden stool. A voodoo doll with black hair and red lipstick. A Strawberry Shortcake doll with a knife through her heart.

"Where's the dart board with my picture on it?" I lean in a little farther.

"It's in the spare room."

It's masculine and dark, lusciously warm, all the walls painted in chocolates and sand. There's a zingy scent of orange. A big squashy couch sits center stage in front of every male's prerequisite giant flat screen, which he hadn't even turned off. He was in a big hurry. I step out of my shoes, immediately shrinking a little more. He disappears into the kitchen and I peer around the corner.

"Have a snoop. I know you're dying to." He begins to fill a shiny silver kettle, setting it on the stovetop. I let out a shaky breath. I'm not about to be ravished. No one boils water beforehand, except maybe in the Middle Ages.

He's right of course. I'm dying to look. It's why I came here. The Joshua I know is no longer enough. Knowledge is power, and I can't get enough at this point. A silent, exhilarated squeal is lodged in my throat. This is so much better than only seeing the sidewalk outside his building.

There's a bookcase lining an entire wall. By the window there's an armchair and another lamp, with a stack of books illuminated beneath it. Even more books on the coffee table. I'm intensely relieved by this. What would I have done if he turned out to be a beautiful illiterate?

I like his lampshades. I step into one of the big bottle-green circles of light they cast on the oriental rug. I look down and study the pattern; vines of ivy curving and twisting. On the wall in his living room is a framed painting of a hillside, likely Italian, maybe Tuscany. It's an original, not a print; I can see the tiny dabs made by a paintbrush, and the gold frame is ornate. There are buildings clustered on the hill; church domes and spires, and a darkening purple-black sky overhead. A freckling of the faintest silver stars.

There are some business magazines on the coffee table. There is a fancy, pretty cushion on the couch made of rows and rows of blue ribbons. It's all so . . . unexpected. Not in the least bit minimal. It's like a real human lives here. I realize with a jolt that his place is far lovelier than mine. I look under his couch. Nothing. Not even dust.

I spot a little origami bird made of notepaper I once flicked at him during a meeting. It is balanced on the edge of the bookshelf. I look at his profile in the kitchen as he arranges two mugs on the counter in front of him. How strange to imagine him putting my tiny folded scrap in his pocket and bringing it home.

On the next shelf down is a single framed photograph of Josh and Patrick posed in between a couple who I assume are his parents. His father is big and handsome, with a grim edge to his smile, but his mother almost glows out of the picture. She's clearly bursting at the seams to have two such big handsome sons.

"I like your mother," I tell him as he approaches. He

looks at the photograph, and his lips press together. I take the hint and move on.

He's got a lot of medical textbooks on the bottom shelf, which look pretty dated. There's also an articulated anatomy statue of a hand, showing all of the bones. I fold the fingers down until only the middle one remains raised, and smirk at my cleverness.

"Why do you have these?"

"They're from my other life." He disappears into the kitchen again.

I hit Mute on the TV remote and the silence drenches us. I creep past him into his kitchen. It's sparkling clean and the dishwasher is humming. The orange scent is his antibacterial counter spray. I notice my Post-it note with the kiss on it stuck to the fridge and point at it.

He shrugs. "You put so much hard work into it. Seemed a shame to waste it."

I stand there in the lightbulb glow of his refrigerator and stare at everything. There's a rainbow of color in here. Stalks. Leaves. Whiskery roots. Tofu and organic pasta sauce.

"My fridge is nothing but cheese and condiments."

"I know." I close the fridge and lean against it, magnets digging into my spine. I put my face up for a kiss but he shakes his head.

A little crestfallen, I look in his cutlery drawer and stroke the arm of the jacket hanging by the door. In the pocket I find a gas station receipt. Forty-six dollars paid in cash.

Everything is neat, everything in its place. No wonder my apartment broke him out in stress hives.

"My place is like a Calcutta slum in comparison to this. I need a basket for my gym gear too. Where's all your junk? Where's your too-hard pile?"

"You've confirmed your worst fears. I'm a neat freak."

I'm the freak as I spend at least twenty minutes looking at practically everything he owns. I violate his privacy so badly I make myself feel a bit ill, but he stands there and lets me.

It's a two-bedroom place and I stand in the middle of what is set up as a study, hands on hips. Huge computer monitor, some huge dumbbells. A closet filled with heavy winter sportswear and a sleeping bag. More books. I look lustfully at his filing cabinet. If he wasn't here I'd read his electricity bills.

"Are you done?"

I look down at my hand. I'm holding an old matchbox car I found in one of the narrow drawers of a bureau. I'm clutching it in my hands like a crazy old pickpocket.

"Not yet." I'm so scared I can barely say it.

Josh points, and I walk over to the remaining darkened doorway. He snaps on the light switch near my ear and I make a strangled gasp of delight.

His room is painted the blue of my favorite shirt of his. Robin's-egg blue. Pale turquoise mixed with milk. I feel a strange unfurling in my chest, like a sense of deep déjà vu. Like I've been here before, and I will be again. I hug the doorframe.

"Is this your favorite color?"

"Yes." There's tension in his tone. Maybe he's been teased before.

"I love it." I sound reverent. It's such an unexpected pop of bright against the dark chocolates and taupes, and I think how *Josh* it is. Something unexpected. Pale pretty blue. The dark brown headboard, plushly upholstered in leather, saves the room from femininity. He's behind me, close enough to lean against, but I resist. The scent of his skin is fogging my brain. His bed is made and the linen is white, and I seem to find that little detail pretty sexy. His bathroom is polished to a high shine. Red towels and a red toothbrush. It looks like an Ikea catalog.

"I would never have picked you as someone who owns a fern. I had one but it went brown and crunchy."

I go back to Joshua Templeman's *bed*. I touch my finger to the edge of his pillowcase.

"Okay, you're getting beyond weird now."

I try to rattle the headboard but it's solid.

"Stop it. Sit on the couch. I made you tea."

I scuttle sideways like a crab into the living room. "How could you stand there and watch me snoop?"

I take the fancy cushion and stuff it in the small of my back. He gives me a mug and I hold it like a weapon.

"I snooped through your apartment. It's your turn."

I'm flustered, but try to hide it with a joke. "Did you find all the pictures I have of you with your eyes scratched out?"

"No, I never did find your scrapbook. I do know you've got twenty-six Papa Smurfs, and you don't fold your bed sheets properly."

He's at the other end of the couch, head rolled gently to the side, lounging comfortably. He lolls in his office chair a lot but I've never seen his body make such stretched-out, loose shapes. I can't stop looking at him.

"Sheets are too hard. My arms aren't long enough."

He sighs and shakes his head. "It's no excuse."

"Did you look in my underwear drawer?"

"Of course not. I've got to save something for next time."

"Can I look in yours now?" I'm losing my wits. The threshold to his apartment is where I left my sanity. I sip the tea. It is like nectar.

"Now, Shortcake. We're going to do something a bit unusual."

He unmutes the TV and takes a sip from his mug and starts watching an old rerun of *ER* like we do this every night. I sit with a pounding heart and try to concentrate. Hey, this is no big deal. I'm sitting on Joshua Templeman's couch.

I roll my head to the side and stare at him for the entire episode, watching the tense surgery scenes and ward conflicts reflected in his eyes.

"Am I bothering you?"

"No," he replies absently. "I'm used to it."

We are not normal. The minutes tick past and he drinks his coffee and I continue to stare. He's got a shading of stubble I don't see during working hours. My chest is tight with anxiety. My body and brain are conditioned for combat whenever I'm in his immediate radius. When he looks over, I jerk back. He puts his hand between us on the couch, palm up, and then looks back at the TV.

It's like he's put out a dish of seed and is now sitting very still, waiting for the cowardly little chicken to make a move. And it does take me a while. I tentatively pick up his hand and lace his fingers into mine. For a scary moment he doesn't react, but as the warmth of his hand begins to glow into my palm, he gives me a deep, delicious squeeze. He lays our joined hands back down, picks up his mug with his other hand, and nods at the screen.

"I watch medical dramas to spite my dad. They drive him insane. You could never have this on in their house."

"Why? Are they inaccurate?" I'm glad to be able to focus my attention on something other than this strange hand-related development.

"Oh, yeah. They're complete fiction."

"I prefer *Law and Order*. I love when a restaurant worker finds a body in a Dumpster."

"Or a dog walker in Central Park." He gestures at the screen with his coffee. "That so-called doctor isn't even wearing gloves." He scowls at the screen like he is offended to his core.

The art of holding hands is underrated and it's embarrassing how much this simple act has me nearly breathless. The pads of each of his fingertips reach across the backs of my hands to my wrist.

Large men have always intimidated me. When I mentally line up my ex-boyfriends, they've all been definitely on the jockey end of the scale. Easier to deal with. More of an even match. There's never been any of the astounding masculine architecture I'm sitting next to now.

The rounded caps of muscle on his shoulders balance on smoothly curving biceps. His elbow and wrist joints are like something from a hardware store. How would it feel to lie underneath a man as big as this? It would be staggering.

Josh watches *ER* and yawns, not at all suspecting I'm trying to estimate how big his rib cage is like a meat-eating predator.

It's possible our size mismatch has added a friction to our interactions during our working hours. I've always tried to make myself stronger in the only way I can: my mind and my mouth. I think he's converted me. I think I'm into muscles now. I've started to breathe a little hard, and he looks at me.

"What's with the weird eyes? Relax."

"I was thinking how big you are."

I look at our joined hands. He carefully strokes the

length of my palm with his thumb. When we look at each other again, his eyes are a little darker.

"I'll fit you just right."

Goose bumps scatter my skin. I press my thighs together and accidentally make a little pony-snort. I'm sexy as hell. I can't resist; I look over my shoulder at his bedroom. It's so close it would take maybe five big strides to be pushed backward down onto his mattress. His tongue could be on my skin in under thirty seconds.

"If you're going to fit me so well, show me."

"I will."

Our palms are slick. The back of my neck feels hot under my hair. I need to be kissed again. This time, I'm going to slide my tongue against his until he groans. Until he presses something hard against me. Until he takes me into his bedroom and takes off his clothes.

The end credits of history's longest episode of *ER* begin to roll. My heart is threatening to pop like a balloon.

He mutes the TV ominously and turns his head until we're playing the Staring Game. I watch his eyes tip into black, breathless for whatever is about to happen. I can feel a pulse point in all the sensitive parts of my body. Between my legs is heavy and warm. I look at his mouth. He looks at mine. Then he looks at our joined hands.

"What happens now?"

He slants me a look. The next word out of his mouth is like the lash of a whip. "Strip."

I flinch and he laughs to himself and turns the TV off. "I'm kidding. Come on, I'll walk you down to your car."

I am getting dangerously high off his smiles. This is my third one now? I'm stuffing them in my pockets. I'm cramming them into my mouth.

"But . . ." My voice is plaintive. "I thought . . ."

His eyebrows pinch together in a fake display of incomprehension.

"You know . . ."

"It's rather hurtful to only be wanted for my body. I didn't even get the date beforehand." He looks down at our hands again.

"From what I can see, you've got a fabulous set of bones. What else should I want you for?" I start holding and squeezing some of his arm joints. It's the worst seduction routine imaginable, but he doesn't seem to mind. His elbow is too big to fit in my hand. My dress helpfully slips down a little when I reach for him, and his eyes trail down to the revealed cleavage.

When we make eye contact again, I realize that I've said the wrong thing.

He swiftly conceals it by frowning. "We're not doing this tonight."

I nearly snap back but as I watch his eyelids close and he takes a deep breath, I realize how badly I don't want this evening to end. "If I ask you a question about yourself, will you answer?"

"Will you do the same?" He's regaining composure, like I am.

"Sure." Everything we do is tit for tat.

"Okay." He opens his eyes and for a moment I can't think of anything to ask that won't be revealing too much of myself in the process.

What do you really think of me? Is this all some elaborate plan to mess me up? How badly hurt will I be?

I try to sound light. "Let's make it a game, like everything else we do. It's easier. Truth or Dare."

"Truth. Because you're dying for me to say dare."

"What are the pencil codes in your planner? Is it for HR?"

He scowls. "What's the dare?"

His scent is fogging spicily around me. The plush, warm couch conspires to tip me closer to his lap.

"You even need to ask?"

He stands up, and stands me up too. My hands curl into the waistband of his jeans and I feel nothing but firm male against the backs of my knuckles. My mouth is nearly watering.

"We can't start this tonight." He takes my fingers out of his jeans.

"Why not?" I think I'm begging.

"I'm going to need a little more time."

"It's only ten thirty." I follow him to the front door.

"You've told me we'll only do this once. I'm going to need a long time." I feel a fluttery pinch between my legs.

"How long?"

"A *long* time. Days. Probably longer."

My knees knock together. His eyes crinkle.

"Let's call in sick tomorrow." I am infatigable in my quest to get his clothes off. He looks at the ceiling and swallows hard.

"Like I'm going to waste my one big chance on a generic Monday night."

"It won't be a waste."

"How can I explain it? When we were kids, Patrick would always eat his Easter egg straightaway. I could make mine last until my birthday."

"When's your birthday?"

"June twentieth."

"What star sign are you? Cancer?"

"Gemini."

"And why wouldn't you eat it straightaway, exactly?" Wow, I sure know how to make things sound filthy.

He strokes my hair away from my shoulder. "It made Patrick sweat. He'd go into my room and obsess over it. He'd ask me every day if I'd eaten it. It drove him insane. It drove my parents goddamn insane. Even they'd beg me to eat it. When I finally did, it tasted better, knowing how bad someone else wanted it."

He slides the shoulder of my red dress a half inch to the right and looks down at the skin, before leaning down and breathing me in. I feel the tickling suck of his inhale and feel a deep stab of empathy for the heavenly torture his Easter eggs suffered.

"It's perverted to be turned on by a childhood story about two brothers, isn't it?"

He presses his mouth to my shoulder and laughs. It vibrates through my entire body. I look over at his beautiful bedroom, all lit up with the light still burning. Blue and white, like a gorgeous Tiffany box. A gift with a ribbon. A room I want to spend days in. A room I'll probably never want to come out of.

"Did you eat it a bite at a time, or did you snap one day and gorge on it?"

"I guess you'll find out. Eventually."

He picks up his keys and stands jingling them while I put my coat on. We don't touch in the elevator. He walks me outside in silence, over to my car.

"Bye. Thanks for the tea." Embarrassment has caught up with me. I've acted like a total nut tonight. Why is it I can act like a normal human with a guy like Danny, but with Josh I end up dorking out? Something is sharp in my hand and I look down. Oh shit, I'm still holding the matchbox car.

"I'm a freak." I put my face in my hands and tiny wheels roll across my cheek.

"Yes." He is gently amused.

"Sorry."

"Keep it, it's a present."

The first thing he's ever given me aside from the roses. I'm honored beyond words and study it afresh. It has the initials JT scratched onto the bottom.

"Is it a childhood treasure? It looks old." I don't think I'd give it back, even if he changed his mind.

"Maybe it's the start of your new collection. I think we've done something kind of monumental for us. We had a ceasefire. For the full length of a TV episode."

"You sure are good at holding hands."

"I'm probably not good at a lot of things, but I will try to be," he tells me. It's the strangest thing to say and I feel another crack forming in the wall between us.

"Well, thanks. I'll see you tomorrow."

"No you won't. I've got a day off." He never, ever takes a day off.

"Doing anything special?" I look up at the apartments above and a wave of loneliness hits me.

"I have an appointment."

Just when I think I've got a handle on this kaleidoscope of weird feelings, it twists and something new surprises me. I feel like I've been told Christmas is canceled. No Josh, sitting across from me like always? I have to bite my lip to silence myself.

Please, I beg myself. *Please hate Josh again. This is too hard.*

"You're not going to miss me, are you? You can manage one little Tuesday on your own." He touches the little toy car in my hand and spins the wheels a little.

I try to be nonchalant, but he probably sees through it.

"Miss you? I'll miss looking at your pretty face, but that's about it."

I hope it landed somewhere in the vicinity of faint

sarcasm. I haul my quivering body into my car. He taps the window to make me lock the door. It takes me several attempts to get the key into the ignition.

Josh stands motionless in my rearview mirror until he's a speck, one person among billions, but I cannot tear my eyes away until he disappears altogether.

When I get home, I still have the Matchbox car in my hand.

Chapter 15

I'm sitting at my desk, eyelids dry and tight, and I'm staring at Josh's empty seat. The office is cold. Quiet. A professional haven. Any of the cubicle inmates downstairs would kill for this kind of silence.

Josh is supposed to be sitting across from me in an off-white striped shirt. He should be holding a calculator, tapping, frowning, tapping again.

If he were here, he'd look at me, and when our eyes connected a flashbulb of energy would pop inside me. I'd label it annoyance, or dislike. I'd take the little flash and call it something I don't think it is.

I look at the clock. I wait for a small eternity, and a minute ticks by. To amuse myself, I roll my new Matchbox car back and forth across my mouse pad, then take out the florist card from underneath.

You're always beautiful.

I look at my reflection in the ridiculous prism of glass surrounding me. I look at the wall, the ceiling, analyzing my appearance from different angles. Those three words now aren't enough to sate me. He's created a monster.

I turn the florist's card over and notice the address.

I have the best idea and cackle out loud. Grabbing my purse, I walk down to the corner to the exact same florist. Before I lose my nerve, I arrange to have a bunch of off-white roses sent to him with a card. I barely know what I'm going to write, until my hand writes out the following for me:

I want you for more than your body. I want you for your Matchbox cars. —Shortcake

Instantly I have a wave of self-doubt, but the florist has already taken the card and carried the bouquet out to their back room.

It's a joke, that's all, these flowers. He did it for me and we hate being uneven. I slide my credit card back into my purse and imagine him opening his door, and the look on his face. I'm basically cannonballing into something I shouldn't.

On the walk back I buy takeout coffee and knock gently on Helene's door.

"Hi. Am I interrupting?"

"Yes, thank God," she exclaims, throwing her glasses down so vigorously they bounce onto the floor. "Coffee. You're a saint. Saint Lucy of Caffeine."

"And that's not all." I take out a flat box of fancy macarons from under my arm, labeled *Made in France.* I've had them in my drawer for a while for an emergency. I'm such a kiss-ass.

"Did I say saint? I meant goddess." She reaches into the cabinet behind her and finds a plate; it is delicate, painted with flowers and edged in gold. Of course.

"It's so quiet out there today. I can hear a pin drop. It feels strange to not be glared at."

"Get used to it. He does stare a lot at you, doesn't he, darling? I've noticed in the last few all-staff meetings.

Those dark blue eyes of his are actually rather lovely. How's the interview preparation coming along?"

She opens the box of macarons with her silver letter-opener and I'm grateful she's momentarily distracted. She shakes the box gently onto the plate and we each choose. I pick an off-white vanilla one, like today's missing shirt, because I am tragic.

"I'm as ready as I'll ever be."

"I'm not on the interview panel so it wouldn't be a conflict of interest if we did some practice together. How's your presentation coming along?"

"I'd love to show you what I've got."

"Bexley has been making all sorts of comments. I don't know what I'll do, Lucy, if for some reason you don't get the job . . ." She looks out the window, expression darkening. She passes a hand through her hair and it settles back into a perfect shining cap. I wish my hair was so obedient.

"He could easily get the job over me. Josh has a money brain. I'm more of a book brain."

"Hmm. I don't necessarily agree. But if you want, we could breed you together and create the next-generation ultimate B and G employee. I've never heard you call him 'Josh' before."

I pretend my mouth is incredibly full. I chew and point to my mouth and shake my head and buy myself twenty seconds of time. I hope the phone rings.

"Oh, well, you know. That's . . . his name I guess. Joshua. Er, Josh Templeman. Joshua T."

She munches, staring with avid interest at my face.

"You've got a rather eerie glow about you today, darling."

"No I don't." She's on to me. My messing around with Josh is catching up to me.

"You're all confused and bunny-in-the-headlights. It's these dates."

"It's all a bit confusing. Danny is nice. He really is."

"All my favorite boyfriends when I was young weren't particularly nice."

There's a bang on the door adjoining Mr. Bexley's office to Helene's. I'm deeply grateful to Fat Little Dick for this interruption.

"Enter," she barks. He bursts in and stops dead when he sees me and the box of macarons on the desk.

"What do you want?"

"Never mind." He lingers, eyes on the desk, until she heaves a sigh and holds the plate in his direction. He takes two, fingers hesitating on a third. I swear I see the faintest hint of amusement in her eyes when he walks back out and shuts the door without a word.

"Lord, could that man *smell* the sugar? I gave him some to encourage the diabetes, darling, no other reason."

"What did he want?"

"He's lonely without Josh. He's going to have to get used to it."

"When should we do a practice presentation?"

"No time like the present. Wow me, darling."

After delivering my introduction, I can see I have her attention. "My presentation is to propose a new Backlist Digitalization project. I've taken a sample of the combined top one hundred books published by Gamin and also by Bexley in 1995, just as an example. Only about fifty-five percent are available in digital format."

"iPads are a fad," Mr. Bexley interjects from the open adjoining door, chewing. "Who would want to read off a sheet of glass?"

"The fact is, the largest growing market for e-readers are those over thirty," I explain, trying to keep my cool.

How long has he been standing there? How did he open the door so silently? I focus on Helene and try to ignore him.

"This is a huge opportunity, for all of us. It's a chance to renew contracts with authors that have gone out of print. It's growth within the company for people who have the skills to pull the content into ebook, the cover designers, and to get older B and G releases back onto best-seller lists. Publishing is constantly evolving, and we need to keep up."

"Please leave," Helene says over her shoulder to Mr. Bexley. The door closes, but I swear I can still see two shadows of his feet under the door.

The rising panic is now fully fledged. If he reveals my strategy to Josh, he could screw me. I click to my last slide.

"If I'm successful in winning this position, I would seek to create a formal project to get the deep backlist into ebook. I have created an initial budget, which I'll get to in a few slides' time. These ebooks will all need to be repackaged with new, updated covers. There will be costs involved with three new cover designers over the course of the two-year project."

I click through my project proposal. Helene questions me on several points, and I can answer her questions and justify my requirements easily. Eventually, I'm at my last slide. Helene stares at the screen for so long I check to see if she's blinking.

"Darling. Very, very good."

I drop to kneel beside her chair. Tears are forming in her eyes and she takes the tissues from my hand, sighing like she feels silly.

"I've been selfish in keeping you out there," she says quietly. "I just . . . I can't do without you. But I see now how wrong I've been. I should have done more to get you into editorial after the merger. You were so upset too, about losing your friend."

I can't say anything. I don't know what to say.

"But every time I started to think about recruiting for your job, I'd think about how good you are at it, how you basically keep this office running and keeping me sane. Then I'd say, maybe another month won't hurt."

"I only do my job," I say, but she shakes her head.

"Another month. And another month. And it did hurt you, Lucy. You've had ambitions, and things you've wanted, and ideas, but I couldn't bear to let you go."

"So the presentation was okay?"

She laughs and wipes her eyes. "It is going to get you this promotion. And we are going to get B and G back into the game with this. Together. I want to be right beside you, working as colleagues. Mentoring you might be one of the best things I ever achieve in my career."

She looks at the last presentation slide and pauses.

"I have to know, though. If there were no interviews, no new job, would this idea have stayed locked up inside you forever? Why keep this to yourself?"

I sit back on my heels and look at my hands. "Good question."

How many other things has this promotion unlocked inside me?

"I thought you knew your ideas were important." She's starting to fret.

"I think maybe I was waiting for the timing to be right. Or I didn't have confidence. Now I'm being forced to go with it. It's a good thing, I think. Even if I don't get the job, this whole thing has . . . woken me up."

I think of last night, kissing Josh under a streetlight, and then remember.

"What if Mr. Bexley tells Josh about my presentation?"

"Let me deal with him. If he turns up dead in the river you'll know to keep your mouth shut and provide me an alibi. Focus on next week. I do have a suggestion."

"Great." I take the USB and sit opposite her again. "Hit me."

"It's a little light in some places. Why not have an ebook ready for the presentation? Get something from the deep backlist catalog into e-format, and have a breakdown of how many man-hours it took, salary costs. The actual cost of creating it. It will prove your budget is right."

"Yes, good idea." I gulp my lukewarm coffee.

"You think numbers are Josh's strength, yes? Here's your chance to prove you're every bit as capable of creating a baseline budget for this new project."

I'm nodding and scribbling notes, my mind racing ahead.

"But to keep things fair, you can't use company resources on this. Get creative. Use your contacts. Maybe someone who can freelance." There's no mistaking that she means Danny.

I jot down a few notes for myself as she turns off the projector.

"I'm going to get this," I tell her with a new certainty.

"No doubt about it, darling." Helene looks to the adjoining door, and I see her mouth start to quirk with mischief.

"Did you give some more thought to your recent battles with Josh? I have an interesting theory." A little cackle escapes her.

"I'm not sure I'm ready to hear this." I lean on her desk.

"It's inappropriate but here goes. Josh thought you were lying about your date because he can't imagine you with anyone but himself."

"Oh. Um. Ah." I try all vowel combinations. Heat is sweeping up my chest, up my throat, face, into the roots of my hair, until I am completely red.

"Think on *that,*" she says and pops another entire macaron in her mouth.

I open my mouth, hesitate, close it, then do it a few more times. She stands up and dusts off crumbs, looking at me shrewdly.

"I've got to run, I have the hot-water man coming at three. Why do they always come at the most inconvenient times? Go home too, darling. You look a bit like a fish."

I sit at my desk after she leaves. The pathway is as clear as day. I should be on the phone to Danny to talk about him freelancing on my ebook, but every time I pick up the phone I put it down again. To keep things professional I dig out his business card and email him a meeting request for tomorrow. I have no idea what he charges but it's all or nothing at this point.

I have a text. My stomach freefalls. My heart soars.

Joshua Templeman: *Glad to hear it.*

He got the roses then. I hug the phone to my chest.

This interview is the worst kind of limbo. So many people have wished me good luck in the hallways. Imagining their sympathetic awkwardness if I fail is unbearable.

If Josh gets this job, I have to walk away.

I look at the cross in my planner that symbolizes next week's interview. As much as my mock presentation boosted my confidence, I also need to plan out the worst-case scenario. It's good business planning to have an exit strategy. I've got some money saved in a sacred account that I never touch. I'd wanted to take a vacation this year, but I guess it's going to be my safety net. Maybe I'd have to go and sit under the umbrella at the front gates of Sky Diamond Strawberries. My parents would probably hug and jump and scream in delight. They wouldn't even have the decency to be disappointed in me.

If Josh gets this job, and I resign, will my bitterness outweigh those little flickers inside my chest when he looks at me? Could our weird, fragile little game survive outside these walls? My friendship with Val didn't survive.

Could we see each other while I hear about his successes at B&G and I'm in the job queue? On the other hand, would he be happy for my success while he's papering this city with his CV? His pride is something I can't imagine he'd lay down lightly.

I'm not completely out of options. I've got some contacts at some smaller boutique publishers that I could possibly approach, but I'd feel disloyal to Helene. I could ask Helene for a transfer into another B&G team. Maybe it is time to start at the bottom of the editorial team. But if I remain at B&G, that would almost certainly mean that Josh was the new COO.

Needless to say, any chance of ever sitting on his couch again would be completely gone.

Life would be easier if I could just hate Joshua Templeman. I look at his empty chair, and then close my eyes, the blue of his bedroom washing through me.

I'm about to lose something that I never had to begin with.

I GO HOME early as per Helene's suggestion, and look for something to occupy myself.

Everything is tidy, thanks to Josh. I check online for any new Smurf auctions, and do a little stock take of my current collection. I count the Papa Smurfs.

I look in my empty fridge, and think of his rainbow of fruit and vegetables. I decide to make a cup of tea and have none. I could go out to the store, but instead I drink a glass of water. I feel cold and bundle myself in a cardigan.

Now that I've seen his apartment, I can't stop looking at my own with new eyes. It's so drab. White walls, beige carpet, the couch a nondescript color in between. No patterned rugs or framed paintings.

I shower and put on makeup, which is ridiculous. Why would I spray perfume into my cleavage? Or put on my nice jeans? There's no one here to see me, or smell me. I've got nowhere to go. It's been so long since I've had someone in the city I could call.

I sit down and my knee is bouncing. My insides are crawling. I feel like a magnet, shaking with the need to move. Is this how addicts feel? I am beginning to realize what's happening, but I can't admit it to myself, not yet.

Has holding a phone and looking at a contact name ever been this terrifying?

Joshua Templeman

I should be sitting here looking at

Danny Fletcher

I should be giving Danny a call, asking him to meet me for a movie or a bite to eat. We could plot and plan my project. He's my new friend. He'd meet me wherever I asked in twenty minutes. I bet he would. I'm dressed. I'm ready.

But I don't. Instead, I do something I don't think I've ever done.

I hit the Call button.

Immediately I hang up and throw my phone onto the bed like a grenade. I wipe my damp palms on my thighs and let out a wheezing breath.

My phone begins to ring.

Incoming: Joshua Templeman

"Oh, hi," I manage to say lightly when I answer. I grind the heel of my hand into my temple. I have no dignity.

"I had a missed call. It rang once."

There's loud pulsing music in the background. He's probably swilling liquor in a bar, surrounded by tall models in stretchy white dresses.

"You're busy. I'll talk to you about it tomorrow."

"I'm at the gym."

"Cardio?"

"Weights. I do weights at night."

The response implies he does cardio another time. He makes a faint grunt, and then I hear a heavy metal clang.

"So what's up? Don't tell me you pocket-dialed me."

"No." There's no point in pretending.

"Interesting." There's a muffled clothing sound, maybe a towel, and then a door closes. The obnoxious pulsing music gets quieter.

"I'm outside now. I don't know if I've ever seen your name on my caller ID. Something happen at work?"

"I know. I was thinking that too." There is a loaded pause. "No, it's not work related."

"That's a shame. I was hoping Bexley had a fatal embolism."

I make an amused honk. Then I fidget. "I was calling because . . ."

I haven't seen you today. I've been feeling mixed up and desperately sad, and for some reason seeing you might help the weird pain in my chest. I don't have friends. Except for you. Except you're not.

"Yes . . ." He is not helping me out at ALL.

"I'm hungry and I have no food. And I haven't got any tea, and my apartment is cold. And I'm bored."

"What a very sad little life."

"You've got lots of food and tea. And your heating is better than mine, and I . . ."

There is nothing but silence.

"I'm not bored when I'm with you." I'm mortified. "But I'd better just—"

He cuts me off. "Better come over then."

Relief floods through me. "Should I bring something?"

"What would you bring?"

"I could grab some food on the way."

"No, it's okay, I've got something to cook. Do you want me to pick you up?"

"I'd better drive myself."

"Probably safer." We both know why. It'd be too easy for me to stay the night otherwise.

I'm already holding my purse, coat, and keys. My feet are in shoes. I'm locking my door and jogging down the hall to the elevator.

"Will you show me the muscles you worked on?"

"I thought you wanted me for more than that." I can hear a car start. At least I'm not the only impatient one.

"Race you there. I want to see you all sweaty. We need to get even."

"Give me half an hour. No, an hour." He's alarmed.

"I'll wait for you in the lobby."

"Do not leave now."

"See you soon," I reply and hang up.

I start laughing when I start my car and pull out into traffic. It's a new game, the Racing Game, with two cars at different points on a city grid, speeding toward a central location. It's scary how I want to be in his apartment on his couch so badly I'm jiggling my knee impatiently at red lights. I'd bet anything he's doing the same.

When I'm jogging up the sidewalk to the entrance to his building, I've basically exhausted all of my weak excuses, caveats, reasoning, and we're down to this. I run into the lobby.

I haven't seen Josh all day, and I miss him.

The elevator has an up arrow above it. I hold my breath. It bings.

He couldn't imagine you with anyone but himself.

The doors snap open and there he is.

Chapter 16

He's ruffled and sweaty, weighed down by gym gear. His brow creases when he spots me, his eyes unsure. He puts a hand out to hold the elevator door.

My. Heart. Bursts.

"I won!" I scream as I run at him. He has enough time to put out his arms as I jump. He hits the back wall with a grunt as I manage to get my arms and legs around him. The doors slide closed and he manages to hit the button for his floor.

"I think technically I won. I was in the building first," I hear him say over my head.

"I won, I won," I repeat until he laughs and concedes.

"Okay. You won."

His sweat smells like rainwater and cedar, leaving a faint rosemary-pine tingle in my nostrils. I press my face against his neck and breathe in, again and again until the elevator bings, and we're on the fourth floor. I try to muster up the strength to let him go, but the addictive press of our bodies together is stronger than my willpower.

"Okay then." He begins to walk down the hallway. I'm clinging like a koala to his front, coat flapping, my bag bumping against his gym bag. I hope he doesn't bump into any neighbors. I lean back enough to see his face and see amusement shining in his eyes as he puts down his bag beside his door and begins sorting through his keys.

"Every man should get a welcome home like that."

"Don't mind me. Go about your business."

I hug harder. His collarbone fits nicely under my cheekbone. He's wearing a hoodie and his body feels humid and damp.

I hear him drop his gym gear into the basket. He toes off his sneakers, which seems a little bit more difficult, and he takes my bag. He presses a button on the heating control.

"Seriously, just pretend I'm not here."

He walks us into the kitchen and bends to look in the refrigerator, making me grip tighter. He fills a glass and I press my ear to his neck to listen to him swallow.

I tighten my legs around him, and he slides a hand to my butt and squeezes it once in a friendly way. Then he gives it a slap. "Ow, what's in your pocket?"

"Oh." I remember now and feel like a nerd. I slither down to my feet. "It's nothing."

"It hurt my hand." He pulls the lumpy shape out of my pocket and cranes to see what he's found. "It's a Smurf. Of course. What else would you fill your pockets with? Why does it have a bow on it?"

"I have, like, ten of him. It's Grouchy Smurf."

"If I didn't know how much you adore Smurfs, I'd be insulted." His mouth quirks and I know I've pleased him. "So what's with the Smurfs, anyway?"

"My dad had a regular delivery over the state line. He'd leave before dawn and be back after I went to bed.

He always bought me a Smurf at the gas station on the way home."

"So they remind you of your dad. That's nice."

"It meant that he was thinking of me." I shuffle on the spot.

"Well, thank you for thinking of me."

"Well, you gave me something of yours, so. We're even."

"Is that so important? Being even?"

"Of course." I notice he has a little whiteboard with a weekly meal plan. He's such a *freak*.

"Okay, well you're clean, and I'm not. I need a shower."

"How do you smell so good after the gym?" I go into the living room and throw myself down onto the couch with a groan. I sink into it like it's made of memory foam. *Hello, Lucy,* the couch tells me. *I knew you'd be back.*

"I didn't think I did," he replies from the kitchen. I'm hearing water boiling and the fridge opening and tea-spoon clinking.

"You do." I pat around for the ribbon cushion. "Like a muscly pinecone."

"I think it's my soap. Mom gives it to me in bulk. She likes making care packages."

He appears, upside down, and I see a slice of heavy bare shoulder revealed by his hoodie sliding off. He's wearing a tank under there. My mouth puddles with drool. He puts a mug near me and hands me the cushion.

"Take the hoodie off. Please. I'll only look with my eyes."

He puts his finger on the zip, and I bite my lip. Then he zips it up to his neck as high as it will go, and I howl.

"Drink your tea, you little pervert." He tosses something on my stomach. He shuts his bedroom door and after a minute I hear the shower. I hold up a box. It's a packaged Matchbox car. I can't help feeling like it's a reproach. Isn't being wanted for his body a man's dream?

I put the ribbon pillow under my neck. It's a little black car this time, quite similar to his. Is this what he did on his day off? Go and buy me a toy? I open the pack and drive the tiny car on my stomach for a while. I imagine him in the shower with his bar of soap like the little perv I am.

As predictably as night follows day, I begin to fret as the minutes pass. I don't know why I'm here again. All I know is this couch is my new favorite place on earth. I should put my shoes on and leave. I touch the side of my mug. Not cool enough to drink.

I need to start behaving normally. I got a little overexcited. I think about what kind of girls he probably dates. Tall, cool blondes. I feel it in my tiny undersized brunette bones. I remember once going to a club with Val, back in the day when I actually did things, before the merger, before the loneliness.

We saw these bored, beautiful icy girls. They were standing beside the bar, ignoring all the men who approached them. Val and I spent the rest of the night imitating them on the dance floor, striking aloof poses and making each other laugh with fierce, steely glances. I might try it now.

When his bedroom door opens and he appears again, I am a mature young woman, legs elegantly crossed, flipping through a medical textbook, sipping my tea. He's got on some soft black sweats, a black T-shirt, and nice bare feet. Can't he have a flaw?

He sits on the edge of the couch, his hair damp and

ruffled in every direction. I turn the page and unfortunately a lurid diagram of an erect penis glares up at me.

"I am trying to be a bit more normal."

He looks at the page. "How's it working out so far?"

"I'm glad this isn't a pop-up book."

He huffs in amusement. I follow him to the kitchen and watch him cut vegetables into ridiculously neat little sticks.

"Omelet okay?"

I nod and glance at his whiteboard. Tuesday: OMELET. I look at what's for dinner for the rest of the week. I wonder how I can score an invitation back.

"Can I do anything?"

He shakes his head and I watch him crack six eggs into a metal bowl.

"So, how was work? You clearly missed me."

I put my hands on my face in embarrassment and he just laughs a bit to himself.

"It was boring." It's the truth.

"No one to antagonize, huh?"

"I tried abusing some of the gentle folk in payroll but they got all teary."

"The trick is to find that one person who can give it back as good as they can take it." He takes out a pan and begins to fry the vegetables in a single, stingy drop of oil.

"Sonja Rutherford, probably. That scary lady in the mailroom that looks like an albino Morticia Addams."

"Don't line my replacement up too quick. You'll hurt my feelings."

The reminder of the likely outcome of this entire scenario makes me decide to lean against him. The middle of his back is the most perfectly ergonomic place to hide my face.

When it all comes to an end, I'm going to remember this.

"You gotta tell me why you're here."

"I got a bit . . . sad today, thinking about everything changing?"

"Doctor Josh diagnoses you with Stockholm syndrome."

"I know, right." I snuggle my cheek into the muscle.

"Maybe you fear change, rather than the prospect of sitting alone in there."

I appreciate he hasn't automatically said I'd be out job hunting.

"I kept thinking about your blue bedroom. I feel like this is something we need to discuss. Before time runs out."

I hear the deep sizzle of the egg being added to the vegetables. He covers the pan and turns.

"You're the sort of person who needs to be eased into things slowly."

I open my mouth to protest, but he silences me.

"I know you, Luce, and you do. Your freak-outs are pretty impressive. Imagine we have sex right now. Right here, on the counter." He slaps his hand down firmly on it.

"You'd be so awkward afterward, you'd never speak to me again. You'd quit ahead of the interviews and go and live in the forest."

"Why would you care? I'd like to live in a forest."

"I need you to compete with me. And maybe we can find a scenario that doesn't involve running out of time." He sighs and checks the omelet. "Do you have one-night stands? Like, do you go to clubs and pick out some hot guy and take him home with you?"

Even as he asks the question, his face grimaces. Maybe I'm not the only one who can imagine faceless suitors.

"Of course not. Unless you count. And I can't even get one night."

He lightly rubs his palm across my shoulders, as kindly as a friend, and all the wiring holding my muscles together gets an inch looser. I step closer and lean all my weight against him. When I press my cheek on his chest, his heat glows against me.

"I'm trying to make sure that when we do, you don't have any regrets."

"I doubt I would."

"I'm flattered." He peeks in at the omelet. "Go back to the couch, put the TV on."

I drop myself into the plush perfection of his couch. I'm going to transform my igloo into a safe, warm little stronghold too. I need lamps, rugs, more shelves, and a painting of Tuscany. I need buckets of paint and a pale blue bedroom. White linen and a fern.

"Where'd you get this couch? I want to get the same one."

"It's the only one on earth." His dry voice floats out from the kitchen.

"Can I buy it from you?"

"No."

"What about this ribbon cushion?"

"One of a kind."

"I think I see your strategy." I watch TV for a bit and Josh hands me a plate and a fork.

"I'm like a little duchess when I'm here. You don't have to wait on me." I kick my shoes off under his coffee table.

"Some horrible monsters secretly enjoy spoiling little duchesses. Should we aim for a two-hour cease-fire? Starting now?"

"Sure, let's do it. Yum, this looks good." I can smell fresh basil. How is he still single?

We watch the news and he takes my empty plate. Then he gives me a bowl of vanilla ice cream. He doesn't have one for himself.

"Why even bother keeping any in your freezer?"

"In case I have unexpected sweet-tooth visitors."

I can't help but grin at the thought. "It wouldn't destroy those abs to have one little spoonful. It's protein, right?"

He looks at the bowl, and sighs. He takes my spoon from me and steals a huge mouthful. "Oh, lord." His eyelids flutter.

"You should treat yourself to something small each night. No point in being cruel to yourself."

"Something small, huh?" He looks at me pointedly. "Okay."

I take another mouthful of ice cream. The spoon slides against my tongue and the intimacy of it is obscene. His tongue, my tongue. I lick it and he watches me, chest expanding, breath leaving him in a rush.

He unfolds a fluffy gray blanket over me and I lie there like a spoiled child. He sits at the far end, near my feet, and I stare at his side profile as he leans forward on the edge of the couch and picks up the medical text book.

"You look sad."

"I'm . . . happy." His expression changes to faint surprise. "Weird."

"Why do you still have those textbooks? This one has so many dicks in it."

"I was originally going to go into the family trade.

I haven't managed to part with them, I guess. And a lot of them are my mother's. They're pretty old, but she wanted me to have them."

He flips to the flyleaf and traces his finger across her handwritten name. I want to ask about his parents, but if I know Josh, he's on the verge of shutting down.

"Doctor Josh, MD. You would have been a sexy doctor."

"Oh, definitely." He discards the book and clicks around with the remote.

"All your lady patients would have had pounding heart rates."

He takes my empty bowl. He kisses the little hinge of my jaw until I gasp, and then finds the pulse point in my wrist expertly.

"Let's see. Think about me in a white coat, sliding a stethoscope into the neck of your blouse."

I can almost feel the freezing cold disc pressed against me. I shiver and I feel my nipples begin to pinch.

"You're giving me a brand-new kink." I say it like a smartass, but he smiles.

"I could probably work with that."

My mind leaps to what our theoretical sex life would be like. We're playing games with each other all day; it stands to reason they'd carry on in bed. The image hits me so powerfully I feel my body squeeze, empty and wanting.

His voice against the back of my ear as we stand in the doorway to his beautiful bedroom.

What shall we play now?

"I'd pretend to be sick every single night."

"Every night?" He's still checking my pulse, staring at his watch, his lips moving as he counts. It's so sexy I know it beats faster. Eventually, he releases me.

"Quite a pounding little heart you got there. And a raging case of Horny-Eye. I think it's quite serious."

"Will I die?"

"I prescribe complete couch-rest under my supervision. But it's touch and go."

"I'd make a sleazy joke about your bedside manner but it would be a little redundant at this point." I snuggle back down under my blanket.

"Can you even imagine my bedside manner? I'd be the worst. I'd scare people into health."

"Is that why you didn't want to be a doctor? Because you hate people?"

"It didn't work out." His voice gets hard.

"Was there anything you enjoyed about it?"

"I enjoyed most of it. I was good at the theory component. I've got a good memory. And I don't hate all people. Just . . . most people."

"What about the practical component? Did you have a bad experience? Did they make you put your finger up someone's butt?"

He laughs even as his nose wrinkles in distaste. "You don't start on live people. And you don't start on butts. What kind of mind thinks of that?"

"Cadavers! I bet you saw cadavers. What was it like?" I think of all the autopsy scenes in *Law & Order*.

"This one time, my dad . . ." He hesitates, looking away, considering.

I don't push him, and after a long silence he continues.

"My dad, in his wisdom, decided to set me up on a bit of informal work experience at his hospital, in the break before I started college. Some of it was okay. Mainly I was passed around by a few doctors who all seemed too exhausted to say no to him. But one afternoon he slaps me on the back, introduces one of the coroners, and leaves us to it."

I am starting to feel terrible. "You don't have to tell me if it's hard."

"No, it's okay. I guess it was the ultimate baptism of fire. I made it through about five minutes before I threw up. The smell of dead person, and chemicals, it left a taste in my mouth. Probably why I started eating all these mints. Sometimes I can't get the smell out of my nose and it's been years."

He lifts my arm and presses my wrist to his nose.

"Your skin smells like candy. Up until that point, it was a given I'd study medicine. My great-great-grandfather was a doctor and it's always been the Templeman chosen vocation. But after seeing someone's rib cage get jacked open, it was the beginning of the end."

"You managed to stay for the rest of the autopsy?"

"I managed to stay for another year. And then I quit." He looks distressed by the memory and defaults to defensiveness. "So you came over to grill me on my life choices?"

I catch his fingertips and hold his hand between mine.

"I didn't want to be anywhere else tonight. I was crawling out of my skin."

I'm proud I had the courage to say it.

He turns back to me and the expression in his eyes is softer.

"My leg was jiggling like this." I demonstrate and he grins. "You should have seen me driving here. I was laughing like I'd broken out of prison. I was completely deranged."

"Do you think you've finally cracked your sanity?"

"For sure. The weird need to stare at your pretty face completely overwhelmed me. I had the energy of twenty atom bombs."

"Why do you think I go to the gym so much?"

A big bubble of happiness fills me. I struggle upright and lean against him, my head falling easily into the perfect cradle of his neck. It's true; he fits me everywhere.

"You never have to explain your choices. Not to me, not to anyone."

He nods slowly, and I cover him in the blanket too.

I could never have imagined one day I'd be sitting on a couch, my mouth tasting like vanilla, with my head on Joshua Templeman's shoulder. It's going to end in disaster. I close my eyes and breathe.

"I want to know why you were so sad today, Short-cake." It's uncanny how he senses shifts in my mood.

"I just was. I was thinking about everything at stake for me."

"Tell me."

"I can't. You're my nemesis."

"You're awfully snuggly with your nemesis." It's true. I'm snuggling.

"I don't want to talk about me. We never talk about you. I probably don't know anything about you."

He laces his fingers into mine and rests our hands on his stomach. I move my fingertips in tiny circles and he sighs indulgently.

"Sure you do. Go on, list everything."

"I know surface things. The color of your shirts. Your lovely blue eyes. You live on mints and make me look like a pig in comparison. You scare three-quarters of B and G employees absolutely senseless, but only because the other quarter haven't met you yet."

He smirks. "Such a bunch of delicate sissies."

I keep ticking things off.

"You've got a pencil you use for secret purposes I think relate to me. You dry clean on alternate Fridays. The projector in the boardroom strains your eyes and gives you headaches. You're good at using silence to scare the shit out of people. It's your go-to strategy in meetings. You sit there and stare with your laser-eyes until your opponent crumbles."

He remains silent.

"Oh, and you're secretly a decent human being."

"You definitely know more about me than anyone else." I can feel a tension in him. When I look at his face, he looks shaken. My stalking has scared the ever-loving shit out of him. Unfortunately, the next thing I say sounds deranged.

"I want to know what's going on in your brain. I want to juice your head like a lemon."

"Why do you even want to know anything about me? I thought I was going to be your one glorious bout of hate sex to cross off your list before you settle down with some Mr. Nice Guy."

"I want to know what sort of person I'll be using and objectifying. What's your favorite food?"

"Vanilla ice cream. Eaten from your bowl, with your spoon. And strawberries."

"Dream vacation destination."

"Sky Diamond Strawberries."

When I level a frustrated look at him, he relents, and points at the frame on his wall.

"That exact Tuscan villa."

"I want to climb inside that painting. What would you do there?"

"Swim in a pool with a tile mosaic on the bottom." He smiles at how much that image delights me.

"Does the pool have a fountain somewhere? Like a little lion spitting water?"

"Yes, it does. After the swim, I lie in the shade eating grapes and cheese. Then I'd have a big glass of wine and fall asleep with a book on my face."

"Basically you've just described heaven. What happens then?"

"I forgot to mention that a beautiful girl swam in that pool with me and slept in that sun too. She's starving. I'd better take her out for pasta. Carbohydrates and oil, covered in cheese."

"I'm enjoying this food fantasy," I manage. I want to be that girl so badly I could howl.

"We'd walk back to the villa in the dark, and I'd pull down the zip of her red dress. I'd feed her champagne and strawberries in bed to keep her strength up."

"How are you coming up with this stuff." I'm so enraptured I'm almost slurring. If this is what his holiday daydream is like, I wouldn't survive his bedroom.

"Then I'd wake up and do it all again the next day. With her. For weeks."

I stare at the painting and imagine standing with him under the glittering dark purple sky, the headlights of faraway cars illuminating the rows of poplar trees lining the road.

I have to say something. Anything. He's looking at me, clearly entertained.

"Lucky bitch."

He laughs out loud at that. I fire off my next quiz question.

"You're shipwrecked onto an uninhabited island. What three things would you take with you?"

"A knife. A tarpaulin." He thinks for a long time on the last item.

"And you. To annoy you," he amends.

"I'm not an object. I don't count."

"But I'd be so lonely on the island," he points out. I think of him sitting alone in the all-staff meeting.

"Okay. So we're crawling up the beach and I'm cursing your name for pulling me away from civilization and hair-care products and lipstick. What then?"

My shiver from the movement of his lips on my earlobe shakes the couch. When I feel the press of his mouth to my throat, I groan out loud.

He turns the TV off, and for a moment I'm certain he's about to walk me out. Or pick me up and throw me on his bed. It's hard to tell. He raises his hands into my hair, softly trailing his fingertips through it, until he reaches my scalp. My eyelids flutter.

"I'd build you a shelter and find you a coconut, and then we'd pass the time."

"How?" My voice is barely more than a whisper.

"Probably like this." He presses his mouth to mine.

Chapter 17

We both suck in a breath and the room has no oxygen left.

Last night he picked me up under a street-light and gave me a kiss that was calculated to leave me wanting more. Now I know what my problem has been today. I've been craving.

Images of us in another life in Tuscany are still behind my eyelids as he kisses my mouth open, touches my tongue with his, and breathes. He *sighs*. He's wanted this. He's been craving as badly as I have. My mouth is vanilla, his is mint, and they combine to create something delicious.

A miracle has occurred, and I don't know when, but I know it now. Joshua Templeman does not hate me. Not a bit. There's no way he could when he kisses me like this.

He loosens one hand from my hair and spreads it across my jaw, stroking my skin, cupping and tilting my face. It's so completely sweet, even as our tongues begin to get filthy.

I slide my knee over his lap, feeling my inner thighs stretch.

"I swore to myself I wouldn't come here tonight."

"Yet here you are. Interesting."

We both look down at my thighs on his, and I can't stop myself from sliding my hips forward.

This new position splices power and adrenaline into my blood. I put my hands on his collarbones and look him over. His hair is still a little damp. I cup the nape of his neck in my palm and press my hand against his heart.

I start a slow slide down to his chest, ribs, testing the density of flesh. He's so firm I can trace the lines between each muscle, even through a T-shirt. I try to tug up the bottom of the shirt but it's pinned under my knees.

Impatience rips clean through me. I nearly tear his shirt off but I force my fingers to loosen. He must see this flash of violent cavewoman, because he closes his eyes and his throat hums in a groan.

"Sometimes you look at me like you're . . ."

He forgets what he was saying when I begin to kiss his jaw. His hands lie palms-up on either side of my calves. He's letting me control this and I like it. I feel him smile when I nibble against his bottom lip.

The couch gives softly underneath my knees, and as our clothes begin to make a warm friction, I feel his arousal, hard and blunt, pressing into the back of my thigh.

"I need it," I tell him and watch his eyes go viciously black. I take huge handfuls of his clothes and we kiss again.

I roll my hips slowly in his wide lap and his hands slide down my body in a series of slow, squeezing pauses. Shoulders, underarms, the sides of my breasts. I shiver, and he slides his hands lower. Ribs, the curve of my waist. Hips. Butt.

His hands slide down my thighs, his long fingers

dragging down the outer and inner seam of my jeans. He traces his fingers along my calves. When I drop my face to his neck, his hands tighten on my ankles, a little reminder he could take control if he wanted to.

"I like how little you are." He sure sounds like he likes my body as he takes another slow, stroking tour.

As I slide my tongue into his mouth, I begin thinking about a board meeting we'd been in, a few weeks back. He'd been sitting by the window and I remember watching the sun slowly slide along the windowsill, across the floor, across the board table as the afternoon dragged on.

He'd been wearing a navy suit I don't see him wear often and the pale blue shirt. I'd sat there opposite him, watching the way the sun slowly crept up his body like a rising tide. I'd breathed in the scent of the fabric warming on his body.

I remember how he'd cut his dark blue eyes to me during the meeting, and it had flustered me, made my stomach twist in half. He'd smirked and resumed his patient staring at the PowerPoint presentation, not taking a single note whereas my scribbling hand was cramping.

Those eyes, flashing to my face, made me jump out of my skin. I hadn't known why. Now I do.

"I was remembering the board meeting a few weeks back." My head rolls to one side as he kisses under the hinge of my jaw. I have a full-body shiver. His hand spreads across my ribs, thumb nudging the underside of my breast. My total focus narrows down to this half inch of contact.

"Yes, what about it? I'm not doing so well if you're thinking about it now."

He returns his mouth to mine and dials it up a little. It's minutes before I can speak again. Possibly hours.

My breath is in little gasping pants, and he bites down gently onto my bottom lip.

His thumb slides up, nudges my nipple softly and continues up to my jaw. I jolt and quiver.

I have to explain myself properly. "You looked at me and . . . And I think I wanted to kiss you. I only just realized."

"Oh, really."

I am rewarded by his other hand sliding up the back of my top. Skin against skin. Fingers playing languidly with my bra strap.

"I was remembering how you gave me this look."

"Like I was thinking about something dirty? I was. You were wearing your white silk shirt with the pearl buttons. And this soft-looking cardigan for the first half of the meeting. Hair up, red lips."

He leans back and trails his fingertips down my throat to the top of my cleavage. His fingertips dip in, I shudder out the only thing I can think of.

"It's a cashmere cardigan."

"You like Doctor Josh . . . I like prissy retro librarian Lucy. Silk-cashmere Lucy. That's *my* kink. A pencil in your hair, grilling a department head on absentee stats for last quarter."

He continues his slide down my torso, fingers pressing into my ribs.

"What a specific kink. I can't believe you can remember what I was wearing. But hey, I can roll with this. I could get some nerd glasses and scold you." I frown sternly and hold my finger to my lips. "Be *quiet*."

He groans theatrically. "I couldn't take it."

"Can you even imagine how it would be between you and me? All day, every night?"

He knows exactly what I mean. "Oh, yeah."

"Like you said just before: The trick is to find someone who's strong enough to take it. That one person who can give it back as good as they get."

"Can you?" His eyes look like he's on drugs. Pupils inked, irises hazy.

"Yeah."

We kiss with a new intensity, sparked by our shared boardroom fantasies. Lucy and Josh starring in graphic, sweat-slicked pornography.

He arches against me. His hard-on is pressing so hard against the back of my leg my hamstring feels bruised.

He breaks the kiss. "Slow up. I want to ask you something."

He sits back a little and we stare into each other's black eyes. His mouth is softened, pink and I want it all over me. Licking and biting mouthfuls of my flesh. My breathing is so loud that I almost can't hear what he says next.

"When you called me tonight, did you nearly call Danny instead?" I start to protest but he smoothes his hand down my arm.

"I'm not being a jealous psycho. I'm just interested."

"You already won that competition with him. He's my friend now. We are only going to be friends."

"You haven't answered, though."

"He's the sensible option. I'm not doing many sensible things with my evenings these days. I'm glad I didn't call him. I'd probably be sitting in a movie, instead of here." I bounce a little on his lap.

Josh tries to smile, but it doesn't quite work. "I'd go to a movie with you. Look, it's getting late."

His hands slide down my back to grip my butt. He tilts me, and drags me down the hardness of his arousal. Then he lifts me off and sets me aside.

He sits forward on the edge of the couch and puts his face in his hands. He's breathing as heavily as I am. It does my ego no harm.

"Fuck." He sighs it. "I am so turned on," he says with an embarrassed half laugh, and I completely understand his desperation.

He's surely got to be wondering why he's subjecting himself to this. He's an adult man, reduced to teenage make-out sessions with his weird colleague.

"Do you want to hear how turned on I am?"

"I'd better not," he manages.

"I guess I should go home." I pray he tells me to stay. He doesn't.

He talks through his hands. "Give me a minute."

I take our mugs and my bowl into the kitchen and rinse the bowl. I look at the frying pan and put it in the sink and fill it with hot water and suds. My legs are trembling and doing a poor job of holding me upright.

"I'll do it," Josh says behind me. "Leave it."

My eyes badly want to drop below his waist, but because I am a lady I resist.

He feeds my arms into my coat and we both put our shoes on. We carefully stand on the opposite ends of the elevator, but we stare at each other like we're one second away from slamming the elevator to an emergency stop to put ourselves out of our misery.

"I feel like your Easter egg."

He catches my hand at the curb and walks across the street with me. When we reach my car, I tilt my mouth up to his. He carefully takes my face in his hands and he kisses me. A simultaneous shocked gasp rocks us. It's like we haven't kissed in an eternity. He presses me against the car door and I whimper. Tongues, teeth, breath.

"You taste like my Easter egg."

"Please, please. I need you so badly."

"I'll see you at work tomorrow," he replies. He turns me in his arms, and presses his mouth against the back of my neck. Even through my hair, the heat of his breath makes me inhale so hard it's more of a snort.

"Is this an asshole control-freak thing?" I wriggle free.

"Possibly. Sounds consistent with my character."

I have a thought. "Are you planning on sexing me comatose on the morning of the interview so you beat me?"

Josh puts his hands in his pockets. "It's worked for every other promotion I've gotten in my life. Why stop now?"

"You want to make sure I'm all over you like a rash at the wedding."

Something about the look on his face makes me step back and press my back to the cold door of my car.

"You haven't lied and told them all about the brain surgeon you're betrothed to?"

He smiles. "Dr. Lucy Hutton, MD. She's brilliant, yet unorthodox."

"I'm serious. Answer the question. I'm coming as me, aren't I? I'm not supposed to be acting?"

"No."

I bite my thumb and look down the street. Why do I feel like he's lying?

"Well, I'm beginning to think you're leaving me horny to make sure I'll keep coming back here. I'm like a cat. You're leaving out a saucer of cream."

Josh laughs, a big proper laugh like I'm hilarious. Delighted, irritated electricity floods me. I'm crackling with it. In this moment, I'm more alive than I've ever been.

Fight with me, kiss me. Laugh at me. Tell me if you're sad. Don't make me go home.

"We'll have to see if it's true. If you're back tomorrow night, I'll concede it's part of a deliberate strategy." He looks down at me with undisguised pleasure.

The thought of returning didn't properly occur to me. The following day now glows with promise.

"One more."

He kisses my cheek and I groan in misery.

"Get outta here, Shortcake. And remember, I don't want to see you freaking out tomorrow."

I can't get my seat belt on properly. I'm so wired it's like I'm having drug withdrawals. He taps my window to make me lock the door.

I'm halfway home when a scary thought crystallizes.

I can't wait for work tomorrow.

TODAY HIS SHIRT is the color of a saucer of cream.

Act natural, Lucy. Walk in there like sex on legs. No awkwardness. Go.

He looks at me, my ankle wobbles, and I drop my handbag. The lid of my lunchbox pops off and a tomato rolls across the floor. I drop to my hands and knees and my stiletto heel gets caught on the dangling buckle belt of my coat.

"Crap." I try to crawl.

"Smooth." Josh gets up and walks to me.

"Shuddup."

He unhooks my coat and gathers up my lunch, before holding a hand down to me. I hesitate minutely before I take it, letting him haul me up.

"Can I rewind my entrance?"

He pulls the coat from my shoulders and hangs it up for me.

Mr. Bexley's door is open and the lights are on. Helene's a late starter. She's probably still in bed.

"How was your evening, Lucinda? You look tired."

My stomach sinks in dismay at his impersonal tone until I look at his face and realize his eyes are lit with mischief. If Mr. Bexley is eavesdropping, he'll hear nothing out of the ordinary.

This is a dangerous new game, the Act Natural Game, but I'll give it a try. "Oh, it was nice enough, I guess."

"Nice. Hmm. Get up to anything interesting?" He's got the pencil in his hand.

"I sat on the couch."

He shifts in his chair and I look at his lap.

"Serial killer eyes," I mouth at him. I sit on the edge of my desk, take out my tube of Flamethrower and begin to apply, using the wall nearest me as a mirror. He looks at my legs with such naked lust I nearly smudge it. "And what did you get up to, Josh?"

"I had a date. At least, I think it was."

"What's she like?"

"Clingy. She really threw herself at me."

I laugh. "Clingy is not an attractive trait. I hope you kicked her out."

"I guess I sort of did."

"That'll learn her." I begin to gather my hair into a high bun before smoothing down my dress. It's a fine cream wool knit, stretchy and warm, and I admit I wore it to match his shirt. He likes prissy librarian Lucy? He's got it today.

He watches my hands. I watch his. They're white-knuckled.

"Not sure if I'll see her again, though." He sounds bored, and he's clicking his mouse on his computer.

When his eyes cut sideways to mine, I flash to last night and my insides clench.

"Maybe take her to your brother's wedding? Always gratifying to walk into one of those situations with a hot date."

We both look at each other, and I ease myself slowly into my chair. The Staring Game has never felt so dirty. The phone rings. I look at the caller ID and the word *FUCK* lights up in neon in my brain.

Josh takes one look at my face. "If it's him, I'm going to—"

"It's Julie."

"A bit early for her, isn't it? You're going to have to be firm with her." The phone continues ringing, and ringing.

"I'll let it go to voice mail. I'm too tired to deal with this now."

"You will not." He dials star-nine and answers my extension. They teach call center operators to smile when they answer a call. People can hear a smile in your voice. Joshua needs to learn this.

"Lucinda Hutton's phone. Joshua speaking. Hold." He hits a button, and points at me with his receiver. "Do it. I'm watching you."

We both watch the hold light flashing.

I'm still that smiling girl in the strawberry patch. Look at me, I'm a good girl. I'm the sweet little thing, adored by everyone. Nothing is too much trouble.

"I want to see you be as strong with other people as you are with me."

I press the flashing button. "Hi, Julie, how are you?" My ear nearly burns from her deep sigh.

"Hi, Lucy. I'm not well. I'm incredibly tired. I don't

even know why I came in. I've just sat down, and already the screen is killing me."

"Sorry to hear that."

I lock eyes with Josh. He intensifies his eyes into narrowed scary blue lasers. He's imbuing me with his powers. I am NOT going to care what excuses or requests she's going to make. "What can I do for you today, Julie?" Professional, but a hint of warmth in my tone.

"I'm supposed to be working on this thing for Alan, which he's going to polish up and send up to you."

"Oh, yes. I need it by close of business."

Josh gives me a sarcastic thumbs-up.

"Well, I'm having a bit of trouble finding some of the old reports in the network drive. It keeps saying shortcut moved. Anyway, I've tried a bunch of things and I think I need to step away, you know?"

"As long as I get it by five, it's fine." Josh looks at the ceiling and shrugs. I thought I was being firm there, but he's unimpressed.

"I was hoping to go home and get it done first thing tomorrow, when I'm fresher."

"Didn't you just get here?" Am I going crazy? I recheck the clock.

"I came in quickly to check my email." Her tone is that of an absolute trooper.

"Alan said it would be okay if I cleared it with you first." She's jingling her car keys in the background.

I steel myself with blue-laser strength. "I'm sorry, that's not going to work for me. I need it by five, please."

"I'm aware of the deadline," she counters, voice sharpening by one degree. "I'm trying to let you know Alan is not going to have it to you on time."

"But it's really you who needs the extension, not Alan." There is a long pause while I wait for her to speak.

"I thought you'd be a bit more flexible on this." Her tone is slipping further into an impressive combination of petulance and ice. "I am unwell."

"If you do need to go home," I begin as I watch Joshua's brow transform into a scowl, "you'll need to take today as sick leave, and bring a doctor's note."

"I'm not going to the doctor for tiredness and a headache. He'll tell me to sleep. That's what I want to go and do."

"I'm sympathetic if you're feeling unwell, but that's the HR policy." Josh smoothes his hand over his mouth to hide his grin. I'm playing the HR Game with Julie.

"Sympathetic? I wouldn't call this sympathetic at all."

"I've been fair with you, Julie. I've given you extensions a lot of times. But I can't keep staying late to finish these reports."

Josh circles his hand in the air. I keep going. "If it's late, I end up having to stay back."

"You don't have any family here, or a boyfriend, do you? Late nights don't affect you like they do for people with husbands and . . . well, people with families."

"Well, I'm not going to get myself a husband or a life if I keep staying until nine o'clock at night, now am I? I'll expect the report from Alan at five."

"You've spent too much time in the company of that horrible Joshua."

"Apparently so. Also, I can't do the internship for your niece, it's not convenient for me." I terminate the call.

Joshua lies back in his chair and starts laughing. "Well, shit."

"I was amazing, wasn't I. Did you see me?" I punch the air and mime giving Julie an uppercut. Josh rests his folded hands on his stomach and watches me shadow-box my reflection.

"Take that, Julie, and your life and husband and your phony sleep disorder."

"Let it all out."

"Take that, Julie, and your me-graines."

"You really were amazing."

"Take that, Julie, and your French manicure."

"Okay." He's smiling at me, openly, in this exact office that was once a battlefield, and I flop back down into my chair and close my eyes and feel the glow of his pleasure from across the marble superhighway. So this is what it feels like. This is what it could have been like, all this time. It wasn't too late.

"No more late nights for me. I've probably totally destroyed my relationship with her, but it was so worth it."

"You'll have a life and a husband in no time."

"No time at all. Probably by next week. I hope he's super nice." I open my eyes and the way he looks at me makes me wish I hadn't said it. We both hesitate, and his eyes flick sideways. I've interrupted our flow.

"Please, let me enjoy this moment. Joshua Templeman is officially my friend." I link my fingers and stretch my arms over my head.

"I'm going for my breakfast meeting. Josh, I need those figures by lunch," Mr. Bexley says, walking in between us. I think we all know this breakfast meeting is with a plate of bacon.

"They're already done; I'll email them through now."

Mr. Bexley harrumphs, I suppose his best attempt at thanks or praise, and then turns to me.

"Good morning, Lucy. Nice dress you've got on there."

"Thanks."

Ugh.

"Got your nails sharpened, do you then? Interviews

coming soon. Ticktock." He ambles to the edge of my desk and peruses me from the neck down. I resist the urge to cross my arms over myself. I don't know how Mr. Bexley hasn't noticed Josh's murderous glare refracted dozens of times. He continues his usual gimlet-eyed assessment of my appearance.

"Don't," Josh says to his boss, voice metallic.

"I'm pretty well prepared for the interview." I look down at my front. "Mr. Bexley, what are you looking at?"

I calmly level my eyes at Mr. Bexley, and he physically jolts. He quickly averts his eyes and begins to comb his fingers through his sparse hair, his face burnished red.

Man, I kick ass today.

Josh clenches his jaw and looks down at his glass desk so angrily I'm surprised it doesn't shatter.

"From the little sneak peek I had in Helene's office, I do think you're well prepared. Doctor Josh, we may need to discuss strategy."

Holy shit. He's going to tell Joshua about my project. I swing my panicked stare to Josh, who looks at his boss like he is an absolute idiot.

And then he reminds me that no, he is not my friend, and no matter how much kissing we do on his couch, we're still in the middle of our biggest competition.

"I'm not going to need any help beating her."

Chapter 18

He's cold as ice and the tone gives me flashbacks. He says it like it is the most ridiculous thing he's ever heard. Silly little Lucy Hutton, impossible to take seriously, and absolutely no match for Joshua Templeman in any arena. I'm a joke. I'm not getting the job, because why would I? I have to be coached through a phone call.

"Maybe not," Mr. Bexley muses. Clearly pleased to have kicked over two beehives, he plods off. As he waits for the elevator, he looks back at us.

"But then again, Doctor Josh, you may want to re-think that."

The elevator door closes as Josh's silently mouthed *Fuck you* fragments around us. Then he looks at me.

"I was lying."

The silence rings like crystal wineglasses touched together.

"Well, you're quite a good actor. I sure believed it." I pick up my bottle of water and sip, trying to ease the angry tightness in my throat. I'm actually grateful to him. This is what I've been missing. We're two race-horses pounding toward the finish line. I've been flagging, but I've just felt the first lash of the whip. I need to hold on to this feeling until I walk out of the interview.

"I always have been. I was mad at him for looking at you like that and it came out wrong. I've got a bad habit of snapping. Look at me, Luce."

When I do, he repeats himself slowly. "I did not mean it."

"It's all right. It's what I needed." I use the same flat, icy tone that he'd just used with Bexley. I have no idea how I can make my voice so cold when anger feels like a blowtorch in my chest. I'm a good actor too.

His forehead has his trademark crease of concern. "You needed that? Me being an asshole? It's all you seem to get from me."

"You've just given me what I needed to hear."

Life is all about perspective, and if I choose to believe I've just received a boost to my motivation from my competitor, I can ignore my bruised pride. I am going to keep my focus forward. My focus is now a laser beam that he has given me.

My computer chimes. Five minutes until I have my meeting with Danny to discuss working on my ebook project.

"Wait. We need to clear this up. I can't quite explain it yet, though." His face twists in agitation. "The timing is all off. I didn't mean it the way it sounded."

"I'm going out." I begin gathering my bag and coat.

"And where are you going? In case Helene asks me," he amends. He looks miserable. "Are you coming back?"

"I'm meeting someone for coffee."

"Well," Josh says after a second. "I can't stop you."

"Thank you for allowing me to do my job." After

spitefully pushing his in-trays crooked I march to the elevator.

I walk to the Starbucks across the street. The thing about being in combat with Joshua Templeman? I never truly win. That's what is so deceptive about it all. The moment I think I've won, something happens to remind me I haven't.

Please, let me enjoy this moment. Joshua Templeman is officially my friend.

It's nothing but win, then lose, lose, lose.

Danny's already at a seat by the window. The fact I'm late is another nail in my professionalism's coffin.

"Hi. Thanks for meeting me. Sorry I'm late."

I order coffee and then briefly outline my idea.

"I've got time this weekend," Danny offers nobly. He's been looking at me with undisguised interest; my tied-up hair, my bare throat and the red of my mouth. I have a bad feeling he's hoping our bad kiss was a blip.

"I'd be paying you out of my own pocket. Can you give me an idea of how much?"

Danny doesn't look concerned. "Why don't we make a deal. Credit my work in the interview and mention my new self-publishing software to Helene. There may be some cross-functionalities that could suit your project. And . . . three hundred bucks."

"That's fine, and of course I will," I rush to assure him. This is something I can do. Give him a little exposure to the exec, and help build his business.

A couple of B&G people are queuing for coffee and look at us with speculative glances. Another walks past on the street and waves at me. I'm sitting in a big glass fishbowl. My cheeks start to burn when I think about everything I've said and done with Joshua on the top floor. The barbs, the insults, the circuit-frying kisses.

In our own isolated little world, everything seemed so normal and acceptable.

"Thanks for thinking of me on this." Danny sips his coffee.

"Well, after our dinner on Monday I knew I could trust you with my little secret. And like you said, I needed some help and you were the first person I thought of."

"Oh, so it's a secret?"

"Helene knows, of course. Mr. Bexley knows about the project *concept* but not the actual finished product I'm hoping to present."

I wish I didn't have to say this next part, and I'm sad at how messed up this situation has gotten.

"I need to ask you to please, don't say anything to Josh. I know you won't see him again, but let's keep it between us. He's so sure he's getting the job. It's more important than ever I beat him."

"I won't. But, actually, he's over there."

"What?" I nearly scream it. I can't turn around. "Act businesslike." I draw a diagram on my notepad and Danny draws some slashy lines on it.

"What is his *deal*? He always looks furious." Danny shakes his head at my notepad and we do a bit more business-miming.

"That's his face."

"You guys have a weird dynamic going on."

"There's no dynamic. No dynamic." I begin swigging at my coffee. It's too hot and a terrible idea.

"But you know he's in love with you, right?"

I inhale my huge mouthful and begin to drown on dry land. Danny leans over and thumps me between my shoulder blades. Tears are streaming down my face. I wish he'd let me die.

"He's not," I wheeze. I use a napkin to wipe my face. "That is the stupidest thing I've ever heard. Ever."

"As your *friend*," Danny articulates with a little smile, "I'm telling you he is."

"What's he doing?"

"Scaring the cashier shitless. People are concerned about how things will be if he gets the job. We know how good at cutting staff he is. A few guys in design are brushing up their CVs, in case."

"I'm sure he'd be fine to work for." I muster my diplomacy. I won't stoop to Josh's level. I stand up and gather my things.

"Let's say hi to him," Danny says and I'm pretty sure he's messing with me. His mouth is lifted into a half smile.

"No, we're going to climb out the bathroom window. Quick."

He laughs and shakes his head. Once again, I'm impressed by his bravery. Everyone else tries to avoid the monster in their midst. But I do know a secret about Josh. I think of him last night, taking my pulse, counting each beat of my heart. Covering me with a blanket, tucking my feet in. It's quite remarkable how he's managed to maintain this frightening façade for so long.

"Hi," we both say in unison as we approach.

"Well, hello," Josh says archly.

"Quit stalking so much." My tone is so aggrieved that the girl at the coffee machine laughs out loud.

Josh fixes his cuff. "Missed each other, did you?"

I am lasering the word *SECRET* into Danny's brain. I raise my eyebrows and he nods. Josh watches this exchange.

"Lucy's talking to me about an . . . opportunity to . . .

work with her." Danny is a genius. Nothing is more believable than the truth.

"That's right. Danny's helping me with my . . . presentation." We couldn't seem more shady if we tried.

"You're working on your presentation. Right. Okay." Josh takes his coffee when his name is called and gives such an accusing look my face nearly melts off. "And were we doing that too, Lucinda? Last night on my couch?"

Danny's jaw hits the floor. I am not amused. If this got out, my reputation would be in shreds. It's too juicy. Danny's still in contact with too many people in design. And he's also a sticky-nosed gossip hound.

"In your *dreams*, Templeman. Ignore him, Danny. Walk back with me."

I tug Danny ahead so he doesn't get tossed into oncoming traffic. Josh follows at a languid pace, sipping his coffee. I'm holding Danny's arm so tightly he winces as I drag him across the road.

"Even if he kidnaps and tortures you, don't tell him what you're doing for me. He'll use every bit of information he can to screw me."

"Wow, you guys really *are* mortal enemies."

"Yep, to the death. Pistols and swords at dawn."

"So he's doing this to try to find out your interview strategy?" Danny says hi to a colleague and checks his phone.

"Exactly!" I let out a nervous whinny. I think everything is covered up. "I'll call you after work once I've worked out what book I want you to format for me."

Josh is nearly upon us. I'm beginning to think I might toss Danny into oncoming traffic myself to end this agonizing little tableau.

"Okay, talk to you tonight. Bye, Josh. Good luck in your interview." Danny continues along the footpath.

Josh and I don't say a word to each other as we get into the elevator. He's so livid it's a visceral thing. Meanwhile, I'm still partially deceased by what Danny said. *You know he's in love with you, right?*

"He's so nice. What a nice guy. I think I get what you see in him." He speaks so sharply I bump backward. "I must have had a vivid dream last night."

"Hey, what can I say? I *lied*. I'm a good actor." I spread my arms wide and push ahead to my desk.

"So, you're embarrassed of me?"

"No. Of course not. But no one can know. I think he's a gossip. Oh, don't give me that sourpuss face. People will talk about us."

"Newsflash, people have always talked about us. And you don't care if people talk about you and him, but not you and me?"

"You and I work ten feet from each other. It's different. I want to reestablish some level of professionalism in this office."

Josh pinches the bridge of his nose. "Fine. I'll play it your way. If this is the last personal conversation we ever have in this building, then I'll tell you now. Bring your bag on Friday."

"What? What's happening on Friday?"

"Bring in your stuff for the wedding. Your dress and stuff."

At my walleyed stare, he reminds me. "You're coming to my brother's wedding. You insisted, remember?"

"Wait, why am I bringing my dress on Friday? The wedding is on Saturday. Is there a rehearsal? I didn't agree to go to the wedding twice."

"No. The wedding is at Port Worth and we have to drive there."

I look at him, doubtful. "That's not too far away."

"Far enough away that we need to leave after work. Mom needs my help with a few things the night before."

I'm filled to the brim with annoyance, terror, hurt feelings, and absolute certainty this is going to be a disaster. We stare into each other's eyes.

"I knew you wouldn't be happy but I also wasn't expecting such complete horror." Josh leans back in his chair and assesses me. "Don't freak out."

"We've never even gone to a movie together, or to a restaurant. I was nervous getting a ride in your car. And now you're telling me I'm driving several hours with you and to bring my pj's? Where are we staying?"

"Probably a seedy hotel."

I am close to hyperventilating. I am this close to running down the fire escape. I've had a fair idea we'd at some point get around to playing the Or Something Game. I imagined it in his blue bedroom, or while hissing hurtful insults at him in the cleaner's closet. But too much has happened today.

"I was kidding, Lucy. I have to talk to my mom about where we're staying."

"I didn't properly think about meeting your parents. Look, I'm not coming. You were a real asshole to me just now, remember? You don't need help beating me, remember? I'd have to be crazy to help you now. Go by yourself like a big loser."

"You made the commitment. You promised. You never break your word."

I shrug and my moral fibers strain uncomfortably. "Like I care."

He decides to play his ace card. "You're my designated moral support."

It is the most intriguing thing he could have gone with. I can't resist.

"Why exactly do you need moral support?" He doesn't answer, but shifts uncomfortably in his seat.

I raise my eyebrows until he relents.

"I'm not dragging you along as my sex slave. I won't lay a finger on you. I just can't walk in without a date. And that's you. You owe me, remember? I helped you vomit."

He looks so grim I have a chill of foreboding.

"Moral support? Will it be so bad?"

His cell begins to ring, and he looks between it and me, torn.

"The issue here is timing. I have to take this."

He walks down the hallway, and I resign myself to looking up the route, because unfortunately it's true. I promised.

ONCE, A TINY eternity ago, I could lie on my couch like any other person. I could watch TV, eat snacks, and paint my nails. I could call Val and we'd go try on clothes. But now that I'm an addict, I have to hang on to the cushions with my chipped fingernails to stop myself from standing up, putting shoes on, and running to Josh's building. The effort is making me ache. I weigh myself down with my laptop on my chest and halfheartedly flick between news sites, my interview presentation, Smurf auctions, and my favorite retro-dork clothing site.

I get a pop-up notification that my parents have just logged into Skype, and I dial so quickly that it's a little embarrassing. My mother appears onscreen, frowning and too close.

"Stupid thing," she mutters, and then brightens. "Smurfette! How are you?"

"Fine, how are you?" Before she replies the screen fills with the fly of her jeans as she stands up and calls out repeatedly to my dad for one very long minute. *Nigel! Nigel!* Even the familiar tone and cadence her voice takes has me shriveling in homesickness. Finally, she gives up.

"He must still be out in the field," she tells me, sitting back down. "He'll wander in soon."

We look at each other for a long moment. It's so rare to have her to myself, without my dad's gale-force personality propelling the conversation, that I hardly know where to start. I can't seem to talk about the weather, or how busy I've been. As her shrewd blue eyes narrow as I choose my words, I realize I'd better ask the question I've been torturing myself with for these last few weeks, and perhaps all of my life. It's something I should have asked her years ago.

"Before I was born, and when you met Dad . . . how could you give up your dream?"

The question clangs in the dead static air between her and me. She doesn't speak for a long moment, and I think maybe I've said something I really shouldn't. When she locks eyes again with me, her gaze is steady and resolute.

"If you're asking me if I regret my choice? No." She sits back into her chair, I sit up properly on the couch, and suddenly it's like there's no screen between us. No frame surrounding her face, or mine, and no strangely intrusive preview screen distracting us with our own faces. I feel like I could reach out and take her hand. It's the closest we've been since I saw her last, when I hugged her at the airport and breathed her shampoo and sunshine smell. I watch her thinking, and the clock is ticking before my dad walks in and interrupts.

"How can I regret it for a second? I have your father, and I have you." It's the answer and the smile I knew she'd give me. How can she say anything differently?

"But don't you wonder where you'd be now if you chose your career instead of him?"

She avoids answering again. "Is this about your job interview? Are you worried about what happens if you miss your big chance?"

"Something like that. I've just started thinking that even if I get it, I could lose out on other . . . opportunities."

"I don't think you need to give up your dream for anything. You want this, I can see it. I can hear it in your voice. Times have moved on, honey. You don't have to give up anything. You don't have to make a choice like mine. You just need to give it your all."

A door bangs in the background on her end of the conversation, and her eyes flick offscreen. "That's your dad."

I'm starting to feel frantic. I can't tell her about the change in my relationship with Josh, our competition, and what I will lose no matter what the outcome is. There's no time. There's only time for this.

"If I were in the same position, walking through an orchard, possibly about to derail myself somehow, what would you tell me to do?"

She looks offscreen and I can hear heavy boots clomping up the stairs to the office. Her answer convinces me of the cherry seed of *what if* that has always been lodged in her heart. "For you? I'd tell you to keep walking. I want things for you. Keep your eye on the prize and whatever you do, just keep walking."

"What's going on?" Dad appears, kissing the top of my mom's head, and he sees me on the screen. "You should have come got me! How's my girl? Ready to beat Jimmy at the interview? Imagine his face when you get it. I can just see it now." He drops into the seat beside Mom and then beams at the ceiling, relishing my fictional victory and his own cleverness.

I can see it on the tiny preview screen; my face falls. It could be seen from space and Mom definitely sees it. "Oh. I see now. Lucy, why didn't you say?"

Dad forges onward without a response from me. Next topic. "When are you coming home?"

I admit I pause for a second longer, for greater effect.

"The long weekend." It's the answer that my heart has been aching to give, and when I watch my dad's face break into his chipped-tooth grin I'm glad I've said it. Mom continues to hold my gaze, steady.

"Just keep walking, unless what's up that tree is as special as this."

"What on earth are you talking about? Did you hear her? She's coming home!" Dad's seat squeaks under the rhythm of his chair dancing, and just like my mom, I'm at the gates of a frighteningly momentous orchard, and I need to focus my gaze forward on the far exit, laser strong, never looking up.

It's Friday. It should be a terrible mustard shirt today, but it's not. I have my bag packed in the trunk of my car, and over the past two days I've been so nervous about this weekend I haven't been able to stomach solids. I've subsisted entirely on smoothies and tea. I slept two hours last night.

It's a relief that we're at this point. The sooner we leave here, the sooner we can get it over with. My mind has run every scenario possible, in my dreams, in my every waking moment. And the only certainty I have is, whatever happens, it will all be over soon.

Josh has been in Mr. Bexley's office for over an hour. There's been raised voices, Mr. Bexley shouting, and silence. It hasn't helped my anxiety level.

Helene went in earlier to intervene. More chillingly, Jeanette hustled past me about forty-five minutes ago and stepped into the fray. Maybe Josh's strategy involves major workforce cuts and she was called in to consult.

When she left, she paused by my desk, and looked at me, and laughed. It was the kind of laugh tinged by hysteria, like she's just heard the funniest thing.

"Good luck," she tells me. "You're going to need it. This is beyond HR."

We've been found out. Someone has seen me and Josh together, and we're busted. Danny has told someone. It's out. This scenario wasn't in the mix. I lean down and press my cheekbone against my knee. *Breathe in, breathe out.*

"Darling!" Helene is alarmed when she walks to my desk. My vision is gray. I try to stand and weave on the spot. She makes me sit back down and hands me my water bottle.

"Are you all right?"

"I'm going to faint. What's going on in there?"

"They're talking about the interviews. Josh's idea for the future doesn't quite align with Bexley's."

She pulls over a chair and sits beside me. I'm about to be fired. I begin wheezing.

"Am I in trouble? Is he doing some kind of pre-interview? Why aren't I doing one? And why was HR involved? I kept hearing shouting. And Jeanette said something spooky. About how I was going to need luck. Am I in trouble?" I end on the same pitiful note I began.

"Of course not. It's a bad argument they're having in there, darling. They have disagreements all the time. I thought it best to bring Jeanette up to remind them of professional etiquette. Nothing worse than two men barking at each other like dogs."

Helene is looking at me strangely. I must look terrible.

"Is he . . ." I bite off the words, but she won't let me get away with it.

"Is he what?"

"Is he okay? Is . . . Josh okay?" She nods, but the thing is, I know he's not. The last two days have been exhausting. Josh has been nothing but grave civility, but I can now read the nuances of his face better than ever. He's worn out. Sad. Stressed. He can't decide what's worse; eye contact, or none.

And I understand. I really do.

I find if I keep my eyes off him, and fixed on my computer screen, there's less chance of feeling my stomach flip. I can keep the butterflies out of my system if I can avoid seeing the blue of his eyes or the shape of his mouth. The mouth I have kissed, over and over. No one can kiss me like he does, and it's more proof the world is unfair.

The hurt over his comment, *I'm not going to need any help beating her,* has dulled into a callus I can't stop pressing. What a shitty thing he said. But if the roles had been reversed, and it was Helene out there tormenting us, who's to say I wouldn't have said the exact same thing? I'm not the blameless little victim in our private war.

We're like this because we've found someone who can take it as good as they can dish it out. And I'll guarantee one thing. I'm going to dish it out at the interview. Even in my dreams, I know the answer I'll give to any question they ask. He sure will need help beating me. Helene is watching me, her eyes soft with empathy.

"It's sweet you're concerned for him, darling, but Josh is a big boy. You should be more concerned about Bexley. I know who I'd put my money on."

"But why is Mr. Bexley—"

"I can't say. It's their confidential business. Let's talk about *your* interview. How did the meeting with Danny go?"

"It's going well. He's going to do that old thriller *Bloodsummer* in ebook for me. It was my dad's favorite book. He's doing it over the weekend, and gave me an incredible rate."

"Well, that's good of him. If the presentation impresses the panel, maybe he'll end up getting some consulting work out of us. How is your dad? When are you going to go home, darling? Your parents must be missing you."

"The long weekend that's coming up. That's when I need to go. Actually, I'd like to take a week." In the pause that follows, I realize that my usual caveat of *if that's okay* didn't attach itself to that statement. The old me is shaking her head in disbelief.

I look at my lovely, generous friend and like I knew she would, she nods. "That's fine. Take a break before the new job begins." Her faith in me has never wavered.

My newfound assertiveness doesn't help me shake the feeling something bad is going on. I look at Mr. Bexley's closed door again.

"Go home, darling. No one should ring this late on

a Friday anyway. It should be illegal. What are you up to this weekend?" I have the weirdest feeling that she's testing me.

Unless it's to Josh, I can't lie properly. "I think I'm going on a road trip with a . . . friend. Actually, not a friend. But I can't quite decide if I should."

The word *friend* feels like a foreign word I've mispronounced. *Frand.* She catches the pause, and smiles.

"You should go. I hope you have a wonderful time with your friend. You need one. I know you've been lonely since the merger, when you lost your Valerie."

Unexpectedly, she takes my shoulders in her hands, and kisses both of my cheeks. "I can see your brain working. I think just for this weekend you need to put it all aside. Forget the interview. One day, this interview will be a faint memory."

"Hopefully a good memory. A triumphant memory."

"It's up to the recruitment gods now. I know you've done all you can."

I have to admit it's true. "As long as the ebook formatting doesn't screw up, I'd be ready to be interviewed now."

"I'm your boss, and I am *ordering* you to live a little this weekend. You're fading away these last few days. Look at your eyes. All red. You look as bad as Josh does. We've driven you both to a nervous breakdown, announcing the promotion." She purses her mouth unhappily.

"There are moments when I wish this had never happened. None of it. The merger. This office. This promotion. It's ending something, and I'm not ready yet."

"I'm sorry." She pats my hand. "So sorry."

"I've been getting my filing up to date, in case I have to leave. I've emailed my CV to five or six recruitment firms. I've cleaned out my drawers. I'm pretty much packed. Just in case."

Helene looks at Josh's desk, which seems even more sanitized than usual. He's been doing the same. You could perform surgery on his desk.

"I can't lose you. We'd find you somewhere else in another team. Somewhere you'd be happy. I don't want you to be fretting all weekend, thinking you have no options."

"But how could I bump into the new COO in the elevator? How humiliating."

I can imagine it now. The heat would rise in my body, and the tiny hairs on my skin would rise in memory. He'd look down at me, eyes coolly professional. I'd greet him politely and remember how he pressed me against an elevator wall once in a total game changer. Then I'd reach my floor and leave him behind to continue his journey upward.

It's better to leave here completely than have to look at him across boardroom tables and glimpse him in the basement parking lot. He'll find a new woman to torment and fascinate. One day I might see a gold ring on his hand.

"Why would I keep torturing myself like that?"

I think my expression must be stark, because Helene makes an attempt to cheer me.

"Live a little, this weekend. Trust me. It will work out for the best."

"I'll put the phones through to my cell and let you know if anything urgent comes in."

I need to go downstairs to my car. I want to open the trunk, look at my packed bag, and try to dodge the big question a little longer. The *how do I feel about Josh* question. My car keys glow in my bag. I could get in my car, and drive.

I pat my pockets and realize I've got a major problem. My cell phone is gone. I look under my desk, in my bag, in folders, and paperwork. I can't even remember the last time I saw it.

I find it beside the sink in the ladies room. When I return to my desk, Josh is emerging from his meeting with Mr. Bexley without a hair out of place.

Chapter 19

W hat was all that about?" I hug the back of my chair.

"Professional disagreement." He lifts a shoulder carelessly, reminding me of what he's wearing. When he walked in today, he was wearing a pale green shirt I've never seen before. I've spent today trying to decide if it's a harbinger of doom, or if I love it.

"What's with the green shirt?"

"Green seemed appropriate, given my little scene in Starbucks."

Mr. Bexley puts his head out of his office, looks at us both, and shakes his head. "Hell in a handbasket. I tell you, hell in a handbasket."

A witchy Shakespearean crone has nothing on him right now.

Josh laughs. "Richard, please."

"Shut your mouth, Bexley," I hear Helene call faintly. He harrumphs and slams his office door. Josh looks at his desk and picks up his tin of mints, pocketing them. He flicks his phone to voice mail and pushes his chair in. It looks exactly like his desk on the first day I met him. Sterile. Impersonal. He walks to the window and looks outside.

It's that first moment all over again. I'm standing by my desk, nerves shredding me from the inside out. There's a huge man by the window with glossy dark hair, his hands in pockets. As he turns, I pray he's not as gorgeous as I think he is. The light catches his jaw and I'm pretty sure.

When those eyes hit me, I know.

He looks at me. Top of my head to the tips of my shoes. *Say the words,* I think desperately. *You're beautiful. Please, let's be friends.*

"Tell me what the hell is going on."

"I'm sworn to confidentiality."

In a clever strategy, he has utilized the one thing he knows I won't argue against.

"Tell me they just didn't informally offer you the job."

"No, they didn't."

I lower my voice to a whisper. "Do they know about . . . us?"

"No."

My two big fears seem unfounded.

"So . . . how are we getting out of here? Do I still have to?"

"Yes. That thing over there"—he points as he unhooks my coat from the hanger—"is an elevator. You've been in it before. With me, in fact. I'll step you through the process."

"What if someone sees us?"

"You say that *now*? Lucinda, you're priceless."

I slap my keyboard to lock my computer, snatch my handbag and clatter after him. I try to tug my coat from his arm but he shakes his head and tuts. The elevator doors open and he tugs me in, his hand at my waist.

I turn and see Helene, leaning on her doorframe, her posture one of casual amusement. She then throws her head back and laughs in delight, clapping her hands together. He waves to Helene as the doors close.

I use both hands to push him to the other side of the elevator. "Get over there. We look so obvious. She heard us. She saw us. You're carrying my coat. She knows you'd never do that." I'm almost hoarse with embarrassment.

"Newsflash, I *am* doing that." He circles his finger over the emergency stop button. I grab his hand in a steely grip. I think he suppresses a laugh.

When we get to the basement I creep out ahead. "We're clear."

I go to my car and unlock the trunk. My suitcase is lying crooked and upside down and it feels like a sign. I want to leap into my car, screech out, and lose him in a high-speed chase. As quickly as the image forms, his hand materializes, reaches, takes my suitcase, and walks off to his car. I snatch up my garment bag, lock my car, and then realize something.

"If we leave my car here, Helene will know. She'll see it."

"Should we hide it under some branches in a forest?"

What an excellent idea. I rub my stomach. "I don't . . ."

"Don't even say you don't want to do this. It's all over your face. I don't want to do this either. But we're going."

He's getting a little terse. My belongings are in his trunk, my handbag is on the passenger seat.

"Can I take my car home?"

"Yeah, right. You'll escape. If anyone asks on Monday, say it broke down again. It's the perfect alibi, because your car is shit."

"Josh . . . I'm freaking out." I have to put my hands on the door of his car to steady myself. If I thought things were going too fast before, it's all hitting warp speed. He pulls off his tie and undoes two buttons. He's beautiful, even in this dreadful basement.

"Yes, that's obvious." His little brow-crease is deepening. "I am too. You look exhausted."

"I couldn't sleep. Why are you freaking out?"

He ignores me. "You can sleep in the car." He opens the door for me. He tries to fold me in but I dig my heels in.

"The interview. The job."

"Fuck it. The interview will happen. We will deal with the outcome." He takes my shoulders in his hands.

"It's not that easy. I lost someone important to me in the merger, my friend Val. I kept my job, she lost her job, and now we're no longer friends. Just as an example," I hastily tack on. I nearly told Joshua Templeman that he is important. I just hinted that we're friends. He narrows his eyes.

"She sounds like an asshole."

"It's why I'm a lonely loser. Look, I'm meeting your family tomorrow. Let's face it, we're almost certainly seeing each other naked sometime soon. Tiny bit of pressure."

He ignores me again. "This is our last chance to sort our shit out."

I still hesitate, stubborn as a mule.

"This weekend is going to be hard for me. But with you there, maybe it won't be so bad."

Maybe it's the surprise of that little admission, but my knees weaken enough to allow me to get into the car and momentarily relinquish control to the last person I ever thought I would.

I feel weak with defeat. Even when packing my bag and buying a dress, I'd felt sure I'd find some last-minute way to escape or get out of it. Only in my worst-case-scenario imaginings did I think I'd be in his car, exiting the B&G underground parking lot.

The sun drops lower in the sky as he drives us through the heavy afternoon traffic. It seems like everyone in the city has had the same idea: It's time to escape into the pale, pretty hills.

I have to break this awkward silence. "So how long is this drive?"

"Four hours."

"Google Maps says five," I say without thinking.

"Yeah, if you drive like a grandmother. Glad I'm not the only one who's done some hometown cyberstalking."

He sighs as a car cuts us off, braking. "Asshole."

"How are we going to pass four hours?" I know what I want to do. Lie here in this warm leather seat and stare at him. I want to lean across and press my face against the firm pad of his shoulder. I want to breathe, and imprint it all into my memory, for when I need it one day.

"We manage it all the time."

"So, where *are* we staying? Please don't say your parents' house."

"My parents' house."

"Oh holy fuck. Why? Why?" I scrabble upright in my seat.

"I'm kidding. The wedding reception's at a hotel. Patrick has made a booking of a bunch of rooms. We mention the wedding when we check in."

"Is it seedy?"

"Sorry, no, not remotely. I'll make sure you get your own room."

Seems he's dead serious about his promise to not lay a finger on me. It's a bucket of cold water on the fire burning in my chest, and I'm left with the charred remains, unsure if I'm relieved.

"Why don't you stay with your parents then?"

He nods. "I don't want to." His mouth turns down unhappily and I impulsively pat his knee.

"I've got your back this weekend, okay? Like at paintball. But the offer stands for this weekend only."

"Thanks for covering for me. You took a lot of hits. I still don't know why you did it, though."

He squints against the sun, and I find a pair of sunglasses in the glove compartment. I huff on them and polish them with my sleeve.

"Well, you'd made me the last person to go for the flag. The most expendable."

"I did it because you looked like you were about to keel over. Thanks." He takes the glasses.

"Oh. I thought it was another one of your little tricks. No one covering for me. Lucy Hutton, human shield."

"I was always covering for you." He checks his mirror and changes lanes.

There's a little candlelight flicker in the vicinity of my heart. "You should see my bruises, though."

"I saw a few of them."

"Oh, right. When you took off my Sleepysaurus top." I rest my cheek on the seat and open my eyes. We're stopped at a traffic light, and I see the little smile line near the corner of his mouth.

"You have no idea how much I regret you seeing my pajama top. My mom gave it to me a few Christmases back."

"Oh, don't be self-conscious about it. It looks great on you."

I laugh and a little of the stress leaves me. The city bleeds into suburbs, and the sun begins to set as we wind through vast tracks of green. I've never been out this far. I need to start living my life, rather than walking the same path, in and out of B&G, like a little highland sheep.

"So you've said I'm coming along for moral support. Will you tell me why? I feel like I need to be forewarned and forearmed."

"I have . . ." he begins, and sighs.

"Baggage?" I hazard. "Who's this about?"

"It's largely just about me. I made some mistakes and didn't try hard enough on something important. Now I have to go and have it rubbed in my face a little. It's just going to sting a bit."

"Medicine." Without thinking I reduce it down to one word. "I'm sorry. That was insensitive."

"You're talking to the king of insensitive, remember?" He rolls his shoulders, desperate to change the subject. I take pity.

"I should come out here on the weekend and do some exploring. I could buy some stuff to decorate my apartment." I look at him sideways. *Fishing for an antiquing pal? Seriously, Lucy, get it together.*

"Well, I'm sure your new good friend Danny would love to drive you."

I cross my arms and we don't talk for twenty-three minutes, according to his perfectly accurate digital display.

I break under the silence first. "Before this weekend is over, I am going to crack open your head. I am going to work out what is going on in your evil brain."

"That's fine."

"I'm serious, Josh. You are destroying my sanity." I lean forward and put my elbows on my knees and rub my face.

"My evil brain is thinking about grabbing some dinner soon."

"Mine is thinking about strangling you."

"I'm thinking if we plunge off a bridge I won't have to go to this wedding." He looks at me, perhaps only half joking.

"Oh, great. Watch the road or your wish will come true." When we do cross a bridge, I supervise him with suspicion.

"I'm thinking about . . . my car's fuel consumption."

"Thank you for sharing these valuable insights into what makes you tick."

He glances at me, considering. "I'm thinking about kissing you, on my couch. I think about it disturbingly often. I keep thinking about how weird it will be to spend my days not sitting across from you."

The thing about the truth is, it's addictive.

"More of your brain contents."

Josh smiles at my demand. "I've never had someone try to do this before."

"What, break your skull open? I'll use a hammer if I have to."

"Get to know me. And I never thought it would be you."

"Do you want me to stop?"

I almost can't hear his reply, it's so quiet. "No."

I swing my head away, pretending to look at the scenery. We park in front of a truck stop diner and he touches my hand. What he says next makes my heart crackle bright with stupid hope, even though I know he's kidding.

"Come on. It's time for a romantic dinner date."

On my first fake date with Joshua Templeman, the booths are taken so we sit side by side at the counter. My feet dangle like I'm five years old as I perch on the stool, which he helped me up onto. We order and I immediately forget what I'm going to have. He rests his chin on his palm and we play the Staring Game to pass the time.

I could get through this weekend if he didn't have such beautiful hands. Or such a lovely scent to his skin. My eyes go on a little walking tour. The tube lights turn anybody else sallow, me included, but somehow he glows with vitality. I notice the faintest smattering of freckles across the bridge of his nose. I must have had my hate-goggles on during most of our working relationship, because in all honesty, I've never seen a man this good-looking in person.

Everything about him is pleasurable. He drips with quality, luxury, everything so exactly right. Every part of him is engineered and maintained perfectly. I can't believe I wasted all this time not admiring him.

"You're like a beautiful racehorse." I sigh, a little garbled. I should have tried to get some sleep last night.

He blinks. "Thank you. Your blood sugar is bottoming out. You're all white."

It's probably true. My stomach makes a goblin noise. A bunch of laughing college guys walk past too close and Josh puts his hand on the small of my back. Just like a real date would; protective, telling them, *Mine*. Then he orders me an orange juice and makes me drink it. I hear a trucker repress a belch and then let it out slowly with a groan. The fryers sizzle in the background like radio static.

"Lacks a certain ambience," Josh says to me. "I'm sorry. Crappy date."

The waitress looks at him sidelong for the fifth time, her tongue licking idly at the corner of her mouth. I touch his wrist and end up holding it.

"It's fine."

Our food arrives and I cram my grilled cheese sandwich into my face, having to remind myself to chew. He's ordered some sort of grilled chicken breast. The next few minutes are nothing but a blur of taste and salt. He steals a couple of fries from my plate like it's the most natural thing in the world.

"Where do you go to eat lunch? I've always wondered."

"I go to the gym at lunch. I run four miles, shower, and have a big protein shake on the walk back."

"Four miles? Are you training for the apocalypse or something? Maybe I should do that too."

"I've got too much restless energy."

"You might snap and kill me if you didn't. Your body is insane. You know it, right? I've barely seen half an inch of actual skin, but it is *insane*."

Josh looks at me like it's the craziest thing he's ever heard. He takes a sip of his drink and looks self-conscious.

"I am so much more than my insane body." There is mock-dignity in his voice, and he sounds so prissy that we both laugh. I smooth my hand down his arm, shoulder to wrist.

"I know. You really are. You're too much for this little pip-squeak."

"No, I'm not. I wanted to ask you if you're still angry about the other day. What I said to Bexley about not needing to beat you."

"What's the saying? Don't get mad, get even." I push my plate away and lick all my fingers. I ate my meal like a barn animal. "You were wrong, you know. You're going to need help beating me. I'm going to fight for it."

I drain my second glass of orange juice, then my water, and then his.

"Duly noted." He scrunches a napkin around his fingertips. "Wow, you eat like a Viking."

"For this weekend? I call a cease-fire. This weekend we're us."

"Who else would we be?"

"B and G employees. Competitors. Forbidden HR rule-breakers. Mortal enemies. Oh man, I feel so much better."

I jump off my stool and immediately appreciate how much stronger my legs feel. "I don't want any surprises, Josh. If I'm walking into some kind of shit-storm, I want to know."

A shadow crosses his face. He picks up the check folded under the edge of his plate and gives me a faint look of disdain when I dig for my purse.

"We're just us. I'm just me." He counts out some bills. "Let's get going."

I go to the bathroom. When I wash my hands I glance at the mirror and nearly jump out of my skin. My color is back. In fact, I'm lit up like the Vegas strip. Neon-blue eyes, cheeks glowing pink, hair blue-black. My mouth is cherry red, but my lipstick is long gone.

A solid meal has clearly revived me, but I wouldn't mind betting I always look like this after a period of Josh's undivided attention.

"Keep. It. Together," I tell myself sternly as a woman walks into the bathroom and gives me a weird look. I dry my hands and run out.

Chapter 20

The evening is perfumed by the thunderclouds overhead. He's leaning against the car, looking across the highway. There's a strange kind of grace in the heavy twist of his body. If I had to label the image, it would be *Yearning*.

"Hey. Everything okay?"

He looks at me with an expression that makes my heart shake. Like he's reminding himself I'm actually here. Like I'm not just in his head.

"Are you sad?"

"Not yet." He closes his eyes.

"I'll drive for a bit." I hold out my hand.

He shakes his head. "You're my guest. I'll drive. You're tired."

"Oh, I'm your guest now?" I put as much menace as I can into my walk and he puts both hands behind his back. I smile at him and he smiles back. I'm surprised the pinprick stars above us don't explode into silver powder. The sadness I caught in his eyes is burned away by a spark of amusement.

"My hostage. My blackmailed, unwilling captive. Stockholm Shortcake."

"Keys." I put my arms around his waist to get them

from his closed fist. Then I lean against him and tighten my arms.

"Let go. Come on." I extract the key, but he hugs my shoulders. We stand there for another long moment. Cars whip past in a steady stream.

"I want you to know I don't expect anything from you this weekend," Josh says above my head.

I lean back and look up at him. "Whatever happens, I'm pretty sure we're going to be alive come Monday morning. Unless your sexuality is as deadly as I suspect, in which case, I'm a goner."

"But," he protests helplessly. I hug him harder and press my cheek against his solar plexus.

"It's going to happen, Josh. We just need to get it out of our systems. I think that's what it's all been building toward."

"You sound a little resigned."

"I can only apologize in advance for the things I'll do to you."

He laughs and shivers and pushes me away.

"Look, it's just one weekend." I keep my voice light. I think I convince us both with it.

I have to jiggle the driver's seat forward about a mile, necessitating quite a lot of jerky pelvic thrusts. He slides the passenger seat back without comment and watches me as I struggle. I snap on my seat belt and angle the rearview mirror down about a mile.

"Want a phone book to sit on? How'd you get so small?"

"I shrank in the wash." I navigate us back to the highway.

"Over halfway there now." His knee has started jiggling.

"Try to relax." I've never known Josh to be nervous before. I feel him turn to stare at me. It's all we ever do.

"Why do we do it? Stare at each other?"

"I know why I do it. But you go first." He thinks I won't call his bluff, so I do.

"I'm always trying to work out what you're thinking." I toss him a triumphant glance, as if to say, *See, I can be honest. Sort of.*

"I stare because I like looking at you. You're interesting to look at."

"Urg. Interesting. Worst compliment ever. My poor shriveled ego."

Immediately I give myself a little mental slap. Fishing for compliments is a cardinal sin. "Never mind, I was only joking. Hey, look at that old farmhouse. I want to live there."

"It's mainly your eyes." His voice hangs in the space between my shoulder and his. A fine mist of rain has started to grit on the windshield. I grip the steering wheel tighter.

"Those absolutely insane eyes. Eyes like I've never seen before."

"Gee thanks. Insane." I feel myself smile anyway. "I guess it's accurate."

"You called my body insane. I mean it in the same way. It sort of helps you can't look at me. I can tell you."

The rain is falling heavier, and I set the wipers on intermittent, trying to focus on the car in front. He switches off the radio, and I don't know why but it feels like a threat. Like the click of a door, locking me in.

"The most gorgeous eyes I've *ever* seen." He says it like he wants me to understand the importance.

I am grateful for the dark because I blush. "Thanks."

A sigh gusts out of him, and when he speaks again it's a strip of velvet rubbing against the sensitive shell of my ear. I try to glance at him but he tuts.

"But your little red Valentine mouth . . ."

He trails off and makes a noise partway between a groan and a sigh. Goose bumps sweep up my arms. I bite my lip in case I respond. Maybe the more silent I am, the more he'll let loose.

"This one time, you wore a white shirt and I could see your bra. It was a colored lace. Maybe, like, pink or pale purple. I could see the faintest outline of it. It was one of the days when we had a huge fight, and you ended up leaving early because you were so angry."

"That could have been a few occasions. You'll have to narrow it down further for me." I wish he wouldn't remind me of moments like that.

"I have lain in bed so many nights thinking about your colored lace bra under the white shirt. How embarrassing," he confides, shifting a little in his seat.

When he speaks again, his voice coils into my ear.

"And the dream you once told me about? You were only dressed in sheets, with some mystery guy pressed up against you?"

"Oh, yeah. My stupid dream."

"I thought maybe you meant it was me in your dream."

"It was all a lie." It falls out of my mouth.

"I see," he says after a long pause. "Well done, I guess. You got me wound up over it."

I've damaged the little momentum he had going and I regret it instantly. He begins to pull himself straighter in the seat.

"I did have the dirtiest dream of my entire life. But it wasn't like I told you."

He sinks back down into his seat. I can sense his face is turned away. I can imagine his embarrassment. If he'd told me about a dream and let me believe it was about me, I'd feel ridiculous, carrying his lie in my head.

"The dream was definitely about you, Josh."

Now it's my turn to talk like he's not there. The sound of my own voice sounds scratched-up and husky and the rain is falling harder as I drive. I can see the reflective eyes of a forest animal on the roadside as I bring the car around a long curve.

"I'd gone to bed thinking about you, and how I wanted to mess with you by wearing the short black dress. I wanted you to look at me and . . . notice me. I still don't know exactly why I wanted to wear that dress. And during the night you showed up in my dream. You, pressing me down, tangling me up in bedsheets."

He breathes out in a rush. I need to get this out.

"It was something you'd said to me during the day at work. You'd said to me, *I'm going to work you so fucking hard.* Any girl would have an erotic dream after you said that to her. Even one who hated your guts."

Silence. I press on.

" 'I'm going to work you so fucking hard.' You said it to me in my dream. And you smiled at me, and I woke myself up on the edge of coming."

"Seriously," he manages to say.

"I almost came from the thought of you pressing me down and smiling at me."

I can see out the corner of my eye his hands are in fists on his knees.

"Is that all it would take? Because it can be arranged."

"I was shocked as hell and I acted all weirded out the next day. Exit the highway here?"

As the off-ramp approaches he makes a sound like a

strangled yes. I indicate and exit. He shifts again in his seat. I glance over at his lap. A streetlight helpfully gives me one gorgeous freeze-frame of a hard, heavy angle.

"So why'd you lie then, about your dream?"

"I didn't want to even say a word, but you wouldn't let up. How could I confess? I was too embarrassed. I thought you'd tease me. So I lied."

"Your tiny little dress . . ." He mutters something to himself. We both do identical squirms in our seats. His eyes slide sideways to my lap, and we both understand each other perfectly.

The main street of Port Worth is wide and divided by wide verges planted with mounds of petunias and geraniums that glow red in our headlights and under brass streetlights. During the day, this place is undoubtedly gorgeous.

"It was the same day I thought you were lying about your date. Left here, then follow the road as far as it goes."

Surely he'll laugh. It's sort of funny when you think about it.

"Yeah, I did lie about it."

There's a pause, and this time I'm in a hell of a lot of trouble.

"Lucinda. What the *fuck*? Why would you do that?" His anger is visceral.

"You were sitting there at your desk, looking at me like I was a loser."

"Fucking hell. Is my face so fucking difficult to read?" When I say nothing, he shakes his head.

"So somehow I caused all of this? Danny sniffing around like a little dog?"

"Yes, it was a lie, but you wouldn't let it go. You said you were going to the same bar too. How could I sit

there alone? I had to go down to design and find someone. He was the one I knew would say yes."

"You wouldn't have been sitting there alone. I would
have been there. It would have been me."

My mouth drops open, and he raises a hand to silence me.

"You think he's your friend, but he wants more from
you. It's painfully obvious. Next time I see him, I'm
going to explain a few things about you and me. Just so
he's clear."

"Is that right? I think you should try explaining
things to me first."

"The entrance is there."

I pull up in front of the Port Worth Grand Hotel. It
glows, opulent and gold, lawns groomed to perfection
in the beam of our headlights. A parking valet signals
to me and I manage to put the car in park and slide out
onto shaky legs, grabbing at my purse.

I go to the trunk, but another hotel guy dressed like a
toy soldier is already taking our bags out. Josh looks on
with a bored, irritated expression.

"Thank you." I tip them both. "Thank you so much."

Josh goes to the reservations desk. The receptionist
visibly flinches when blasted by his blue laser-eyes. I
turn a full circle in the lobby. Everything is in shades
of red; strawberry, ruby, blood, wine. A giant tapestry
with a faded medieval scene hangs down one wall. A
lion and a unicorn both kneel before a woman. A chan-
delier hangs above me from the center of an elaborately
corniced ceiling. There is a spiral staircase above me,
scrolling up about four floors in concentric circles. It's
like being inside a heart.

"It's something, huh?" A man in a suit says to me
from the bar nearby.

266 • Sally Thorne

"It's gorgeous." I have my hands clasped in front of me like a schoolgirl. I look for Josh, but I can't see him.

"It looks even better from here at the bar," the suit guy says, gesturing me over.

"Nice try," Josh says sharply, joining me. He scoops an arm around me and walks me toward the elevator. I hear a laughed apology—*Sorry, pal!*—behind us.

"How many keys do you have in your hand?" He presses the elevator button and he holds up a single swipe card like he's got the winning poker hand.

"Only a certain number of rooms were reserved for the wedding. I tried to get you your own room but the entire hotel is booked. This is Patrick's idea of a joke."

I know when he's lying, and he's not. He's completely irritated. I look over my shoulder at the receptionist, who is being comforted by his supervisor.

When we find our room, he takes four tries to get the swipe card into the door handle. I take two attempts to get past him when he holds the door open, but when I accidentally bump into him every rounded girly part of me bumps across him like a ball in a pinball machine. Boob, hip, ass.

Our bags are deposited. Josh tips. The door shuts and we are alone.

Chapter 21

The way he lays the swipe card on the dresser to his left is slow and deliberate. I briefly feel fear. He's a huge, dark, shaking mass walking toward me, atoms vibrating, blurring my vision as he steps to me and presses his toe against mine.

The Staring Game has never before taken place in a locked hotel room.

He releases the button on my coat with the snap of his fingers. The traitorous garment flips open, as if to say *Help yourself, mister!* He slides his hands inside, and his eyelashes droop a little when I arch into his touch. He anchors his fingers at the small of my back, fingers digging softly into my spine.

"Let's do this." I should write sonnets. I hook my hand into his belt and tug him toward the bed. He lowers me down carefully onto the edge of the mattress and cuffs my ankle with one hand. I can feel him shaking. He takes my shoes off and puts them beside the bed tidily.

It's been forever since I last felt a man's skin against mine. For as long as I've known Josh, I've been celibate. I probably have some confusion in my eyes when I realize it. He sees it, and strokes his finger under my chin.

268 • Sally Thorne

"I was more angry at myself just now."

He kneels down between my feet. A nice boy, kneeling beside his bed, about to say his prayers.

His dark blue eyes are stubborn when he looks at me again. I am certain he's about to kiss my cheek and leave, so I hook one leg around his waist and tug him into the cradle of my thighs. A noise like *oof* falls out of his mouth and I take his jaw in both of my hands and kiss him.

Usually, he likes kissing soft. Tonight, I like kissing hard. I press his mouth open the moment our lips touch. He tries to slow me, but I won't let him. I nip at him until he pushes his hips against me. I feel a solid thud against me.

If I ever thought I was an addict before, it was a vast understatement. I want to OD on him. By the end of this weekend, I'll be legless in a back alley, unable to say my own name. At least I understand this lust. I can deal with this, and frankly, it's the only outlet we've got. I am holding him with my legs and arms in an iron grip and it's a surprise when I feel a dropping sensation. I open my eyes and realize he's standing up, taking me with him.

"Are you going to kill me tonight?" he asks against my mouth, and I kiss him again fiercely.

"I'm going to try."

My last boyfriend, the last man I had sex with forever ago, was only about five-six. He could never have picked me up. He'd have ruptured a disc in his fragile, boy-sized spine. Josh sinks down onto a beautiful wingbacked armchair I'd only dimly registered when we first came in.

My whole life, before Josh, I've scoffed at guys who made displays of their strength. But maybe a little part of me still exists who loves to be carried and coddled. My skirt has slid up so high he can probably see my underwear, but his eyes don't stray down. The word *gentleman* flashes through my mind.

He raises a hand and once upon a time I would have flinched, but now I lean into his palm.

"Slow down."

I shake my head in disbelief, but he looks me in the eye. "Please."

Doubt begins to spread through me. "Don't you want to?"

He rolls his hips. The heavy, painfully hard proof is against me. He wants me so badly his eyes have gone their signature serial-killer black. I press my eyebrow to his. We breathe against each other, lips barely touching.

He wants to press his mouth against my skin. Bite. Eat. Devour. He wants me, hands and knees. Wet skin and cold air. Fingers sliding into me. His whispered words barely audible over my labored breathing. Tears of frustration and wet mascara marking a Rorschach pattern on the pillowcase.

I already know what I'll get from him. Coaxing, tormenting, a darkly worded warning when I get too close. I'll be rolled into whatever position he feels like, bossy hands cupping, tilting, tightening, and gentling.

But I also know he'll make me laugh. Sigh. He'll tease me, chide my theatrics, make me smile even when I want to strangle him. My defiance will earn me a delay. My acquiescence, a kiss.

It's what he is creating, of course. Delay. He wants to play with me until my orgasm hits me, hours after the first touch. He's going to make this little Easter egg last for days. Shard by shard. Melting on his tongue. He wants to do it so many times that we lose count, and probably die in the process. He wants to make sure I'm addicted to him. I know what I'll get from him in bed, all right. It's what I've always gotten from him.

Every single pornographic image is flickering in my eyes because he's licking his lips and his eyes drop to the sheer lace at the tops of my stockings. He tries to speak but can't.

I'm unbuttoning his shirt very clumsily, dragging each button through until I hear a thread snap.

"Why do all colors make your skin so lovely? Even the horrendous mustard." I drop my mouth to his neck. "Beautiful man, inhumanly pretty under fluorescents in the office."

"Green, the color of envy. I've been a jealous psycho lately."

"Mustard, the color of Colonels. Let's burn it."

"Sure, Shortcake. You can burn my shirt. In a barrel, in an alleyway."

He's laughing and then sighing against my throat, not making it remotely easy for me as I get as many shirt buttons open as I can. I slide my hands inside.

"You're like an anatomy poster under all this perfectly ironed business attire. I always suspected it. Clark Kent."

"Slow down." He takes both my hands out of his shirt. I struggle a little, but he holds me gently cuffed, and tilts his face to mine.

We begin kissing again; soft as silk, lighter than I could have believed was possible after my rough little paws mauled him so.

His thumbs are pressing gently into my wrists and I'm arched a little, breasts pressed into his chest as we kiss each other, achingly slowly. The wild impatience

I was feeling has been checked a little, because maybe he's selling me on the concept of delay.

"You've rushed things in the past, I think," he tells me, as if reading my mind. "What's your hurry?"

Being kissed by Josh, his lips tender and ripe, is a pleasure on par with sex. He's thinking of nothing but me and my reactions, learning what I like, withholding and giving and talking to me wordlessly. When I open my eyes a fraction to take a peek I see he's doing the same thing.

My stomach bottoms out when he smiles against my lips.

"How You Doing?" he whispers and I bite the words softly off his tongue.

"How would you say I'm doing?"

His hands fall away from my wrists tentatively. When he is satisfied I can be trusted to keep our lazy rhythm, he cups my ass and gives it a firm squeeze.

"You're doing great. Goddamn, Luce."

"You betcha." It's exhilarating, knowing I can now lay my mouth on him whenever I want. I look over his skin like a warlord, and he's my new territory. He shivers under my perusal.

"Let's play a special game," I tell him. "It's called Who Comes First."

"Also known as Gold Medal, Silver Medal."

We're laughing. I'm unbuttoning his cuff when his cell phone begins to ring. He ignores it, drawing my mouth back to his. My bottom lip is given a little pinch with his teeth.

"So pretty," he tells me. "Just so pretty."

The phone rings on and on. It stops and I let out a sigh of relief. Then it starts ringing again. He flicks his eyes to mine, and I give him a frustrated shrug and climb off.

"I'll turn it off."

He digs in his pocket and I survey my handiwork. He's sprawled in the chair, legs everywhere, shirt unbuttoned, hair completely wrecked, eyes hazed and black.

"You look like a hot virginal dork who's been defiled in the backseat of my car."

His eyes spark with amusement. "That's how I feel." He unearths his cell and glances at it dismissively, but then looks at it again.

"It's my mom. Oh, shit. I forgot her."

I go into the bathroom to hide. Shyness takes hold at the thought of meeting her. I'm not sure what to do next, and I listen to his placating tone through the door. I wash my hands and press my swollen lips and stare at myself in the mirror. I look like the porno version of myself.

He speaks through the door. "Luce. I'm sorry, but I have to go downstairs for a few minutes."

I open the door. "Is everything okay?"

"Mom's downstairs. She made table centerpieces from her rose garden apparently, but she can't find any hotel staff to help her carry them all in and she's getting upset. Fucking hopeless. I need to go down there and kick someone's ass." He rebuttons his shirt.

"Of course. Go on. Make some young hotel worker cry. Do you want me to come and help?"

"No, you're tired. Do you want me to order you any room service? Bring you back some coffee?"

"No, it's okay. I might have a shower while you're gone. I'm sure I'll be draped seductively across the bed in something lacy for when you get back."

He winces and adjusts his pants a little. He's so torn, I feel sorry for him.

"You can't leave her down there struggling."

"I don't know how long I'll be, hopefully a few minutes. But relax, and I'll be back soon."

"It's okay. There's no way I'm interested in making out with a guy who wouldn't go help his upset mom. Go."

The bathroom is nearly the size of my bedroom. I shower and wash my face. When I'm brushing my teeth, I look at my face, pale and devoid of any makeup, and remind myself he's seen me like this. In fact, he's seen me even worse.

He's seen me sweating, vomiting, feverish, and asleep. He's seen me angry, frustrated, scared. Horny, lonely, heartsick. No matter how I look, it never seems to faze him. He always looks at me exactly the same way. Knowing this gives me the confidence to walk out in my SLEEPYSAURUS T-shirt and sleep shorts. It seemed like a funny idea at the time, but I catch a glimpse of myself in the dresser. I look about ten years old. Oh, well. Negligee Lucy would be a fake.

Silence stretches on. I check my phone. Nothing. I push back the comforter and slide into the bed. I can't hold in the groan of relief. After the stress and tension of the last few days, this isn't as scary as I imagined it would be. The sheets quickly grow warm and I paddle my tired feet in pleasure.

I lean back against the pile of pillows and turn the TV on. I find a channel playing *ER* and it is strangely comforting. Josh has probably seen this one. I try to watch for medical inaccuracies, but when my eyes become dry and tired I close them. To calm my nerves, I hit Play on my memory and bite back a yawn.

I'm there again. The night I swallowed my goddamn pride and went to his apartment. My own personal happy place in my mind. I'm curled on his couch, the soft deep cushions cradling my back. I feel the dipping weight of him sitting down beside me, and I know as long as he's there, I will be okay. I don't know how long we do this. I sit here holding hands with the most intensely fascinating man I've ever known. He's looking at me with fierce tenderness in his eyes. Eyes like he loves me.

Now I know I must be dreaming.

I WAKE WHEN the sun slices through the center of my pillow through a gap in the hotel drapes. My first thought is, *No. I'm too comfortable*.

My second thought is: *I finally get to see Josh asleep*.

Lying face-to-face with our pillows touching, we've been playing the Staring Game all night with our eyes closed. Each eyelash curves against his cheek, glossed and dark. I'd kill for lashes like those, but they always seem to be lavished upon the most masculine of men. He's hugging my arm like a teddy bear. I don't hate him. Not even a bit. It's a disaster that I don't. I smooth my fingers over his brow and he frowns. I press away the crease.

I prop up onto my elbow and see the bedside clock reads 12:42 P.M. I have to check several times. How did we sleep past noon? Our mutual exhaustion from the last few days has resulted in a pretty impressive sleep-in.

"Josh." No point sticking with the formality of his full name when we're asleep in the same bed. "What time's the wedding?"

He jolts and opens his eyes. "Hi."

"Hi. What time's the wedding?" I try to slither out of bed but he hugs my arm tighter.

"Two P.M. But we have to get there earlier."

"It's getting close to one. In the afternoon."

He's a little shocked. "I haven't slept this late since

high school. We're going to be late." Regardless of this, he nudges my elbow like the kickstand of a bike and I flop back down onto the mattress. I manage to glimpse some bare arm. He's wearing a black tank.

"Nice arms."

I slide my hands down one, watching them undulate along each taut, defined curve. Then I do it again. He watches, and the next time I use my fingernails. Goose bumps. Mmmm. I bend my head to kiss them.

"You are something else, Joshua Templeman." I push his hair away from his forehead. It's ruffled and messy. I spend a few minutes grooming him.

"Am I trying too hard to seduce you?"

He rolls me closer. I never imagined Josh would be a cuddler. "Well, you could always try *harder.*"

He's so sweet. Lying in bed with him is pretty luscious. Without thinking I ask something I've always wanted to know. "When was your last girlfriend?"

The question clangs like I've struck a gong. Well done, Lucy. Bring up other women while lying in bed with him.

"Um." There's a long pause. So long I think he's either asleep or about to explain he was married. He's too young. Surely. He tries again. "Well. Um."

"Don't tell me you're waiting for your divorce to come through or something."

His arm slides up the middle of my back, and my head rolls slowly onto his shoulder. I can barely keep my eyes open, I'm so comfortable. So warm. Surrounded by his scent, and cotton sheets.

"No one would be masochistic enough to marry me."

I'm a little indignant for him. "Someone would. You're completely gorgeous. And you're neat. Tall and muscly. And employed. And have a nice car. And perfect teeth. You're basically the opposite of most guys I've dated."

"So they've all been . . . hideous messy trolls . . . unemployed . . . and smaller than you? How could that even be possible?"

"You've been reading my diary. The last guy I dated was so small he could wear my jeans."

"But he must have been nice. To be my opposite, he must have been so darn nice." He looks at the wall.

"He was, I guess. But you can be nice. You're being nice right now."

I feel teeth on my collarbone, and I snort with amusement.

"Okay, you're never nice." The teeth are gone and a soft kiss is pressed against the same spot.

"So when did you break up with this miniature man?" He begins kissing my throat, lazily, with care and gentleness. When I tilt my head to let him have better access I see the clock radio again. Real-world o'clock is fast approaching. I wonder if I have a granola bar in my purse.

"It was in the couple of months prior to the B and G merger. It hadn't been working for a while. It was such a stressful time at work, and I didn't see him as much, and we agreed to take a break. The break never ended."

"That's a long time."

"Hence me dry-humping you constantly. But you never answered me. Wait, don't tell me, I don't want to know." The thought of him pleasuring another woman is too much.

"Why not?"

"Jealous," I groan and he begins to laugh softly, but

then sobers. He's painfully awkward when he finally explains.

"I was seeing someone, but we broke up in the first week of moving to the new B and G building. She ended it."

"B and G ruins another relationship." I want to bite my tongue but the words won't stop. "I bet she was tall."

"Yeah, pretty tall." He reaches to the side table and retrieves his watch.

"Blonde."

He buckles it and doesn't look at me. "Yes."

"Goddamn it, why are they always Tall Blondies? I bet she has brown eyes and a tan, and her dad is a plastic surgeon."

"You've been reading *my* diary." He looks faintly disturbed.

I press my face into his shoulder. "I was guessing she's my polar opposite too."

"She was . . ." He lets out a wistful sigh and my heart twists. The territorial little cavewoman inside me appears at the entrance to her cave and scowls.

"She was just so nice."

"Ugh, nice. Gross."

"And her eyes were brown." He watches me mull this over.

"Sounds like a legit reason to break it off. You know what? Your eyes are too blue. This just isn't going to work." I was hoping for a clever retort, but instead, his tone is withering.

"You've actually thought that this would work?"

Now it's my turn to say *um*. I'm halfway recoiled into my own shell when he blows out a breath.

"Sorry. It came out wrong. I can't help being such a cynical asshole."

"This is not news to me."

"It's why I don't have a girlfriend. They all trade me in for nice guys."

He looks at the ceiling with such deep regret in his eyes I have an awful thought. He's pining for some-one. Tall Blondie broke his heart when she moved on to someone less complicated. It would certainly explain his bias against nice guys. I try to think of how to ask him, but he looks at the clock.

"We'd better hurry."

Chapter 22

Please give me a crash course on the key players in your family. Any taboo topics of conversation? I don't want to be asking your uncle where his wife is, only to find out she was murdered." I rummage around in my bag.

"Well, before last night when I carried forty-five individual flower displays into the hotel because they couldn't find her a fucking cart, I hadn't seen my mom in a few months. She calls me most Sundays to keep me up to date with the news of neighbors and friends I never cared about. She was a surgeon, mainly hearts and transplants. Little kids and saintly types. She's going to love you. Absolutely love you."

I realize I'm pressing my hands over my own heart. I want her to love me. Oh, jeepers.

"She'll say she wants to keep you forever. Anyway. My dad is a cutter."

I flinch.

"It's the nickname for surgeons. When you meet my dad, you'll understand why. He was mainly on call for emergency room surgeries. I'd hear all sorts of things over breakfast. *Some idiot got a pool cue through the throat.* Car crashes, fights, murders gone wrong. He was forever dealing with drunks with gravel rash, women with black eyes and broken ribs. Whatever it was, he fixed it."

"It's a hard job."

"Mom was a surgeon too, but she was never a cutter. She cared about the person on her table. My dad . . . dealt with the meat."

Josh sits on the sill lost in thought for a minute and I search in my bag for clothes, giving him some privacy. I start swiping on makeup in the bathroom.

After a few minutes, I peep through the gap in the door. In the reflection of the dresser he's shirtless, gloriously so, and he's unzipped my garment bag. He holds the dress between two fingers with his head tilted in recognition. Then he rubs his hand over his face.

I think I've made a mistake with my blue dress.

My Thursday lunchtime dash to the tiny boutique near work seemed like a good idea at the time, but I should have worn something I already had. But it's too late now. He unfolds an ironing board and flaps his shirt over it.

I slide the door open with my foot. "Yowza. Which gym do you go to? All of them?"

"It's the one in the bottom of the McBride building, a half block away from work."

I have to swallow a mouthful of drool. "Are you sure we have to go to your brother's wedding?"

I have never seen so much of his skin, and it glows with health; honey gold, flawless. The deep lines of his collarbones and hips are an impressive frame. In between are a series of individual muscles, each representing a goal set and box ticked. Flat, square pectorals with rounded edges. The skin of his stomach pulls tight across the kind of muscles I usually stare at during Olympic swimming finals.

He irons his shirt and *all* the muscles move. His biceps and lower abdomen are ridged with those blatantly masculine veins. Those veins ride over muscle and tell you, *I've earned this.* His hips have ridges that point down toward his groin, obscured in suit pants.

The amount of sacrifice and determination to simply maintain this is mind-boggling. It's so Josh.

"Why do you look like this?" I sound like I'm about to go into cardiac arrest.

"Boredom."

"I'm not bored. Can't we stay here, and I'll find something in the minibar to smear all over you?"

"Whoo, are those some horny eyes or what." He waggles the iron at me. "Get finished in there."

"For a guy who looks like you, you're awfully bashful."

He doesn't say anything for a bit, stroking the iron over the collar. I can see how much effort it is taking him to stand shirtless in front of me.

"Why are you self-conscious?"

"I've dated some girls in the past . . ." He trails off.

My arms are crossed. My ears are about to start whistling with steam. "What sort of girls?"

"They've all . . . at some point made it pretty clear my personality is not . . ."

"It's not what?"

"I'm just not great to be around."

Even the iron is steaming in indignation. "Someone wanted you only for your body? And they told you that?"

"Yeah." He redoes one cuff. "It should feel flattering, right? At first I guess it did, but then it kept happening.

It really doesn't feel good to keep being told that I'm not relationship material." He bends over his shirt and analyzes it for creases.

I finally understand the Matchbox car code. *Please see me. The real me.*

"You know what I honestly think? You'd still be amazing, even if you looked like Mr. Bexley."

"You've been drinking the Kool-Aid, Shortcake."

He's smiling a little as he keeps ironing. I'm almost shaking with the need to make him understand something that I don't fully know myself yet. All I know is, it hurts me to think he feels bad about such a fundamental aspect of himself. I resolve to objectify him less, and turn away until he puts on his shirt. It's robin's-egg blue.

"I love that color shirt. It matches what I'm going to wear, um, obviously." I cringe at my dress again. I go to my handbag and dig in it, finding my lipstick.

"Can I see something?" He's got his tie flapping loose as he takes the tube from me and reads the bottom.

"Flamethrower. How appropriate."

"Do you want me to tone it down?" I rattle my handbag, searching.

"I fucking love your red." He kisses my mouth before I start to apply. He watches me applying the lipstick, blotting, reapplying, and by the time I'm done he looks like he's endured something.

"I can barely take it when you do that," he manages to say.

"Hair up or down?"

He looks pained. He gathers it up, and says "Up."

He lets it fall and scoops it in his hands like snow. "Down."

"Half up, half down it is. Quit fidgeting, you're making me nervous. Why don't you go and have a drink at the bar downstairs? Liquid courage. I can drive us to the church."

"Be down in, like, fifteen minutes okay?"

Once he's gone and the silence fills the hotel room like a swelling balloon I sit on the end of the bed and look at myself. My hair falls around my shoulders, and my mouth is a little red heart. I look like I'm losing my mind. I strip down, put on my support underwear to smooth out any lumps, hook my stockings up and look at my dress.

I was going to buy something in a muted navy, something I could wear again, but when I saw the robin's-egg-blue dress I knew I had to have it. I couldn't have color matched it better to his bedroom walls if I tried.

The sales assistant had assured me it suited me perfectly, but the way Josh rubbed his hand over his face was like he'd realized he's dealing with a total psycho. It's undeniably true. I'm practically painting myself in his bedroom blue. I manage to zip myself up with some contortionist movements.

I decide to take the huge sweeping spiral staircase down instead of the elevator. How many opportunities will I ever have? Life has started to feel like one big chance to make each new little memory. I walk in downward circles toward the gorgeous man in the suit and pale blue shirt at the bar.

He raises his eyes, and the look in his eyes makes me so shy I can barely put one foot in front of the other. *Psycho, psycho,* I whisper to myself as I plant myself in front of him and rest my elbow on the bar.

"How You Doing?" I manage, but he only stares at me.

"I know, what a psycho, dressed in the same color as your bedroom walls." I self-consciously smooth down the dress. It's a retro prom-dress style, the neckline dipping and the waist pulled tight. I catch a whiff of lunch being served in the hotel restaurant and my stomach makes a pitiful little whimper.

He shakes his head like I'm an idiot. "You're beautiful. You're always beautiful."

As the pleasure of those three words lights up inside my chest, I remember my manners.

"Thank you for the roses. I never did say thank you, did I? I loved them. I've never had flowers sent to me before."

"Lipstick red. Flamethrower red. I have never felt like such a piece of shit as I did then."

"I forgave you, remember?" I step in between his knees and pick up his glass. I sniff.

"Wow, that's one strong Kool-Aid."

"I need it." He swallows it without a blink. "I've never gotten flowers either."

"All these stupid women who don't know how to treat a man right."

I'm still agitated about his earlier revelation. Sure, he's an argumentative, calculating, territorial asshole 40 percent of the time, but the other 60 percent is so filled with humor and sweetness and vulnerability.

It seems I've drunk *all* the Kool-Aid.

"Ready?"

"Let's go." We wait for the valet to bring the car. I look up at the sky.

"Well, they say rain on your wedding day is good luck."

I press my hand on his jiggling knee after we drive a few minutes.

"Please relax. I don't get why this is a big deal." He won't reply.

The little church is about ten minutes from the hotel. The parking lot is filled with cold-looking women in pastels, hugging themselves and trying to wrangle male companions and children.

I'm about to start hugging myself against the cold as well when he gathers me to his side and swoops inside, saying, *Hello, talk to you later* to several relatives who greet him in tones of surprise before flicking their eyes to me.

"You're being so rude." I smile at everyone we pass and try to dig my heels in a little.

His fingers smooth down the inside of my arm and he sighs. "Front row."

He tows me up the aisle. I'm a little cloud in the slipstream of a fighter jet. The organist is making some tentative practice chords and it's probably Josh's expression that causes her to press several keys in a foghorn of fright. We approach the front pew. Josh's hand is now a vise on mine.

"Hi." He sounds so bored I think he's worthy of an Oscar. "We're here."

"Josh!" His mother, presumably, springs to her feet for a hug. His hand falls away from mine and I watch his forearms link behind her. You've got to hand it to Josh. For a prickly pear, he commits completely to a hug.

"Hi," he tells her, kissing her cheek. "You look nice."

"Cutting it a bit close," the seated man on the pew comments, but I don't think Josh notices.

Josh's mom is a little lady, fair hair, with a soft cheek-dimple that I've always wished for. Her pale gray eyes are misty when she pulls back to look up at her huge, gorgeous son.

"Oh! Well!" She beams at his compliment and she glances to me. "Is this . . . ?"

"Yes. This is Lucy Hutton. Lucy, this is my mother, Dr. Elaine Templeman."

"Pleased to meet you, Dr. Templeman." She's roping me in for a hug before I can blink.

"Elaine, please. It's Lucy at last!" she says into my hair. She pulls back and studies me. "Josh, she's gorgeous!"

"Very gorgeous."

"Well, I'm going to keep you forever," she tells me, and I can't help but break into a dorky grin. The look Josh shoots me is like, *see*. He wipes his palms on his suit pants and almost has a crazy look in his eye. Maybe he has Churchphobia.

"I'm going to keep her in my pocket. What a doll! Come and sit up front with us here. This is Josh's father. Anthony, look at this little thing. Anthony, this is Lucy."

"Nice to meet you," he replies gravely, and I blink in shock. It's Joshua on time delay. Still ridiculously handsome, he's a stately silver fox, gravely upholstered in heavy tailoring. We're the same height and he's seated, so he must be an absolute giant when standing. Elaine puts her hand on the side of his neck, and when he looks up at her the faintest smile catches at his lips.

Then he swings his terrifying laser-eyes to me. Genetics never cease to astonish me.

"Nice to meet you," I return. We stare at each other. Perhaps I should try to charm him. It's an ancient reflex and I press pause on it. I examine it. Then I decide against it.

"Hello, Joshua," he says, redirecting his lasers. "Been a while."

"Hi," Josh says, and snags me by my wrist, pulling me in to sit between himself and his mother. A buffer. I remind myself to admonish him for it later.

Elaine steps between Anthony's feet and strokes his hair into a neater formation. Beauty tamed this particular Beast. She sits down and I turn to her.

"You must be so excited. I met Patrick once, under less than pleasant circumstances."

"Oh, yes, Patrick told me on one of our Sunday phone calls. You were quite unwell, he said. Food poisoning."

"I think it was a virus," Josh says, taking my hand and stroking it like an obsessive sorcerer. "And he shouldn't discuss her symptoms with other people."

His mother watches him, looks at our joined hands, and smiles.

"Well, whatever it was, I was completely steamrolled by it. He probably won't even recognize me today. I hope. I was grateful to your sons for getting me through it."

Elaine glances at Anthony. I've brought Josh too close to the big elephant in the room; his lack of a stethoscope.

"The flowers are lovely." I point to the huge masses of pink lilies on the end of each pew.

Elaine drops her voice to a whisper. "Thank you for coming with him. This is hard for him." She shoots Josh a worried look.

As mother of the groom, Elaine soon excuses herself to greet Mindy's parents, and help several terrifyingly old people into their seats. The church is filling up; delighted cries of surprise and laughter filling the air as family and friends reunite.

Frankly, I don't see what is so difficult about this situation. Everything seems fine. I can't see anything amiss. Anthony nods to people. Elaine kisses and hugs and lights up everyone she speaks to.

I'm just a little lonely book in between two brooding bookends. Anthony is not the sort of man to appreciate small talk.

I let father and son sit in silence on a polished plank of wood, and I hold Josh's hand and I have no idea if I'm being remotely useful until he catches my eye.

"Thanks for being here," he says into my ear. "It's already easier."

I mull this over as Elaine takes her seat, and the music starts to play.

Patrick takes his place at the altar, casting a wry glance at his brother, his eyes skating over me as though assessing my recovery. He smiles at his parents and huffs out a breath.

We all stand when Mindy arrives in a big pink marshmallow dress. It's insanely over the top, but she looks so happy as she walks down the aisle, simultaneously grinning and weeping like a lunatic, so I love it too.

She takes her place in front of Patrick, and I get a good look at her. *Holy moly. This woman is stunning. Go, Patrick.*

Weddings always end up doing something weird to me. I feel myself getting emotional when their friends read special poems, and the minister reflects on their commitment. I get choked up during their vows. I take the Kleenex offered by Elaine and dab at the corners of my eyes. I watch with suspense as the ring is slid onto each finger, and sigh with relief when they fit perfectly and go on with ease.

And when the magic words *you may now kiss the bride* are uttered I let out a happy sigh like I've seen THE END scrolled over the top of this perfect movie freeze-frame.

I look at Elaine and we both let out identical delighted laughs and begin clapping. The men on either side of us sigh indulgently.

They walk out down the aisle wearing their brand-new gold rings, and everyone stands up, talking and exclaiming until the strains of the ancient organ are almost drowned out. For the first time, I notice some speculative glances at Josh. What *gives*?

"They go for photographs down on the boardwalk. I hope the wind doesn't blow Mindy clean away," Elaine tells me, waving politely to someone. "We'll all go to the hotel now, have some drinks, then an early dinner and speeches. We'll borrow Josh for some family photos at some point."

"Sounds good. Right, Josh?" I squeeze his hand. He's been vacant for the last few minutes. With a jolt, he drops back into his body.

"Sure. Let's go."

I throw a look over my shoulder to his parents, which hopefully looks bemused rather than alarmed as I'm hooked into his right arm and swept out of the church.

"Slow down. Josh. Wait. My shoes." I'm barely able to keep up. He slides down horizontal in the passenger seat and lets out a groaning sigh.

I'm having trouble trying to time my reverse. Everyone is piling out of the parking lot simultaneously.

"Do you want to go straight back? Or do you want me to drive around for a bit?"

"Drive around. All the way back home. Take the highway."

"I am an independent observer. I assure you, it went pretty well."

"You're right, I guess," he says heavily.

"Pardon? Could you possibly repeat that in a moment, so I can record it? I want it as my text message alert noise. Lucy Hutton, you're right."

Teasing him will get him out of his little funk. He looks at me.

"I could do the voice mail message too if you want. You've reached the voice mail of Lucy Hutton. She's too busy crying at a stranger's wedding to take your call right now, but leave a message."

"Oh, shut up. I must watch too many movies. It was so romantic."

"You're kinda cute."

"Joshua Templeman thinks I'm kind of cute. Hell has officially frozen over." We grin at each other.

"You must have cried for a reason. You're dreaming of your own wedding?"

I look at him defensively. "No. Of course not. How lame. Plus, my fiancé is invisible, remember."

"But why would a stranger's wedding make you cry, then?"

"Marriage is one of the last ancient rites of civilization, I guess. Everyone wants someone who loves them so much they'd wear a gold ring. You know, to show everyone else their heart is taken."

"I'm not sure it's relevant these days."

I try to think of how to explain it. "It's so completely primal. He's wearing my ring. He's mine. He'll never be yours."

The slow procession of traffic takes us all back to the hotel. I hand the keys to the hotel valet and Josh attempts to steer me to the side of the building.

"Josh. No. Come on."

"Let's go to the room." He's putting on the brakes. He weighs a ton.

"You're being ridiculous. Explain what is going on with you."

"It's stupid," he mutters. "It's nothing."

"Well, we're going in." I take his hand firmly and march him through the doors held open for us.

I take the deepest breath my lungs can manage, and walk through into an entire room half filled with Templemans.

Chapter 23

In a pretty room adjoining the ballroom, we spend nearly two hours mingling in various states of awkwardness in an endless champagne reception. When I say mingling, I mean me carrying Joshua through a succession of social encounters with distant relatives while he stands beside me, watching me glug champagne to dull my nerves, which burns my empty stomach like gasoline. Every introduction goes like this.

"Lucy, this is my aunt Yvonne, my mother's sister. Yvonne, Lucy Hutton."

When his duty is completed, he begins occupying himself with stroking my inner arm, spreading his hand across my back to find the bare skin under my hair, or linking and unlinking our fingers. Always staring. He barely takes his eyes off me. He's probably amazed by my small-talk ability.

After a while, he is taken by his mother out into the side garden, and I watch through the window as he poses with various combinations of family. His smile is forced. When he catches me spying, I'm beckoned out, and he and I pose together in front of a charming rosebush. When the shutter clicks shut, the old version of me shakes her head, wondering how we ever got to this point. Me, and Joshua Templeman, captured side by side in the same photograph, smiling? Every new development between us feels like an impossibility.

He turns me and cups my chin in his palms, and I hear the photographer say, *Lovely.* Another shutter click, and I forget the world in the instant his lips touch mine. I wish I could shake off my old mistrusts, but this all feels too much like a summer afternoon daydream. The sort I might have had once, and then hated myself for it.

I watch Patrick and Mindy across the lawn, now clinched together romantically in front of another camera and I realize that I'm clinched in a fairly romantic pose myself. The man who's hated me for so long is now showing me off, tugging me close to his side. When we go back inside, he kisses me on the temple. He drops his mouth down to my ear, and tells me I'm beautiful. I'm turned another ninety degrees, presented to another set of relatives. He's showing me off.

What I haven't worked out yet is, *Why?*

In every introduction, after discussions on how lovely Mindy looked and how nice the ceremony was, the inevitable question always comes next.

"So, Lucy, how did you meet Josh?"

"We met at work," Josh supplied the first time when the silence stretched too thin, so it becomes my default answer.

"Oh, and where do you work?" is the next question. None of his family has even the slightest idea where he works, or what he does. They're awkward about it; like being a Med School Dropout is something to be deeply ashamed of. At least a publishing house sounds glamorous.

"It's so lovely seeing you with someone new," another great-aunt tells him. She gives me a Meaningful Look. Perhaps he's also rumored to be gay.

I excuse us and pull him aside behind a pillar.

"You have to make more of an effort. I'm exhausted. It's my turn to stand there and feel you up while you talk." A waiter passes and offers me another tiny canapé. He knows me by now because I've eaten at least twelve. I'm his best customer. I'm obsessed with dinner, which I've been promised by the waiter is at five o'clock sharp. I watch the hands on Josh's watch, knowing I'll probably die of hunger before then.

"I can't think of anything to say." He notices a paint-ball bruise on my upper arm and begins silently fussing over it.

"Ask people about themselves, it usually works." I am acutely aware of how many people keep taking little peeks at us. "You need to tell me why everyone's looking at me like I'm the Bride of Frankenstein. No offense, you big freak."

"I hate being asked about myself."

"I noticed. Nobody knows a flippin' thing about you. And you didn't answer my question."

"They're looking at me. Most of them haven't seen me since the Big Scandal."

"Is that why you want me to play girlfriend? So everyone forgets you're not a doctor? You'd do far better to hand out your business card. Quit touching me. I can't think straight." I tug my arm.

"I can't seem to stop now I've started." He gathers me closer and dips his mouth down to my ear. "Are you this soft all over?"

"What do you think?"

"I want to know." His lips brush my earlobe and I can't remember what we're talking about.

"Why are you acting so kissy and boyfriend-y?" I watch his eyes closely, and when he answers, I know with deep certainty that he is not telling me something.

"I've told you. You're my moral support."

"For what? What am I missing?" My voice gets a little sharp and some heads close to us turn. "Josh, I feel like I'm waiting for the other shoe to drop."

He strokes his hand down the side of my neck. I shiver so hard he sees it. When he bends to press a kiss against my lips, my eyelids drop shut, and there's nothing in the world but him. I want to exist only here; in the dark, the feel of his forearm in the small of my back. His lips telling me, *Lucy, stop fretting.* It's an unfair move.

I open my eyes and a couple who I think are Mindy's parents are clearly talking about us. Both have busybody speculative eyes as they inspect me.

"Quit trying to distract me. We need to get through dinner. And you're going to come up with some topics of conversation and talk to your family. Why are you being so shy?" As soon as I say it, I understand. "Oh. Because you *are* shy."

My new revelation gives me a slightly different angle to view him from. "All this time I thought you were just an arrogant asshole. I mean, you are. But there's more to it. You're actually incredibly shy." He blinks and I know I'm right on the money.

A strange sensation stirs in my chest. It unfolds, grows twice as large, then again. It doesn't stop; it gets faster, bigger, feathers and fluff stuffing my chest like a cushion. I don't know what's happening, but it's filling up my throat and I can't find any breath. He seems to know something is happening with me, but he doesn't press me on it; instead, his arm rises to hug my shoulders, his other hand cradling my head. Again, I try to speak but I can't. He just holds me and I squeeze my hands uselessly on his lapels and the red foyer in the far distance sparkles like a jewel.

"Josh," Elaine says. "Oh, here you are." Her voice warms. Josh pivots without releasing me, sliding my shoes along the marble floor.

Her eyes are a little too bright when she looks at us both. "When you're ready, would you like to join us inside? You're at our table."

"I'll bring him right in."

The unfolding in my chest crumples a little when I realize his mother is happy to see him with someone. I straighten up and his hands slide to my lower back. People shuffle in to take their seats and I see heads crane as they walk past to look at us.

"Who am I?" I try one last time. "Your housekeeper? Your piano teacher?"

"You're Shortcake," he says simply. "You don't need to make up anything. Come on. Let's get this over with."

I feel some trepidation as I approach our table and Josh stiffens up. We ease into our chairs and spend a few minutes studying the table decorations and our name cards. The others are typed, but mine is handwritten, I'm guessing due to the late RSVP.

The table seats eight. Me, Josh, his mom and dad, Mindy's parents, and Mindy's brother and sister. I'm at the head family table. If I had known this would happen when I brashly offered my services as Josh's chauffeur, I would have punched myself in the face.

I chat a little to Mindy's brother, seated to my left. Glasses are clinked. I'm praying Josh will say something, anything. I'm about to aim a little jab at the side of his thigh when the silence is broken by Elaine. The dreaded question.

"Lucy, tell everyone how you met Josh."

Inwardly I shriek. I've answered this same question at least eight times today, and it never gets any easier. "Well. Well, uh . . ."

Oh crap, I'm sounding like a priced-by-the-hour escort who hasn't thought of a good enough lie. What did we agree again? I'm Shortcake? I can't tell them that. If I ever was going to humiliate Josh, now would be the time. I can almost imagine saying it. *He forced me to come.*

"We work together," Josh says calmly, ripping his dinner roll in half. "We met at work."

"An office romance," Elaine says, winking at Anthony. "The best kind. What did you think of him when you first laid eyes on him?"

I know a born romantic when I see one. She's a mother who will take any compliment of her offspring as a compliment to herself. She's looking at him now with her heart in her eyes, and I cannot help falling a bit in love with her myself.

"I thought, good grief, he's tall." Everyone except Anthony laughs. He's studying his fork, checking for cleanliness.

"How tall are you, Lucy?" Mindy's mother, Diane, asks. Yet another dreaded question.

"Five whole feet." My standard answer that always gets a laugh.

Waitstaff are beginning to pass out the starters and my stomach makes a hungry gurgle.

"And what did you think when you saw Lucy?" Elaine prompts. We may as well be sitting in the middle of the table like decorative centerpieces. This is getting ridiculous.

"I thought she had the best smile I'd ever seen," Josh

replies, matter-of-fact. Diane and Elaine both look at each other and bite their lips, eyes widening, eyebrows rising. I know that look. It's the Hopeful Mom look.

But even I can't stop myself from blurting, "Did you?"

If he's lying, he's absolutely outdoing himself. I know his face better than my own, and I can't pick it. He nods and gestures at my plate.

I learn that Patrick and Mindy are going to Hawaii for their honeymoon.

"I've always wanted to go there. I need some sun. A vacation sounds good right about now." I push away my plate, which I've practically licked clean, and remember that a trip to Sky Diamond Strawberries is on the near horizon. I start to tell Josh, because he's so fascinated with that place, but his mother interrupts.

"Is work busy?" Elaine asks.

I nod. "So busy. And Josh is just as busy."

I notice Anthony make a little snort, looking away dismissively. Boy, is that expression familiar. Josh goes rigid, and Elaine gives her husband a frown.

The main courses are served and I begin dismantling it with gusto. Tiny hairline cracks of tension are starting to run through the meal. I must be incredibly slow, but I can't work out the source of it. True, Anthony hasn't said much, but he seems like a nice enough man. Elaine is growing more tense, her smile more forced, as she attempts to keep the mood light. I can see her starting to glance at Anthony, her eyes imploring him.

As the waitstaff clear the plates after our main courses, I can see all the major players getting ready for their speeches. Anthony takes an index card from his inner pocket. As they test the microphone, I tug my chair a little closer to Josh and he drops one arm over my shoulders. I lean back into him.

There's a speech from the best man and Mindy's maid of honor. Her father makes a speech welcoming Patrick to the family, and I smile at the sincere ring in his voice. He talks about his pleasure in gaining a son. Josh hugs me closer and I let him.

Anthony takes the podium and looks at his index card with an expression bordering on distaste. He leans down to the microphone.

"Elaine wrote me some suggestions, but I think I'll wing it." His voice is slow, deliberate, with a pinch of sarcasm I'm beginning to understand is hereditary among the Templeman males.

A laugh scatters through the room, and Josh sits up straighter. I don't need to look to know he's frowning.

"I've always expected great things of my son." Anthony holds the edges of the podium and looks at the crowd. His choice of words also implies that he has only one son. Maybe I'm just reading too much into it.

"And he hasn't disappointed me. Not once. Never have I gotten the call every parent dreads. The 'Hey, Dad, I'm stuck in Mexico' call. Never got that from Patrick." Bigger laughs from the crowd now.

"Not from me, either," Josh mutters into my ear.

"He graduated in the top five percent of his class. It's been a privilege watching him grow into the man you see here," Anthony intones. "His range of experience has gone from strength to strength and he's well respected by his peers."

I can't detect any particular emotion in his voice, but he does look at Patrick for a fraction too long.

"I must say, the day he graduated med school, I could see myself in Patrick. And it was a relief, knowing we'd continue the medical dynasty."

Behind my ear, I hear Josh draw in a sharp breath.

His arm feels increasingly viselike around my shoulders.

Anthony lifts his glass. "But I believe you're only as strong as the person you choose to live your life with. And today, by marrying Melinda, he's made me a proud father yet again. And Mindy, might I say, you've chosen an outstanding Templeman to marry. Mindy, welcome to our family."

We raise our glasses, but Josh does not. I look over my shoulder and see two people, heads together, whispering and watching us. Mindy's mother looks at Josh with raw pity.

Mindy and Patrick cut the cake and feed each other a square. I've been looking forward to some cake for most of the day, and I'm not disappointed. A huge wedge of something chocolate and heavy is placed in front of me.

"Great speech. Thanks for that little remark," Josh tells his father.

"It was a joke." Anthony smiles at Elaine, but she's not pleased.

"Hilarious." Her glare turns glacial.

I know when a subject change is in order. "This cake looks like death by chocolate. I hope it's not too naughty."

"You would be amazed by the damage to arteries caused by high-fat diets," Anthony pipes up.

"Would you say the occasional treat is okay? I hope so." I'm forking the cake into my mouth.

"Ideally, no. Saturated fat, trans fats, once they go into your arteries, they aren't coming out. Unless you have a heart attack and someone like Elaine has to fix you."

"He's a little strict with himself," Elaine assures me

as I drop my fork with a clatter and press my hands to my chest. "Treats are okay. They're better than okay."

"She asked my opinion," Anthony points out gravely. "And I gave it."

I notice he's got no cake in front of him. I'm reminded of the all-staff meeting. Josh didn't eat any cake then, either. I glance sideways, and to my surprise Josh picks up his fork and begins eating cake too. It's a great big giant fuck-you to his dad. Over and over we fork cake into our greedy faces until Anthony's forehead pinches in distaste, clearly unused to having his sage advice ignored.

"Self-indulgence is a tricky thing. It can be hard to get yourself back on track once you begin indulging trivial little impulses." Anthony is not talking about cake. Josh drops his fork with a clatter.

Elaine looks wretched. "Anthony, please. Leave him alone."

"Come with me," I tell him, and to my mild surprise he rises obediently and walks with me to the shadowed edge of the empty dance floor.

"Can you please explain what's going on? This tension is excruciating. I'm sorry, but your dad is being a dick. Is he always like this?"

He jams a hand into his hair. "Like father, like son."

"No, you're not like this. He's being bitchy and your mom is upset. His speech was so weird." Every single time I feel protective of Josh, the realization pings me right in the solar plexus. I take his hand, which is folded into a fist, and smooth my hand over the knuckles.

He watches my fingers. "Dinner's over. We've gotten through it. That's all I care about."

"But why does it feel like all eyes are on you? It seems

like everyone in this room is looking at you, wondering if you're coping okay. It's like, *Hang in there, sport.*"

"I think they'll assume I'm not suffering too badly." He loops a hand around my waist, and the glow of his flattery hits my bloodstream, along with probably two thousand premium cake calories.

"They're wrong. No one makes you suffer like I do." I receive a smile for my cleverness. "Are you okay? Please tell me about this Big Scandal that they're all whispering about. I cannot fathom that you deciding to not be a doctor could cause such a fuss."

It's rare to see Josh procrastinate, but he does now. "It's a long story. Bathroom first."

"If you climb out the window, I'm going to be really mad."

"I'll be back, I promise. I'll tell you the whole sorry tale. Will you be okay for a minute?"

"I've had to make friends with half the people in this room, remember? I'm sure I'll find someone to hang out with." I watch him go and strike the most casual pose I can manage.

I haven't actually spoken to Mindy yet. Outside, she was always being moved around by the photographers, but she'd smiled at me and I have the impression that she is nice. She's nearby speaking animatedly to an older couple. When they move away, I smile and wave tentatively. I feel bad she has to have strangers at her wedding.

"Hello, Mindy, I'm Lucy. I'm Joshua's, ah, plus-one. Thank you so much for having me here. The ceremony was lovely. And I love your dress."

"Nice to meet you. I've been dying to." She smiles broadly, her dark eyes lit with undisguised interest as she looks me over.

"You're the girl who's melted the ice man."

"Oh! Um. I don't know about melted . . . Ice man?" I'm at my articulate best.

"You know Josh and I dated for a year?" She waves her hand quickly as if it were nothing.

"What? No." My stomach folds in half. And in half again. She puts one hand to her hair and smoothes the already perfect style. It's blond. She's tall, tan, and brown eyed. She's Tall Blondie.

My mouth is probably a perfect circle. I am speechless. It is all dropping into place. How humiliating would it be to go alone to your ex-girlfriend's wedding? Especially when she's marrying your brother?

"How long ago did you meet Patrick?" I am trying to keep my voice modulated. I sound like my car's GPS.

"I'd known him while dating Josh, of course. When all that business with Josh's work going through the merger, I started talking to Patrick to try to understand why Josh was being so distant. He isn't much of a talker, as you know."

I look at all the strangers who have been staring at Josh all night. They've been wondering how he's coping with seeing this beautiful woman marry his brother. A year. They would have definitely slept together. This willowy, immaculate blonde has lain in his bed. Kissed his mouth. I swallow acid.

"Patrick and I just clicked. It's been a bit of a whirlwind; we only got engaged six months ago. I still feel bad about it, but Josh and I were not a good fit. I found his moods to be scary sometimes. I still hardly know what to talk to him about. I'm sorry, I'm being rude. Please don't tell him I said that."

I feel like I'm about to burst into tears and Mindy watches me with growing alarm.

"I'm sorry, Lucy, I thought he would have told you. He's so happy with you. I never would have imagined he'd be so completely smitten. He never was with me. I suppose it does make sense. Intense men like him usually fall pretty hard, when they eventually do."

I force myself to smile, but it's not convincing. I can't be responsible for ruining Mindy's happy wedding buzz, but inside I'm breaking. How could I have been so stupid to think he was walking me around, showing me off, for nothing? I'm moral support while he attends his ex-girlfriend's wedding. If that isn't the definition of a rent-a-date I don't know what is.

"Oh, Lucy. Sorry to upset you, especially if you two are early days. But Josh is yours."

I manage a weak laugh. He's really not.

"Patrick is especially surprised. What did he say? Something like, *I've never seen Josh look like he has a heart.*"

"He has a heart." *A self-serving heart, but a heart nonetheless.*

A wedding-planner-type person indicates to Mindy and she waves.

"His heart is all yours," Mindy says and pats my arm. "I'll be tossing the bouquet now. I'll aim right for you."

She weaves through her guests, as poised and gorgeous as I'll never be.

Arms slide around me from behind. A kiss on the back of my neck, diluted by my hair. The effect is still so potent I have to gulp. The DJ has begun calling the single ladies onto the dance floor. The freak-out is building in my gut. My palms sweat. I need to get out.

"Hi. Where's all your new friends?" He begins to push me into the growing group of contenders.

"No, Josh. I can't."

People are watching us. I'm on the knife-edge of needing to make a scene but knowing I can't. The tears and panic are welling up inside me. Usually perceptive, he doesn't see them this time.

"Where's your competitive spirit?" Josh gives me one last firm push and I'm propelled into a ragtag bunch of females, ranging from a lisping flower girl to a woman in her early fifties who seems to be doing hamstring stretches. Everyone looks at the bouquet. It's lovely. We all want it.

I see Josh's mom on the sidelines. She smiles at me, and then it fades, concern filling her eyes. Who knows what my face looks like. Mindy catches my eye and I can see her genuine regret that she has upset me. Josh repositions for a better view and he and his mother swap glances. She gestures to him, he bends his head and she tells him something. He looks at me sharply.

It's all too much.

"Here we go!" Mindy turns her back on us and mimes doing some practice swings. The bouquet is a pink-lily confection.

I hardly register the slap of the flowers against my chest. They drop down into the waiting arms of the flower girl, who screams in delight. The entire audience is shaking their heads and laughing at my lack of coordination. Everyone turns to the person next to them and says, *She could have caught that.*

I'm so disappointed in *not* catching them the freak-out is triggered in full.

I politely laugh and manage to walk slowly from the other end of the dance floor, weaving through the spectators. Now I'm running. I need to get out of this room. I know he'll be coming after me, so instead of choosing the most obvious sanctuary—the ladies room—I go down the waitstaff passageway and find myself in the garden beside the hotel.

A few boys in white shirts and ties are smoking and fiddling with their cell phones. They look at me with bored expressions. I pick up my pace until I'm trotting, running, the spikes of my heels barely touching the ground. I want to run until I reach the water. I want to leap into a rowboat and sail to a deserted island.

Only then will I be able to face up to it.

I have feelings for Joshua Templeman. Irreversible, stupid, and ill-advised feelings. Why else would this hurt so much? Why did everything in me ache to wrap my arms around the wedding bouquet and see him smile? I dither along the water's edge.

The footsteps approaching come too fast. I bite back a swell of impatience and open my mouth to give him a piece of my mind.

Then I see it's Joshua's mother.

Chapter 24

"Oh, hi," I manage to say. "Just . . . getting some air."

Elaine looks at me, and opens her purse and finds her pack of Kleenex. I'm confused by it until I press it to my eye and it comes away wet.

We stand, looking at the water glittering darkly under the fading sunset sky. I'm too upset to comprehend I'm about to unload to his mother. Any sympathetic ear at this point will do me. It's not like I'll ever see her again.

"He never told me about Mindy."

She is aggrieved, and frowns back across the lawns. "He should have. You shouldn't have found out this way."

"It all makes so much sense. I can't believe I've been so stupid. The way he's been acting has been pretty unbelievable."

"Like he's in love with you."

"Yes." My voice breaks a little. "He told me once he's a good actor. I can't believe this."

She says nothing and puts her hand on my shoulder. Every single glimmer of foolish hope feels extinguished in this moment.

"I don't think he has been playing a game." Elaine's mouth twists.

The word *game* only crystallizes further the hurt in my gut.

"Oh, I'm sorry, but you have no idea how good at games he is. Every day of our working relationship, Monday to Friday. This has got to be the first time he's played me on the weekend, though."

Elaine looks past me, and I can see Josh's silhouette pacing along the side of the building in agitation. She shakes her head and he stops.

"Why did you come today?" She is genuinely curious.

"I owed him a favor. He told me I was coming along for moral support. I didn't know why, but I came anyway. I thought it was something to do with him dropping out of medicine. And now I find out his ex-girlfriend is marrying his brother? I'm in a soap opera right now."

Elaine steadies me with a hand on my elbow. When she speaks, she's got a fond smile teasing at the edge of her lips.

"I speak to him on Sundays, and I've known you for as long as he's known you. A beautiful girl, bluest eyes, reddest lips, blackest hair. He describes you like a fairy-tale character. He's never quite decided on princess or villain."

I put my hands into my hair and make two fists. "Villain. I feel like the world's biggest idiot to even believe for one day he could be so . . ." I can't finish.

"You're the girl he calls Shortcake. When I first heard your nickname, I knew. I will tell you now, he's never looked at anyone the way he looks at you."

I am starting to feel irritated with this lovely woman. It's pretty clear she's so biased I can no longer use her as a sounding board. She cannot believe her son would do anything so hurtful. I open my mouth but she silences me firmly.

"He dated Mindy. I'm so glad to have her for a daughter-in-law. Sweet as pie. Cinderella hasn't got anything on Mindy."

"She's lovely. She's not my issue."

"But she never challenged Josh. You have since the first day you met him. You make him angry. You've never been scared of him. You've taken the time to try to understand him, just to get the upper hand in your little office skirmishes. You *notice* him."

"I've tried not to."

"Neither Josh nor his father are easy men. Some men are a delight. Patrick, for example. Reasonable, calm, ready with a smile. Josh has a nickname for him, too. Mr. Nice Guy. It's true. He is. It takes a strong woman to love someone like Josh, and I think it's you. Patrick's an open book. Josh is a safety-deposit box. But he's worth it. You won't believe me, and I can't blame you tonight, but so is his father."

Elaine waves Josh over and he begins striding toward us.

"Please go easy on him. You could have caught the bouquet," she admonishes me. "If you'd put your arms out a little."

"I couldn't."

She kisses my cheek and hugs me with such kind familiarity I close my eyes.

"You will one day. If you decide to stay, we're having a family breakfast at ten A.M. in the restaurant. I'd really love to see you both." She walks back down the path, where she intercepts Josh.

They begin urgently conferring. Great. She's giving the enemy a warning of what he's in for. I am so tired of being in this place, by this water, under this sky. I go and sit on a low concrete bench and try to cram my heart back into my chest. Even his mother thought Josh was in love.

"You found out about the Mindy thing." In the twenty yards it took for him to get to me, he's no doubt framed his argument.

"Yep. Well done. You sure fooled me."

"Fooled you?" He sits beside me and reaches for my hand but I pull away.

"Cut the shit. I know you've been parading me around in front of Mindy and her family. Maybe you should have hired someone better looking than me."

"Do you seriously believe that's why you're here?" He has the audacity to look shaken.

"Imagine being in my position. I take you to my ex-boyfriend's wedding and I'm all over you like a rash. I make you feel special. Important. I make you feel beautiful."

There's a tremor in my voice. "And then you find out, and suddenly you're left wondering if it was real."

"You being here has nothing to do with Mindy. At all."

"But she's the Tall Blondie you broke up with after the merger, right? She's the one we talked about in bed this morning. Your big old heartbreak. Why didn't you just tell me this morning?" I put my hands over my face and lean my elbows on my knees.

Josh turns sideways in his seat. "We were in bed, and you were just starting to look at me like you didn't hate me. And she's not my heartbreak."

I cut him off. "I could handle being a rent-a-date, but you really should have been clear with me up front. That was a dick move, and frankly, I'm mad at myself for not expecting you'd do something like this."

Josh's urgency is growing. He puts his hand on my

shoulder and turns me gently toward him. We stare into each other's eyes.

"I wanted you here because I always want you with me. I don't care that she's just married Patrick. It's ancient history to me. How could I tell you this morning, and ruin the moment? I knew how you'd react. Just like this."

"You're damn right I'm reacting like this." Like a teary fire-breathing dragon. "Didn't I specifically ask you if there was any touchy subject I needed to know about, so I'd be forewarned? You could have told me back in the office. Days ago. Not now."

"You would never have agreed to come under those circumstances, had you known. You would have refused to believe this weekend could be anything more than an act. Whatever your reaction, it wouldn't have been good."

I grudgingly admit to myself that he's probably right. Even if he had managed to get me to come, I probably would have invented a character and I definitely would have worn false eyelashes.

He touches a fingertip to my wrist. "I've had my focus on other things, believe it or not. Mom's flower arrangements. Dad's mood. Your blood sugar. Telling you about this just faded away to the edges." He looks across the water and pulls his tie loose. "Mindy is a nice person. But I didn't bring you here to show her how well I've moved on. I don't care what she thinks."

"I don't believe you can be so cool about this situation." I can't detect any emotion in his eyes at all as he casts his eyes back across the water, contemplating.

"She was never going to be my wife, put it that way. We were wrong for each other."

Hearing his voice say *my wife* makes me go too still.

Eyes frozen and unblinking. Pupils dilated to black coins. Terror and panic and possession torches my throat dry. I don't want to examine why I feel this way. I'd rather jump in the water and start swimming.

He looks at me sideways, his face tense. "Now that I've promised that you're not here as some part of an elaborate revenge scenario, can you tell me the real reason this bothers you so much? Other than my lie by omission, and people staring at us? People that you never have to see again?"

This is skating way too close to my tangled-up new feelings. I try for several long moments to come up with an answer that sounds even halfway credible, but when I can't I get to my feet and walk so fast back to the hotel he has to lengthen his stride to keep up.

"Wait."

"I'm getting a bus home." I try to close the elevator door on him but he shoulders in easily. I press the button for our floor and dig for my phone to look up a bus schedule. I have no idea what time it is. I have several missed calls. Josh tries to speak but I put my hand up until he crosses his arms, exasperated.

I click through them distractedly; Danny has been trying to get ahold of me a couple of times throughout the afternoon. I have a few texts along the lines of, *Do you have a font preference? . . . I'll choose then . . . Could you call me back when you can?*

The elevator bings.

Josh looks like he's one second away from going stark-raving insane. I know the feeling.

"Leave me alone," I tell him with as much dignity as I can and walk to the far end of the corridor, where a pair of armchairs are arranged beside a bay window. During the day, this would be a nice spot to sit with a book. In the evening, as the last peach glows of sun leave the sky, it's the perfect place to fume.

I sit down and dial a local bus company. A late-night express is leaving at seven fifteen, and they are already stopping by the hotel to pick up someone else. The gods are smiling upon me.

Going back to the room will mean having to finish things with Josh, and I am burned-out. A husk. I have nothing left. I need to procrastinate.

Danny answers on the second ring.

"Hi," he says, tone a little stiff. Nothing more annoying than an uncontactable client, I imagine. Especially one you're doing a favor for.

"Hi, sorry I've been out of touch. I've been at a wedding and my phone is on silent."

"It's okay. I just finished."

"Thank you so much. Did it all go okay?"

"Yep, for the most part. I'm at home now checking it on my iPad, flipping through the pages. The formatting looks good. Whose wedding is it?"

"The brother of a complete asshole."

"You're with Joshua."

"How'd you guess?"

"I had a feeling." He laughs. "Don't worry. Your secrets are all safe with me."

"I hope so." I couldn't care less at this point. It would serve me right to be humiliated in the halls of B&G.

"When are you back? I'd like to show you the final product."

"Tomorrow at some point. I'll call you when I'm back in town and I can meet you."

"If you come over on Monday evening it would work for me. I've kept the spreadsheet that you wanted. It breaks down the time it took, along with what I think costs would be by a designer in a usual commercial setting, but also a salaried staff member."

"I'm impressed. Maybe I should bring you a thank-you pizza."

"Yes, please." Danny's voice drops a cheeky half octave. "So, what did you wear to this wedding?"

"A blue dress?" I see Josh's reflection over me in the window and jump in fright. He takes the phone out of my hand and looks at the caller ID.

"It's Joshua. Don't call her again. Yes, I'm serious." He hangs it up and slides it into his pocket.

"Hey. Give it *back*."

"No fucking chance. He's who you had to sneak off and call?" The look in his eyes is getting sharper, blacker.

"It's work related!"

He tugs on my hands to make me stand up. A door opens near us, too close to other rooms to indulge in one of our signature yelling matches. We both purse our lips and march into our room. I try not to slam the door.

"Well?" Josh crosses his arms.

"It was *work related*."

"Sure. A work-related call. Dinner? What are you wearing?" He skates narrowed eyes over me, like he's contemplating ripping the skin right off me. I can relate. I want to punch him in the face. Energy and anger are making the air almost sulfuric. The thing about Joshua is, even when he's furious, he's still exquisite to look at. Maybe even more so than usual. He's all glittery black eyes and an angry tensing jaw. Messed-up hair and a hand on his hip, pulling his blue shirt tight. It makes being angry back with him just that little bit harder, because I have to try to not notice. It's an unachievable endeavor that I have always struggled with, as long as I've known him. But still, I persevere.

"You've got no right to lecture me. I knew this was a disaster the second I got into your car." I kick off both my shoes across the room. "I'm leaving soon. There's a bus." I grab at my bag and he stops me with a raised hand.

"In between Danny and Mindy, we've kind of had our fair share of jealous revelations today, don't you think? I'm going to crack if you don't just listen to me for once." He wrenches out his cuff links and tosses them on the dresser and shoves up his sleeves, muttering to himself. "Little fucking asshole. What is she wearing? That guy has a fucking death wish."

The expression on his face makes me wonder if I've got a death wish too. I try to position myself behind the armchair, just to give myself the illusion of space, but he points between his leather shoes.

"Don't hide. Get over here."

"This better be good." I cross the room to stand in front of him and put my hands on my hips, just to puff myself up. He takes a few long moments to decide how to proceed.

"Two simple issues first. Danny and Mindy." He looks like he's taking control of a board meeting. He practically has a presentation slide behind him.

"Do you care about Danny? Could you love him one day?" Those eyes belong to the king of the serial killers.

"I called Danny about something for work. Something to do with my *interview*. You already know this! Forgive me for not wanting to spill my secrets to the person I'm competing against."

"Answer my question."

"No, and no. He's helping me with something I'm using in my presentation. It's a design job, and he's a freelancer now. He's doing me a massive favor, working over the weekend. But I couldn't care less if I never saw him again."

His insane eyes dial down a few notches. "Well, I couldn't care less about Mindy. It's why she left me for my brother."

"You could have told me. Back in your apartment, on your couch. I would have tried to understand. We were almost friends then." I realize something else that's bothering me. He didn't trust me with this.

"I finally have you coming over to sit on my couch and you think I'm going to tell you about how I was such a terrible boyfriend she ended up with my brother? It's not really a glowing endorsement of my character. Gee, wouldn't you want to stick around after hearing that?" I can spot the faint wash of darker color on his cheekbones. He's embarrassed as hell.

"Why am I even here? Moral support, remember?" I watch him try and fail several times to start.

"If anyone has broken my heart, it wasn't Mindy. It was my dad." He puts his hand over his face. "You were always right about why I needed moral support. No big conspiracy. It's medicine. Me quitting, failing, disappointing. You're here because I'm scared of my own fucking dad."

"What did your dad do?" I can barely ask it. When I think of dads, I think of my own. A big, funny sonic boom since I was a kid, always surprising me with Smurfs and beard-burn cheek kisses. I know there are bad dads. When I see the look on Josh's face, I wish to god he didn't have one.

"He's ignored me my entire life."

It sounds like the first time he's spoken those words. He looks at the ground, miserable. I creep closer to him. Another weird kaleidoscopic twist? His hurt makes my own heart hurt.

"Has he hit you? Has he forced you into medicine?"

Josh shrugs. "The British royal family have an expression. The heir and the spare. I'm the spare. Patrick was firstborn. Dad's not one of those people who's willing to dilute his efforts, if you know what I mean. They were only ever planning on having one kid too. I was a surprise."

"You would have been wanted." I have his crumpled cuff in my hand now, and I give him an awkward little shake. "Look at how much your mom loves you."

"But to Dad, I was not in the plan. Patrick has always been his focus, and look where he is now. The best son, effectively the only son, making Dad proud on his wedding day."

He won't meet my eyes. We're mining some old, deep, painful territory here.

"Nothing I did rated a mention. Dad wouldn't pay a cent toward my tuition, but Mom did. I studied my ass off, like a complete sucker for punishment. Nothing pleased him." The bitterness in his voice sounds like it is choking him.

My anger has steamed out of my pores now and I can't do anything but put my arms around him and hug until my arms ache.

"I thought if I could become a doctor too, maybe . . ."

"He'd notice you." Just like his mom said.

"And meanwhile perfect, golden child Patrick, who can do no wrong, was making it look easy. The thing about Patrick is, he's so nice. He's so goddamn nice.

He'll do anything for anyone. Even get up in the middle of the night and drive over to help me with you. Man, can he be any nicer? It makes it impossible for me to hate him. And I want to. So bad."

"He's your brother." I link my arm into his. "It's obvious he'd do anything for you."

"There's a perfect son, and then there's me. I may as well be the best at something, even if it is being an asshole. I'll never be nice. You need to imagine what it was like growing up with a parent like him. I've had to make myself this way."

I think of him stomping around at B&G, trying to hide his shyness and insecurity behind that mask.

"I hate to break it to you Josh, but underneath it all, you're nice too."

"I've got no interest in being the second best at anything. I'm never being second again."

His voice is iron-clad with determination. I think of the promotion, and some deep part of my brain sighs, *Oh fuck it.*

"Is this why you've always hated me? I'm so nice. I'm way too nice and you've always hated it." I tug the sleeve of my dress a little straighter.

"It killed me to watch you try your heart out for people who were using your kindness. It made me want to stand up for you, and protect you from it. I couldn't though, because you hated me, so I had to get you to stand up for yourself."

"And my niceness made it impossible to hate me?" Hopefulness has rendered me pathetic.

He puts a thumb under my chin and tilts my face. "Yeah."

"Well, this is a sad story." When he kisses me on the

cheek, I know it is an apology, and I suspect that I'll probably accept it.

"Don't get me wrong. I didn't have some traumatic childhood or anything, I always had a roof over my head and so forth. And my mother is the best," he says, affection in his tone now. "I can't complain."

"Yes you can."

He looks at me, surprised.

"No one should ever be ignored, or made to feel unimportant. You've achieved a lot of things in your career, and you should be proud of yourself." I emphasize the last word. "You can complain all you want. I'm Team Josh, remember?"

"Are you?" I hear some of the tension melt out of him a little. "I never thought I'd hear those words fall from your Flamethrower lips. Not after tonight."

"You and me both. So what happened after you completed premed? Surely your dad must have taken notice of you then."

"Mom made the biggest fuss ever. She threw a party. It seemed like everyone who'd ever known me was invited. It was at our house here. It's on the beach. I suppose it was a great party, in retrospect. But Dad wasn't there."

"He skipped it?" I hug him, resting my cheek on his chest. I feel his hands slide up my back, like he's soothing *me*.

"Yeah, he didn't bother to swap shifts at the hospital like Mom had asked him to. He skipped it entirely. When Patrick completed premed Dad gave him our grandfather's Rolex. For me, he couldn't even bother turning up. He's always known I wasn't cut out for it. Watching me try so hard made me pathetic."

"So him not turning up to the party means you

haven't spoken to your father properly for five years? You've got to see it's hurting your mom. She's got permanently sparkly eyes from trying not to cry."

"That night I got incredibly drunk. I was sitting down there by myself on the sand by the water, emptying this bottle of whiskey into my mouth. Alone. Melodramatic. Behind me is the house, filled with people, but no one had noticed the guest of honor was gone."

He looks a little amused, but I know underneath it is a deep hurt. I remember looking at him once in the team meeting, a thousand years ago, and wondering if he ever felt isolated. I know the answer now.

"So you sat out there? Drunk? What did you do? Go in and make a scene?"

"No, but I realized something I'd worked so hard for— his approval—had resulted in absolutely no outcome. I'm like him, maybe. Why try? Why bother? I decided then and there to quit trying. I'd go and get the first job I could."

He turns me a little in his arms, and when he holds me close again, he's rubbing my shoulder like I'm the one who needs comfort.

"I stopped making any kind of effort to engage with him, and it was like the biggest source of stress in my life was removed. I stopped. I thought, when he wants to be a father to me, he'll make the move."

"And he hasn't?"

Josh keeps talking like he hasn't even heard me.

"The thing that gets me is, when I switched to doing an MBA at night while working at Bexley, he was unimpressed. Like he'd had any kind of opinion. Like I wasn't even noticed or acknowledged enough to disappoint. But I have. Over and over, my entire life. My career is a joke to him."

I'm surprised by how angry I'm getting. I think of Anthony, his face permanently twisted into a sarcastic expression.

"He's lost something special in you. Why is he like this?"

"I don't know. If I knew, maybe I could change it. He's just been that way with me, and most people."

"But Josh, this is what I don't get. You're so over-qualified for what you do at B and G."

"We both are," he tells me.

"Why do you stay?"

"Prior to the merger, I nearly quit every day. But I already had the family reputation as a quitter."

"And post merger?"

He looks away, and I see the edge of his mouth beginning to curl in a smile.

"The job had a few good things about it."

"You enjoyed fighting with me too much."

"Yeah," he admits.

"How did you end up working at Bexley, anyway?"

"I applied for twenty jobs in a fit of rage. It was the first offer I got. Richard Bexley's lowly servant."

"You didn't even care? I wanted to work for a publisher so badly I cried when I heard I'd got the job."

He has the grace to look guilty. "I suppose you'd think it was unfair if I got the promotion now."

"No. The process is based on merit. But Josh, you've got to know. It's my dream. B and G is my dream."

He doesn't say anything. What *could* he say?

"So you really didn't bring me along to show Mindy you'd moved on with some hot little dweeb?"

I know his face better than my own, and I can't see a trace of a lie. When he speaks, there is none.

"I couldn't face him without you. I am an embarrassment. Dropped out of med school, administrative job, lost the girl to my brother. I'm nothing to him. Mindy and Patrick can have ten children and be married for a hundred years for all I care. Good luck to them."

I let myself say it. "Okay. I believe you."

We sit in silence for a moment before he speaks again. "The worst thing is, I keep wondering what I'd be now if I'd stuck with medicine."

"I've got so much inside me I have no idea about. I'm like the mayor of a city I've never seen."

He smiles at my phrasing. "If you knew the kind of little miracles happening every moment you breathe in, you wouldn't be able to handle it. A valve could close and not open; an artery could split, you could die. At any moment. It's nothing but miracles inside your tiny city." He presses a kiss to my temple.

"Holy shit." I clutch at him.

"You wouldn't believe the stats on people who go to bed one night and never wake up. Normal, healthy people who aren't even old."

"Why would you tell me this? Is this what you think about?"

There's the longest pause. "I used to. Not so much anymore."

"I think I preferred it when I thought I was full of white bones and red goo. Why am I now thinking about dying tonight?"

"Now you see why I can't do small talk. Sorry Dad scared you about the cake. He's jealous he can't let himself go enough to enjoy something. I don't think I've eaten cake in a few years. Man, it was good."

"Filthy little pigs, the pair of us. Want to go downstairs and see if there's any left?"

He looks at me with guarded hope. "You're not leaving?"

I remember my plans to get the bus home. "No, I'm not leaving."

It's helpful he's still sitting on the dresser. It means when I step closer and take his face in my hands, I can reach him with only a little tiptoeing. It means I can feel the tingling sparks jumping in the air between our lips, his sigh of relief that tastes sweeter than sugar. His pulse jumps under my fingertips. It's a pretty convoluted game we've played to make it to this moment.

It's helpful he's still sitting on the dresser, because I can pull his lips to mine.

Chapter 25

When I kiss him, his exhalation is long, until he's surely completely empty. I want to fill him back up. I don't realize it until a few dreamy, melting minutes have passed that I've been talking to him with my kiss. *You matter. You're important to me. This matters.*

I know that he understands, because there is a fine tremor in his hands as he slides one fingernail up the side seam of my dress, across my shoulders to my nape. He tells me things, too. *You're who I want. You're always beautiful. This really matters.*

He toys with the zipper of my dress for a tiny, jingling eternity, and then pulls it down. It makes a sound like a needle dragging across a record. He deepens the kiss, and I push closer in between his knees, and wild horses could not drag me away from this man and this room. I will kiss him until I die of exhaustion. When I feel the sharp edge of his teeth on my lips, I know I'm not alone in this.

I let the dress drop and step out of it, bending to pick it up. Self-consciousness prevails and I hide behind it a little, until I look so silly that I have no choice to hold it aside. I had to wear an ivory bodysuit under the dress, like a little swimsuit, to give it a smooth line, and it has little suspenders holding up my stockings. Sleepy-saurus, it ain't.

Josh looks like he's been stabbed in the gut.

"Holy shit," he says faintly.

I hand him the dress and put my hand on my hip. His eyes eat every line and curve of me, even as his hands neatly fold my dress in half. My legs are ridiculously short, and I don't have the benefit of my heels, but the way he looks at me makes my tiny knees weak.

"You've gone a bit quiet on me here, Josh." I slide my finger under the shoulder strap of this ridiculous thing I'm wearing, and pause. I see his throat swallow.

I put my hands on his neck, squeeze briefly in a strangle, then slide them down. He's so solid, heavy, the heat radiating from within the muscles flexing under my palms. I step in closer, and put my face into his throat, and breathe him in. I close my eyes and beg myself to remember this. *Please, remember this when you're a hundred years old.*

His hands slide down my waist to take my butt in both hands, and when I begin to kiss his throat he squeezes me tighter.

"Shirt off. Come on now." My voice is rough and cajoling. He begins unbuttoning his shirt, looking dazed. When he shrugs out of the shirt I can see his back in the reflection of the dresser mirror. "You've still got paintball bruises. I do too."

My free hand is groping along his chest, and I break off the kiss to watch myself do it. The muscles are all stacked together like LEGOs. I press my fingertips to watch his flesh give. His hands haven't moved from my ass, but his fingertips have slid down to stroke the little ribbons holding up my stockings. To stop myself from making an embarrassingly loud moan I kiss him again, wriggling closer to him.

"I had it all planned." He finally finds his voice again, moving me backward smoothly to the bed. He hauls the coverlet away and lays me back against the sheets with easy strength.

"It was going to be a little more romantic than a hotel room."

Josh, thinking about romance? My heart can't take it. He captures my mouth in a kiss, and it's so gentle I could cry.

"See," he says into my mouth. "I don't hate *you,* Lucy."

His tongue touches mine, tentative, shy. He drops himself down on his elbows, caging me with his biceps, and it triggers the memory of him pressing me against a tree, shielding me, covering me.

I was always covering for you.

I sigh, and he breathes it in. "That's it . . ."

I stretch and wriggle underneath his weight. "You're so big. It gets me hot."

"And you're so tiny. It makes me wonder about all the ways we'll fit together. It's all I've been thinking about since the day we met."

"Oh, sure. The momentous day you looked at me, head to toe, then out the window."

He's giving my throat the softest bites imaginable. He slides his fingers into mine above our heads and we're now holding hands. How did we get back here? To this tender place after the blaze of anger burned us both up? It's so sweet, so completely soft and gentle and *Josh.*

"If we do this tonight, I'm not going to let you get weird on me." His eyes are solemn as he braces himself up a little. "Are you going to have one of your infamous freak-outs?"

"I don't know. Very possibly." I try for a joke but he's not remotely amused.

"I wish I knew how much I have of you. How much do I get?" He's kissing me on the throat again, fingers tightening on mine.

"Until the interviews, you get it all," I say into his skin, and he lets out a shaky breath, like I've offered him forever, not a few days.

We begin kissing again, and the friction of my thigh against his groin is spurring him into a slightly heavier rhythm. His mouth is wet, soft, delicious. The moment he stops, even to take a proper breath, I tug him back.

After an eternity, he tangles his hand in the strap on my shoulder. He runs it lasciviously through his fingers pulling it taut, releasing it with the faintest snap, and then does it again.

"The zip's at the side," I tell him. Technically I think I begged him.

He ignores me completely and instead slides his finger down to the bow between my breasts. "The smallest bow I've ever seen." He dips his head and bites it.

We're going so slowly, I wouldn't be surprised to open my eyes and see daylight. He's always completely different from what I expect. Soft instead of hard. Slow instead of fast. Shy instead of brash. My previous boyfriends and any of their egg-timer foreplay attempts are distant memories now that I'm experiencing the intense pleasure of lying underneath Josh.

He slides a hand into my hair and the scrape of his nails against my scalp makes my skin break into goose bumps. He licks them. He coils up smoothly to kneel between my feet, seemingly just for a better view. It works for me. I watch his stomach flex, and I make a sound like *ohhgah*.

"How do you even look like this?"

"I don't have anything better to do than go to the gym."

"You do now."

I sit up too and drag my mouth across the muscles, and I do what I've always wanted to. I get my hands on his ass, and it is fabulous.

His hands slide into my hair and I begin making out with his stomach. I can't help myself. I find a little bit of hair, and look up to see he's got a light dusting on his chest, in a line down, disappearing beyond the waistband of his suit pants.

"Horny eyes," he tells me shakily.

"No kidding. I want to snort you. You always smell amazing." I press my nose into his skin and breathe in as hard as I can, and he begins to laugh. I look up at him and grin.

His fingers are resting on the zip at my side.

"I'm completely covered in bruises," I say by way of a disclaimer. I suck my stomach in, looking at his abs.

"You're cute when you get shy. I'll go slow." He eases one strap down, lets it rest against my arm. He does the same with the other one. He bites his lip. "I'm going to sit down. I feel too tall."

There's a brief reshuffle when he leans against the headboard and I settle between his legs and rest back against him. His hands spread over my shoulders, and my eyes close as he begins to rub, the sweetest, most strangely timed massage. Most men would be unzipping and feeling by now, but he's not most men.

"You sat like this when you were sick."

He continues to massage, the friction between us blooming outward. He scoops my hair away and presses his mouth on the side of my neck. I'll barely be able to remember my own name at this rate.

He slides his hand into the satin and weighs my bare breast in his hand. Slowly, gently, his fingers pinch.

"Oh, yeah," he groans, and presses his mouth back to my neck.

I hear the sound I make. The kind of harsh intake people usually make from extreme pain. Except I feel like I'm halfway to orgasm.

"Imagine all the things we're going to do," he says, almost to himself.

"I don't want to imagine. I want to know." My feet are scrambling uselessly against the sheets, like I'm being electrocuted.

"You will. But tonight isn't enough, I can already feel it. I've always told you, I need days. Weeks."

I barely notice the zipper sliding down. He's easing me out of the stretchy satin, because the feeling of his big palms smoothing over me is sublime. I'm being coddled and patted, skin warmed, everything admired. When I manage to open my eyes, his breath is steaming hot underneath my ear and the cream fabric is puddled at my waist. He unclips my stockings and leans over my shoulder to look at me.

"Mmm." He hooks his fingers into the sides of the fabric at my hips, tugs it down my legs and I'm naked except for my stockings.

I see the leg of his suit pants, which makes my nudity feel even more vulnerable. I bring my knees up, trying to hide myself, but there's no point. He makes kind, soothing sounds against the back of my ear. His huge hand strokes down my hip, my thigh, then clasps my waist. The other hand follows suit.

"Lucy," is all he can seem to say. "Lucy. How am I going to walk away from tonight? Seriously. How?"

I get goose bumps. I'm wondering the same thing. I let my head drop to one side, and we kiss.

I'm hoarse and breathless. "I'm gonna die tonight. Please take your pants off."

"I want that embroidered on a pillow," he says, and I laugh until I'm gasping.

"You're so funny. I've always thought so. I could never laugh, but I wanted to."

"Ah, so that's one of your rules." He slides off the bed, hand on the button at his waistband. "So the aim of the game is to not laugh?"

"The aim is to make the *other* person laugh. Come on. I'm getting cold." I'm getting impatient, more like. He pulls the sheets and blankets over me when I shiver and I watch him like a lecherous creep as he manages to ease the zip down on his pants.

"I have my own rules. And the aim of the game is different for me."

Watching Josh take off a pair of suit pants is on another level. He's in these stretchy black trunks. They're badly bent out of shape in front.

"Do tell. Come on."

He slides those shorts down, and my mouth drops open. Seems that even my fevered imagination was woefully inadequate. I'm about to tell him that he is *glorious* when he snaps the lamp and we are plunged into darkness.

"No! Josh, that's absolutely not fair. Light on. I want to look at you."

I flail my arm at the lamp but when he slides into the blankets and I register the warmth of his body against mine, we make identical sounds of disbelief. Skin to skin. The heat of it.

I have no idea where he is precisely. He's all over me. I think I feel his breath in my hair, but we roll a little and when he sighs it's down near my rib cage. It's disconcerting and erotic and I nearly jolt out of my skin when he slides one hand across my ribs.

Another hand is dispensing with my stockings, smoothing down my legs. He's touching my ankle and gently pinching at the little curve of my waist. I've got hands sliding all over me.

"You're so soft it's ridiculous. Everywhere my hand slides, you fit me. I was so right."

He demonstrates. Throat. Breast. Ribs. Hips. Then he shows me his mouth fits perfectly too. My skin heats with every kiss and press. He licks at the sheen of sweat beginning to mist across me, and I hear a faraway sound that I realize is me. Whimpering, begging noises. He takes no notice and shows no pity. He presses his perfect mouth on whatever section of skin he pleases. Inch by inch, he is charting me like a map. Which is all very well, except that Josh has a body that I need to get my hands on. When he's partway through traversing the upper curve of my spine, my pleading whispers begin to wear him down.

"Please let me touch you."

He relents and rolls me over, and I run my hands down his neck to the big muscles at the tops of his arms. I squeeze. I bite. I use both hands to stroke down one bicep, weighing the muscle in my hand. It's such a pleasure, to be touching someone else. It's satin, this skin. My palms tingle from stroking it. My mouth fits everywhere that I can kiss him. My eyes are adjusting, and I can see the glint in his eye as I take my time, testing every new muscle, tendon, and joint that I encounter.

In the dark, I slide my body against his, feeling his sighs, and I tug him down to lie on me properly.

"I'm pretty heavy. I'll flatten you."

"I've had a good life."

He laughs, husky and pleased, and obeys me, pressing me down so firmly into the mattress I lose half the air in my lungs.

"Oh, so good. So heavy. I love it."

He kneels up after another minute because I am gradually dying. I reach down between us and take hold of his intriguing hardness. He lets me fondle and play until his every broken breath convinces me of the fact that he's falling apart at the seams, and it's because of me. I can't think of anything more I could win. But then I feel his mouth against my hip bone, and then he starts kissing my thighs.

I have to laugh, both from the tickling of his stubble and the memory of our uniform argument from a lifetime ago. He kisses my thighs in openmouthed reverence, whispering things I can't properly hear. They feel like they must be complimentary words; the hot breath punctuated with licks, bites, more kisses. I could never withstand the soft pressure of this mouth, and there's no doubting his intention. My legs fall open, and I stare into the dark at the ceiling.

The first touch is a swirl. The kind of lick you'd make to the top of a melting ice cream cone. I breathe in so hard I nearly snort, and he kisses my inner thigh, a reward. I can't form any human words.

The second is a kiss, and I think of his signature first-date kiss; chaste, soft, no tongue. The promise of everything to come. I hug a pillow and decide he's never going on a first date with anyone, ever again.

The third is a kiss again, but it disintegrates from chaste to dirty so slowly I barely know when it's changed. He's got all the time in the world and with each minute ticking by, my body simultaneously relaxes and winds tighter. I find my voice and manage to sound crisp and prissy.

"I don't think there's anything about doing this in the HR manual."

I can feel him shiver and groan. "Sorry," he tells me. "You're right." He doesn't stop, but continues to flaunt the HR regulations for an untold number of minutes.

I'm shaking closer and closer to the blinding personal explosion I feel nearby on the horizon. Frankly I'm surprised I've lasted this long. I put a hand down and sink my fingers into his hair and tug.

"I can't handle it. Please. I need more. Way, way more." I slide away, clutching at him, pulling him up by the arm with superhuman strength. He sighs indulgently and kneels up, and I finally hear that magic foil-rip.

His voice would sound authoritative when he speaks next, except it has a shaky, breathless edge, totally undermining his efforts.

"I'm finally having you."

"I'm finally having *you*," I counter.

He drops down and I'm surprised when the lamp flicks on. Dazzled, I close my eyes, and when I open them, he's looking at me. The black-sapphire facets of his eyes are doing strange things to my heart.

"Hey, Shortcake." Our fingers tangle again above my head.

The first press he makes is gentle and my body takes, and then takes some more. He's pressing his temple to mine, making desperate sounds, like he's in pain, like he's trying to live through this. I involuntarily clench and he jerks forward, hard. My head nearly hits the headboard and I laugh.

"Sorry," he says, and I kiss his cheek.

"Don't apologize. Do it again."

Chapter 26

We've never played the Staring Game with you inside me." His hips flex a little, and my eyelids start to flutter.

I was expecting the pleasure and pressure, given that he's huge and I'm small, but it's emotion now tightening my throat until I can't reply. It's his eyes, and the expression in them as he begins to roll his hips, slick and easy. There's no hard impact, no teeth-chattering thuds. He moves against me with measured control. This is the hottest moment of my life. I can't process each sensation. A feeling similar to freaking out is beginning to fill my chest.

I can't keep my composure under his eyes. Passionate eyes. Intense, fierce, fearless eyes. He wants me to hand over everything. He won't take anything less from me.

"Talk to me." He touches my nose with his. His breath is heavy and even.

"You were right . . . you fit me, somehow. Oh, that's so nice." I can barely speak. "I'm freaking out slightly."

"Nice, huh?" He looks at me with amusement. "I can always do better than nice."

He lets go of my fingertips, slides a hand under each of my thighs and lifts me a few inches off the bed.

"Nice is good, nice is good," I babble. My next sound is a groan.

Joshua Templeman really, *really* knows what he's doing.

My eyes roll back into my head. I know they do, because he smiles a bit and moves his hips again. The blankets fall away, and I'm front row, looking up his gorgeous flexing muscles, to his face.

"I'm not nice," he tells me. Slowly, we begin to stretch against each other, and it's more rolling friction. I've never felt anything like it. It confirms that no guy I've ever been with has done it right. Until now.

He's frowning a little in concentration. It's got to be the angle he's created so easily that seems to nudge a little switch inside my body.

"Hey." He hits it again, and the pleasure is so intense a sob catches in my throat. Again and again. I've never played this game before.

I have no strength to raise my arms to his shoulders. Every distinct slide of his body into mine is taking me one step closer to something I'm fairly sure will kill me.

"Are you tired?" I try to be considerate but instead he picks up the pace.

Sweat begins to mist my skin. My hands scrabble for purchase on the sheets. If I'm a deadweight, it doesn't seem to bother him. All I can do is press my shoulders against the mattress and try to survive this.

"I'm dying," I warn him. "Josh, I'm dying."

Josh lifts one of my ankles to rest on his shoulder. His arm hugs my leg, and he studies my face with interest as he increases his pace further. His eyebrows pinch together. The Staring Game is the absolute best when Josh is hitting my lifelong nonexistent G-spot. The one that exists now.

"Holy. Holy . . . Josh."

When he laughs in response it's nearly my undoing.

Here's my problem. This doesn't happen. First sex with someone is awkward and you take turns and try to work out each other's likes and dislikes. There's no simultaneous wet dirty screwing and trying to *delay* your orgasm. But I am. And he knows it.

"Lucy. Quit holding off."

"I'm not," I protest, but for my lie he increases his force. I babble a thank you.

"You're welcome," he tells me and angles me higher. I have no idea how he's not tired. I will write a thank-you card to his personal trainer. If my hand can ever grip a pen again. I bite my lip. I can't let this end. I tell him so.

"Forever, do this forever," I beg. I'm near tears. "Don't stop."

"Stubborn aren't you, Shortcake."

"I can't let this end. Please, Josh. Please, please, please . . ."

He presses his cheek against my calf in such a sweetly affectionate gesture.

"It won't end," he tells me.

I can see he's starting to lose himself a little. His eyes are lit in a bright haze, and I see him raise them to the ceiling, praying for something. His gorgeous skin is glowing gold in the lamplight.

It's a smooth, deep rolling thrust like any of the others, but I break.

It's not a sweet, tame thing sweeping over me. My teeth snap together, I grip on to him and wring myself out. The anguished sound I make probably wakes every single person in the hotel, but I can't hold it in. It's violent. I nearly kick him in the jaw but he grabs my foot and holds on to me. The pleasure boils over, my body twists, squeezes, shakes me out, and I'm out-of-my-mind crazy for Joshua Templeman. He's right. This will not be enough. I need days of this. Weeks. Years. Millions of years.

I'm falling, completely falling, and I look up as he falls too.

He leans down against my leg and I feel him shaking in release. He looks down at me, eyes suddenly shy, and I raise my hand to stroke his cheek.

He lowers me down carefully. I can't imagine how I'll let him go. I wrap my arms around his shoulders and press my mouth to his eyebrow and my chest has a cleaned-out feeling like I've run a few miles. He must feel like he's done a triathlon.

He looks up at me. "How You Doing?" he whispers softly.

"I'm a ghost. I'm dead."

"I didn't know I was lethal," he says and begins to pull away from me, achingly slowly. I beg and plead and say, *No, no, no.* I'm an addict, completely hooked, already wanting my next fix while the current one is still running brightly through my veins. My body tries to hold on to him but he kisses my forehead and apologizes.

"I'm sorry, I gotta," he says and walks away into the bathroom. I watch his backside and drop back into the pillows.

Best sex of my entire life. Best backside I have ever seen.

"Is that a fact?" he says from the other room. Seems I said it aloud.

I lay my forearm over my eyes and try to regulate my

breathing. I feel the mattress dip and he pulls the blankets up over my chilling skin, and turns off the lamp.

"Now you're going to be unbearable. But goddamn, Josh. Goddamn." I'm slurring.

"Goddamn, yourself," he says, and I'm tugged into the cradle of his arms. I press my cheek against him, delighting in his sweat.

"Let's work out a game plan for when we wake up. I can't handle it if you go weird on me."

"We'll say good morning politely, then we'll do it again." I sound like I've had a stroke. I fall asleep with my ear pressed to his chest, listening to him laugh.

I SOMEHOW SURVIVE until morning. I'm washing my hands when I glance up at the mirror.

"Oh, shit."

"What?"

I open the door a crack. The room is dimly lit by strobes of light through the heavy curtains.

"I forgot to take off my makeup. I look like Alice Cooper again."

My eye makeup is smudged black and it makes my eyes look milky-blue and lurid.

"Again? You've looked like Alice Cooper before?"

"Yeah, the morning after I was sick, I nearly screamed when I saw myself." I brush my teeth and get my hair into a bun.

"I like you when you look a little wrecked."

"Well, you'd like me right now then."

I'm in the shower and trying in vain to get the tiny packet of soap open when I hear the door creak and he's joining me, calmly, like we do this every day. Lust electrifies me; the strangest mix of joy and fear.

"It's a Shortcake-sized soap," he comments, taking it from me and biting the package. He pinches the little coin of soap out and holds it up between forefinger and thumb.

"I am going to enjoy this."

I am so dazzled by the sight of his velvety gold skin being streaked with water I can't do anything for a few minutes except stare, my tongue peeking out the corner of my mouth like a hungry dog. The water channels down between each muscle, before overflowing and sheening the flat planes.

The shading of hair begins in the center of his chest, fanning outward to his nipples, and moving downward in a thin line toward his navel. After being bombarded with a million billboards of shiny men in their underwear, I nearly forgot men have hair. I follow the water down, the thicker hair, the imposing jut of his erection. All of it wet. Beautifully veined, enough to make my knees lose their strength. He was inside me. I need it again. I need it so many times I lose count.

"You are . . ." I shake my head. I have to close my eyes, to remember how to speak English. He's too much. I can't have possibly captured this big golden creature inside a glass hotel shower, and he's looking at me with those eyes I love so much.

"Oh, no, I'm hideous," he whispers, mock tragic, and I feel the soap press against my collarbone. It starts to swirl in a little circle, sticky then slick.

"My personal trainer was so sure this disguise would help with women. What a fucking waste of time and energy."

I drag my eyes open, and they must look like I've been in an opium den because he laughs.

I press my thumb into the smile line on his cheek. "You're gorgeous. Beautiful. I can't believe you."

I back away until I'm pressed against the tiles, to get a better view, and now it's his turn to look at every wet inch of me. My arms ache with the effort it takes to not cover myself. His perfect muscles make me look very squishy in comparison. His eyes darken as he looks at me from head to toe.

"Get over here," he says faintly. I take his hand when he holds it out.

What a way to start the day. Showering with my colleague and nemesis.

As soon as the thought materializes, I know it's so outdated I can't keep lying to myself. He tugs me away from the freezing tile and faces me toward the spray, rechecking the temperature before he pushes me under. Then he puts his arms around me from behind and gives me what can only be described as a cuddle. I press back firmer against his arousal to feel him groan.

"How You Doing? Not weird? Freaking out?" He smoothes lather under my breasts, down my ribs. He lifts my arm to inspect it, and we compare hand sizes.

"No, I'm fine. How come we don't have to worry about you getting weird? Most girls have to worry about guys making up an early-morning training session so they can escape. And in this case it's not implausible."

"I've been ready for this for a lot longer than you have," he says. He seems to know I don't want to get my hair wet, and turns us a little. His slippery hands coast along my hips.

"Oh."

"Yes."

"How long?"

"A very long time."

"I never guessed."

"I'm very secretive." He is gently amused.

I capture the soap, which is fast on its way to becoming a translucent sliver. I stick it to my palm, and it gives me a good excuse to stroke over his body, while his tongue licks at the water droplets on my jaw.

We look at each other, nose to nose, eyes half shut, and everything spirals out. The edges are nothing but cold air, but underneath this spray we get hotter and hotter, until I'm sure I'm nearly sweating. It's this kiss.

The minutes and hours fade away when I'm kissing Josh Templeman. There's no arc of the sun rising into the sky, no emptying hot water tank, no checkout time. He takes his time with me. He's a rare man; achieving the almost impossible. He kisses me into the present moment.

It's something I've always had difficulty with in past relationships: turning off my brain. But here, it's only us. Our lips find a rhythm; the gentle upswing of a pendulum, dropping away to the lightest curve, again and again, until there's nothing left for me in this world but his body, mine, and the water spilling over us, destined to refill a cloud.

He makes words like *intimacy* seem inadequate. Maybe it's the way he uses his thumb to tilt my face, the other fingers splayed behind my ear, into my hair. When I try to gasp a mouthful of air, he breathes it into me. My head rolls to the side, dreamy and heavy, and he cups my jaw. I look up at him, and a starburst of emotion expands inside me. I think he sees it in my eyes, because he smiles.

Nothing reminds me of how big his hands are like having them on my body. He cups my ribs in his palms, then slides up to show me how perfectly I fill his hands. When I can't handle much more, he turns me to the wall and his fingers splay wings across my shoulder blades.

Nails scratch down smoothly and he's whispering against my neck.

He's telling me I'm beautiful. The most delicious strawberry shortcake. I'm the taste he'll never get out of his mouth. And that he wants me to be sure, completely sure, before I make a decision about us.

He's licking the water from my shoulders as he eases one broad palm in between my thighs. I feel my foot slide across the tiles an inch. Two. I shiver and he puts an arm across my collarbones.

At the first touch of his fingertip, I hear the sound I make echo around us. He begins to wind me tighter with each gentle circle he draws, and I reach behind me, capturing him in return. Our joint moan creates a cavernous buzz against the tiles.

"Give everything to me," he says into my ear. I repeat it back to him. I've got nothing but wet, hot muscle against me, all around me, his mouth nipping at my earlobe and his strong thrust into my inadequately small hand. He doesn't seem to mind; in fact, he's starting to groan.

I've got problems of my own. Like trying to not make so much noise people outside our room can hear me. It's surprisingly difficult, given the heavenly amount of friction he is giving me. *Shush,* Josh half laughs. I begin to teeter, and his teeth scrape the nape of my neck. I tighten my grip on him. We both stretch taut and snap at virtually the same moment.

This one is an unfurling bloom. His cheek is resting on the tile above me, and we wordlessly look at each other as we shake. It's a strange thing, watching each other come apart. I have a feeling I could get used to this.

There's no possible way to adequately end a moment like this. How does one transition back to reality? This hotel room needs a commemorative plaque.

"Oh shit! Breakfast is soon. We gotta hurry. I need to pack my bag."

"Let's skip it." His hands toy with the curve of my waist and hips. Up, down. In, out.

"Your mom'll be waiting. Come on."

"No," he yowls unhappily, and his hands slide up my shoulders.

"No," I tell him in return and get out of the shower, evading his hands. I wrap myself in a towel and check the time beside the bed.

"Come on, fifteen minutes. Hurry, hurry."

"I'll book the room for another day. We can stay for hours. We could live here."

"Josh. I like your mom. And I don't know if I'm lame for wanting to make her happy, and I don't know if I'll ever see her again after today. I know she misses you. Maybe that's my role in this whole weekend. To force you to be with your family again."

"How sweet. Forcing me to do things I don't want to. And of course you'll see her again."

"Fine. Put it this way. I was invited to breakfast and I'm going. I'm starving. You sexed all of my energy out. You do what you want."

I manage to get some mascara on and half of my top lip done in Flamethrower. Then he eases up behind me and I look at us in the mirror.

The differences between us have never been more stark, or more erotic. The contrast of me against his large, muscled glory almost breaks my resolve. He gathers my hair away from the side of my neck and drops his mouth in a kiss. We make eye contact in the mirror and I let out a broken breath.

I want to tell him, yes, rent this room for the rest of our lives. If I had more time, I could make you love me. The realization has me by the throat.

I'd have to be blind to not see the light of affection in his eyes as he wraps his arms tighter and begins kissing the side of my neck. I'd have to be a thousand years old to forget the way he kisses me. It's the fresh new bud of something that could one day be something remarkable, but I have severe doubts that it could survive in the real world. This bubble we're in? It's not reality. I wish it was, and I wish we lived here. All of this, I should say out loud to him, but I don't have the courage.

I close my eyes. "We can have breakfast and then drive back to your apartment at warp speed."

"Fine. Nice lipstick, by the way."

I manage to get the rest done and I blot once. He takes the tissue before I can scrunch it up. He holds it up to admire it.

"Like a heart."

"How about you buy a little white canvas and I'll kiss it for you. Something to remember me by."

I give him a cute wink to keep the tone light. The sarcastic rejoinder that I am expecting never eventuates, and instead he turns and walks out of the bathroom. When I come out a few minutes later with my makeup bag under my arm he's dressed in jeans and a red T-shirt.

"I've never seen you in red. How come every color in the flippin' rainbow suits you?"

He puts my cell phone near my purse, and the white rose he saved from his lapel.

"You just think they do." He zips his bag and stands at the window, looking out at the water.

I dig in my bag for my own jeans and the black cashmere sweater I'm glad I packed. The air down here is colder, fresher than I'm used to. I'm getting dressed and he's not watching. I hop slightly to get the jeans zipped up and he doesn't turn. I loudly squirt perfume into my cleavage and he doesn't even flare a nostril.

"Breakfast is going to be fine."

"Yeah, sure," he says faintly.

I stick my feet into some flats and decide to leave my hair in its big messy damp bun. I walk up behind him and hug his waist, resting my cheekbone against the lower curve of his shoulder blade.

"Tell me what's wrong."

"I'm a one-night stand. This is everything I've been trying to avoid. I've been trying to build something, not give you some sense of closure."

"No! Hey. How have I made you feel this way?" I tug on his elbow until he faces me.

"You're constantly talking like it's already over. A lipstick kiss to remember you by? Why am I going to need reminding, exactly?"

"We're not working together much longer."

"I haven't wanted you this long, and gone through so much, and given up so much, to have you for one night. It's not enough."

He's right, of course. The interview result hangs over us like a scythe. A flash of impatience hits me.

"Can I stay at your place tonight?" It's all I can think of to say. "Can I sleep in your bed?"

"I guess," he says sulkily, and I tug him by the loops on his jeans over to his suitcase.

I look back at the bed. How so much could have

changed in one space? Maybe he's thinking the same thing. He kisses my eyebrow so gently I feel tears begin to prick behind my eyes.

I catch a glimpse of the receipt when we check out. It was roughly a week's rent for this magical hotel room. He slashes his signature like Zorro onto it, and hugs me close. My cheek presses against his perfect pectoral.

"And did you have a nice stay?"

The elegantly groomed receptionist is smiling a little too widely at Josh as she processes the checkout. She seems to be willfully ignoring my presence, or maybe she's just dazzled. I look at her slicked-back blond-coil hairdo. Her chalky pink lipstick is too bright against her tan. Hotel Barbie.

"Yes, thanks," he replies absently. "Great water pressure in the shower."

I look up at his face and watch the corner of his mouth quirk, the little smile line deepening.

The receptionist is definitely imagining him in the shower. Her eyes stray from bicep to computer screen. Screen to his face. She staples and folds and searches for the perfect little envelope for his receipt, even though the customer at the next counter didn't get one.

She fiddles and does a dozen other little things so she can look at little segments of him. She tells him about their loyalty program and how his next check-in will be with a free bottle of wine, and probably her, draped across his bed. She reconfirms his address and phone number.

I'm gimlet-eyed with annoyance. He doesn't notice, and begins kissing my temple. Who can blame her, though?

A man built like this, with a face like this, being so ridiculously sweet and tender? I'd die a little too, watching this, and I'm the one on the receiving end. It's like seeing a bruised nightclub bouncer cuddling a tutu-clad toddler, or a cage fighter blowing a kiss to his sweetheart in the front row. Brute, raw masculinity contrasted with gentleness is the most attractive thing on earth.

Josh is the most attractive thing on earth.

I watch her eyes harden speculatively as she glances at me. I spread my hand across his chest. It says, *mine*. The tiny jealous cavewoman in me can't resist.

"Shall we bring your car?"

"Yes," Josh says at the same moment I say, "No."

"No, we're having breakfast. Can we leave our bags here?"

"Of course." She checks Josh's bare left hand. My bare left hand.

"Thank you, Mr. Templeman."

"I need a fake wedding band on you if we ever came back," I grumble as we walk through the lobby to the restaurant.

Josh nearly trips over his own foot. "Why on earth would you say that?"

We walk past the ballroom and I can see cleaners taking down the huge bunches of Mindy-pink balloons.

"The receptionist wanted to jump on you. I can't blame her, but sheesh. I was standing right there. What am I, invisible?"

Josh looks at me sideways. "How primal."

We push through the glass double doors and he pulls me to one side. I crane around the doorframe. I can see his family. I raise my hand to wave but he tugs me back and scolds me unintelligibly.

"It's a buffet." My delight is evident in my voice. "Look at those croissants, plain *and* chocolate. Quick, there's not many left."

"I am going to appeal to you one last time. Let's just go. Things went pretty well yesterday, family-wise. Let's cut our losses."

"And what, screech out of here like Thelma and Louise?"

"They all loved *you*."

"I'm immensely lovable. Josh, come *on*. Croissants. I'm here with you. No one will hurt you as long as I'm here. I've got my invisible paintball gun. Take me in there, feed me pastry, and then drive me back to your pretty blue bedroom."

He presses a little kiss to my lips. I look over my shoulder at the reception desk.

"Come on, be brave. Forget about your dad and focus on your mom. Be a gentleman. I'm going in."

I weave through the room and I have no idea if he's following. If he's not, this is going to be a little awkward.

Chapter 27

At the table by the window sits Elaine and Anthony, and Mindy and Patrick. Everyone stops talking when I approach. I wave like a dork. Everyone looks surprised.

"Hi."

"Lucy! Hello!" Elaine recovers first and looks at the table. Oh. There are no spare chairs. We're barely five minutes late. They clearly weren't expecting us to turn up. Josh is dawdling, thankfully.

"Quick, quick!" I start looking around at other tables.

"More chairs," Elaine gasps. She understands perfectly. If he walks over here and there are no seats for us, he'll shrivel up.

Anthony sits at the daddy-end of the table and continues reading his folded up newspaper. No wait, medical journal. Jeez. He makes no indication he's aware of any other people in the room.

There's a great deal of shuffling and I manage to borrow spare chairs from a nearby table. By the time Josh arrives with a plate of croissants and a cup of tea, we're all sitting as casually as we can, trying to slide the plates back in front of their original owners.

"Good morning," everyone chimes.

"Hi," he says cautiously, and puts the plate and tea in front of me. "I got you the last ones." It's a plate filled with croissants and strawberries. He strokes his hand down the side of my neck.

"Sweet of you. Thanks."

"I'll just get something," he says, and retreats. Elaine watches him, part sad, part amused, and looks at Anthony.

I smile at Mindy to show I'm not upset anymore. I probably have a nuclear post-orgasmic glow. She tentatively smiles back.

"How do you feel, Mrs. Templeman?"

I didn't put too much thought into the question, but the words *Mrs. Templeman* make her physically jolt. Maybe I'm exceptionally empathetic, but I feel like I've dropped a bombshell. The words ring in my ears, off the walls, right through my bones.

Mrs. Templeman. How primal, indeed.

"Wrecked. I'm so tired I feel like I'm dreaming. But in a good way." She breaks into a smile and looks at the tablecloth.

"Mrs. Templeman. It sounds so . . ." She covers her face with her hands and sighs and laughs and dorks. Get out of my head, Mindy.

"Sorry we took a smaller table," Elaine begins, but I shake my head.

"It's okay. I had to use my lasso to get him down here." I mime swinging a rope over my head and the women burst out laughing. The men sit silently, reading and eating.

"I can imagine it. Little cowgirl dragging him behind her, bucking and snorting."

"I don't know why he makes such a big deal of everything," Patrick interjects mildly, taking a quick wincing mouthful of his coffee.

I have a feeling he's always so busy he eats all of his meals in painful scalding gulps and swallows. Maybe it's a doctor thing. Ingest the fuel rather than enjoy it.

"He's shy. Leave him alone."

Patrick frowns at my kid-sister impudence, and then laughs. He glances at Josh.

"Shy. Huh." I can see the realization dawning across his face, like it did mine yesterday. Shyness takes so many different forms. Some people are shy and soft. Some, shy and hard. Or in Josh's case, shy, and wrapped in military-grade armor.

"Josh, Lucy, thank you for the gift," Mindy says when Josh takes his seat. She catches my eye and smiles, clearly thinking I chose it.

"I never did see what he ended up choosing." I take a huge bite of croissant. He's got one arm across the back of my chair, his warm hand spread across my shoulder.

"The most beautiful set of Waterford crystal champagne glasses, engraved with our initials. And two bottles of Moët."

"Good job, Josh."

"The wedding was nice," Josh tells her. I look at his eyes as they assess each other. It's probably the first time they've faced each other since the breakup. I almost quiver with concentration, trying to detect any residual heartbreak, lust, resentment, loneliness. If I had whiskers, they would be twitching.

"Thanks," Mindy replies. She looks at her wedding ring again and then at Patrick with such helpless devotion I look at Josh sharply. If ever he was going to react badly it would be now. He smiles, looks at his plate, and then looks at me. He kisses my temple and I'm convinced.

"How have you kept Lucy a secret from us all?" Mindy says as she cuts her grapefruit.

"Oh, you know. I keep her in my basement."

"It's not as bad as it sounds. He's made it comfy down there." Everyone laughs, except Anthony, naturally.

I have a refreshing realization. I'm not trying. It explains why I'm so comfortable sitting here, eating with strangers. If they like me, fine. If not, I can live. But I feel the same relaxed slouchy feeling I get when sitting with my family. If I tilt my head just right, I can't see Anthony at all.

Mindy lists some of the other gifts they received. Patrick's new gold band winks in the pale sunshine filtering in through the clouds, and he occasionally curls his thumb in to touch it. Mindy watches him, tenderness in her eyes.

Josh's breakfast is two poached eggs, a slice of wheat toast, and a heap of wilted spinach. He drinks his coffee in two swallows. I look at my own plate and pinch my stomach under the table. His body is a temple. Mine will be a hut made of butter at this rate.

"More coffee?" I get up and decide to bring myself back some more fruit. I can't just sit there eating pastry. He snags my wrist and looks up at me.

Stay, his eyes tell me. I pat him kindly and he reluctantly relinquishes his mug.

"I'll be right back. Anyone else?"

I take my time fiddling with the coffee machine. Everything's a little stilted and it does occur to me that I'm essentially an intruder. I'm the only one at the table who's not a Templeman.

As I struggle with the long plastic tongs to get another slice of watermelon, I am dimly aware of sharp tones. I'm piling my plate with a bunch of grapes when realization dawns. Oh shit.

I hurry back to the table and put down my plate and Josh's mug. Mindy is frozen, eyes frightened, and Patrick looks resigned.

"But what I want to know is, why would you throw away premed? Any monkey can get an MBA." Anthony has laid aside his breakfast reading and is staring down Josh, gimlet-eyed.

Seriously, I was away from the table for maybe two minutes. How did this escalate so quickly? I suppose a nuclear bomb has one red button, and that doesn't take long to press. I put my hand on the back of Josh's neck, like I'm holding an attack dog by the collar.

"For fuck's sake. If you knew anything about it, you'd know it's almost impossible to complete an executive MBA while working full-time. And I did it. And I was in the top two percent. I got four job offers, and two of those companies still call me."

"I'm surprised you finished it, if it was so hard," Anthony says. "I thought your favorite hobby was quitting."

"Hey," I blurt. I'm still standing, and I realize I have a hand on my hip.

"Lucy, they're just . . ." Elaine is unsure of what to do. "Maybe you should talk to Josh outside, Anthony."

People at nearby tables are all sitting with cutlery lowered in various stages of avid interest or awkward avoidance.

Josh laughs meanly. "Why, so we can have a good old-fashioned fistfight? He'd just love that."

Anthony rolls his eyes. "You need to—"

"Toughen up? Is that what you're about to say to me? What you've said to me for as long as I've been alive?" Josh glances up at me in exasperation. "Now can we go?"

"I think maybe you should talk this out." Another five years might go by.

"She's one of those touchy-feely types," Anthony says to Elaine. "Fantastic."

Josh's eyes narrow dangerously. "Don't talk about her."

"Well, she can't resist bringing herself into it."

"Be quiet," Elaine says to Anthony. She's furious. "All I asked was for you to be civil. Keep your mouth shut."

I look at Anthony and he looks at me. His eyes are full of derision as he runs his eyes from the top of my head, down. Then he sniffs and looks out the window, obeying his wife, mouth pursed shut.

Oh boy. I'm not putting up with this twice in my life, and certainly not from another Templeman. My temper snaps.

"Your son is incredibly talented. Focused. Ridiculously intelligent. He is instrumental in keeping a publishing house running."

"What, licking stamps? Answering phones?" We lock eyes.

I bark a laugh. "Is that seriously what you think he does?"

"I'm not going to sit here and be spoken to like this by *you*, young woman. I've seen his email signature block. Assistant TO the CEO. I don't know who you think you are."

He's attempting to reestablish his authority. Maybe I'll sit down and be a good little girl. Josh's instinct to protect me is making him rise up out of his chair but I wave him back.

I got this.

"I'm the person who knows your own offspring better than you do. He's the person the finance and sales divisions report to. They're scared fucking shitless of him. I once had a forty-five-year-old man beg me in the hall outside the boardroom to pass on the documents so he wouldn't have to attend. I've seen entire teams scurrying like ants, double-checking, triple-checking their figures. Even then, Josh will always find the mistake. Then usually someone takes a stress day."

Anthony begins to bluster something, but I cut him off. I'm so worked up I could strangle him. Honestly, I could wrap my hands around his neck and squeeze.

I am Lara Croft, guns raised, eyes blazing with retribution.

"The reason Bexley Books didn't completely implode before the merger is Josh recommended that their workforce be reduced by thirty-five percent. I've hated him for it. It was cold-blooded. And he can be, you have no idea. But it meant another one hundred and twenty people kept their jobs. Paid their mortgages. So don't you *dare* try to make out like he's nothing. Oh, and I know for a fact Josh was integral in the merger negotiations. One of the corporate lawyers told me in the kitchen he was, quote, '*a fucking hardass.*'"

I can't seem to stop. It's like I'm purging something.

"His boss, who's the co-CEO in title only, is a fat, sleazy toad so out of his mind on prescriptions he can barely tie a shoelace. Josh is who keeps it all running. Both of us do."

I look at them all. Josh is digging his fingers into the waistband of my jeans.

"I'm sorry I'm making a scene. And I like all of you. Except you." I cut a look at Anthony.

"I spend more time with him than anyone, and I have to tell you, you don't know what you've got. You've got Josh. He's an awkward, difficult asshole. I hate him almost half the time and he drives me mental, and it's clearly hereditary. You gave me the exact same look Josh first did when I met him. Top to bottom, out the window. You know everything about me? You know everything about him? I don't think so."

"I have been trying to give him a boost. Some people need a push," Anthony says.

"You can't have it both ways. You can't completely neglect him, yet trash his choices."

Anthony raises a hand to his brow and rubs it like he's getting a headache. "My father pushed my younger brother."

"And how did he enjoy that?"

His eyes flick sideways. Not too much, I'm guessing.

"He's not a doctor. *Deal with it.*"

Anthony goggles at me.

"But I want you to know something. He could be, if he wanted to. He could be anything he fucking wanted to. Nothing is by mistake. Nothing is because he's not good enough. It's his choice."

I sit down in a huff. Mindy and Patrick look at each other, mouths open. Hell, the entire room is sitting with their mouths open. I hear someone start to clap, then hastily stop.

"I'm sorry, Elaine." I take a huge mouthful of tea, nearly spilling it down my top. My hands are shaking.

"Don't apologize for defending him like that," she says faintly. I suppose what she means by *like that* is like a rabid lioness.

I find the courage to look at Josh. He looks completely shell-shocked.

"I . . ." Anthony trails off and I level my best stare on him. The same withering, emotionless glare I've given his son a thousand times before.

"I . . . er." He clears his throat and looks at his cutlery.

"Yes, Dr. Templeman? Care to share?" My audacity is breathtaking.

"I don't know much about your work, Josh." Everyone's jaw drops even further. Mine doesn't. I will never give him the satisfaction. I stare into his eyes and mentally twist a rusty fish knife into his gut. I raise an eyebrow.

"I'd . . . be interested in talking to you more about it, Josh."

I interject. "Now that you know he's successful? Now you know that he'll almost certainly be promoted to chief operating officer of a major publishing house? You've got something to tell your buddies at golf now."

"Squash," Patrick tells me in an aside. "He plays squash."

I have given Anthony the dressing-down of a lifetime. He is unable to speak. It is wonderful.

"You should love him and be proud of him even if he's in the mailroom. Even if he were unemployed and crazy and living under a bridge. We're leaving now. Elaine, it was a pleasure, I loved meeting you. Mindy, Patrick, congratulations again and enjoy your honeymoon. Sorry I made a scene just now. Anthony, it's been real."

I stand up. "*Now* we screech out of here like Thelma and Louise." Josh stands and goes to kiss his mother's cheek. She grasps helplessly at his wrist.

"But when will I see you?" She looks up at Josh, but she also looks to me.

I can see Josh's jaw tightening, and I can almost hear the excuses forming on his tongue. He might drop off the radar for the Templeman family altogether. The next thing I say surprises even me. Especially given the fact I've essentially just said good-bye to them all for the last time.

"If you can come up to the city soon, we could meet you for lunch. We could go see a movie after. Anthony, you're invited too."

His jaw, which has been hinging loosely, sways in the breeze.

"But only if you're prepared to be civil and start to get to know your son again. I think you know there's going to be no more ragging on Josh. Except by me, because he loves it."

"You and I are going to have a discussion. Outside. Now." Elaine gets to her feet and points to a French door leading to the side gardens. Anthony looks like a man walking to the gallows. I know a fellow rabid lioness when I see her.

I take Josh's hand and we weave through our spellbound audience.

"No charge," the cashier tells me. "Lady, that was better than theater."

I retrieve our bags from the receptionist, thankfully not the lustful blonde this time. I probably would have roundhouse-kicked her head off. Walking together, matching our footfalls, we exit the lobby like two television district attorneys gunning for justice.

I ask the valet for our car, and turn.

"Okay, let me have it." I just made an incredibly embarrassing scene. I can see people talking about me as they wait for their taxis. I'm going to star in twenty different retellings of That Restaurant Incident.

Josh picks me up off the ground. "Thank you," he tells me. "Thank you so much."

When we kiss, I hear some applause.

"You're not mad I rescued you? Boys don't need rescuing."

"This one did. And I'll even let you choose which you wanna be. Thelma, or Louise," he tells me, setting me on my feet as the car arrives.

"You're the good-looking one, I guess you're Thelma."

He slides the driver's seat back. We drive about half a block before Josh bursts out laughing.

"You told my dad it had 'been real.'"

"Like I was a bad TV scriptwriter who thought that's how kids talk."

"Exactly. It was so priceless." He wipes a tear away with his thumb.

"I feel bad about your mom, though. She looked so completely stricken."

"Don't you worry, she is going to kick the shit out of him for that."

"I have no doubt. It's why she and I get along so well."

He thinks for a few moments while driving. "I don't know how I can move on from this, with my dad."

"Nothing's insurmountable." I try to believe my own words.

I roll down the window a little so the breeze is on my face. The sun is warming my legs and Josh is smiling again.

I do not even let myself think about how it is all going to end.

IF THE DRIVE normally takes five hours, I swear Josh cuts it down to three. But the hours mean nothing to us as we wind through the countryside, leaving the sea-salt wind behind us.

The memory is lit by the sun through the trees we drive through, nothing but lemons and copper tones scattering across our arms, lighting our eyes up blue; his sapphire, mine turquoise. I see my face in the car's side mirror and I barely recognize myself.

I've changed. I'm someone new today. Today is a momentous day.

I'll always remember the drive home as a movie montage, and I knew I was in one. Each detail was vividly bright. I knew I'd need the memories one day.

This montage is directed by someone French. A convertible would have been their preference, but the windows are down, so that's something. The air is unseasonably warm and scented like honeysuckle and cut grass.

The montage stars this pretty girl, Flamethrower-red mouth smiling over at a beautiful man. He's looking so achingly cool in his sunglasses you immediately buy a pair for yourself.

He lifts her hand to his mouth and kisses it. Tells her something charming and makes her laugh. It's the sort of moment you want to hit pause on and buy whatever it is they're selling.

Happiness. A better life. Red lipstick and those sunglasses.

The soundtrack should be a lilting indie affair; equal parts hopeful and with a broken, bittersweet lyric hook that makes your heart hurt for some unknown reason. But instead it's scored by the 1980s hair metal I found in an incriminating iPod playlist titled *Gym*.

"You seriously got those abs while listening to Poison and Bon Jovi," I crow, and he can't deny it. It's just us, windows down, stereo cranked, the road curling in front of us like a tongue.

We sing along. The lyrics for songs I haven't heard in years fall out of my mouth. His fingers drum the steering wheel. Life right now is easier than breathing.

We never stop the car. It's like if we stop, even for a rest break, reality will catch us. We're bank robbers. Kids running away from boarding school. Eloping teenage sweethearts.

There's a bottle of water in my bag, and Josh's tin of mints. We share, and it's better than a banquet.

I will eventually confess to myself why this montage means so much. I could try to believe it was because of Monday morning looming, and the one prize dangling above two worthy recipients. Maybe it was because of how alive I felt. So completely young and filled to bursting with the scary, thrilling certainty my life was about to change in a big way.

Possibly it was the thrill of sticking it to the man and the heady rush of standing up to someone terrifying. The thrill of rescuing someone. Being the strong one. Carrying someone; coddling and protecting, defending like a lioness.

Maybe it was the smell of spring in the air; the field of four-leaf clovers we pass. Red roses against a fence. Leather seats and Josh's skin.

No, it was something else; the new knowledge of something irreversible, permanent. It cycled through my head with each revolution of the car's wheels, each pulse of blood in my frail whisper-thin veins. At any moment a tiny valve could buckle under the pressure of the cholesterol from my croissants. At any moment I could die.

But I don't. I fall asleep, my cheek against the warm

seat, my face turned toward him, like it always has been. Like it always will.

I open my eyes a tiny crack. We're in a parking garage.

"We're home," he says.

I think the unthinkable. I should have been thinking it all along. My eyes slide closed and I feign sleep.

"You need to wake up," he whispers. A kiss on my cheek. A miracle.

I love Joshua Templeman.

Chapter 28

We walk into his apartment and he puts my overnight bag with his in the bedroom, like I am returning home. I use the bathroom and when I come out, he's making me a cup of tea with the concentration of a scientist.

He takes one look at my face. "Oh, no. Don't tell me."

My stomach drops out of my body and I grip the edge of the counter. He knows. He's a mind reader. My eyes are love-hearts.

"You're completely freaking out," he states flatly. I can't do anything but make awkward eye-slides and lip-nibbles. I look at his front door. I can't get past him, he'll be too quick.

"No chance. Get on the couch," he scolds. "Get. Go on."

I slip my shoes off and go and scrunch myself in a ball on his couch, hugging the ribbon-cushion.

He's right, I am completely freaking out. It's the mother of all freak-outs. I've completely lost my voice.

I talk to myself in the privacy of my head.

You love him. You love him. You always have. More than you've ever hated him. Every day, staring at this man, knowing every color and expression and nuance.

Every game you've ever played has been to engage with him. Talk to him. Feel his eyes on you. To try to make him notice you.

"I'm such an idiot," I breathe.

I open my eyes and nearly scream. He's standing over me with a mug and a plate.

"I simply can't condone this level of freak-out," he says, and gives me a sandwich. He puts the mug on the coffee table. He disappears for a minute then comes back with my gray fleecy blanket.

It's like he *knows* I've had some kind of shock. He tucks me in on all sides, brings me an extra pillow. Who knows what my face looks like. I avoided looking at myself in the bathroom.

My teeth begin to chatter and I reach for what is quite a good-looking sandwich. No shoddy workmanship here. It's even cut in half diagonally; my favorite.

I chew like a chipmunk, using my tiny prehensile paws to rip off the crust. I've got bright, shifty button eyes and puffed-up cheeks.

"You have not said a word to me since I woke you up. You look shell-shocked. Your hands are shaking. Low blood sugar? Bad dreams? Carsick?"

He discards his plate, his sandwich untouched.

"You're still tired. You have stomach pains." Josh begins to rub my feet through the blanket. When he speaks again, it's so low I can barely hear.

"You've realized what a mistake you've made, being with me."

"No," I blurt through my mouthful. I close my eyes. The worried line on his brow is killing me.

"No?"

I feel terrible. I'm ruining what was the beautiful bubble of energy from our drive home.

"Today is Sunday," I respond after a lot of deliberation.

"Tomorrow is Monday," he returns. We both sip from our mugs. The Staring Game has commenced, and I am welling up with questions I am dying to ask, but I have no idea how to go about it.

"Truth or Dare," he says. He always knows the exact right thing to say.

"Dare."

"Coward. Okay, I dare you to eat the entire jar of hot mustard I have in my fridge."

"I was hoping for a sexy dare."

"I'll get you a spoon."

"Truth."

"Why are you freaking out?" He takes a bite of sandwich.

I sigh so deeply my lungs hurt. "I wasn't ready for this, and I am having some scary feelings and thoughts."

He studies me, looking for any trace of lie. He can't find any. It's abbreviated, but it's the truth.

"Truth or Dare?"

"Truth," he says, unblinking. There is some low afternoon light coming through the windows and I can see the cobalt facets of his eyes. I have to close mine a moment until the pain of his beauty eases.

"What are the marks in your planner?" It pops into my head. He didn't answer last time; I doubt he will now.

He smiles and looks at his plate. "It's a bit juvenile."

"I'd expect nothing less of you."

"I record whether you're wearing a dress or skirt. *D*, or *S*. I make a mark when we argue, and I make a mark when I see you smile at someone else. Also, when I wish I could kiss you. The dots are just my lunch break."

"Oh. Why?" My stomach trills.

He considers. "When you get so little of someone, you take what you can get."

"How long have you done it?"

"Since the second day of B and G. The first day was a bit of a blur. I've always meant to compile some stats. Sorry. Saying it aloud sounds insane."

"I wish I'd thought of doing it, if it makes you feel better. I'm equally insane."

"You cracked the shirt code pretty quick."

"Why do you even wear them in sequence?"

"I wanted to see if you noticed. And once you did notice, it pissed you off."

"I've always noticed."

"Yeah, I know." He smiles, and I smile too. I feel him take my foot in his hands and he begins to rub.

"Those days-of-the-week shirts have been oddly comforting." I lie back and look at the ceiling. "No matter what's going on, I know I'm going to walk in and see white. Off-white. Cream. Pale yellow. Mustard. Baby blue. Bedroom blue. Dove. Navy. Black." I'm ticking them off on my fingers.

"You forgot, poor old mustard has been replaced. Anyway, you won't be seeing my stupid shirts soon. Mr. Bexley has told the interview panel to have a decision by Friday."

"But that's only a day after the interview." I'd thought maybe there would be a week or two of deliberation. I'm going to either be victorious or unemployed next Friday? "I feel sick."

"He's told them if they haven't worked out who's the right candidate five minutes into the interview, they're morons."

"He better not try to sway the interview panel. We need this to be fair. Ugh, I hadn't thought about reporting to Mr. Bexley directly, without you as the buffer. I tell you, Josh, the man has x-ray eyes."

"I want to blind him with acid."

"You keep a vial of acid in your drawer?"

"You should know. You've been snooping in my desk and planner."

There is censure in his tone but his eyes remain friendly as he slides his thumb into my arch and makes me purr.

"You'd resign, if I got the job?" He says it gently.

"Yes. I'm sorry, but I'd have to. At first it was my pride making me say it. But now it's clearly the only option. I want you to know, that if they decide you're a better fit for the role, I'll resign happily. I'll be happy for you, Josh, I swear. I know more than anyone how hard you've worked for it."

I arch a little and sigh. "You'd be my boss. It'd be hot as hell, making out with the COO every chance I got, but we'd get caught for sure."

"But if you get it?"

"I can't expect you to resign, but I can't be your boss. I'd give you inappropriate tasks and Jeanette would have a stroke."

"And if I were your boss, I'd work you so fucking hard. *So* fucking hard."

"Mmmm. I'd have dirty dreams all night."

"You told my parents I was probably about to be chief operating officer. Did you mean it, or were you just adding to your long list of brags about me? It's okay if you didn't mean it."

"If I were the recruiting panel, I'd look at our CVs side by side and you'd probably edge me out. You're so good at what you do. I've always admired how well you work."

I rub my hand on my chest to try to relieve the ache.

"Not necessarily. It's not just the CVs. There's the interviews. You're charming. There's not a person alive who doesn't adore you instantly."

"Says you. I've seen you in action, when you're making an effort. You're like a 1950s politician. Smoother than smooth."

He laughs. "But you love B and G. And everyone there hates me. That's your advantage over me. Plus you have your top-secret weapon Danny is spending his weekends on."

"Yeah." I dart my eyes away.

"It's got to do with ebooks, I'm not an idiot," Josh says.

"Why can't you be an idiot for once? Just once, I want to keep a secret from you."

"You're keeping a secret from me right now. We haven't gotten to the root cause of your freak-out."

"And we're not going to." I pull the blanket over my head altogether.

"Very mature," he comments and swaps my feet, squeezing my toes and circling his thumbs. "You can't keep secrets from me for long. I know you too well. I'll get it out of you."

"Well apparently I'm a complete open ebook." I groan in the dark. "Did Mr. Bexley tell you about my digitalization project? Please don't screw me on this, Josh. Please. My entire presentation is based on it."

"Do you seriously think I'd do that to you?"

"No. Well, maybe."

I expect a whip-crack response. He says nothing, but continues to massage my foot.

I flip the blanket off my face. "Why didn't you smile at me when we first met, and say, *Pleased to meet you*?

We could have been friends all this time." It feels like a tragedy. I've lost so much, and we have no time left.

"We could never have been friends."

I try to pull my foot back but he holds on to it.

"So that's a sore point." He squeezes the arch.

"I've always wanted to be friends with you. But you didn't smile back. You've been one-up ever since."

"I couldn't. If I'd let myself smile back, and be friends with you, I probably would have fallen in love with you."

It's all the past tense of that statement that kills the leap of joy inside. Because he didn't, and he isn't. I try to brush over it.

"You said that to me after the elevator kiss. We'd never be friends."

"I was angry at the time. I was delivering you to Danny, and you were looking hotter than hell."

"Poor Danny. He's so nice. You'll have to apologize for how you hung up on him. He's been nothing but nice to me and all I've done is give him two shitty dates and made him lose a Saturday."

"He got to kiss you." When he says that, Josh looks like he wants to destroy planets. "And he's not doing the freelance work completely out of the goodness of his heart."

"Under different circumstances he'd be a great boyfriend."

Josh is making black scary serial killer eyes at me. "Different circumstances."

"Well, I'm assuming you're going to chain me in your basement and keep me as your sex slave."

This conversation is like a tightrope. One misstep and he'll know. He'll know I'm in love, and then I'll wobble and fall. No safety net.

"I don't have a basement."

"Too bad for me."

"I'll buy us a house with a basement."

"Okay. Can I come with you when you house hunt?"

I smile despite the doomed sensation dripping into my blood. I love the energy we create between us when we banter like this. It's the most intense sensation of pleasure, knowing he'll always have the perfect response ready. I've never known anyone like him; as addictive to talk to as he is to kiss.

"Truth or Dare," he says after a bit.

"It's not my turn."

"Yes, it really is."

"Truth." I have no choice. He'll dare me to eat the mustard again.

"Do you trust me?"

"I don't know. I want to. Truth or Dare?"

He blinks. "Truth. It's all truth from this point forward."

"Have you ever lived here with a girlfriend?"

"No. I've never lived with anyone. Why do you ask?"

"Your bedroom is girly."

Josh smiles to himself. "You're such a moron sometimes."

"Thanks. Hey, should I go home? I don't have anything to wear tomorrow."

"Would you believe, I own my own washer and dryer."

"How newfangled." I go into his bedroom and kneel on the floor to unzip my bag. "I hope Helene doesn't notice I'm in the same outfit."

"I'd say the only person at B and G who notices that much about you will be the same one who laundered those walk-of-shame clothes."

I sit up on my heels and look at his bedroom. He's put the Smurf I gave him beside his bed. There's also white roses, petals unfurled and loose. He didn't have a vase, so he used a jar. I close my eyes. I can't move for a bit.

I love him so much it's like a thread piercing me. Punching holes. Dragging through. Stitching love into me. I'll never be able to untangle myself from this feeling. The color of love is surely this robin's-egg blue.

When his feet appear in the doorway I take my dirty clothes and hug them to my chest. "No looking at my underwear."

"That would be rude," he agrees. "I will close my eyes."

I sit on his bed. I smooth my hands over the covers, twiddling the silky thread count. I push one fist into his pillow. He dreams. He lives. And he will do it all without me. He finds me sitting there with my head in my hands.

"Shortcake," he says, and I know he is genuinely regretful.

It's the strangest sensation. I need to confide in him. He's the one person I should not trust, but I'm nearly bursting with the secret that I love him and it is hurting me.

"Talk to me. I want to know why you're upset. Let me work this out."

"I'm scared of you." I'm scared of him finding out my biggest, newest secret.

He doesn't look offended. "I'm scared of you too."

When our mouths touch, it's like it's for the first time. Now that I have this pale blue love running through me, the intensity is too much. I try to pull back but he smoothly lays me back.

"Be brave," he tells me. "Come on, Luce."

My mouth is filled with my heart and his breath when we kiss again. I can feel myself trembling as he tastes my fear.

"Ah," he says. "I think I'm beginning to see what the issue is."

"No you don't." I twist my face away. The sun is setting outside on this confusing day, and the light filters through his filmy drapes, pearlescent and pretty. The entire moment is frozen, date stamped and slotted into my memory vault.

He kisses me like he knows me. Like he understands me. I raise my hand to push him away, and he links his fingers into mine. I bite him, and he smiles against my lips. I slide my knee up to get enough leverage to slide away, and he hooks a hand under my leg.

"You're beautiful when you're scared," he tells me.

I can't speak as he trails his mouth to my ear. He sighs. My world narrows down a little more. When he kisses my pulse, I know he is thinking about all of my tiny inner miracles and the first tear wells up in my eye. It slides down my cheek, down my neck.

"We're getting somewhere now," he tells me as he licks my tear.

I raise my hands into his hair, and press him to me as he presses soft kisses like stamps down my neck. Each pushes me deeper in love. When he smoothes his hand down my torso I wince.

"Let Doctor Josh take a look," he says, pulling off my sweater and T-shirt in one motion.

He smoothes a steady hand down my throat, over my bra, between my breasts, to my belly. The light in here is brightly diffused, and he can see every vein and pastel paintball bruise as he looks down at me, eyelashes fanned so perfectly I feel the next tear coming.

I love him so much I can't hold it in much longer. I'm vibrating from it. I'm showering sparks. He makes it even harder to hold on when he speaks, fingers stroking my marred skin.

"I'm sorry you've been bruised so often because of me. I should have protected you from myself. I've been set to a default for a long time. Sort of like, I attack before I can be attacked. You've been on the receiving end, days, weeks, months, and you've handled it like no one else ever could have." I try to speak but he shakes his head and continues.

"Every day, every minute, I've only ever been sitting there, looking at you. What I've done to you has been the worst mistake of my life."

"It's okay," I manage to say. "It's okay."

"It's not. I don't know how you've coped with me. And I'm sorry." He drops his mouth to the bruise on my ribs.

"I forgive you. You forget, I've been a complete bitch to you."

"But you never would have been, if I'd just smiled back."

"I wish you had." My voice breaks traitorously. I may as well have said, *I wish you loved me.* I hold my breath. With his crazy-intelligent brain, I know he's joining the dots seconds behind me. I struggle up the bed, but he crawls easily over me, and lays my head on his pillow.

"It made no difference. I loved you the moment I saw you."

I'm falling backward, through his bed. He loops an arm around my waist. I jerk like he's caught me.

"You love . . . What? Me?"

"Lucinda Elizabeth Hutton. One and the same."

"Me."

"Lucy, heiress of the Sky Diamond Strawberries dynasty."

"Me."

"Could you show some ID so I can be certain?" His eyes are lit and the smile I love best of all is glowing on his face.

"But I love *you*." I can hear how incredulous I sound. He laughs. "I know."

"How do you always know everything?" I kick my feet against the mattress.

"I only figured it out a few minutes ago. Your heart has been breaking."

"I can't hide anything from you. It's the worst." I try to put my face into the pillow.

"You don't need to hide anything from me." He takes my chin in his fingers and kisses me.

"You're scary. You'll hurt me."

"I guess I'm a bit scary. But I will never hurt you again. Anyone who ever does will find out about scary."

"You hate me."

"I never have. Not for a second. I have *always* loved you."

"Prove it. There's no way you can." I am satisfied that I've thrown out the unwinnable challenge. He rolls onto his side and rests his cheek on his bicep. My heart is pounding.

"What's my favorite color?"

"Easy. Blue."

"What kind of blue?"

"Bedroom blue!" I point at the wall. "The walls. Your shirt. My dress. Pale Tiffany blue."

He tugs me to sit, then goes to the end of the bed. He opens his wardrobe door, and I see all of the shirts hanging in color sequence.

"Josh, you dork." I start to laugh and point, but he grabs my ankles and drags me to the end of the bed. There's a full-length mirror, and I see myself, at long last sitting on the bed in his robin's-egg bedroom. His walls are the blue of my eyes. I've been a bit slow.

"But that's the prettiest blue in the world!"

"I know. Good lord, Lucinda. I thought I'd be busted the moment you saw this room."

He sits on the bed behind me, one knee up, and I fall back into the perfect cradle of his body.

"How somebody can't recognize their own eyes, I'll never know."

"Seems I didn't recognize a few things. Hey, Josh."

"Yes, Shortcake."

"You love me." I see him smile in our reflection at the confusion and wonder in my tone.

"Since the moment I saw you. Since the moment you smiled at me, I felt like I was falling backward off a cliff. The feeling has never stopped. I've been trying to drag you down with me. In the worst, most ill-conceived and socially stunted way possible."

"We've been so awful to each other." I feel his cringe, and his hands begin to stroke me. "I mean, how can we even begin to start again?"

"Time for a new game. The Starting Over Game."

I smile. Eyes bright, dazzling, full of hope and certainty this merger will be the most exciting, passionate, challenging thing ever to happen to me. "Nice to meet you. I'm Lucy Hutton."

"Joshua Templeman. Please, call me Josh." I see the blinding flash of his smile in return, and now I'm properly crying. Tears running down my neck.

"Josh."

"Sounds like heaven coming out of your mouth."

"Josh, please. We've been colleagues for one minute, you're rather flirtatious. Let me hang my coat."

He unclips my bra. "Allow me."

"Thank you." We are playing the Staring Game in the mirror, and his eyes begin to darken. He fills his hands with my white skin.

"I grew up on a strawberry farm. It's named after me."

"I love strawberries. I'm so lovesick, I eat them constantly. Can I nickname you Shortcake? It'll be a dead giveaway that I love you."

"You love me! We've only met a minute ago."

"I do. I'm sorry, but I work fast. I hope it's not too forward of me to say, but your eyes are incredible, Lucy. I die when you blink."

"You're smooth. What do you know. I love you too. So much. Every time your dark blue eyes hit me, I feel like I get a mild electric shock."

I reach behind me to tug off his T-shirt. He helps me out and pulls it off.

"I've been wondering since I met you—granted, only minutes ago—what you've got under this shirt. My goodness, your body. But I want you for your mind, and your heart. Not this impressive disguise."

He looks at the ceiling. "I think I'll paint my bedroom this weekend. I'll probably feel annoyed the whole time I do it. And I'll happily farewell my current girlfriend, a tall boring blonde called Mindy Thailis. She's not you and it eats me up. It makes the fact I sleep alone and desperately celibate in this Lucy-blue room even more romantic when I eventually tell you."

He slides me in between his sheets and spoons behind me. My cheek is pillowed on his bicep, and he kisses the side of my neck. I'm shivering.

"Sounds like a good plan. It'll pay off. Desperately,

huh? So, pray tell, what is the aim of the Starting Over Game?"

"The same as all the others. For you to love me."

"Mine was to make you smile. How lame."

"I laughed my ass off every day on the drive home from work, if it makes you feel any better."

"I guess. But you've won. I'm going to have to know forever you've won all the games." I'm sure my mouth probably has a sulky pout to it. He rolls me onto my stomach and begins to kiss up my spine.

"Do you trust me now that you know everything?"

For a moment we shimmer against each other; my skin trembling for the touch of his lips.

"Yes. And if you get the job, I will be happy for you."

"I already resigned. My last day was Friday. Jeanette came in and did the paperwork. I'm on vacation now."

"What the *fuck*?" I blurt into his bed.

"I don't want anything that means I can't have you. There's nothing worth it."

"But I didn't have a chance to compete against you." I don't know whether to laugh or scream.

"You still have to do your interview against the other candidates. From what I've heard, one of them is a real contender. The independent panel might decide you're completely incompetent."

I elbow him and he laughs.

"But you'll always know you could have gotten it. When we fight I'll be worried you'll bring it up."

"I've worked out a solution. Something so Machiavellian even you will deem it a perfect solution. It retains all of the competitive bullshit we thrive on."

"I'm scared to ask."

"I'm the new divisional finance head of Sanderson Print. B and G's most bitter rival."

"Josh. What? No."

"I know! I'm an evil mastermind!" He drops a kiss to my nape and I squirm away and roll over.

"How on earth did you manage that?" I feel faint.

"They've been pestering me for ages about coming over for a chat. So I did, and I told them I wanted to work on their completely fucked-up financial situation before they completely fold. They said okay. No one was more surprised than me, but I hid it well."

"Is that why you took a day off?"

"Yeah. And I needed to buy you a Matchbox car. They took forever to give me my formal offer. That's why I never needed help to beat you. I didn't want to beat you."

I smooth my hand over his shoulder, the glorious curve of his arm. "So that's that."

"I had to make a few conflict of interest statements."

"Such as?" I watch his eyes crinkle in memory.

"I disclosed that I'll be in love with the soon-to-be chief operating officer of B and G."

I can just imagine him telling them, cool and calm.

"You didn't. Were they okay with that?"

"My new boss seemed to think it was kind of sweet. Everyone's a romantic. I had to sign some nondisclosure stuff. If I tell you anything, I will be sued. Luckily, I have a good poker face when it comes to you."

"Oh man, how angry was Mr. Bexley? He's not a romantic."

"Furious. He was on the verge of calling security. Thankfully Helene came in and defused things. Once I told them my reasons for leaving, they were pretty understanding. Helene said she's always known it."

"Reasons."

"I had one weekend left to make you love me."

I gape in horror. "You didn't tell them that."

"Yes. You should have seen Jeanette's face."

"Pretty big gamble, Josh. Hell in a handbasket."

"It paid off, thankfully."

He's pressing his mouth to my skin and sighing, breathing, like I'm a dream he never wants to wake from. He's breathing me in like he's a filthy addict.

"Can you be sure that you won't resent me one day? You've given up a big chance, Josh."

"I'll be buried in numbers all day long. I can continue my crusade to save one publishing house from financial ruin at a time."

"Please try not to make people cry anymore. It's time for you to be your true self. You're a Mr. Nice Guy."

"I make no guarantees. But for me, this role at Sanderson is honestly a better fit. The best part is, it means I'll be coming home to you on my couch every night. I couldn't have gotten this decision more right if I tried."

"Every night? Well, I can't on the long weekend. I'm going to Sky Diamond for the week. I don't suppose you're busy then."

"Take me with you," he says in between kisses on my shoulders. "I know the way. I've mapped the journey. Flights and hire cars. I'll grovel to your dad. I know exactly what I'll say."

"I don't get it with you and that place."

"I need to go there so I can start at the beginning. So that I can know everything about you."

"You sure do love strawberries."

"I love you, Lucy Hutton. So much, you have no idea. Please be my best friend."

I'm so ridiculously in love. I decide to try it out loud. "I'm in love with Joshua Templeman."

His reply is a whisper in my ear. "Finally."

I pull back. "I'm going to have to change my computer password."

"Oh yeah? To what?"

"I-love-Josh."

"4 eva," he replies.

"You cracked my password?"

He rolls me onto my back and smiles down at me with eyes bright with mischief.

There's nothing else I can do. When the white flag of his sheets settles on my skin, the Hating Game is over. It's primal. It's a miracle. And it's forever.

"Yeah, all right. Forever. What game should we play now?" I look up at him and we play the Staring Game until his eyes spark in memory.

"The Or Something Game really intrigued me. Can you show me how it works?"

He tosses the blankets over us, blocking out the entire world. He's laughing, my favorite sound in the world.

Then there's nothing but silence. His mouth touches my skin.

Let the real games begin.

Epilogue

It's a red dress kind of day.

It's Friday afternoon. I'm sitting in my office at Bexley & Gamin and I can see my reflection in my floor-to-ceiling window. Outwardly I look remarkably corporate, but on the inside I'm forever an immature little weirdo. I cross my legs and begin to play the Mirror Game with myself. The Staring Game. Even a whispered How You Doing Game. It's just not the same without my opponent.

It's been a shitty day. I spent the afternoon fighting a valiant battle against Mr. Bexley over electronic distribution royalties, and then I found out that there's a bug in our latest e-library app. I'm so tired I can feel my own skeleton. I need to be lying on my perfect couch but it's not going to happen tonight. It's so quiet I can hear the fluorescent tubes buzzing.

The elevator bings.

Whoever's just arrived on the tenth floor needs to be kept out of my office so I can get the hell out of here. Scott, our executive officer, is a pretty good gatekeeper. I can hear muffled conversation, and then there's a rap on the door. There's only one person in the world who can put so much short, sharp love into a single knock.

"Come in," I say. The door swings open and there he is.

Joshua Templeman is dressed in black. Everything, from his underwear to his cufflinks to his tie, is ink-black midnight. He enjoys the drama of it on a Friday, sliding into people's office doorways like Dracula just as they're loosening their ties and thinking about their weekends. All he needs is some devil horns and a pitchfork. I feel vaguely bad for whoever he's been terrorizing today.

He leans against the doorjamb and we're playing the Staring Game for a minute until his dark navy eyes spark. "Shortcake," he breathes like he can't believe I'm real. "I missed you so bad."

My. Heart. Bursts.

I stand up and go to him. He picks me up off the ground, kissing my jaw, my cheekbones, his fingers stroking my nape. He turns me in a circle and I cross my ankles prettily. The tiredness falls out through my feet and dissolves.

He's here, and I'm lit up. It's the kind of light that never fades.

People in the opposite building might be able to see us. Motorists at the traffic lights below can probably make out the silhouette of a ridiculously large man twirling around a ridiculously small woman. During one slow revolution I catch sight of Helene and Mr. Bexley, standing near Scott's desk. They're all looking at us like we're the most gorgeously silly couple in the world. It's accurate. We are.

Helene glances at Mr. Bexley with a wry expression, and I swear I see a little moment of connection between them. I've been suspecting it more and more. I know love-hate when I see it.

I speak into Josh's neck. "I hate not being able to stare at your pretty face all day."

I breathe in his addictive, perfect scent. Deciduous trees in the sun. Evergreen trees in the snow. A pencil sharpened to a razor point, pressing into fresh white paper.

"It's against HR policy to stare at your corporate rival all day."

I hug him harder. "Whose HR policy?"

"One of them, I'm sure. I'll look it up." Josh sets me down and kisses my cheek again. Once he starts, he can't stop.

In the elevator I'll wipe off my Flamethrower lipstick so I can get my proper hello kiss. If I'm lucky he'll hit the emergency stop button, although we've been pissing off the security guards with that.

I treat myself to a nice squeeze of his torso before I remember the door is ajar. "Who have you made cry today, Overlord?" At the Sanderson Christmas party, I overheard his nickname and had to laugh. He earned it.

"Nobody," he tells me with adorable sincerity and a blink. "Not a single person. I'm a changed man."

I'm trying to teach him how to be more approachable. More understanding. More like me.

At the first Sanderson Christmas party, I stood alone and awkward for an excruciating two minutes, during which time I was the subject of speculation. I felt like the word *how* was said a lot. I could hear their drunk, high-pitched whispers. *She looks normal. Sweet. So small! How does she cope with that . . . monster? We should rescue her.*

Maybe he keeps her chained in his basement.

I waved like a dork to show that I was not shackled and was there of my own free will. They shrank back, then fell totally silent as their chief financial officer, aka the Overlord, approached me with a glass of wine. His eyes were soft with tenderness and my heart stopped beating until he restarted it with a kiss. The Overlord snuggled me into his side, fitting us together just right. Hard and soft. Darkness and light. Good cop, bad cop.

I registered the jaws dropping. *He's smiling!*

He's the Overlord, he calls them his Underlings, but I can see the little signs that he's getting better at this. At a lot of things, actually.

"Did you remember your dad's present?"

"Yep. We'd better get going if we're going to make the party. Mindy and Patrick have been texting me obsessively. *Don't be late, don't be late.*" He's sarcastic but I know how much this means to him.

I give his arm a stroke and a squeeze. "We won't be late."

I can't lie on the couch tonight because I'm needed in Port Worth. I'm Josh's little lucky charm. When I'm there, he and his dad don't fight. Luckily for them both, I'm always there.

"Got quite a collection by now, Shortcake," Josh says, looking at the rows of Matchbox cars on the shelf behind me. He forgets our hurry and takes a red Volkswagen beetle out of his pocket, sliding it into one of the gaps.

"My toys have given me a reputation for being quirky and approachable."

"No one would guess this strawberry-sweet exterior hides a complete hard-ass."

"I learned from the master. I'm known for being firm but fair."

"Mmm. Tell me more." He loves sitting at my desk to look at everything I surround myself with, and he lowers himself down into my chair like it's a milkmaid stool. His eyes are lit with a creepy kind of devotion as he looks at the castle of books against the wall, and the Smurf hidden in one of the battlements. He finds my bottle of perfume and smells the lid as he strokes my computer mouse.

"That's where you've been," he says in a scolding tone to the cardigan slung on the back of my chair. He folds it into a breadslice square on his knee.

I've turned him into such a total freak.

I'm an even bigger freak when I visit his office. I once touched the speed dial button on his phone marked *SHORTCAKE* just to make my cell phone ring. Then I was jealous of myself. That's a sensation I feel a lot.

How am I living this life? How did I win so much?

Like he can read my mind, Josh picks up the framed photograph on my desk. It's us together in the strawberry fields. Our eyes are summer bright, and I am sitting between his legs leaning back against him. Around us is a carpet of green, studded with red. The picture is a tiny bit crooked because my dad was a little overexcited by the secret he was keeping.

Five minutes after this photo was taken, Josh said, "Hey, it's an old Smurf in the dirt."

He knew nothing would make me drop to the ground faster. I scratched frantically through the leaves. *Where? Where?* What I found in the vines at Sky Diamond Strawberries was a Tiffany blue box. Then I realized he was kneeling down, too.

Lucy blue. True-love blue.

Even as he squeaked the box open and began to speak, I was dimly aware of cheering from the house. My parents were spying from the office window.

After I brushed the squashed berries from the back

of his T-shirt, I learned that Josh had become an expert in diamonds. Carat, cut, color, clarity. He shivered with delight as he described staring at imperfections through a loupe. I could just imagine his laser eyes crumbling stones to ash. The way he tells it, he searched through a pile of worthless pebbles until he found something worthy of my tiny finger. I tell him it's too big, too much, too perfect. He just laughs and says, *I know,* then makes me forget whether we're still talking about the diamond.

I think my cheeks are going pink right now. When he looks me in the eye, he smirks. He's definitely a mind reader.

"We need a vacation," he decides, his finger straightening the terra-cotta tile I use as a coaster. I got that tile in Tuscany. "I'm taking you back. Cheese and wine and sleeping in the sun." His eyes follow the line of my dress down my body. "Red dresses and champagne and carbohydrates." A pause, and there's a little vulnerability in his expression now. "I didn't go crazy and dream it all, did I?"

"I have frequently assured you that I'm real." I take his hand in mine and use it to pinch my forearm. "I was there for every incredible second. I always will be. Now, quit talking about carbohydrates. You're turning me on."

He laughs. "We'd better get out of here." He grabs my coat and walks out to chat with Helene and Mr. Bexley.

I log off and lock away the stack of slush pile manuscripts I've been reading as my own little treat. I lock my door and just watch his reflection bounce around off the slick, glossy surfaces that make up level ten. The only thing better than having one Josh is having a hundred.

I look at the plaque on my office door as I lock it.

It says, *Chief Operating Officer,* and usually it has me grinning like a dork. But right now, I'm smiling over something else.

The gold ring on Joshua Templeman's left hand has set off a shower of firework sparkles in this huge black prism. Each time I focus on one particular reflection, it fractures and doubles. It's a kaleidoscope of his love around me now. There are a hundred gold rings. A thousand. It's still not enough. I want to spin around while they circle me like fireflies. That's how he makes me feel, every day of our life.

It's wonderful. It's primal. It's nothing short of a miracle.

My name is Lucy Templeman.

Keep reading for a sneak peek at
Sally Thorne's next novel

Second First Impressions

**Coming April 2021
from William Morrow**

Time to saddle up and hit the trails on this gleaming borrowed steed. For the journey, I'll be needing:

- My cool cardigan (it has foxes and mushrooms)
- A freshly retightened bun with no escaping wisps of hair
- Brushed teeth and some pink lip gloss
- Some courage, which I know is weird

Hold on to your hat, partner, we're about to ride out into the valley and . . . who am I kidding? I'll sit here and simmer in my own nerves. I once googled how much the Parlonis' car cost, and my brain instantly forgot the amount like I'd experienced a trauma. I hate leaving here. What if something happens? Someone falls, a hydrant explodes? A tortoise sprains its ankle? I make myself start the (very valuable) engine, because the sooner I leave, the quicker I can get back for tonight's episode of my favorite show.

I haven't told a real-life soul this, but I'm one of the founding creators of the longest-running *Heaven Sent* online forum, Heaven Sent You Here. *Heaven Sent* is about Pastor Pierce Percival; his wife, Taffy; their studious teen daughter, Francine; plus twin eight-year-old girls (Jacinta and Bethany), who are always up to mischief.

The forum hosts an annual global rewatch of the entire show. Tonight we're up to season two, episode eight. That's the one where the homesick twins think they've seen the face of Jesus singed onto a marshmallow at Bible camp. When I get back from my errands for the Parlonis, I need to rewatch this episode to refresh myself on it and start a discussion thread.

With this goal in mind, I begin the trip. Holy moly. I'm in the outside world. I'm filling the car with liquid gold at the less-busy gas station when I realize I am staring at the back of a young man. He has very long black hair that puts Melanie's hair extensions to shame. Resplendent, gleaming hair is wasted on men. I bet he doesn't even condition or get the ends trimmed. He sits there sideways on his motorbike, ankles crossed, that unearned glory lifting on a breeze in an inky swirl.

He's oblivious to my presence. Fine by me.

This particular specimen is in his twenties. His skin sits tight on his body, inked all over with tattoos. I see a scorpion, a knife and fork, a diamond ring. It's like his body is the page he's been doodling on while on hold to the electricity company. An upward trail of butterflies, a switchblade, a donut. The artistry is lovely. This is a guy who took a lot of care getting trivial, unrelated things printed all over himself.

Nothing's been colored in, and I want to unzip my pencil case and get to work. I'd start on that big unfurled rose on the back of his arm. Actually, I think I'd use a pink lipstick. The slanted tip would be just the right size for the petals, each the size of a woman's kiss.

He turns his head, feeling my eyes like an animal would, but he doesn't look back at me. I stare at the concrete until he resettles. I put my hand on my neck; I can feel my heartbeat. This is an interesting development: My body knows it's twenty-five.

Melanie told me to take a chance and smile at a guy. I look down at myself. Mom told me once that I have nice calves and my reflection in the car's window is perfectly fine, maybe even pretty when I soften my face.

Imagine being a guy. How would it feel to sit on a neat butt that doesn't spread out like a hen when you sit? If I was turned into a man for a day, I'd spend the first hour carrying around hay bales, making myself sweat. Then I'd muster the courage to unzip my pants to make a decision on whether seeing a penis is a worthwhile priority moving forward. As the minutes tick on, the Rolls-Royce guzzles and he continues to sit motionless. I can't see a second helmet. He does have a very full backpack. I worry for that zipper.

I lock the car. Then I check each individual door. I say under my breath: "I locked the car doors." I mostly believe myself as I walk inside to pay.

As I'm deliberating over what soft-looking chocolate bars I'll get for Renata, my ears tune in to the gas station clerk's hushed telephone conversation. "He's going to steal it."

I rush to the window to check the car, but Tattoo Guy's sitting where I left him. I lay my purchases on the counter.

The clerk says into the phone, "It's been more than ten minutes. He's filled his bike, can't pay for it, and he's deciding what to do." He begins scanning my items and mouths my total at me. "Yeah. As soon as he touches the ignition, I'm calling the cops."

I look through the dusty windows. It's evident from the set of this guy's shoulders and the stark deliberation on his face that he is sitting inside a terrible moment. I was oblivious as I admired his butt. Then I suspected him of theft. Is it true that he has no money? I was in a similar situation once. I was only a few weeks out of home and my card kept getting declined. My neck was hot from bottling up the tears. A motherly type paid for me and disappeared into the night. All she'd said was, *Pay it forward.*

Time to settle my karmic debt. "I'll pay for him. How much?" I dig out my special hundred-dollar bill.

The clerk hangs up the phone. "Twenty dollars. Aren't you nice?" The way he says it doesn't make me feel that nice.

I'm almost back to the car door when the clerk says over the loudspeaker: "Pump number two, please thank your Good Samaritan. Your gas has been paid for and you can leave."

We are the only customers. So much for me just melting away into the night. I give it a try anyway. Tattoo Guy says behind me, "Ma'am, thank you so much."

"No problem." I fumble with the car keys and drop things. "Don't mention it."

"You've just saved my ass—I mean, my butt. I'm having the worst day ever." He's closer behind me when he adds, "I left my wallet somewhere, but I always find it. The world's full of Good Samaritans, just like you. If you give me your details, I'll pay you back as soon as I can."

"Not necessary," I say, but now he's right behind me. I smell the cotton on his body when a breeze blows through it. When I look down at my loafers, there's big inked hands picking up my dropped groceries.

No way am I going to say *Pay it forward*. Men probably think that's girlie nonsense. But I'll try to have an exciting story to tell Melanie. I turn on the balls of my feet.

"Here you go," he says when all the chocolate is gathered up. When he straightens to full height, he's obviously surprised. After a beat, he lets out a big joyful howl. Up at the sky, he yells at full volume, "Oh my God, you look absolutely amazing!"

Did Melanie pay a gorgeous local actor to perk me up?

"Oh shit, too good. You got me." When I don't reply, he continues, "I can tell you, from the back, you've absolutely nailed it." His smile is white and lovely as he drags his hair back. "I love costume parties. Can I come?" His slender-muscly body shakes from laughing. It's a full-body workout. He's standing so close, for a moment I don't process the words. Then I feel the slice.

"Excuse me?"

He is staring at my chest with open appreciation. The glasses that I wear for computer work are still hanging from a chain around my neck. "Perfect," he says reverently before dissolving into laughter again. "Are you going as one of the Golden Girls?"

"No—"

"You just need a string of pearls and a walking stick. Look at those granny shoes." He says it like a fond scold and taps my toe with his. "You've even got the old-person car to match. You've thought of everything." He wipes a tear from his eye. "You look like Tweety Bird's granny."

"You don't need to be rude." The prim words are out of my mouth before it occurs to me that I should just say, *Sure, I'm headed to a big party, I hope my costume wins.*

I don't think I've helped someone who really needs it. Tattoos are expensive and he's covered himself in a fortune. His unusual biker-guy jeans have a lot of seams and diagonal lines, the result of skilled craftsmanship. My thrift-store eyes spot a tiny logo on his pocket: BALMAIN. Very, very pricey.

He's noticed my attention and the corner of his mouth lifts in a mischievous way. "So how old are you? Are you an eighty-year-old with a facelift?"

"How old I am is none of your business." The words I've ached to say to all the residents at Providence, and I blurt them in the face of a tattooed guy with a motorbike? "I paid for your gas because I thought you were in trouble. But I can see you don't really need it."

"I was just psyching myself up to call my dad." This guy scratches his jaw and I can't read the word printed across the knuckles. "I try to fuck up during business hours, so I can speak to his assistant instead. Less of a lecture that way."

"I'll give you my PayPal address. You can pay me back and I'll find someone who actually needs the money." I can't write on the Parlonis' receipt. I have one of Sylvia's business cards in my pocket. I cross out her email and write mine. The gas station attendant gives me a grinning thumbs-up and I burn red with humiliation.

He studies the business card I put into his palm. "A retirement villa?" His eyes spark. The irises are mixed colors—familiar, but I don't know what they remind me of. He is holding a new laugh in. "What's going on with you, anyway?" I cram myself into the car and lock it. "Wait, wait," the guy shouts. Now his *I'm sorry* is muted and faraway. I'm sorry too. Funny how fast a good deed can turn bad in the outside world, like time-lapse footage of rotting fruit.

While I wait for a gap in the traffic, I look in my rear-view mirror, praying he doesn't try to follow. The heel of his palm pressed to his temple is universal language for, *I fucked that up.* At least he realizes it. Most people who hurt my feelings never have a clue they did. I just invested twenty dollars for a reminder of why I stay at Providence and tucked in my safe little forum in the far corner of the internet.

Outside World Shields Up.

"YOU'VE BEEN SO quiet today," Melanie says behind me. "Did I say something, or . . . ?"

"I got my feelings hurt a bit last night. Not by you." I keep staring at the parking lot, watching for a car.

After I sorted out the Parlonis and left them asleep on the couch, holding hands, I stood in front of the mirror in my bedroom. Then I used a second makeup mirror to look at myself from behind. That guy was right: From most angles, I am an old lady. I messaged my forum admin friends Austin, JJ, and Kaitlynn. The group chat was a big chorus of outrage—*what a dick, that's so RUDE, of course you're not old*—but the reassurance didn't feel authentic because none of us have ever actually met in person.

"Here's what I know. You're a good person, Ruthie," Melanie says so kindly. "And you don't deserve hurt feelings. Tell me who did it and I will kill them."

"A complete stranger. Someone I'll never see again." I recheck the time and sidestep the tight squeeze of emotion in my throat. "I need to focus on the meeting. I wish I knew what it was about."

"I'm sorry," Melanie says. "I know I screwed up big-time."

When I was up a ladder replacing a blown bulb outside the recreation center this morning, Melanie took a message for me. All she wrote down was:

- *Jerry Prescott*
- *Today @ 3 P.M.*
- *Maintenance something?*

"Jerry Prescott owns Providence," I told her, with sheer terror coursing through my veins. "You spoke to his assistant?" She shook her head no. "You spoke to the owner of Prescott Development Corporation? PDC? PDC?"

"He sounded nice, I think," she replied.

I have tried everything—even an improvised hypnotism session in the darkened office—but Mel swears she can't recall any more details than that. Jerry's assistant never called me back.

A motorbike turns into the parking lot.

"Nope." I'm looking for a rental car. The rider takes off his helmet, shakes his head back, and looks up at the office. I'd know that phenomenal head of hair anywhere.